# SOMEWHERE
## *To* BELONG

# SOMEWHERE

# JUDITH MILLER

# $\mathcal{T}$o BELONG

❧ DAUGHTERS OF AMANA ❧

BETHANYHOUSE
MINNEAPOLIS, MINNESOTA

Published by Bethany House Publishers
11400 Hampshire Avenue South
Bloomington, Minnesota 55438

Bethany House Publishers is a division of
Baker Publishing Group, Grand Rapids, Michigan.

Printed in the United States of America

ISBN-13: 978-1-61664-294-5

Dedicated to

Mary Greb-Hall . . .
for the many years of
friendship and valuable assistance.

Books by
# Judith Miller
FROM BETHANY HOUSE PUBLISHERS

*www.judithmccoymiller.com*

*with Tracie Peterson

JUDITH MILLER is an award-winning author whose avid research and love for history are reflected in her novels, many of which have appeared on the CBA bestseller lists. Judy and her husband make their home in Topeka, Kansas.

Come with me from Lebanon, my bride,
come with me from Lebanon. Descend from the crest of Amana,
from the top of Senir, the summit of Hermon,
from the lions' dens and the mountain haunts of the leopards.

SONG OF SOLOMON 4:8 NIV

# CHAPTER 1

March 1877
Amana Colonies, Iowa
Johanna Ilg

Rigid as a barn pole, I stood planted in the parlor doorway with my gaze fixed upon the pink feather-and-plume bedecked hat. Sparkling pins held it atop wavy dark tresses that crimped and coiled. The girl's hair reminded me of the curly leaf lettuce we forced to early growth in our hotbeds each spring. An artificial rose peeked from beneath the curvy brim like a vigilant watchman. Although the visitors to our villages sometimes adorned themselves in outlandish costumes, the hat perched upon this young lady's head surpassed anything I'd ever seen. She appeared rather young to be wearing such an ornate headpiece. Not that I could imagine anyone attaining any age where they thought that hat becoming.

Touching her fingers to the garish chapeau, the girl's lips curved in a patronizing smile. She'd obviously noted my attention. "The latest fashion from England. My parents purchased it for me on their last visit."

My mother waved me forward. "Come in and meet our guests, Johanna." I tried to force myself to look away from the hat, but my eyes betrayed me as I stepped into the room. I couldn't stop staring at the unsightly mixture of fabric and fluff. My mother cleared her throat. "Come, Johanna. Meet Dr. and Mrs. Schumacher and their daughter, Berta. They arrived only a short time ago. You remember we've been expecting them."

I turned toward the well-dressed couple who sat side by side on our horsehair-stuffed divan. Berta, who looked to be sixteen or seventeen years old, had obviously inherited her dark curls and fine features from her mother. As if prepared to take flight at the earliest possible moment, the girl sat balanced at the edge of her chair. And given the size of her hat, it would take only a slight wind to carry her aloft.

"I am very pleased to welcome you to Amana. I hope you will be happy living among us."

Berta's dark eyes widened to huge proportions. She shook her head with such fervor I expected the decorations to tumble from her hat. "Living?" She glanced around our parlor with a look of disdain. "We are merely vacationing for a short time. My father's family is from Germany, and we have a distant relative living in Middle Amana. My father thought this would be a pleasant place for our family to *visit*. I think he wanted to provide us a glimpse of his homeland without the expense of a voyage to Europe. Isn't that correct, Father?" When Dr. Schumacher didn't immediately reply, Berta leaned forward in her chair, her eyes flashing with impatience. "Well, *isn't it*, Father?" Her voice had raised several decibels and panic edged her words.

One look at my mother confirmed that I'd misspoken. I longed to stuff the welcome back into my mouth, but that wasn't possible.

The damage had been done. Yet no one had forewarned me. How was I to know Berta hadn't been advised of her father's plans to move his family to the Amana Colonies?

The multistriped woven carpet that covered the parlor floor muffled the stomp of Berta's foot. I arched my brows and glanced toward my mother. The girl was behaving like an undisciplined two-year-old.

*"Father?"*

"Now, Berta, please. You must remain calm." Mrs. Schumacher unclipped a hand-painted fan from her waist and handed it to her daughter. "Use this. I don't want you fainting and embarrassing yourself."

Berta grabbed the fan from her mother's hand and slapped it atop her skirt. "I don't need a fan. What I need is an answer to my question." She waited only a moment. "Well, Father? How long will we be visiting in Amana?"

Dr. Schumacher shifted toward his daughter and inhaled a deep lungful of air. "We will be making our new home here in Iowa, Berta. I trust you will remain quiet until we can speak in private. I should have told you before we embarked on the journey, but I wanted to avoid a scene."

"Did you?" Berta jumped to her feet, a horror-stricken look in her eyes. "You don't really believe I'll agree to live in this place, do you?"

Before either of her parents could respond, our parlor door opened and my father entered the room with his flat felt cap pressed between his calloused fingers. A few pieces of straw clung to his dark work pants. He smiled, and crinkles formed along the outer edges of his sparkling eyes. Today his eyes appeared green.

When I was five or six years old, I'd asked him about the color of his eyes. He'd told me they were hazel, but my mother said they were brown. I argued they couldn't be both.

"Hazel is light brown," he'd explained before scooping me onto his lap. "But hazel eyes change and look different colors depending on what you wear. Sometimes they look green, and at other times you can see golden flecks." He'd nuzzled my neck. "Some people call them cat eyes. Do you think I look like a cat?" he'd asked. Remembrance of that long-ago conversation warmed me. I was glad Father was home. Perhaps his easy manner would calm Berta.

He extended his hand and stepped toward the doctor. *"Willkommen!"* His deep voice filled the room. "We are pleased to have you join our community and to have another doctor in the villages."

Berta glared at my father as though he'd committed a crime. "We won't be staying in Amana, Mr. Ilg."

My father's brow creased. I was certain he was expecting Berta's father to reprimand her for such rude behavior. Instead, Dr. Schumacher held a finger to his lips. "We will discuss this once we are settled in our rooms, Berta."

"First, you must tell me we aren't going to stay here more than one night," Berta said before tightening her lips into a pout.

The doctor stood. "If you could show us to our rooms where we can have a private family discussion, I would be most grateful."

My mother signaled me. "Johanna will be pleased to show you to the rooms. We must depart for evening prayer service soon. You are welcome to join us."

"Not this evening," Mrs. Schumacher said. "Another time."

As I led the Schumachers upstairs, I couldn't help but compare Mrs. Schumacher's gown to the blue, black, or gray calicos that were woven in the Amana mills and worn by the women of our colonies. No one longed to wear the bright calicos woven for those living outside the colonies—at least no one ever spoke of such a desire. We didn't object to the sameness of our plain waists or the wide-banded full skirts. Even our shawls, aprons, and caps were worn without thought to their sameness. Would Mrs. Schumacher, in her pale green silk dress, adapt to our ways with more enthusiasm than her daughter?

I pushed down the metal latch and opened the door leading into the rooms that would be the Schumachers' living quarters—for how long was anyone's guess. If Berta had her way, they would be gone before sunrise. "The rooms are sparsely furnished, but I'm sure when you add some of your own belongings, they will seem more like home."

"This will never be my home!" Berta flung herself onto the overstuffed forest green divan with a theatrical flair that defied protestation.

I motioned toward the bedrooms. "Your sleeping rooms are to the rear." I backed toward the door, certain my work here was done.

Mrs. Schumacher motioned that I should remain. "The kitchen?"

Dr. Schumacher grasped his wife's elbow. "Don't you recall that I explained we will be eating our meals in a communal kitchen? There will be no need for you to cook or wash dishes. Isn't that grand?"

"Given that I've done very little cooking in my life, I suppose it is grand. Especially for you and Berta." Mrs. Schumacher rubbed the back of her neck.

Berta arched forward and glared at her father. "Why are you even discussing where we will eat? I am *not* living here!"

I took another backward step. "I must go downstairs. I don't want to be late for prayer service. We won't be gone long. The meeting is short—usually no more than twenty minutes or half an hour each evening." Reaching behind my back, I unlatched the door.

"You have prayer services *every* night?" Mrs. Schumacher took a step toward me.

I turned toward the doctor. "Did the *Bruderrat* not explain our ways before you arrived?" Surely, the council of elders who guided our village would have told them what to expect in their new life among us.

"Yes, of course. I received information from the *Grossebruderrat*, as well," Dr. Schumacher replied.

I tried to hide my confusion, but I didn't understand. If he'd been informed about life in the Amana Colonies, why did his wife and daughter appear so angry and bewildered?

Seeming to sense my confusion, Dr. Schumacher said, "There are many details I haven't shared with my wife, as of yet. I didn't want to burden her unduly."

Mrs. Schumacher crooked her finger and beckoned me forward. "Why don't you explain, Johanna? I'm certain you can more easily clarify these terms and rules. Exactly what are the Bruderrat and Grossebruderrat?"

"Each village has a Bruderrat, which is composed of a group of local elders and a trustee." I glanced at the doctor. He offered a feeble smile and slight nod.

"Do go on, Johanna," Mrs. Schumacher said.

"The members of the Bruderrat meet and appoint the foremen for our industries and discuss crop planting schedules, construction projects, work assignments, and such. In spiritual matters, the head elder has the final word, but in matters related to work duties, the trustee has the final say."

Mrs. Schumacher nodded. "And the Grossebruderrat? What is that?"

"They are the trustees who oversee matters that affect all of the colonies."

"Like what?" She leaned forward in her chair.

"When we build factories, they decide which village it should be built in and when the construction should begin. When the millrace was dug, they decided the place and how we would complete the work. They also settle disputes that are appealed from the Bruder-rat. The Grossebruderrat meets once a month, taking turns among the different colonies."

Mrs. Schumacher glanced at her husband, then back at me. "Thank you for taking time to explain, Johanna."

I bobbed my head, mumbled a hasty good-evening, and hurried down the stairs, glad to be away from the anger and confusion that swirled within the upper rooms.

"*Ach!* I thought you were never going to return. What took you so long?" Before I could reply, Mother handed me my woolen shawl and propelled me toward the front door. "We must be on our way. Put your wrap around your shoulders. It may be March, but the air is still cool in the evenings."

"*Ja,*" my father agreed, leading the way.

I took the shawl without argument. Although I'd turned twenty-one last month, my parents sometimes treated me as though I were still a child. A fact I sometimes disliked but at other times found endearing. Tonight I disliked the admonition and decided some of Berta's hostile attitude must have rubbed off on me.

"The doctor and his family appear to know little about our ways." Though I walked beside my mother, I spoke loudly enough to ensure Father could hear me. Since he was a member of the council of elders, I knew he would have been involved in the decision to grant the Schumachers permission to move into our village. I hoped he would shed some light on the odd situation.

"Dr. Schumacher understands our ways as well as any new arrival to the colonies. Eventually his family will do well."

"I am surprised the family wasn't sent to live in Middle Amana with their relatives," my mother said. "It would have made things less painful for Berta, don't you think?"

My father shrugged. "We already have Dr. Zedler in Middle. There's no need for two doctors in one village. Dr. Schumacher knew they would be living in Main Amana rather than in Middle. Brother Gustav, Dr. Schumacher's second cousin, vouched for them so that they would be easily accepted into the colonies, but I doubt living in the same village with him would make this change easier for Berta."

I silently agreed. Berta Schumacher wasn't going to adapt easily to our ways—relatives or not. To make matters worse, I had been assigned to assist Berta through the transition into our village. She would be working in the kitchen with me. Although the *Küchebaas* was in charge, I would be expected to teach Berta. Just as the young girls who finished school and then transferred into our many kitchens and gardens throughout the villages, Berta would need to be trained.

"What if she resists her training, *Vater*? What am I to do?"

"Pray for guidance, child, and I will do the same. The girl needs a good influence in her life, and you are the perfect choice."

*Perfect choice?* If Father knew some of my private thoughts and feelings, I doubted he would think me a suitable choice for the task at hand. Truth be told, I worried Berta would sway me more than I would influence her. Though I loved life in Amana, those feelings didn't stop me from desiring a peek at what lay beyond the confines of the twenty-six-thousand acres owned by our people. I didn't want to move away permanently, not like my brother Wilhelm, who had left our village to make Chicago his home. But there were places outside the seven villages I longed to see, and Wilhelm hadn't proved a valuable source of information because he seldom returned home to visit.

Through the years, I'd daily traversed the wooden sidewalks of Amana. I'd been in most of the communal residences, attended the Amana school, and knew most of the families in our colony by name—not all five hundred residents, but at least their family names.

Granted, I didn't know as many people in the other six villages that formed our colony, but still I cared deeply about their welfare and safety. No matter if they lived in East or Middle or High Amana. What difference if I lived in Main and they called South or West or Homestead their village. A common cord of love and belief in our Lord united us. The few miles between each of our villages hadn't unraveled our group while we lived in New York, and it had continued to hold fast in Iowa. So why did I want to know about other places?

For a time I'd thought it was because I'd never seen our previous home in Ebenezer, New York, where our people had settled and created six villages. I'd heard my parents talk about how they had moved from New York to the new settlement in Iowa, and they'd told me many stories about life in Ebenezer, but it wasn't the same as seeing or experiencing the old community for myself.

When I'd spoken to Mother, she'd said, "All young people go through a time when they think they'd like to see how people live outside the villages. As you grow older, such thoughts will flee from your mind."

I'd seen fear in Mother's eyes. After all, such thoughts hadn't fled from the mind of Wilhelm. He'd left the community and had no wish to return and live among us. My mother had lost one son to death and another to the outside world. I knew she didn't want to think of losing me.

Much to my father's relief, we arrived for prayer service on time. The small brick building where we attended evening prayers was not far from our home. Unlike our Sunday church meetings, prayer service was held in small meetinghouses in each neighborhood. I sat down on one of the hard wooden benches beside my mother, and soon more women joined us.

On the other side of the room, the men gathered on their

benches, but before we began our prayers, my father stood. "Our new doctor and his family have arrived. I would ask that you pray that these new arrivals will easily settle into our community."

I noted the surprise on several faces. The women were obviously full of curiosity, but this was a time for prayer, not questions.

The moment the final prayer had been uttered and we'd been dismissed, Sister Schmitt grasped my mother's elbow. "So the doctor is living upstairs from you, ja?"

Mother gathered her shawl tightly around her shoulders. "Ja."

"Seems not such a *gut* place for a doctor—living upstairs like that," the old woman said.

"The Bruderrat assigned their living space, not me. You should ask them if you question their decision, Sister Olga."

"Ach! I was not questioning, Sister Emilie. Just making a simple statement. No need to take offense. How many in the family? Any young people to help in the fields or the kitchens?"

"One daughter. She has been assigned to work in the kitchen." My mother patted my arm. "Johanna will help her learn her duties."

Sister Schmitt's smile revealed several missing teeth, and she quickly covered her lips. "Then she will do fine. Johanna is a gut worker, for sure."

I wasn't certain how Sister Schmitt could judge my work. Once she'd become unable to perform the heavier duties in the kitchen or garden, she'd been assigned to the woolen mill, where she tied threads as they were wound onto the large reels. The old woman's transfer had occurred before I began working in the kitchen, but my mother had worked with her in the garden. A few years ago she'd insisted upon helping cut the cabbages for sauerkraut, but it had taken only one day before she'd decided that a return to thread tying was in order.

I was thankful when my father motioned for us to join him. I didn't want to answer any questions about Berta. I feared I'd say more than my parents considered appropriate. Although he appeared calm, my father walked more slowly than usual, and I wondered if he was worrying about what might greet us upon our return home. I considered asking but knew it would serve no purpose.

Father would tell me worry was for those who didn't trust the Lord, while believers placed their burdens at the throne of God. That's where I placed mine. At least I tried to. But unlike my father, I hadn't learned to leave them there. Instead, I gathered my bundle of worries back under my arm and carried them around with me. I wasn't sure about my mother. Sometimes she appeared free from all worry. Yet other times, like when I'd spoken of my desire to see Chicago or Iowa City, I'd seen concern in her dark brown eyes.

My father lifted his nose heavenward. "Smells like rain—the fields could use the water." He'd been the farm *Baas* for our village since I was a little girl, and it seemed he could predict every change in the weather. Sometimes he could even forecast a morning fog. Most of the time he was correct, but occasionally he missed the mark. When that happened, Father would laugh and say God had to fool him once in a while to keep him humble.

I didn't smell rain, and I silently hoped this was one of those times when God was keeping Father humble. Not that I wanted our crops to suffer. But rain meant the garden workers would crowd into the kitchen to help once they'd cleaned their tools. And though they did their best to assist, too many hands and too many bodies in a space that was too small created more problems than help. Besides, with Berta in tow, rainy weather would make my task even more difficult.

Father tapped my shoulder as we approached the front of

our house. "Please look in on *Oma* Reich and see if she needs anything."

"Yes, Vater." The old woman wasn't my grandmother, but she'd requested I use the familiar endearment when she moved into the two rooms adjacent to us after the Bruderrat declared her too frail to live on her own. There were times when I wondered if those knowing men had miscalculated Oma Reich's disability, for I'd seen her summon enough energy to put many a younger woman to shame.

I continued down the hall to the old woman's door. After tapping lightly, I quietly called her name.

"Come in, Johanna. Is no need to whisper."

I opened the door, and Oma pointed to the pale blue plaster ceiling. "That one up there, she is screaming and yelling and stomping the feet ever since you left for prayer service. I should have gone with you."

"I thought you told Vater you were too weak to walk to the meetinghouse."

"Ja, is true I am too frail. But easier it would have been to walk a mile than to listen to such weeping and wailing." Once again, the old woman jutted her finger toward the upper rooms. "That one up there is going to be trouble."

I didn't attempt to disagree. I knew Oma was right.

# CHAPTER 2

Berta Schumacher

Neither my tears nor my foot stomping had obtained the desired effect. My father stood firm in his decision: We would remain in Amana. I'd pushed too far, and now I would pay the price for my impudent behavior. If only I hadn't slipped off for an evening of fun with that silly John Underwood. Father thought I'd run away to wed the foolish fellow, when all we'd done was set off for a bit of merriment playing pranks on several of our friends. Granted, we'd been out until near morning, but nothing horrible had occurred. At least not between John and me. Even though I'd told the truth, my parents didn't believe me. They remained certain I had a romantic interest in John Underwood. How they could believe such nonsense was beyond me. Who would want to tie herself to a man at the age of seventeen?

Yet because they wouldn't believe me, this place was to be our new home. I directed a beseeching look toward my mother. "Surely you don't agree that we should live here, Mother." I grasped her hand. "I apologize for my dreadful behavior and promise I'll never again disobey."

My mother's shoulders sagged, and for a moment I thought I'd won her to my side. But before she could speak, my father intervened. "How many times have we heard that same promise, Berta?"

I shrugged my shoulders. "I don't know, but I truly mean it this time. If you'll just agree that we can leave, I'll never again cause you problems."

Father wagged his head. "It will not work this time. Your promise falls empty on my ears. I love you too much to permit you to continue down this path you've chosen."

"But I haven't chosen a path, Father. That's what I'm trying to tell you. Our evening was simply an adventure. I don't care a whit about John Underwood. He's simply a young man who loves life and enjoys having a good time. Girls should be permitted the pleasure of an occasional adventure, shouldn't they?"

"Sneaking out of your room, destroying other people's property, and imbibing alcohol may be an adventure, but those activities aren't what I consider loving life and having a good time. That is not how respectable young ladies behave. You've left us no choice."

"So your solution is to banish the entire family to a confinement worse than boarding school?" I didn't argue that I hadn't destroyed property, at least nothing that couldn't be easily repaired. And I'd tried only a sip of alcohol. John and one of his friends had been the ones who'd downed several bottles of the nasty-tasting brew.

"This isn't confinement. This is our new home. If you'll simply give it a chance, I believe we'll all be very happy. I'll have more time to devote to you and your mother, and we can all devote more time and energy to the Lord."

I stared in disbelief. I'd never before heard my father express any eagerness to spend more time with the family or with God. "But we could do those things at our home in Chicago. Why do we need to be in this place?"

He sighed. "Because this is the place your mother and I have decided is best for all of us. Isn't that right, Helen?"

My mother's nod didn't bear much enthusiasm, but from the set of my father's jaw, I knew I was losing ground.

"You will be working in the kitchen house with Johanna. She will assist in your training. I would like your word that you will do your best to perform the tasks as you are instructed."

My father's request required an immediate answer. If I was to ever gain his agreement to leave this place, I must show him I could change. "You have my word, Father."

He stood and opened his arms to me. "Thank you, Berta."

As he surrounded me with a warm embrace, I peered across his shoulder and viewed the same multicolored rug I'd seen on the floors downstairs, wondering if I could keep my word. How could a person ever enjoy life in a place where there was nothing but sameness, hard work, and church services to fill each day? If it weren't for those occasional letters from Father's second cousin, Heinrich, Father would never have known of the Amana Colonies. How I wished Heinrich still lived in Germany!

When we'd first arrived that afternoon, I'd thought the village somewhat quaint. The balding man who managed the general store had pointed out the lovely calicos and woolens. When my mother stopped to admire the fabrics, he'd been quick to mention that the fabrics had been designed and created at the Amana mills.

Strolling down the aisles, I'd been impressed when the man had followed along and told my mother that folks in Amana produced almost everything they needed to survive. Of course, that was before I knew I'd be living here. Now, even the wondrous smells from the bakery didn't hold enough power to sway me.

Did these people not long to be different, long for pleasure and excitement? Perhaps no one had ever shown them how to include adventure in their lives. That thought gave me a glimmer of hope. These people could teach me how to pare potatoes, but I could teach them how to have a good time!

"I heard the Ilg family return from prayer service." My mother's voice broke into my thoughts. "Why don't you go downstairs and ask Johanna what time you must meet her in the morning."

I hadn't anticipated beginning work tomorrow. In fact, I thought I'd have a few days for exploration before I began my assigned duties, but I didn't press the issue. When I easily agreed, my mother stared at me, her disbelief obvious.

"Would you like me to go with you, Berta?"

Reaching forward, I pressed down on the iron door latch. "I can go by myself. Unless you're going to be working in the kitchen, too?" No one had mentioned what kind of work my mother would contribute to the community, but on the train ride from Chicago, Father had told me that every able-bodied person over the age of fourteen was assigned to a job in their village. Strange how long ago that train ride now seemed.

Mother shook her head. "I won't be working in the kitchen. The elders thought it would create too much chaos for the kitchen boss if she had two new workers at the same time. I will be helping in the nursery, caring for toddlers while their mothers work."

I couldn't believe my ears. My mother had been in on this arrangement long before we'd arrived. "So both you and Father concocted this idea. And I thought you enjoyed our life in Chicago. What of your friends, Mother? What about your charity work?"

My mother pressed her fingers along the folds of her silk dress, a practice she exhibited when uncomfortable or nervous. "I did enjoy living in Chicago, but I have my reasons for wishing to live a more simple life." She directed a wounded glance toward my father before continuing. "Living in Amana will take adjustment, but my duties here will benefit others as much as any charity work I performed in Chicago—maybe more."

My father patted her hand. "And you know how much your mother loves children. She requested an assignment where she could surround herself with little ones."

It was true that my mother loved children. She had often expressed dismay that she'd not been blessed with at least one more child. I, on the other hand, had never desired siblings. My friends all agreed that brothers and sisters were tattletales of the worst sort. "Then it seems I am the only one who needs further advice. I'll go downstairs and speak with *Sister* Johanna. It seems that I have been instantly blessed with a multitude of brothers and sisters."

I'd reached the bottom step when Johanna exited a room farther down the entry hall. With a pretty dress and decent hairstyle, Johanna would be a beautiful woman. Perhaps I could convince her to let me fashion her ash blond hair into an attractive new style that would accent her delicate features and deep blue eyes. I hurried toward her, my excitement mounting. "You have a bedroom that opens into the hallway?" Like dandelions in spring, my mind ran wild with possible schemes. With such a bedroom, it would be possible to enter and exit the house without being noticed.

My excitement diminished when Johanna shook her head. "No. Those are Oma Reich's rooms. She's a widow without family, and her health is failing. She lives in two small rooms, and we assist her as needed. Sister Stilson and her son, Rudolf, live in the other rooms upstairs."

I swallowed hard. "I didn't know so many people lived here. So we will have only those three upstairs rooms?"

Johanna nodded. Though she told me our family was fortunate to have two bedrooms with such a small family, I found her words difficult to believe.

"Many do not receive separate bedrooms, and almost always the children must share the same room."

Her comment made me happy I didn't have any siblings. My bedroom was too small for even one person. "How is that possible? Where do they store their belongings?"

"We don't need space for fancy dresses and hats. Our attire is simple." Johanna glanced toward the front door. "It's already dark outside. Were you going somewhere?"

"No. I've come for some instruction about tomorrow." Knowing she'd observed my earlier behavior, I wasn't surprised when she exhibited a lack of enthusiasm. Nevertheless, she invited me into their rooms.

Mrs. Ilg sat near a cast-iron stove that was a perfect match for the one in the upstairs parlor. She welcomed me, but I saw the wary look in her eyes. She probably feared I'd returned to create another scene. I did my best to set her at ease, but she appeared unable to concentrate on the handwork she held between her short, thick fingers.

I leaned forward to better examine what she was creating. "Making socks?"

She shook her head. "I am crocheting a new head covering for Oma Reich. In the wintertime, the children knit socks and mittens for all of us who live in Amana." I arched my brows and the older woman continued. "During the afternoons, the younger ones learn to knit and crochet; the older children are taught a trade. Once they complete their schooling, they are prepared to serve the community with their skills."

"I'm not good with handwork."

Johanna's mother didn't appear surprised by my revelation.

"They tried to teach me needlepoint at finishing school, but I was a miserable failure. My thread was always in a knot."

"Perhaps with the proper attitude, you will conquer your earlier inabilities. Johanna could help you in the evenings if you'd care to learn."

I offered a fleeting smile. When I was younger, my mother's knitting needles had occasionally proved to be wonderful weapons for poking a playmate, but I didn't want to learn to tat or knit or crochet. In fact, I didn't want to learn to use a needle of any sort—at least not for fancywork.

"First I believe I must learn about the kitchen work. My parents said I should ask what time my work begins tomorrow morning."

Johanna cleared her throat. "I am cooking breakfast this week, so we must be at the kitchen by five o'clock to light the stove and make the coffee before the others arrive."

"Five o'clock in the morning?" My voice cracked. Did people really get up at that time of day?

"Next week we don't have to be there until six o'clock," Johanna hastened to add.

I stared at her in disbelief. "Six o'clock isn't much better. I'm unaccustomed to rising at such an early hour. I'd like to ask those elders if I can begin later in the morning. How do I do that?"

Johanna's mother inhaled with a slight gasp. "You cannot do such a thing. If you don't adhere to the proper hours, the food will not be ready to eat at the scheduled time and work cannot begin on time."

"Has anyone ever considered changing the schedule, Mrs. Ilg? What about beginning later in the day and working a little later into the evening? I'd guess there are many people who'd prefer to sleep longer."

The older woman placed her crocheting in the basket near her chair and folded her hands in her lap. "Nearly five hundred people live in this village, and you want them to change the schedule for you? I think it works better for you to change the hour you get out of bed in the morning, ja? And you may address me as *Sister* Ilg."

She had forced each word through tight lips. Clearly, I'd offended her. "Merely a suggestion," I said, hoping to make amends. I didn't want her running upstairs and telling Father I was creating more problems.

"I'll wait for you by the front door in the morning." Johanna motioned for me to wait. "Before you go upstairs, let me give you your clothes." I waited while she scuttled off to the other room and returned with a stack of folded dark calico. "You'll receive several additional dresses, but tomorrow you can wear this one." She offered quick instructions on how I should tuck the cotton shawl into the wide waistband of the skirt. "There are work aprons at the kitchen to protect our clothing."

I wasn't at all sure the dress needed protection. I didn't think a few splashes of food would do it any harm. To my way of thinking, the plain garb could use a little color, but I didn't say so. Instead, I asked what work I would be expected to perform the next day. "I've had no experience working in a kitchen."

Sister Ilg tipped her head to the side. "I would guess you've had little work experience of any kind."

"I've become fairly accomplished at climbing trees, but I don't think you'd count that as work."

"Not unless you were picking apples while you were up there," the older woman replied. She reached down and retrieved her thread and crochet hook from the basket.

"I don't think I ever gathered enough for a pie. Then again, I don't know how many apples it takes to make a pie." There'd been a few occasions when I'd picked an overripe apple or pear to toss down on unsuspecting schoolmates passing below, but I didn't think that was what Sister Ilg had in mind.

"Well, you'll soon learn how much fruit it takes to make nine or ten pies. That's how many are needed so that each person receives a nice slice at the Muhlbach *Küche*."

Johanna took note of my confusion and quickly explained that the Muhlbach Küche was the kitchen in our neighborhood. The one where I would work. "Each kitchen house bears the name of the Küchebaas, the kitchen boss. We serve forty or fifty people three meals each day as well as a light midmorning and midafternoon lunch of bread and cheese, or sometimes leftover pastry."

Sister Ilg pointed the crochet hook in my direction. "You suit yourself, but if you are as smart as I think you are, you'll behave yourself in Thekla Muhlbach's kitchen."

"I'll try my best." I still hadn't learned what would be expected of me the following morning, but I decided it might be best if I didn't know in advance. I sidestepped toward the door. I couldn't imagine cooking for myself, much less for forty or fifty other people. What did that many people eat for breakfast? One thing was certain. If I prepared their breakfast, they would all become ill. Then again, such an event would permit Father to earn his keep by caring for them.

Clothes in hand, I returned up the stairs and into the parlor, where my parents sat waiting. My father scooted to the edge of his chair.

"Well, how did it go? Did you learn about your new duties?"

"I learned I am to meet Johanna by the front door shortly before five o'clock tomorrow morning. She promised to bang the broom handle on the ceiling to waken me."

My mother gasped and covered her mouth with her palm.

"Oh, Berta, I didn't realize you would be required to rise so early in the morning."

"If you're truly concerned, we could still go home."

My mother's look of regret immediately disappeared. She might pity my circumstance, but she wasn't willing to change it.

# CHAPTER 3

Johanna Ilg

Where was Berta? As promised, I had tapped on the ceiling with the broom handle and waited until I'd heard footsteps overhead. Now I wondered if she'd gone back to bed. Or maybe the footsteps had been those of Dr. or Mrs. Schumacher. Resting my hand on the latch, I leaned my shoulder against the door. I'd give Berta two more minutes. After that, she'd need to find her own way. Never before had I been late for work, and I wouldn't begin this morning. Even now, we would have to run in order to arrive at the kitchen on time.

At the sound of a slamming door, I stared up the flight of stairs. My eyes had adjusted to the darkness, and I watched for Berta's appearance. I didn't have to wait long. Within seconds she skidded down the steps, clutching the stair rail. Skirt and shawl askew, she landed at my feet with a resounding thud.

"I missed the first step," she hissed.

Leaning forward, I grasped her arm and pulled her up. "No need to whisper. I'm certain you've awakened the entire household. Are you all right?"

She gyrated into positions I'd never before witnessed and then gave a firm nod. "Nothing broken, but I'd be glad to remain at home until my father declares me fit for duty."

Ignoring her suggestion, I pointed to her head covering. "Straighten your cap and tie the strings so it doesn't blow away. We're going to be at least five minutes late now." I hurried her out the door, and though it was difficult, I refrained from breaking into a fast run. If we arrived at the kitchen completely exhausted, we'd never complete our chores on time.

The moon glistened overhead, not yet prepared to give way to dawn. Even though my pace remained even, my heart thrummed at breakneck speed, and I wondered if my chest might explode from the pressure. Like all of the other kitchen bosses, Sister Muhlbach and her family lived in the rooms that adjoined the communal kitchen. There was no doubt she would be out of bed and more than a little concerned when she discovered we hadn't arrived. Yet Berta dallied, obviously in no particular hurry to begin her work. "Can you walk a little faster? The fire should already be started in the stove."

"Who will know if we're a few minutes late? Tell the Küchebaas the wood was damp and it took longer than usual to start the fire."

I couldn't believe my ears. She was encouraging me to tell a falsehood! "It isn't our way to tell lies, Berta. I'm sure you've read admonitions against such behavior in the Bible."

With a giggle, she looped her arm through mine. "I know

what the Bible says, but I don't believe for a minute that the people who live here don't tell lies. Everyone tells lies—even you, *Sister* Johanna."

If I had denied her remark, it would be a falsehood, for during my lifetime I had told lies. Still, I didn't want to agree with her. I feared she would use such a statement against me in the future. "I do my very best to tell the truth. And those times when I have failed, I have asked forgiveness."

"Well, there's your answer. Just tell the Baas the firewood was wet and ask God to forgive you for lying. Seems simple enough to me."

I shook my head. "I'm sure it does." I didn't take time to explain we had a woodbox in the kitchen to prevent such a happenstance. Berta would simply think up some other untruth.

Besides, we had arrived at the kitchen, and I didn't have time to argue about her flawed thinking. There was work to be done, and I would need Berta's assistance if I was to have my tasks completed before the others arrived. I motioned her to follow me as I lit one of the oil lamps mounted on the kitchen wall and then instructed her to complete the task while I lit the fires in the large brick hearth stove and the wood-fired oven. The polished tin sheeting above the hearth glimmered and winked at me as the fire sparked to life.

The well wasn't far from the back door of the kitchen, but Berta would be hard-pressed to locate it in the dark. It would take longer to explain its whereabouts than to fetch the water myself. But then I reminded myself that she needed to learn.

Certain the fires had a good start, I called to Berta. "Come along. We need to fetch water for the coffee. I'll show you where the well is located, and you can finish lighting the lamps in the dining room later." I'd never seen anyone take so much time to light the lamp wicks. I pointed to the row of wooden pegs near the door. "You can hang your woolen shawl here in winter and leave your apron on the hook when you depart in the evening." I lifted an apron from the hook and handed it to her. "We don't do laundry until Monday, so you best put this on and then grab one of the buckets."

"Who does the laundry?" She slipped the apron over her head and tied the strings around her waist.

"Each family does their own. There's a washhouse behind most of the houses. Either you or your mother will be responsible for your family's. The kitchen workers are responsible for the laundry of the single men who eat in their kitchens." I bent down, picked up another bucket, and headed out the door with Berta on my heels.

"My mother and I don't do laundry. We'll have to send it out to someone else," she said.

Though I doubted she could see me in the predawn light, I smiled at her solution. "There is no one to send it to, Berta. You'll need to learn by doing."

She grabbed hold of the pump handle, and with each downward stroke, a surge of water gushed into the bucket. To my amazement, she filled both of our containers in no time. When Sister Muhlbach entered the kitchen a short time later, the aroma of freshly brewed coffee filled the kitchen, the potatoes had been peeled for frying, and Berta was making her first attempt at slicing bread.

"So you are Berta Schumacher, the new helper, ja?" Before Berta could respond, Sister Muhlbach slapped her palm to her forehead. "Ach! Not like that!" She reached around Berta and clasped her thick fingers overtop Berta's hand. "There—you see? You must slice, not hack. And try to make the slices even." She held up one of Berta's uneven slices and waved it back and forth. "Not thick on one side and thin on the other. This is not gut work. We cannot serve those uneven slices." She slapped the bread onto the table.

Strands of unruly graying hair had already escaped the knot of hair hidden beneath her black cap.

"They still taste the same, don't they?"

Sister Muhlbach bent forward until she and Berta were nose to nose. "We do not serve undercooked food, we do not serve burned food, we do not serve spoiled food, and we do not serve uneven slices of bread. We serve only the best we can prepare. Think of your work as an offering to God."

Berta shrugged. "I'm not sure God cares if the slices are uneven, but if you don't want me to serve the bread, I won't serve the bread."

I was surprised the Küchebaas didn't reprimand Berta for her offensive response. Instead, she sent her to pour milk into the pitchers and prepare the butter dishes. All of the remaining kitchen workers had arrived by five thirty, and the room now hummed like a well-oiled machine. Metal utensils rang against pots and pans while sausage sizzled in cast-iron skillets. The thinly sliced potatoes would soon be tender and fried to perfection.

By the time the village bell rang at six o'clock, we were exactly on schedule. Well-scrubbed benches lined each side of the long oilcloth-covered tables that had been properly set with plates and utensils. Once the dining room doors opened, I heard the clatter of feet. The men migrated toward their tables, and the women and children took their places at separate tables.

While the morning prayer was being recited around the dining tables, I heaped fried potatoes into large serving bowls and set them on trays.

Most of the tables had been served when Sister Muhlbach signaled for Berta. "Take this platter to the far table."

I noted the glint in Berta's eyes as she looked toward the men seated at the distant table. One or two were attired in business suits, others in unfashionable work clothes that didn't resemble those worn by the men who lived in our community. She turned toward Sister Muhlbach. "Who are they?"

Sister Muhlbach discreetly nodded toward the well-dressed men. "Those two are here to conduct business. They come to buy woolen goods from the mills." Her chest swelled. "They prefer to eat in *my* kitchen rather than at the hotel."

The pride in Sister Muhlbach's voice surprised me. It was good that members of the Bruderrat hadn't been within earshot. Any appearance of pride among the members was frowned upon.

"The others are hired men. Some work out on the farms to help with the livestock. The two at the far end are assigned to assist with heavy chores in our kitchen and garden. Unless it concerns their breakfast, there's no need for you to talk to them."

While Berta sashayed off with a tray bearing a bowl of fried potatoes and a platter of sausage, I returned to the stove. I was refilling another bowl with potatoes when I heard Sister Muhlbach gasp and stomp across the room. I turned to see Berta sitting at the far table. She had filled a plate and was eating breakfast with the men. My voice caught in my throat, and I slapped my palm over my lips. Not only was she eating with them, she was engaged in conversation. During a meal!

I stared in disbelief, my brain unable to register what my eyes beheld. Then, to my utter horror and dismay, I spied Berta's bright pink gown sticking out from beneath her dark calico skirt. From the workers' chuckles and stares, I knew they, too, had discovered the offending piece of clothing.

I wanted to race across the room and ask her what she was thinking, but I'd already concluded that Berta didn't think, at least not about the proper way to behave. Eyes agog, everyone focused upon the unfolding scene. Except for a few muffled giggles from the children, no one said a word. I glanced around the room, seeking my parents. My father was seated at the east side of the room with a group of the men. Mother was at one of the women's tables and offered me a sympathetic look.

Where were Berta's parents? I hoped one of them would step forward, but I couldn't locate either of them. I didn't know whether to go and inquire about the Schumachers' whereabouts or remain near the stove. I didn't wonder for long.

Moments later, Berta was dancing on tiptoe as the Küchebaas held her by one ear and escorted her across the dining room. The two of them came to a halt in front of me. "This one is your responsibility, Johanna. Take her out back and explain the way of things in the Muhlbach Küche. Make certain she knows that *I* do not intend to become the laughingstock of the village. Understand?"

I bobbed my head at the older woman and then glared at Berta. "Follow me!"

She grasped my arm as I stormed from the room. "Don't be angry, Hanna."

I tugged her along until we were away from the sisters who were cleaning and paring the vegetables for our next meal. For years, the women assigned to the job had been designated "paring-knife sisters." When weather permitted, they sat on the back porch with their wooden trays on their laps and talked or sang hymns while they worked.

This was one time I didn't want them to hear what I had to say. When we'd neared the garden shed, I swirled around. "My name is Johanna, *not* Hanna." My tightly clenched jaw ached.

Berta shrugged and grinned at me. "Then I'll call you Johanna. I don't understand why you and Sister Muhlbach are so angry. I was eating breakfast. Don't I get to eat?"

"Yes, you get to eat, but you do not eat with the men. Didn't you see the men were seated at tables separate from the women and children? Wasn't it clear to you that we do not eat at the same tables? And didn't Sister Muhlbach tell you to refrain from conversing with the men?" I pointed to my ear. "Do you have a hearing problem?"

Berta rubbed her ear. "I didn't used to, but who can tell by now. Did you see the way that woman pulled me up from the bench? I think my ear stretched at least two inches. Does it look any longer than the other one?"

As she turned her ear toward me, I could see she genuinely expected me to check it. "You aren't hurt. And that's not the least of what will happen to you if you continue this behavior. Perhaps you're better suited for some other work." I pointed at the hem of her skirt. "Why are you wearing that silk gown beneath your calico?"

"Those clothes you gave me are too large, so I put them overtop of my own gown. It makes for a better fit. Besides, a bit of color is a good thing, don't you think?"

"That's exactly the problem, Berta. You're not thinking. We do not wear bright colors; we don't feel the need to be different." Though I spoke with authority, my conscience gnawed at me. Sometimes I wanted to be different, too, but I dared not tell Berta about my deep longing to visit other places and experience life beyond the boundaries of Amana.

"Well, I do. And I want to wear beautiful things. I look around the room and every woman looks the same. The calico is either black or brown or dark blue with tiny little white designs. Is that little indistinguishable design supposed to be a nod to prettiness? If so, it misses the mark."

She plopped down on a bench near the shed and tightened her lips into a firm knot. I sat beside her, uncertain how I could win her to my side. I needed to convince her that she would be happier if she would conform to our ways. Still, she hadn't been reared among our people. She knew what existed beyond the perimeter of our villages, and I didn't think I could convince her that this life was better. Like my brother Wilhelm, she wanted more than Amana could offer.

"Before you pass judgment, perhaps you should do your best to follow instructions and learn how we live." When Berta didn't respond, I leaned closer. "Your parents appear determined to remain in Amana. Wouldn't it be easier on all of you if you'd at least make an effort to be happy?"

"We were happy in Chicago. At least I thought we were." Her brows furrowed. "I got in trouble from time to time, but I'm beginning to wonder if there was some other reason they decided to come here. Besides me, I mean."

"I'm sorry, but I have no idea."

With a stubborn glint in her eyes, she thrust her arms around her waist. "You wouldn't tell me if you knew."

"I wouldn't lie to you. The truth is, such matters are discussed and decided by the elders and trustee. Private information isn't shared."

I couldn't tell if Berta believed me, but I'd spoken the truth and could do no more to convince her. Right now I needed to get her back into the kitchen before Sister Muhlbach came looking for us. That thought had barely skittered through my mind when the back door slammed and the older woman tromped toward us.

She stopped directly in front of us and planted her fists on her hips. "Did the two of you decide to spend the day out here enjoying the spring weather while the rest of us perform your duties? If you don't want to help in the kitchen, Berta, perhaps you'd like to work in the garden? I can speak to the Bruderrat."

I couldn't predict what Berta would say, but I poked her with my elbow and hoped she'd understand she should refuse the garden work. Instead, she turned her gaze toward the east, where the sun was slowly ascending into a billowy blue sky.

I knew what she was thinking: Outdoors would be better

than being cooped up in the kitchen. But she didn't know the *Gartebaas.*

Berta would never survive under the supervision of Sister Rosina Nusser. Though small in stature, the garden boss was filled with more energy than any woman in Amana. The wiry mother of five worked hard and expected the same from every person who worked for her. Even the hired hands requested new assignments after a day or two of Sister Nusser's commands.

"Berta is going to do better in the kitchen. She's going to try very hard, aren't you, Berta?" Once again I jabbed her in the side.

She rubbed her fingertips along her waistline and glared in my direction. "I'll give it a try."

Sister Muhlbach motioned toward the kitchen. "Then go inside and help Sister Dickel wash the dishes, Berta."

When I jumped to my feet, the older woman shook her head. "Not you, Johanna. We will speak privately before you return to work."

My heart hammered against my chest like an anvil striking iron. When Berta had returned indoors, Sister Muhlbach pointed to the bench. "Sit down, Johanna." She settled beside me, and the stern lines around her mouth softened. "You've been burdened with a difficult task, one that will try your patience and mine. There is no doubt this is an impertinent young woman who has little desire to live here or learn our ways."

"So it would seem." I didn't want to disparage Berta, but I couldn't lie, either.

She pinched the bridge of her nose. "For your sake, I will give her a little latitude, but I cannot have her creating chaos in the kitchen. You must do your best to bring her around, and quickly. Do I make myself clear?"

I nodded. "Yes, Sister Muhlbach. Very clear."

"Gut. Now let's get back to work."

She walked by my side until we neared the kitchen door. With a viselike grip, she held my arm. "One more thing, Johanna. Make certain Berta never again wears that bright pink skirt!"

# CHAPTER 4

Berta Schumacher

My father folded his arms across his chest and stared over the top of his spectacles. "I'm told you created quite a ruckus in the kitchen this morning."

There was no reason to deny it. My father had obviously heard all of the details. I couldn't help but wonder who had told him, though. Johanna? Probably Brother Ilg, I decided. He was an elder as well as Johanna's father. He'd be eager to tell my parents that I was a misfit in this strange new world. "I didn't follow the rules. I've already been reprimanded." I glanced at my mother. "Where were you? I didn't see either of you come to the dining room for breakfast. Did the two of you receive a reprimand for breaking the rules?"

"No, Berta. Rather than break the rules, we gained permission to be absent in advance. Some of my medical equipment arrived on the train last week and had been delivered by wagon from Homestead. I wanted to check over the items and ensure that nothing had broken. We received permission to eat breakfast at the hotel kitchen, since it is close to the office where I'll be working."

I was weary from the day at work and thought my brain hadn't properly registered what my father had said. "Did you say your equipment arrived last week? How is that possible?"

Mother inched closer beside me on the divan and patted my hand. "We'd begun making plans to move here earlier than you probably surmised."

"How *much* earlier?" I pulled my hand from her grasp.

"We'd been talking for a month or two," she whispered.

"A month or two?" I jumped to my feet and mentally calculated dates. "That's before the trouble with John Underwood." I glanced between them. "You said that was why we were moving here, but now I discover you told me a lie!" With each word, my tone elevated a notch.

"No need to shout, Berta. Sit down and let's discuss this like sensible folks."

My father's placating tone further infuriated me. "Why? Everything has already been decided. I had no choice in this matter. You and Mother made me believe we moved here because of John Underwood, but now I discover that can't possibly be the case."

"It *is* part of the reason. The fact that you and John hadn't yet been involved in that last bit of mischief changes nothing. The two of you had certainly caused us worry by then." My mother retrieved a handkerchief from her pocket and blotted her eyes.

I stiffened at the sight. She needn't think her tears would soften my anger. The two of them had plotted and schemed behind my back and made me believe that living in this strict community was due entirely to my outlandish behavior.

"I know I haven't been the best daughter, but there's something more to this move than my antics with John Underwood. Something you've decided to keep secret." I didn't fail to note the quick glance exchanged by my parents. I yanked the apron from around my waist and stomped toward my room.

"We have prayer service in a few minutes. You need to remove that pink gown and gather your shawl," my father said.

*Prayer service!* The thought irritated me like the prickly wool blanket that covered my bed. Unless I could escape this place, I'd be required to attend prayer service every night for the rest of my life. And as if every night wasn't enough, Johanna had told me there were a total of eleven meetings each week. I'd nearly fainted. *Eleven!* Who ever heard of such a thing! Not only did they meet every night, but they added a meeting on Wednesday, Saturday, and Sunday afternoons. And, of course, there was Sunday morning service, too. The idea of all that praying baffled me. Couldn't they just do it all at once and be done with it?

I gathered my shawl and hiked up the skirt of the pink silk, careful to tuck the waistband tight beneath the calico. Hemming was out of the question. There wasn't time. Besides, I didn't know how to hem a skirt. Later I'd get the scissors from Mother's sewing box and snip off an inch or two. I wasn't yet ready to discard my vestiges of the outside world. Satisfied the fabric was now hidden from sight, I returned to the parlor. With a sweep of his arm, my father gestured toward the door. The three of us exited the parlor with my mother in the lead, my father at the rear, and me sandwiched between them.

Father had turned to close our door when a young man and a middle-aged woman exited their apartment. The young man grinned at me.

*"Guten Abend."*

My father stared at the fellow as if taking his measure. "Good evening."

Their neighbor extended his hand. "I am Rudolf Stilson, and this is my mother, Hilda Stilson."

The woman was holding her son's arm in a possessive grasp. "So, we finally meet the new doctor and his family. I thought Brother Frank would bring you up to meet us when you arrived, but . . ." Her voice trailed off as if she expected my father to respond, but when he said nothing, she continued. "My Rudolf hopes the Grossebruderrat will consider sending him to school to become a doctor or maybe a pharmacist. He is a smart boy."

"I thought pride was frowned upon in the community," I said.

"Berta! You forget your manners." My mother grimaced. "My daughter isn't herself this evening."

I wanted to tell them that I hadn't been myself since we set foot in this town, but I held my tongue. Such a comment would only meet with another reprimand. We followed Rudolf and his mother down the stairs and outside. I was surprised when, before long, Rudolf had worked his way back until he was walking beside me.

"I saw what happened in the Küche this morning," he said. "It takes time to adjust. You'll learn."

"I don't want to learn. I want to return to Chicago, where I can enjoy myself," I whispered.

A straw hat topped his thick dark hair, but it was the glint in his chocolate brown eyes that captured my attention. He appeared to be a young man who could learn to take pleasure in life—with a little help. "Did you grow up in Amana?" I kept my voice low, fearful the others would discover we were talking and pull me away from Rudolf's side.

"Most of my life. We lived on the outside for about a year, but when my Vater died, *Mutter* and I moved back. She's content here. It is her home."

My heart fluttered with excitement. At least I'd connected with someone who knew what living out in the world was like. The fun, the excitement, the adventure. "Don't you miss the outside life?"

"Not so much. Our life out there wasn't so gut. We worked on a farm, and the owner expected too much work for too little pay. When Vater was injured and died, we knew this was where we belonged, so we returned."

The joyful flutter in my chest disappeared even more quickly than it had arrived. I'd misjudged Rudolf. He was like all the rest of them. Content with the dull sameness of this place. But after hearing a few motivating details, he might be convinced there could be more excitement in his future. More beyond the perimeter of the Amana villages, more beyond the farm where he'd been mistreated, more to life than he'd even imagined.

I tugged on his sleeve. "We need to talk. You didn't see Chicago. It's a wonderful place. You would like it very much."

"But here in Amana, I am content. And my Mutter would be sad if I chose to leave. I like my work. It is a gut life here. You will see."

He'd said the proper words, the words anyone living here would expect to hear from him. But I'd detected a shadowy doubt in his eyes that made me wonder if he truly was convinced this was where he belonged. Unfortunately, there wasn't time for further conversation. Sister Stilson waved him forward. He obediently rushed to his mother's side, but I decided Rudolf displayed promise. With a little work, he could be convinced a better life awaited him outside the confines of Amana, Iowa. I was certain of it.

My breath caught when Johanna grasped the fabric of my calico skirt between her thumb and forefinger the following morning. She lifted the fabric only an inch from the floor before allowing it to drop back into place. "I'm pleased to see you did as you were instructed."

I didn't respond. I'd be accused of lying if I agreed, and if I disagreed, I'd have to remove the pink silk skirt. Instead, I offered a bright smile. "And I'm on time, as well."

"Indeed you are. It's heartening to know my prayers are being answered."

I didn't respond to that remark, either. I looped arms and leaned close, pretending we'd been dear friends for years. "I've studied all of the single men who dine at our Küche, and I can't decide which one you plan to marry." Hoping to view Johanna's reaction, I released her arm and danced along beside her. My skirt whispered through the dew-kissed grass as we cut around the house to the rear kitchen door.

The waning moon filtered slivers of light through the budding tree branches and cast eerie designs across her pale complexion. "You are too bold with your questions, Berta. A girl of your age shouldn't be dwelling upon marriage."

"I'm not thinking about my own marriage, only yours. After all, you're getting quite old. At your age most young ladies have several suitors."

"Quite old?"

There was no doubt I'd offended her, but at least we'd moved along to a topic other than my pink skirt. "Indeed. Most young women your age would be distraught if they didn't have an excellent marriage prospect."

She unlatched the kitchen door and gestured toward the lamps.

"You should know that marriage is never deemed acceptable by the elders until a young woman has attained the age of twenty-one, and young men must be twenty-four. For your information, I turned twenty-one not long ago."

I struck a match against the hearth. The glimmering flame revealed the displeasure in Johanna's eyes, but that didn't stop me. "Still, I would think if there is someone who interests you—"

She waved me off as she would a pesky fly. "Finish the lamps and then go fetch water while I light the fire."

Moments later I halted my lamp-lighting duties. "I guess you'd prefer someone from another village. Most of the unmarried men in Amana are quite solemn, don't you think? I believe a sense of humor is important in marriage."

Johanna pointed overhead. "Keep your voice down. Sister Muhlbach will hear. Private matters are not to be discussed. I don't want her to think I'd engage in unacceptable conversation with you. Besides, what does a girl your age know of marriage!"

"My parents are married, and I think they could use more humor in their marriage. Father used to laugh a lot but not so much anymore." I lit the final lamp. "Why are you so worried about getting in trouble? Your father is an elder. He can simply tell them you weren't at fault, and all will be fine. That's what Father usually did when I got in trouble at school."

A piece of firewood slipped from Johanna's hand. "You were disobedient, and your father lied for you so you wouldn't suffer consequences for your bad behavior?"

She made it sound as though Father had committed some horrid crime. "Sort of," I mumbled.

"That won't happen here in Amana. If you misbehave, you must tell the truth and be prepared to take your punishment."

I picked up the bucket and stifled a giggle. What could be done to make my life any more miserable? As if she could read my mind, Johanna said, "Believe me, you don't want to be banned from meetings."

I stopped in my tracks and swiveled around as though spinning on ice. "*That's* the punishment? You can't attend prayer meeting every night?"

"Or on Sunday, either. If the infraction isn't quite so bad, you're relegated to children's church. But since you've not yet advanced, I imagine you would be banned from all church services."

I wasn't certain what she meant by advancing to other services on Sunday. So far, I'd only been to the nightly prayer meeting. Even though I dared not tell Johanna, I considered the punishment more of a reward. Armed with this latest unexpected news, I unlatched the door and skipped outside to fetch water.

Sister Muhlbach arrived in the kitchen a short time later. When I readily agreed to go to the cellar and check the cans of milk for spoilage, she eyed me with suspicion. "You'll be helping to make cottage cheese today," she called after me. I turned and flashed a smile in her direction. Her forehead scrunched with tiny wrinkles. My cooperative behavior had obviously confused her. The thought warmed me like a cup of hot chocolate on a cold day.

Once I entered the cellar, my jubilant thoughts evaporated as quickly as they'd arrived. The dank, dark rooms were enough to set my teeth on edge. In my haste to comply with Sister Muhlbach's request, I'd forgotten the lantern. I stood at the bottom of the wooden steps and hoped my eyes would adjust to the darkness. Unfortunately, the milk was stored far across the room, away from any sliver of light. If I circled behind the steps, I could possibly edge my way along the wall and get to the large water-filled concrete vat that held the milk cans. I stood there and imagined spiders and bugs lurking among the jars of canned fruits and vegetables or a mouse hidden behind a barrel or basket. I should go upstairs, retrieve a lantern, and return to check the milk. That was the easiest solution. But I remained a little longer, unwilling to go upstairs and admit my forgetfulness to Sister Muhlbach.

"Berta! Are you still down there?"

"Coming." I hastened up the steps and shaded my eyes from the bright sun that had begun its ascent into a clear blue sky.

Johanna grabbed my hand and pulled me along. "Sister Muhlbach thought you'd gone to sleep down there."

"Who could sleep in such a place? I'm sure it's full of all kinds of creatures."

"A few spiders and maybe a snake or two—or perhaps a weasel." With lightning speed, she snatched my arm in a quick pinch.

Heart pounding, I jumped backwards. Johanna's laughter rang in my ears, and anger swelled in my chest. "That wasn't funny! You frightened me."

"I'm sorry, but I thought you were the girl who loved to play pranks and have fun."

Sister Muhlbach waved us inside. "Come along. There's breakfast to cook. What about the milk? Sweet or sour?" Her eyebrows arched high on her forehead.

"Sweet."

She stared at my empty hands. "You did not bring any upstairs for breakfast?"

"You didn't tell me. I didn't think I was supposed—"

"Ach! That's the problem. You didn't think. Now go fetch a can of milk and fill the pitchers. I'll slice the bread for you."

This time I grabbed the lantern before I hurried out the back door and down the cellar stairs. What did she mean that she'd slice the bread for me? If I was supposed to slice the bread, why had she sent me to the cellar? No doubt I'd be assigned to dishwashing again this evening. I lifted one of the cans from beneath the heavy rugs used to help keep the milk cold and hiked back up the steps.

The bell had sounded, and soon the tables would be filled with hungry men, women, and children. Sister Muhlbach pointed to the empty pitchers. After filling them, I placed one on each of the tables and returned to the kitchen for further instruction.

Hands on hips, Sister Muhlbach watched my every move. Just looking at her tart expression was enough to make me squint my eyes and purse my lips. "Each table needs bread and syrup. Then come back for the oatmeal."

I dutifully placed platters laden with bread, pitchers of syrup, and tureens of oatmeal first on the men's tables, then on the women's tables, and then on the table occupied by the older children. I'd deposited the last of the oatmeal and had nearly made it back to the kitchen when one of the elders motioned to me.

"Please tell Sister Muhlbach I wish to speak with her immediately—and please remove the pitchers of milk from the tables on your way to the kitchen."

His request could mean only one thing—the milk was sour. Perspiration dampened my palms, and I swiped them down the front of my apron. Spilling sour milk on the elders certainly wouldn't help my plight. When I stopped at the women's table, I could see the concern in my mother's eyes. "Spoiled milk," I whispered in her ear as I lifted the pitcher. "I'll be in trouble for sure."

Mother's chest deflated like a balloon losing air. "You must learn to behave, Berta. I don't want any trouble. Do you understand?" She hissed the words through clenched teeth.

I reared back. Her words felt like a slap. Why did she want to stay in this awful place? What had happened to the mother I'd known in Chicago? The one who attended luncheons and balls? The one who enjoyed seeing the latest fashions when they arrived from Europe? The one who loved purchasing and wearing those fashionable gowns? Within hours of arriving in Iowa, she'd transformed into an unfashionable matron content to care for other women's children and eat in a dining hall isolated from her own husband and daughter.

Pitchers in hand, I hastened to the kitchen and delivered the message to Sister Muhlbach. I didn't have to tell her the milk was sour. I carried the evidence with me.

# CHAPTER 5

Johanna Ilg

There was no controlling Berta. She had an excuse for everything. Yet over the past days her carefree spirit had warmed my heart in an inexplicable way I'd seldom experienced. I'd lain awake for several nights, contemplating exactly why I frequently came to her defense, for she certainly didn't deserve my help. She'd learned little from the incident with the spoiled milk. Even two days of churning butter and making cottage cheese hadn't deterred her from sneaking off to hide behind the shed and take a nap.

Something deep inside compelled me to protect her, yet I couldn't decide what it was. We were in the washhouse helping with the family laundry, and each time our mothers carried a basket of wet clothes to the lines, Berta would tell me something more about Chicago and her life before arriving in Iowa. It was then, when I'd least expected it, I received my answer. Berta represented a link to my brother Wilhelm, in Chicago. When I listened to her talk about the city and the many places she'd been, I imagined Wilhelm doing those very same things. Not shopping for pretty dresses or attending teas, but I could picture him dining at a fine hotel, attending an outdoor concert in the park, or strolling along the shores of Lake Michigan. How wondrous his life must be—and how different from what he'd left behind here.

It took little to prompt my thoughts toward the many places I longed to visit before I died. No doubt my mother would be overwrought if she knew how often my thoughts lingered on the outside world. Not long ago I'd gathered courage and told her of my desire to visit Wilhelm in Chicago. Her complexion had turned pale, and she'd dropped to her chair in a near faint. "Your Vater and I will never consider such a thing. There is nothing gut for you in the outside world," she'd said. But she hadn't changed my mind.

I daydreamed of fashionable people like those who visited our villages. As visitors strolled through our village, staring at us in wonderment, I viewed them with the same curiosity. It seemed unfair that they could enter our world, yet I could not take a peek into theirs. If only mother would relent and let me visit Wilhelm in Chicago. Then I could cross one city off my list of places to see. Maybe Wilhelm would consider taking me to see some other cities, as well. My thoughts skittered in random directions: Boston, New York, even Omaha would be welcome.

Wearing a pair of the wooden shoes we routinely donned on washday, Berta shuffled to my side. After walking out of the clogs and soaking her stockings several times, she'd begun dragging her feet to keep the shoes in place. "Why doesn't Sister Muhlbach report me to the elders? Each day I am certain she'll speak to them, but each day I'm disappointed."

*"What?"* Berta's foolish question interrupted my thoughts of Wilhelm and Chicago. "Why would you want her to do such a thing? You should be thankful Sister Muhlbach has been patient with you. If you'd been assigned to any other Küchebaas, you would have been reported to the elders and banished from church meetings for at least a week or two—maybe more." I'd barely uttered the words when realization struck me like a clap of thunder. Berta *wanted* the elders to ban her from attending church and prayer meetings. For a young woman of seventeen years, she was wily, willful, and set upon getting her way, even if it meant angering Sister Muhlbach.

Her chuckle angered me, and all feelings of compassion instantly evaporated. I grasped her cheeks and squeezed until her lips puckered.

"You're hurting me," she sputtered.

"Not nearly as much as you deserve." I released my hold and silently asked God's forgiveness for my unkind behavior. This girl's conduct pained me as much as a festering carbuncle. "So you're hoping to avoid church, are you? Well, you can rest assured that once I tell Sister Muhlbach what you're up to, she'll not speak to the elders. She'll mete out her own punishment." Berta attempted to lodge a complaint, but I shushed her. "The elders would view her inability to train you as a disappointment—and as a failure on my part, as well."

"But you told me that was the punishment for improper behavior." She tossed an armload of clothes into the water.

Quickly I scooped the clothes out and tossed them to the floor. "Not those, Berta. We wash the dark clothes last."

"There are so many rules you can hardly expect me to remember all of them." Pointing her index finger heavenward, she said,

"Monday is washday, so we get away from the kitchen for part of the day. But only to perform more work." She held up another finger. "Tuesday is the day when foods made with flour are served." She grinned. "I like Tuesdays."

"Of course you do. All children enjoy filling their stomachs with potato dumplings or doughnuts and applesauce."

"Don't forget cream puffs and waffles. Those are my favorites."

"Then you'll be sorry to hear that once springtime is over and the hens aren't laying lots of eggs, we don't prepare so many of the pastries you love."

Berta wrinkled her nose and let out a huff, clearly annoyed by the news. I shaved soap into the wash water and half listened while Berta returned to the recitation of duties associated with each day of the week.

She had all five fingers pointing heavenward. "And then there's Friday. Who wouldn't be delighted with Fridays? We receive the wondrous privilege of cleaning the kitchen."

No one could deny Berta's disdain for the Friday cleaning ritual. She'd grumbled until Sister Muhlbach had finally sent her to the far corners of the dining room to scrub floors by herself. Even that hadn't stilled Berta's complaints. She'd continued to grumble until the rest of us joined our voices in songs to the Lord to drown out her protests.

She poked my arm, obviously aware I'd quit listening to her onslaught. "Our lives are controlled by food and work."

I shook my head, eager to help Berta understand our ways. "Our lives are centered upon worshiping God. When work is completed in an orderly fashion, it permits us more time to seek God."

"God knows where to find me. I don't think He's interested in Berta Schumacher and whether she's baking coffee cakes or serving spoiled milk."

"But He is, Berta. God is interested in all of us. You need only spend time with Him to discover His love for you. Read the Bible and pray. You'll discover that He has much to say to you."

Mouth agape, she stared at me. I wasn't certain what she was thinking, so I clamped my lips together and returned to scrubbing the wet clothes. Her silence gave me hope that she would take my words to heart. But my expectations were dashed when she tapped my arm and said, "I saw a good-looking fellow down at the barn with your father yesterday. I think he'd be a good match for you."

I sighed and dropped another petticoat into the wash basket. "Do you think only of young men, Berta?"

"No, but I do think about them a good deal. Especially where you're concerned." She peeked around the doorway and then stepped closer. "I heard your father talking to the man—about you."

Heat warmed my cheeks, and I turned away. This girl knew no boundaries. My mother reappeared for another basket of wet clothes, so I had a few minutes to regain my composure. The moment she exited the washhouse, I wheeled around to face Berta. "You should not be eavesdropping on other people's conversations. What were you doing at the barns? You have no business down there." Though I'd done my best to remain calm, I hadn't managed to control the angry tremble in my voice. Berta stared at me, and I decided she was likely trying to decide if she should tell the truth or tell another one of her famous falsehoods. "And don't fib to me."

"I went to the barn because Rudolf said he'd meet me there after he completed the milk deliveries."

"So now you're going to blame Rudolf?"

"No! I'm telling you why I went to the barns. We didn't think anyone would see us. We hid in one of the stalls. Just to talk," she hastened to add. "About the time we were preparing to leave, your father and this other fellow walked inside the barn. We didn't have any choice but to stay put."

I could feel the blood drain from my face. "So Rudolf heard this conversation, as well?"

"Yes, but he didn't mean any—"

I waved my hand to silence her. "Who was this man? Did you hear his name?"

Berta quickly closed the distance between us. "So you are interested? I knew you would be. Rudolf told me his name is Carl Froehlich, and he lives in High Amana."

I didn't need further explanation. I knew the Froehlich family. Carl's father had been in charge of the barns in High Amana until he unexpectedly passed away the year Carl turned fifteen. He'd been too young to succeed his father as farm Baas, and the position had been assigned to Herman Miller. When Brother Miller would become too old to capably act as manager, his son, Edward, would step in.

Had Carl decided he could eventually become farm Baas in Main Amana by requesting a move? Or had he decided the succession would more easily occur if he was a member of our family? The thoughts raced through my head like a cat giving chase to a fleeing mouse.

From time to time my father had mentioned Brother Froehlich's death and Carl's dilemma. Probably because he saw irony in the situation. Though he'd fathered two sons, neither would step into my father's position as farm boss. Had Pieter lived, I wondered if he would have remained in Amana or if he would have followed Wilhelm to Chicago. One day I'd asked my father that very question. Tears had pooled in his eyes when he told me it did no good to dwell on matters that couldn't be changed.

After that he never again mentioned Carl or a possible successor as farm boss.

"Tell me exactly what was said. And don't change the conversation to suit your fancy."

Berta cast her gaze toward the floor.

"Look me in the eye so I can see that you're speaking the truth." I reached forward and lifted her chin.

"I didn't hear everything," she whispered. "Rudolf said Carl wants to move from High and work for your father."

"And? What else?"

"Your father said he would speak to the Grossebruderrat about his request."

"That's all? Nothing about me?"

"Not exactly. At least nothing I could hear. But why else would he want to come here and work? I'm sure you were mentioned."

My heartbeat slowed and relief flooded over me. "So when you said they were talking about me, you made that up?" I wanted a positive affirmation she'd been lying.

"Well, maybe you could say that."

"Just tell me yes or no, Berta. Tell me the truth. Did my father or Carl mention my name or speak of me in any way?"

"No. But I'm sure that if he comes to work for your father, he'll want to marry you. The two of you would be a fine couple."

"You need to cease your meddling ways." I motioned for her to bring me the work pants. "And if you sneak off to the barn again, I'll report you to Sister Muhlbach. If she discovers that you're meeting Rudolf, she'll have you scrubbing floors until your knees turn raw."

I considered threatening to tell her parents but knew that would do little good. It had taken no time at all to realize Berta had her parents wrapped around her little finger. Neither of them would be of assistance. I didn't know if I should speak to Sister Stilson. If I did, Rudolf would suffer dearly. His mother was as strict as the Schumachers were lenient. No, I'd speak privately to Rudolf and warn him he shouldn't accept any further invitations from Berta.

I could only pray the elders would never again appoint me to oversee a new member of the community.

On her first day in the kitchen, Berta had been assigned to deliver Oma Reich's meals. To anyone else, delivering food would have been of little consequence. But on that first delivery day, Oma Reich had made it her business to tell Berta what she thought of young ladies who shouted and stomped and created upheaval—especially when the upheaval took place in the rooms above Oma Reich's dwelling place.

When Berta had returned, she requested someone else be assigned the deliveries. But Sister Muhlbach had been unrelenting. Three times a day Berta carried Oma's meals across the street and down the block to our residence. As the days wore on, Berta's complaints had subsided, and now she said nothing when she was sent on her way. In truth, I knew Berta had begun to enjoy the temporary reprieve from the kitchen. And after only a few days, Oma Reich had confided she thought Berta was beginning to change her ways.

I hadn't argued. I'd let the old woman believe she could change Berta into a steadfast member of the community. Personally, I doubted anything would change Berta, but only time would tell.

Today when Sister Muhlbach covered the tray of food with a clean linen cloth, she instructed Berta, "No time for wasting today. Come straight back after you deliver Oma Reich's meal. Spring cleaning begins after breakfast, and every hand is needed."

I came alongside Berta as she lifted the tray. "I know you don't want to help clean, but you must hurry back. Otherwise, Sister Muhlbach will have you scrubbing long after everyone else has gone home this evening."

Though Berta promised a speedy return, I didn't hold out hope. It seemed the girl forgot her promises as quickly as they were made. But for now, my own kitchen chores required completion. Only then could the window washing begin. The only noise to be heard in the dining room was the clatter of utensils striking plates or the occasional shuffling of feet on the wooden floor. I surveyed the tables for any bowls that might need to be refilled, gathered two, and returned to the kitchen.

"More oatmeal," I announced, handing the bowls to Sister Dickel, who dipped a ladle into the oversized kettle.

"They're extra hungry this morning," she said.

"Or your oatmeal is particularly good today." I hurried off with the steaming bowls before she could reply and returned them to the tables.

A shrill scream cut through the morning solitude, and all heads turned as the front door to the dining hall flew open. Eyes wild with fear and cap askew, Berta searched the tables wildly. "Father! Father! Come quick!" She yanked on her father's arm with a ferocity that defied her small frame. "It's Oma Reich. She needs your help."

While her father extricated himself from the bench, I hurried to Berta's side and grasped her arm. "Come sit down, Berta."

Body trembling, she wrested out of my hold. "No, I have to return with Father. Oma Reich is ill. Come with us. *Please*. You can help. She knows you. She'll respond to you."

"Berta's right. I may need help." Dr. Schumacher glanced at my father. "You don't object, do you, Brother Frank?"

"No." My father gestured toward the door. "Go along with them and do what you can to help, Johanna."

We'd cleared the front door when Berta yanked on my hand. "I think I killed her," she hissed.

I couldn't take another step. My feet dug into the ground as if they'd been nailed in place. "What did you do?"

"Come on, girls. There's no time to waste." Dr. Schumacher's urgent command propelled me forward.

"I delivered her tray as usual. I called to her, but when she didn't answer, I went into the bedroom."

Silence hung between us until I poked her with my elbow. "And?"

"I thought she was asleep so I called her name again. When she didn't respond, I grabbed hold of her arm." She captured her lip between her teeth for a moment, and tears welled in her eyes. "I think I pulled too hard, because she fell on the floor."

"What?" I hadn't meant to shriek.

Dr. Schumacher had run several feet ahead of us, but he glanced over his shoulder. "Is something wrong?"

"No, nothing," Berta said. "We're coming." And then to me, "Please don't tell."

I hastened my step. "Was she breathing? Did you check to see?"

"I . . . I don't think so." A gush of tears followed Berta's stammered response.

"Stay out here," I commanded when we entered the parlor. "I'll go in with your father."

Dr. Schumacher was on his knees when I stepped into the bedroom. I stooped down beside him and reached for Oma's hand. The doctor shook his head. "She's gone. From the appearance of her body, she probably died sometime during the night. Looks like she might have gotten up to call for help and couldn't make it."

"You think it was her heart?" I asked. Oma had complained of pains in her shoulder and back over the past month.

"It's difficult to know for sure, but that might be the cause." He lifted the old woman in his arms and placed her body on the bed. "Do you know who we should summon to prepare her?"

"She has no family members. I'll fetch my mother. She'll see to the body."

I returned to the parlor and motioned for Berta to follow me. Neither of us spoke until we were outside. The budding trees throughout the village heralded a season of new life, yet Oma's death had diminished all beauty of the season.

"What did Father say?"

"She died sometime during the night. You weren't responsible for her death. Come on. We need to return to the kitchen."

"You're angry with me. I can tell."

Mud squished beneath the soles of my shoes as I stepped off the board sidewalk and out into the street. "I'm not angry, Berta. I'm sad. I loved Oma Reich. Even though I know she's in a better place, it doesn't mean I won't miss her."

Berta clung to my side while I delivered the news to my parents. The village carpenter would be summoned to Oma's room, where he would measure the old woman's body before he prepared a simple pine box for her burial. The wood shavings would be saved and used in Oma's coffin pillow. My mother would wash the woman's body and dress her in a white muslin gown, a shawl, and knit stockings. Oma's gray hair would be tucked beneath a finely knitted white cap and then covered with a plain white muslin cap before the silk ribbons were tied beneath her wrinkled chin and she was placed in the wooden box.

The ritual remained the same for each member of the community: White clothing for both the men and women, burial in a plain wooden box that was neither too large nor too small, a place in the ground next to the last person who had died, and a simple headstone with the name of the deceased and the date of death.

Just as the community had provided equality in life, it provided parity in death.

By the next morning our parlor had been cleared of all furniture save a small doily-covered table, the casket, and a clock with the hands stopped at midnight to signify Oma Reich's approximate time of death. Though the weather was not yet overly warm, my mother had placed canning jars filled with ice inside and beneath the coffin—just in case. "You never know. It could turn hot," she said when I questioned her. "Better safe than sorry."

Since there were no surviving relatives, my parents greeted the visitors and accepted condolences on Oma's behalf. One after another families appeared, walked to the casket, offered a brief prayer, and departed. Everyone was now gone except Berta. She'd been standing in a far corner of the room for over an hour. She'd neither approached the casket nor said a word to anyone.

I padded across the multicolored wool carpet. It seemed strangely out of place on such a somber day as this. "Would you like me to go with you to the side of the casket, Berta?"

"No. I can see from here." Her gaze drifted toward the pine box. "She doesn't look very good, does she?"

I forced a smile. "She's dead, Berta. No one looks good in death. Why don't you go back upstairs with your parents. There's no reason for you to remain down here."

After one final glance at the coffin, Berta shuffled from the room. Clearly the girl still believed she'd played some part in Oma Reich's death.

Berta and her parents attended the funeral service the next day for Oma Reich. Following our custom, Berta and her mother had made their way to the cemetery with the women while her father took his place with the men. She remained silent, quietly observing the ritual—at least that's what I thought until I observed her slowly working her way to the rear of the crowd until she stood next to Rudolf. Though their exchange was brief, my stomach lurched at the sight. Berta was up to something.

# CHAPTER 6

Berta Schumacher

Throughout the days following Oma Reich's funeral, Johanna guarded me like the village watchman who protected the town against fire. Rudolf and I had arranged to meet after the funeral, but Johanna foiled any opportunity to sneak away. Though I'd done my best to shake her from my side, she hadn't been deterred. Instead of sneaking off to enjoy Rudolf's company, I'd been forced into the frenzy of spring cleaning. Since we already cleaned every day, I didn't see the necessity of spring cleaning, but my opinion wasn't considered.

After scrubbing and scouring every inch of the kitchen and its contents, I learned the same was expected in our rooms at home. The very idea of more cleaning set my head spinning with fresh thoughts of escape. Beating rugs, carrying out mattresses, washing windows, and pressing freshly washed curtains was beyond what anyone should expect from me. Yet my mother and father ignored my complaints. By the time we'd completed the cleaning, my hands were raw, and I'd discovered muscles I didn't know existed. And all of them ached.

Finally Monday arrived to signal the beginning of Holy Week. I looked forward to helping prepare for Easter, but my excitement waned at the prospect of attending yet another church service each day at noon. Had there not been other excitement within the Küche, I would have sorely protested. I hoped the fun of dying Easter eggs would outweigh the boredom of the extra church meetings.

"If you would listen to the elders during the church meetings, you would learn a great deal. And you would grow closer to the Lord, which would be a very good thing," Johanna said when I lodged yet another complaint on our way to the kitchen. "Besides, I thought you were the girl who enjoyed any escape from work."

Rubbing my arms, I crossed the street alongside Johanna. "Escape from one confinement to another isn't escape." The cold March wind whistled through the tree branches, and I shivered beneath my heavy shawl. I hadn't totally adapted to rising at this early hour, but I did derive a small sense of pleasure from the silence that cloaked the village before it bustled to life each day.

"You can rest your feet while you worship the Lord. At least you must admit there is a bit of pleasure in that," Johanna said.

"I think I will find more pleasure in dying eggs for the children. Sister Muhlbach said I could help if I didn't get in trouble the rest of the week."

Johanna patted my shoulder. "That's quite an order, isn't it?"

"I made it through yesterday without any problems, but she said we wouldn't boil and dye the eggs until Friday and Saturday. I wish it could be sooner."

"Good Friday is the best day. We won't be preparing much food, so there will be more time."

More time because Good Friday would be a day of fasting—a concept I didn't understand in the least. Although bread and water could be consumed, very little food would be prepared in the Küche on that day. What would it be like to smell cookies in the oven and be unable to taste them? Maybe baking cookies wouldn't be so much fun after all.

Very few eggs had been cracked during the past week. Each Küchebaas had to have enough dyed eggs to fill the baskets of the children who were served in her kitchen. Sister Muhlbach took that message to heart and had been abundantly clear: There would be more than enough cookies and eggs to fill every basket.

With all the chickens at each kitchen house, I didn't see how there could possibly be a shortage, but Sister Muhlbach had ordered that eggs would be used only for baking coffee cakes and other desserts. The excess were stored in large crocks in the basement, where they would remain cool. I had been assigned the task of carrying the eggs to the basement every afternoon.

With each passing day, I'd performed my tasks and kept my lips sealed. I wanted to help with baking the cookies and dying the eggs, and Sister Muhlbach knew it! When Friday finally arrived, I knew I'd passed the test. After early morning church we returned to the kitchen.

"First we must boil the eggs. While they cool, we can begin work on the cookies." Sister Muhlbach waved in my direction. "Go to the cellar and bring up the eggs, Berta—one crock at a time. We don't want any broken eggs."

I would have preferred to remain in the kitchen and watch how the water was prepared for the eggs, but I didn't argue. Any disagreement and Sister Muhlbach would surely ban me from the kitchen. Lantern in hand, I descended the stairs and entered the cavernous cellar. After making my way across the room, I counted the crocks. My legs would be aching by the time I completed the task.

With each trip to the kitchen, I'd peek to see if the onion skins had been added to the boiling water or the flour measured for the cookies. But if I lingered for even a few seconds, Sister Muhlbach waved me out the door. Once again, I descended the steps and lifted the lantern high. Four crocks remained. I now wished our two hundred chickens hadn't been quite so productive. None of the crocks was quite full. I might be able to rearrange the eggs and reduce the number of containers to three. After a hasty attempt, I gave up on the plan. The eggs simply wouldn't fit. But if I ignored Sister Muhlbach's warning and carried two at a time, I would only need to make one more trip. I could place them outside on the porch and then carry one crock at a time into the kitchen.

Cradling a heavy crock in each arm, I dangled the lantern from two fingers. With careful steps, I crossed the dirt floor and made my way up the stairs. Today, all of the women were busy inside the kitchen. No one to observe my disobedience. I heaved a sigh and placed the two bowls on the edge of the porch before returning downstairs. After securing a crock in each arm, I continued up the stairs, settled one container on the porch beside the other two, and carried the remaining one inside.

The pots of water were beginning to simmer. "How many more?" Sister Muhlbach asked.

I'd opened my mouth to answer when a barking dog and the distinct sound of breaking pottery sent me careering toward the back door. *"No!"* My shrieking admonition did nothing to frighten the furry black-and-white dog. I waved my arms at the animal. "Get away from there!" Paying me no heed, he continued to lap the egg yolks from amidst the pile of broken shells and scattered earthenware.

The other women rushed outside, and their chorus of shouts sent the animal running toward the shed, where he stopped long enough to eye the remaining mess. But when Sister Hillmer rushed after him with a broom, he disappeared.

"How did this happen, Berta?" Thick fingers surrounded my upper arm, and I turned to face Sister Muhlbach.

My lips moved, but my mouth felt as though it had been filled with cotton batting. The dog peeked out from alongside the wood shed, and I considered breaking loose of the woman's grasp. It would be far safer to hide with the dog than face her wrath. "I'm n-n-not sure," I gasped.

"Why were the crocks sitting out here on the porch? And whose dog is that? The only dogs permitted in the village belong to the shepherds. That dog isn't one of ours."

Her words sounded more like an accusation than a question. Did she think I'd enticed the dog into the yard? Couldn't she see my fear and concern? "I've never seen it before. I don't know where it came from," I croaked.

The answer didn't satisfy. She pointed at the mess. Only one crock remained safe on the porch. "Why were the crocks sitting out here?" Deep lines creased her forehead, and anger flashed in her dark eyes.

My mind whirled. What to do? I looked into Sister Muhlbach's dark eyes. "Things were busy with so many women in the kitchen, and I decided to bring the remaining crocks to the porch before I carried them inside. I thought it would cause less confusion." Her eyebrows dipped low. She was doing her best to make sense of my explanation—at least that's what I hoped. I relaxed when I saw a faint glint of understanding in her eyes.

"We will make do. But the next time I give you a job, don't try to improve on my instructions. Do as I tell you." She signaled for Johanna and one of the other sisters to gather the two remaining crocks. "Once you've cleaned up this mess, come inside."

I'd set to work picking up pieces of shell and shards of crockery from the slimy mess when I glanced up to see the black-and-white dog inching toward me. I raised my arm to wave the dog forward when fingers circled my wrist in a tight hold. "Don't do that, Berta."

"Rudolf! What are you doing here?"

"Delivering milk. What else?" He stomped his foot, and the dog backed up several paces. "Don't let that dog eat the eggs, Berta. If he gets a taste for eggs, he'll be trying to raid the chicken coops, and you'll be blamed." He stooped down beside me. "What happened?"

I explained the mishap while I pushed the slippery glob onto a piece of the broken crock. "Sister Muhlbach blames me, but it's the dog that's at fault."

Rudolf lifted his cap and scratched his head. "If you'd followed her orders—"

"Shh." I held my finger to my lips. "I didn't tell her about carrying two crocks at a time. That's just between us. She'd never let me back inside to dye eggs if she knew the full truth."

"Either way, you were wrong. The lying just makes it worse, but I'll keep your secret." He leaned across and scraped the remaining mess into another shard. After dumping the mess into the trash barrel, he wiped off the knees of his pants. "Just pump a little water and scrub with a broom. Soon it will be clean as a whistle."

I pointed toward the woodshed. "And get rid of that dog before he causes even more trouble."

While I scrubbed away any evidence of the broken eggs, Rudolf shouldered the cans of milk and carried them to the basement. The dog remained at a distance, watching my every move until

Rudolf reappeared. "I'll put the dog on my wagon and turn him out when I get over to East. Maybe one of the shepherds can turn him into a sheep dog."

"Oh, thank you, Rudolf. I'm grateful." If all those women hadn't been in the kitchen, I would have kissed him. "You are a true friend."

With an exaggerated flourish, he doffed his cap and bent at the waist. "I'm always pleased to help you, Berta."

"How long will the meeting last on Easter morning?"

Johanna grinned as we walked toward the kitchen on Saturday morning. "You're as eager as the children."

"I admit I'm looking forward to a few hours of fun tomorrow afternoon. I hope it won't rain." Sister Muhlbach and Sister Nusser had both predicted bad weather.

"Either way, the children will have fun. We can hide the eggs inside if it rains. One year when I was a little girl, it snowed on Easter. But it didn't dampen our spirits. It's the tradition that matters. We brought these customs with us when we came to this country."

I liked both of the customs, especially the soft, sugary cookies that had been cut into the shape of rabbits, squirrels, chickens, lambs, or deer. Sister Muhlbach had given permission for each of us to sample one of the treats yesterday. Today we would color the remaining eggs with dye from the woolen mill's dye works.

Yesterday's eggs had been quite lovely, with the onion skins providing a rich honey color to the white shells. Sister Hillmer had shown me how to make patterns by tying string around the eggs before dropping them into the tinted water. I'd even used a wax stylus made by the beekeeper to write names on some of the eggs.

Still, I was eager to see what today's eggs would look like when they were completed.

It was fear of being banned from the kitchen during egg dying that caused me to complete my morning chores without complaint. I didn't want to risk being relegated to cleaning out the chicken coop or some other horrid task while the others enjoyed coloring eggs.

My excitement mounted when Sister Muhlbach motioned me to the stove. "You can help me prepare the dye since you've never done this before."

Her willingness to include me came as a surprise, especially because I'd been responsible for the bowl of broken eggs. Pots of boiling water sat atop the stove.

"Put one color of dye in each of these smaller pots. We will mix in the glue from the woodshop, then set the smaller pan on top of the boiling water, and you must stir."

"How will I know when it's ready?" My stomach lurched at the thought of making a mistake on such an important task.

"Ach! You are always rushing. Before you finish one step, you must know what is next." She placed the bowl of red dye and glue over the boiling water and handed me a long-handled spoon. "Stir until it bubbles. Then pour it into the custard bowls and let it cool and thicken."

Her explanation evoked more questions, but I doubted Sister Muhlbach wanted to hear them at the moment. Besides, I was now stirring the blue dye with my right hand and the red with my left. Never before had I considered the difficulty of keeping both hands moving at the same time.

Soon the older children arrived to help color the eggs. The little ones would have their fun hunting for the eggs tomorrow. Sister Muhlbach pointed them to their places at the tables and gave them explicit instructions. "You color one egg at a time, and you will move from one table to the next. There is a different color at each table." With exaggerated motions, she rolled the egg in the jellied substance and lifted it for all to see. To my amazement, the color held fast and the egg turned a brilliant red.

"You can make some, too," Johanna said. "I'll show you how to make a rainbow egg."

When all the eggs had been colored, they were aligned on the table in a stunning display of bright colors. If only for this brief time, I was pleased to be in Amana.

Easter morning I fastened my pink silk before topping it with dark calico. To me, it seemed perfectly fitting to wear a bright color on this morning when Christians celebrated the risen Savior. After tucking my hair beneath my cap and grabbing my shawl from the foot of the bed, I hastened to meet Johanna. Even on Easter, we were expected to cook. Unless you were ill, there was no day of rest for the kitchen workers.

Sister Muhlbach had ordered us to be at the kitchen even earlier than usual. Today we would serve the special Easter meal. Much work must be completed before we departed for church. Yesterday I had offered to remain behind during the service, but my offer had been immediately rejected.

"You need church more than most," Sister Muhlbach had replied. And that had ended any aspiration of missing what would likely be one of those longer-than-usual meetings like the ones we'd attended in Chicago on Christmas and Easter.

Then again, a comparison between the Chicago and Amana churches would be silly. The two were as different as a cat and a dog. There was no huge edifice or expensive pipe organ in Amana. No worshipers wearing festive hats or riding to the church in fancy carriages. No hand-carved pulpits or stained-glass windows could be found in any Amana church. In fact, until Johanna had pointed out the meetinghouse, I'd thought it just another home. Simplicity and uniformity ruled in Amana, and the meetinghouse was no exception.

With its whitewashed walls, bare floors, and long unpainted benches, the interior of the structure was as simple as the exterior. Instead of standing behind a pulpit, the presiding elder sat at a plain wood table. The people sang hymns without organ accompaniment, their voices blending in perfect harmony. Instead of vociferous entreaties, prayers were offered silently.

Johanna was waiting at the bottom of the steps. "I'm glad to see you're on time."

"I wouldn't want to get in trouble. Sister Muhlbach said I could help hide the eggs and cookies."

The early hours were hectic, but by the time we departed for church, Sister Muhlbach was pleased with our progress. "You did a good job this morning, Berta. You may help Gertrude hide the eggs while we are serving dinner." In spite of her earlier prediction, there was no sign of rain. We would hide the eggs outdoors, and while the children hunted for them, we would hide the cookies in the kitchen and dining room.

"The children have such fun hunting. They each have their own Easter basket, hand-woven by Brother Snyder and presented to them when they are old enough to hunt the eggs." Johanna grinned. "I'm too old to hunt eggs, but I still have the basket Brother Snyder made for me."

In Chicago my Easter basket hadn't been made by a basket weaver. In fact, I'd received a new one each year, and I had no idea where any of them were now. I was surprised when a stab of jealousy knifed through me. Why should I be envious of an Easter basket?

Instead of listening during meeting, I pondered that question. Though I'd not come up with any answer, I had been correct in my earlier expectation of Easter morning. The church service was longer than usual, but with an afternoon of fun looming ahead, I managed to maintain proper decorum. Finally the church service ended. I came alongside Johanna and Gertrude, and the three of us hurried back to the kitchen. Sister Muhlbach and some of the other women were there when we arrived.

The hearty smell of smoke-cured ham filled the kitchen. "Umm. It smells wonderful," I said.

"And now you see why we had to come early and get the hams in the oven and the potatoes peeled." Sister Muhlbach pointed at the pegs near the door. "Get your apron on. We have only an hour before dinner must be served."

Sister Muhlbach called out orders, and we all jumped to do her bidding. By the time the village bell rang to signal dinner, Spätzle soup had been ladled into tureens, the ham sliced, the mashed potatoes topped with toasted bread crumbs, and the green beans seasoned with crispy bacon.

"The meal won't be as gut without fresh lettuce or radish salad," Sister Nusser lamented.

"Ach! It will be fine. No other kitchen in all the colonies is serving radish salad or fresh lettuce. Easter is early this year. No one expects lettuce; they will be happy with *Quark*."

Sister Nusser frowned. "Cottage cheese is no substitute for fresh lettuce!"

"There is no time to argue about salads. The milk pitchers need to be put on the tables." Sister Muhlbach thrust a pitcher at me and motioned toward the dining room.

When everyone had taken their place in the dining room and the prayer of thanks had been recited in unison, Sister Muhlbach ordered the platters and bowls of food delivered to the tables. After directing the other women, she signaled to Gertrude and me. "You two can take the colored eggs and hide them in the back and along the sides of the house. I'll be out to check on your progress after the serving is completed."

Gertrude and I agreed that she would hide her bowl of eggs along the sides of the house and I would go to the backyard. I'd hidden over half of my eggs when I found an excellent spot near the woodshed. Kneeling down on my hands and knees, I stretched forward to place an egg amidst a clump of shaded grass when something wet nudged my arm. With a yelp, I jerked around and jumped to my feet.

The black-and-white dog from yesterday had returned. He wagged his tail and nudged my hand. "Now look what you've done! I've ripped my skirt." I lifted the hem of my calico to examine the damage.

"Sister Berta! What is that?" Sister Muhlbach came marching toward me like a soldier on a mission.

What a silly question. Couldn't she see? "It's a dog—the one from—"

"Not the dog!" She came to a halt in front of me and tugged the fabric of my pink silk skirt between her fingers. "So you are again wearing the pink skirt!"

My mouth turned drier than a parched desert, but Sister Muhlbach didn't expect a response—no excuse would save me now.

# CHAPTER 7

Johanna Ilg

"Sister Johanna!" Taking two exaggerated steps, I hastened to the open door, where I spied Sister Muhlbach in the backyard. She waved me forward, her arm gyrating like a windmill blade. "Come here!"

I held an empty bowl high in the air. "There are bowls that need to be filled. I'll come out when—"

"Now!"

From the stern look on her face and the tone of her command, I knew she would brook no argument. I ran down the porch steps and raced across the yard, scanning the area for Berta. When I didn't see her, I knew this had something to do with the girl, and my stomach churned at the idea.

I sucked in a breath of air. "Where are Gertrude and Berta?"

"Gertrude is hiding eggs." Using her thumb as a pointer, Sister Muhlbach motioned toward the tool shed. "Berta is in there taking off that pink skirt. The one I forbade her to ever again wear in my kitchen."

I bowed my head, unable to bear Sister Muhlbach's harsh look. "She disobeyed again?"

"Ja, that's for sure. I even let her hide the eggs, and still she doesn't obey."

Just when I thought Berta was going to change her ways, she'd proved me wrong. When would I learn that the girl was as immature as the children in *Kinderschule*!

Moments later Berta emerged from the shed, the pink fabric draped across her arm like a decoration.

Sister Muhlbach grasped the skirt. "What has happened out here will remain between the three of us." She thrust the skirt into my arms. "Sister Johanna, you will get rid of this."

Berta stared at me with pleading brown eyes, but I forced myself to turn away. Ignoring her desire to cling to the pink silk would prove difficult, especially since I yearned to visit distant cities and see such finery for myself. Yet I would never challenge Sister Muhlbach's command. No matter how sad Berta looked, she wouldn't convince me to disobey the order. To do so would betray my years of training and cause my parents deep pain and embarrassment.

"Go inside and begin to wash the pots and pans, Berta. Your days are going to be filled with much scrubbing and cleaning." After one final, pleading look, Berta shuffled back inside. "With the arrival of spring, there is more work in the garden, and Sister Nusser will be happy to have some extra help when Berta completes her kitchen duties. You'll be expected to supervise her, Johanna."

I wilted at the thought.

"Make certain you do away with that pink skirt."

"As soon as dinner is complete, I'll see to it."

We remained in the kitchen far longer than usual. Berta was cleaning and scrubbing long after the others had departed. Sister Muhlbach had given the other kitchen workers the rest of the afternoon to enjoy with their families while Berta cleaned and I supervised. There would be little time to return home before the next service, but I couldn't take Berta's skirt to church. I considered digging a hole and burying it in the backyard, but knowing Berta, she'd see me and dig it up. Even though she'd apologized, I feared I couldn't trust her.

Spotting an empty flour sack, I folded the skirt into a tight bundle and shoved it inside. "Come along, Berta. We must leave. The bell is ringing, and I must stop at the house before church."

"Please, Johanna. It was my very favorite. At least let me cut the fabric and make it into a pillow to decorate my bed."

I clutched the bag tight against my chest. "I understand your desire, but I won't suffer any more punishment because of this skirt. You could have made it into a pillow after the first incident, but you chose to wear it again. Now it's too late."

"If that silly dog had stayed away, it wouldn't have ripped, and Sister Muhlbach would have never found out." We crossed the street, and our shoes clunked in rhythm on the sidewalk. "Besides, Rudolf promised he'd take the dog to the shepherds over in East Amana."

Now she was blaming a stray dog and Rudolf for her misdeed. "This is your fault alone, Berta. You made a choice. Now you must suffer the consequences." She continued to beg until we neared the house, but I remained steadfast. "Remember what Sister Muhlbach told us. This is not to be discussed with anyone else." I doubted she'd admit today's wrongdoing to her parents, but with Berta there was no certainty.

The house was empty when we arrived. While Berta waited in

the hallway, I took the bag into my room. A corner of the pink silk poked out of the sack. For a moment I savored the softness between my fingers. Though I'd never tell Berta, I thought the color quite lovely. Pushing the thought from my mind, I tucked the bag into the small chest at the foot of my bed. I'd dispose of it later.

The following weeks proved even more difficult. As usual, I was required to inspect all of Berta's work as well as complete my own. In addition, Berta and I now delivered the midafternoon coffee and cake to Sister Nusser and the women who worked in our three-acre garden. Though her gardening skills were nonexistent, Berta had been instructed to offer her services to Sister Nusser each afternoon. And Sister Nusser cheerfully accepted the offer. Today she said to me, "Go back to the Küche and finish your work. I can handle Berta. I'll have the handyman drive us back when we're finished. And I'll make certain she returns in time to scrub the pots." A lighthearted chuckle escaped her lips as she wiped the dirt from her hands.

Although Sister Nusser knew Berta was being punished, the Gartebaas didn't know why. Her curiosity had gotten the best of her, and she'd asked me about it on two occasions. Now I wondered if she thought Berta would tell once they were alone. Sister was a hard worker, and her produce outshone every other garden in Amana, but she did like to share news—that was what she called it—sharing news. The elders called it gossip and frowned upon the practice. *"Speak with as few words as possible, so your tongue doesn't create problems."* That's what I'd been taught as a little girl.

I didn't follow the rule as closely as recommended, but I did try to avoid gossip. I leaned down beside Berta, who was intent upon pulling a clump of weeds. "I'm returning to the kitchen. Sister Nusser will bring you back later. Remember, you are not to tell about your pink skirt. Sister Nusser may ask why you are being punished."

Berta giggled. "She already has—several times, but I haven't told."

At least the girl had followed one instruction. I headed off toward the Küche, not confident I was doing the right thing. It was difficult to know if I should follow the orders from Sister Muhlbach or from Sister Nusser. Each woman reigned supreme in her own domain, but right now I straddled both of their worlds.

Sister Muhlbach looked up when I entered the kitchen. Her eyes immediately darted to the door. "And where is Berta?"

"Sister Nusser said she would deliver Berta in time for her to clean the kitchen."

The bang of Sister Muhlbach's metal spoon atop the cookstove echoed her displeasure. "*Humph.* Of course she will. She'll bring her along when she comes to eat supper. What about the dishes and pots Berta should be washing before supper ever begins? Sister Rosina doesn't know how many utensils and dishes I need washed up while we're preparing a meal or how much other work must be completed. Now that spring has arrived, all she thinks about is getting the garden planted."

"Maybe you should explain that this arrangement isn't working."

Sister Muhlbach spun around from the stove and pointed the long-handled spoon in my direction. "And have Sister Sister Rosina tell everyone in the village that I'm incapable of operating my Küche because one inexperienced young girl is gone for a few hours each afternoon?" She waved the spoon back and forth in the air. "And you know that's what she'd do. Sister Rosina's tongue wags like a dog's tail." Her eyes opened wide, and she clapped her free hand across her lips.

I hurried across the room and patted her shoulder. There was no doubt she longed to snatch back the words she'd spoken in anger and haste. "I'm sorry, Sister Muhlbach. I shouldn't have suggested you retract your offer."

She smoothed the front of her apron. "Do not blame yourself. I am in charge of the words I speak, not you. I'll need to ask the Lord's forgiveness." A slight blush colored her cheeks.

"Would you like me to begin the dishes?" Not wanting to cause her further embarrassment, I started toward the dirty pots and pans.

"Ja. That would be good."

She withdrew into silence while supper preparations got under-way. As I carried the final pan of lukewarm dishwater out the back door, I glanced at the paring-knife sisters. "Sister Muhlbach said to tell you she'll need the potatoes."

Shoulders wrapped in dark shawls, the threesome glanced up from the wooden trays that captured the vegetable peelings while they worked. The one closest to me shook her head. "She knows we'll bring them in when we've finished our work. She worries too much. There's plenty of time before supper." The oldest of the three leaned forward in her chair and pointed the tip of her paring knife toward the path leading to the back porch. "If I were Sister Thekla, I'd worry about that instead of the potatoes."

With a small shuffle step, I turned to see what she was referring to. I couldn't believe my eyes! The handyman lifted Berta down from a wagon and then Berta tucked her arm into the crook of the handyman's arm. They were strolling toward the house as though their behavior were perfectly acceptable. Berta knew better! What was she thinking? My thoughts tangled in a knot of anger and confusion as I jumped off the porch.

"What are you doing?" I grasped the sleeve of Berta's dress and yanked her arm.

Pointing a finger, I turned on Matthew. "I doubt you'll have a job come morning." His nonchalant shrug further infuriated me. He was hired help and not a member of the community, but he knew there were rules to be followed.

"Where is Sister Nusser?"

"She ain't feeling so good and said she needed to rest for a while before supper. It was her that told me to escort Miss Berta back here. I s'pose she'd be the one to decide if I done somethin' wrong." He grinned and touched a finger to the brim of his flat cap. "Thanks for your fine company, Miss Berta." He strode off with a jaunt to his step.

I wanted to call after him and say he'd have to answer to more than Sister Nusser if he didn't obey the rules, but he was out of sight before I could gather enough gumption to speak.

"He's nice looking, don't you think?"

My frustration moved from a slow simmer to a raging boil. Eyes shining with curiosity, the paring-knife sisters leaned forward to watch as I yanked Berta up the porch steps and into the kitchen. "Don't forget the potatoes, Sisters." I pointed at the pile of unpeeled vegetables. All three dropped back into their chairs and glared at me.

Sister Muhlbach crossed the kitchen, her heavy feet thudding across the wooden floor, and her focus square upon the two of us. "Now what has she done?"

Before I could respond, Berta twisted from my hold and jutted her chin. "I followed Sister Nusser's directions. She isn't feeling well and said the handyman should escort me back to the Küche."

"I'm sure she didn't say you should walk arm in arm with the hired help."

Sister Muhlbach gasped. "You did not do such a thing."

This time I didn't give Berta a chance to respond. "Yes. She did."

The older woman's complexion visibly paled, and she dropped

into a nearby chair. "This is something I don't want to believe you would do, Berta."

I bobbed my head. "That's exactly what I said." The other women cast curious stares in our direction, one or two dallying in the kitchen longer than necessary.

"Come with me." Sister Muhlbach stood and waved us toward the door that led to her private living quarters. Once inside, she pushed the door until the latch clicked in place. "Sit down. Both of you." We didn't hesitate.

"I don't know why this is such a concern. Matthew is very nice. We did nothing wrong. We traveled directly from the acreage, past the woolen mill, and down the main street until we turned toward the kitchen."

Sister Muhlbach cupped her palm to her wrinkled cheek. "You rode in the wagon with him by yourself? Did you at least ride in the back of the wagon?"

Berta shook her head. "No. I rode beside Matthew. Riding atop the wagon was great fun, and there's a much better view." She smiled as though we should be pleased. "He helped me up and down, of course."

"Of course." Sarcasm dripped from the older woman's terse reply. She turned her attention to me. "There is no way to keep this from the Bruderrat."

I nodded. "They've probably already heard. But this is not your doing, Sister Muhlbach. If anyone is to blame, it is me. I shouldn't have left her. The elders assigned me as her supervisor."

"Perhaps. But Sister Nusser is the one who should be held to account. She told you to return to the kitchen, and she told Berta the handyman could escort her. The decisions were improper."

"No, you're wrong. Sister Nusser's stomach was upset. She promised I would be back in time to help, and she needed to rest before supper." Berta clasped her arms to her midsection as if to emphasize the garden boss's illness.

Sister Muhlbach's eyes flashed with anger. "Sister Rosina doesn't need you to defend her decisions. Go to the kitchen and begin your duties. Your work in the garden has ended. I can find enough work right here to keep you busy from sunup to sundown."

Mouth half open, Berta hesitated, but Sister Muhlbach raised her finger in warning. "Don't say one more word."

The minute Berta was out of earshot, the older woman shook her head. "Never have I seen one girl so difficult to manage. And who would believe Sister Rosina would behave in such a foolish manner. Do you think the girl is lying?"

"I don't think so, but with Berta I can never be sure."

"Talk can wait. Supper cannot." Lifting her ample body from the chair, she motioned me to do the same, and I hurried from the room to continue meal preparations, a welcome respite from further discussion.

Thankfully, supper was completed on time. Otherwise, Sister Muhlbach's mood would have gone from bad to worse. The prayer of thanks for our meal had been recited and I was serving the men's table when Sister Nusser opened the front door and quietly slid into her regular place at one of the women's tables. Immediately turning to find the Küchebaas in the kitchen, I didn't miss the look that passed between Sister Muhlbach and Sister Nusser. Fur would fly after this meal—of that there was no doubt.

Berta did her best to capture my attention while I rushed back and forth, refilling and serving the bowls of food. When I slowed my pace for a moment, she grabbed my arm with a sudsy hand. "Do you think she'll change her mind and let me return to the garden?"

I heaved a sigh and shook my head. "I doubt that will happen. After being instructed to keep your distance from the hired men, why did you sit beside Matthew in the wagon and then walk arm in arm with him? You knew such behavior was improper, Berta. You enjoy creating havoc."

She grabbed a towel and wiped her hands. "That's not true. I just like to have fun. And riding on top of the wagon was fun."

There wasn't time to argue. Besides, it would do little good. I picked up two bowls of rice pudding and carried them to one of the women's tables. As I drew near, Sister Nusser crooked her finger and beckoned me closer. "Did Berta return to help in the Küche?"

"Ja. She is scrubbing pots and pans."

"Then why is Sister Thekla looking at me with such anger?"

No matter what, it seemed I was going to be stuck in the middle of this conflict. "You should ask Sister Muhlbach, not me." I plopped the bowl in front of her, but she grasped my hand.

"Tell her I was sick. She needs to know that is why I sent Berta back with Matthew."

I nodded. "She knows. And you should talk to her yourself. I'm pleased to see you have returned to good health in such quick order."

A scowl creased her face. "Tell Sister Thekla I will speak to both of you when supper is finished. And Berta should be there, too."

I doubted such a command would sit well with Sister Muhlbach. She didn't like anyone else issuing orders in her domain. And given the circumstances, I was certain she'd be disgruntled. Entering the kitchen, I decided to temper Sister Nusser's order just a mite.

"What did she say to you?" Sister Muhlbach whispered the question as soon as I cleared the threshold.

"She asked if we could meet with her after the others leave the dining room—to explain."

"Explain? What's to explain? Sister Rosina's decision was wrong."

"But you have a forgiving heart, Sister Muhlbach. I know that you can bring the matter to resolution. Then if the elders come to you, you can tell them it has already been settled to your satisfaction. They will be pleased that you have remembered what our Lord says about peace and unity among the body of believers." I was doing my best to offer a solution. Neither of the older women would want to appear the loser. "You'd prefer to avoid a meeting with the Bruderrat, wouldn't you?"

"Ja, of course. And since she asked so nice . . ."

I picked up a bowl of rice pudding and hurried from the room before she could finish the sentence. *Please don't let Sister Muhlbach discover the meeting was a command rather than a request.* The aroma of the sweet-smelling dessert drifted heavenward in tandem with my prayer.

The end-of-meal prayer was recited, followed by the clatter of dishes and shuffling of feet. Sister Muhlbach shooed the other workers from the dining room and kitchen much earlier than usual.

"To what do we owe this special privilege?" Sister Hillmer asked.

"To my kind disposition, but if you'd prefer to stay and work, I can accommodate you." Sister Muhlbach's remark was enough to send the workers, both young and old, skittering out the door. All except Berta and me—and Sister Nusser.

Once the four of us had gathered around a table, I said, "I think it would be wise if we prayed before our talk." The three of them glanced at me and then at one another. To disagree would appear ungodly. Without a word they bowed their heads, and we prayed.

When the meeting concluded a half hour later, the two older women had arrived at an agreement. They would accept equal responsibility for what occurred, but Berta would no longer help in the garden. When Berta attempted to object, I tromped on her foot.

Sister Nusser pushed away from the table. "The matter is settled."

We all nodded.

Unless the Bruderrat decided otherwise.

# CHAPTER 8

Berta Schumacher

The following morning when Rudolf arrived at the Küche to deliver milk, I managed to sneak outside and meet him. "I want to know how I can make a request to the Bruderrat."

He stared at me as though I'd spoken a foreign language. *"You?"* He pointed his finger at me. "You want to go before the Bruderrat?" He clapped his hand over his mouth to stifle his laughter.

I slapped his arm. "I didn't expect this from you!" I turned, but he lunged forward and captured my hand.

"Wait!" He stepped closer. "Why would you want to go before the Bruderrat?" He tugged on my hand. "Please tell me. I promise not to laugh."

"The elders are the ones who decide where people live, isn't that correct?"

"Ja. You want to move to another house?"

I heard the disappointment in his voice, and it pleased me. "No, not another house. But I've been thinking that since no one has moved into the two rooms that were occupied by Oma Reich, they might assign them to me."

"To *you*?" His voice cracked. "Assign two rooms to a seventeen-year-old girl? They would never consider such a suggestion."

"You haven't heard the entire plan. I would tell them it would be easier for my father to see patients late at night if he had use of the extra rooms. Then I would convince my father to let me use the rooms as my own."

Rudolf didn't let me go any further. "They would never agree. And even if they did, your father would not agree to such dishonesty, would he?"

I shrugged. "I won't know if I can't ask the Bruderrat."

"It doesn't matter, because Oma Reich's rooms will soon be occupied."

Rudolf's curt reply startled me. "How do you know?"

He tapped his index finger against his right ear. "I hear things, but I'm not sure I should tell you."

I scrunched my eyes together and did my best to glower at him. "Because you don't know anything. You're just trying to make me think you do."

He shook his head and grinned. "I know."

He'd spoken with such authority that I could no longer doubt what he was saying. "Tell me who it is, and I promise we'll be friends forever." When he hesitated, I pointed my nose toward the heavens and turned on my heel.

"Wait! I'll tell you." He sighed. "It's Carl Froehlich who is moving into the rooms."

"Nooo. Is that the truth?"

"Ja. When I returned the milk wagon to the barn a couple days

94

ago, Brother Ilg told me Carl would be moving into our house next week."

Without thinking, I leaned forward and pecked Rudolf on the cheek. "Thank you for telling me." I glanced toward the Küche, hoping no one had seen me.

He touched his cheek with his fingers. "I will never again wash my face."

"That's not a good idea. At least not if you want me to kiss you again."

"If that is all I need to do, let me get water from the cistern and I'll scrub my face this very minute."

Even though nothing had been said that day in the barn, maybe my idea about Johanna's father arranging a marriage between Carl and Johanna had been correct. Yet the members of the community believed a single life superior to marriage. If that was their belief, why would Brother Ilg seek a husband for his daughter?

"Did Johanna's father seem pleased with this new arrangement?"

"Who can say? But he is a member of the Bruderrat. If he didn't like the plan, he could have asked the other elders to assign Carl to another house."

"I wonder what Johanna will think."

The milk wagon blocked the sun and cast a shadow across Rudolf's face. "Why would Johanna care where Carl lives?"

*Men!* They didn't understand anything at all. If Rudolf hadn't figured it out, I wasn't going to take time to explain. "I'd better go back inside before Sister Muhlbach comes looking for me. I can hardly wait to tell Johanna."

Rudolf grasped my arm. "No! You cannot tell her."

I wheeled around. "Why not?"

"It is not your information to share. Brother Ilg told *me*, not you. He will tell Johanna, just as he told me, when he believes she should know." He stepped closer. "Promise you won't betray my trust, Berta."

I hiked up on tiptoe and brushed his cheek with a parting kiss. "Oh, all right. I promise."

Rudolf had been mistaken.

Carl Froehlich didn't move into Oma Reich's rooms the following week. He moved in the following day. I was delighted. Not because he'd moved in, but because I didn't think I possessed the willpower to keep my promise to Rudolf. Although I'd not yet discovered my best qualities, I did know many of my failings. And keeping secrets was one of them.

The day was warm and the air cooled a modicum as we neared the millrace that powered the woolen and flour mills for the village. Probably just my imagination, but the mere sight of water cooled me on even the hottest of days. Johanna and I were on our return from delivering the midafternoon repast to the garden workers, a task Sister Muhlbach had yet to reassign. I was thankful, but I knew Johanna disliked the twice-daily trips.

A budding lilac branch stretched into the path, and I lifted it to my nose. "What do you think of him?"

Johanna arched her eyebrows. "Who?"

"Carl, of course."

"I don't think about him at all. Why should I?"

"Because he's a good age for you. He's tall and very good-looking. Your father appears to like him, or he wouldn't have agreed to have him come to work in the barns with him. He'd make a perfect husband." I nudged her with my elbow. "Don't tell me you haven't thought the same thing."

She lifted one shoulder in a nonchalant shrug. "I haven't had any such thoughts. I know it's difficult for you to believe, but marriage is not what most young women in Amana think about."

I skipped ahead, then twirled around and faced Johanna as we walked across the bridge that spanned the millrace near the woolen mill. "What else is there to think about? We can't go shopping or discuss the latest fashions."

"You could think about ways you can serve God. You could think about ways to help others. You could think about ways to better accomplish your work. You could memorize Bible passages—a good way to avoid dwelling upon marriage or young men."

The beautiful spring day begged human appreciation, but I'd been a complete failure at convincing Johanna to slow her pace and enjoy the day. "When I lived in Chicago, I would spend entire days doing nothing but wandering the aisles of the stores along State Street. Mother and I would discover the latest arrivals from Paris or London. We'd compare the quality of fabric and lace or inspect the latest hats and gloves, and then we'd move on to the next store."

"Did you see any of our Amana fabrics in the stores where you shopped?" She tipped her head and met my gaze. There was a moment of hesitation. "My brother, Wilhelm, was a salesman of our woolens and calicos before he left Amana. He would go to the cities, both large and small, and sell our fabrics. Like you, he is very fond of Chicago."

"Is? Does your brother live in Chicago?"

"Yes."

"Wait!" I planted my feet on the dusty road, unwilling to move until she answered my questions. "Did he run away?"

With a glance over her shoulder, she waved me forward. "No. He was a grown man who could make his own choice."

Sadness weighed my shoulders into a slump. "So you've never seen him again."

"Of course I've seen him. He comes to visit occasionally. If he ever wanted to return, he could do so. This isn't a prison. Wilhelm was an adult, and he chose to leave. If he ever wants to return, he will be welcomed back."

Johanna's explanation sounded rehearsed. I was certain there must be more to Wilhelm's departure. "Were your parents very displeased with him?"

"We won't speak of this any further, Berta. Hurry up or Sister Muhlbach will assign us extra duties."

# CHAPTER 9

Johanna Ilg

*Not again!* Ever since Carl had moved into Oma Reich's rooms, my parents had been inviting him to visit in our parlor each evening after prayer meeting. And now my mother had invited him to join us Sunday afternoon, as well. "I don't know why he has to be with us every free moment."

My mother frowned and touched her index finger to her lips. "Hush, Johanna. Carl will hear you."

"He and Vater are discussing repairs for the barn. They don't hear a word we say." I leaned close to her ear. "I'm going to my room to mend my stockings."

"You will stay here and behave like a proper young woman. I think Berta's rude behavior is beginning to have an effect on you."

"I don't see why I must be present when you're the one who initiates these visits. Carl and Vater discuss farm equipment and the barns. Why must I listen to such uninspiring talk?"

Berta's influence couldn't be blamed for my conduct, but she had certainly questioned Carl's frequent visits. Ever the romantic, she wanted to believe Carl was madly in love with me. She still didn't believe the visits had been initiated by my mother. I'd given up any attempt to convince her otherwise.

My mother sighed. "Carl is lonely and has no family here in Main Amana. We are his neighbors, and your Vater is his supervisor. It is only right that we make him feel welcome."

"But it was his choice to leave High. If he didn't want to be alone, why didn't he stay there—or bring his Mutter with him?" Our hushed whispers had finally captured the men's attention, and my father looked in our direction.

"What interesting talk are we missing?" His eyes twinkled with curiosity.

"Just women's talk, Vater. Don't let us interrupt you."

Grasping the armrests of the overstuffed chair, he pushed to a stand. I knew all hope of further discussion with my mother had come to an end. "There is a meeting of the Bruderrat that I must attend, but Carl has offered to take the two of you fishing this afternoon."

Fishing? With Carl? I had always enjoyed fishing with Wilhelm, but the idea of spending the remainder of the afternoon with a veritable stranger didn't appeal. I turned toward my mother. Surely she could read the silent plea in my eyes. Surely she would refuse.

"Oh, that sounds wonderful." Mother folded her hands in her lap and preened.

*Sounds wonderful?* I'd never before heard her speak in such a manner. Was she attempting to impress Carl?

"Thank you, Carl, but I have mending to finish. I'm sure Mutter will keep you company."

"You can bring your mending along, Johanna. I know you probably don't want to touch worms or handle fish. I'll find a shady spot where you can sit and enjoy the breeze while you finish your stitching."

"Ja. That's a gut plan." My father gathered his Bible and hat. "You go with them, Johanna. And if you finish your sewing, maybe Carl can teach you how to catch a fish." He winked at me before he turned and opened the door.

I'd been left no choice. I couldn't disobey. There was little doubt my father held high regard for Carl. The two of them had forged an excellent friendship, and they worked well together—as if they'd known each other for a lifetime. Without warning, realization struck and I understood what was happening. Little by little Carl was becoming Wilhelm's replacement. Eventually Carl would become the son my father had hoped for. That's why Father was sending us fishing with Carl. Soon Carl would be inserted into every part of our lives—everywhere that Wilhelm should have been.

Well, Carl would not replace Wilhelm. Not for me. We were sister and brother, connected by blood, born of the same parents. No one could replace Wilhelm. The very thought caused a tear to form in the corner of my eye. Before the others could notice, I swiped it away with the back of my hand.

"I'll get my fishing pole from my room and meet you on the front porch. Is five minutes enough time?" Carl's broad smile caused a twinge of guilt. I shouldn't blame him for what my father was doing. He couldn't know he was being groomed to become a substitute son. Then again, maybe he would cherish the idea.

"I will need at least ten minutes."

He flinched at my terse reply. "Whatever you need will be fine. I'll wait outside."

I should have tempered my curt response, but I still hadn't completely digested all that was happening. Besides, I needed to visit the outhouse and then collect my mending.

It was closer to fifteen minutes by the time Mother and I finally gathered all our items. In addition to her handwork, she decided we would need a blanket to keep our skirts free of grass stains or dirt. Obviously, she didn't plan to fish, either.

After a quick inspection of the items, Mother said, "I think this is everything we should need."

A tap on the front door let me know we'd taken longer than Carl had anticipated. "Coming." I yanked open the door and took a backward step. "Berta! I wasn't expecting to see *you*."

She grinned. "I know. Carl's at the buggy talking to Rudolf. He said you're going fishing."

"We are." My mother came alongside me, the blanket and her sewing basket tucked in one arm.

Berta clapped her hands. "Oh good. You're going, too, Sister Ilg. My mother said Rudolf and I could go along if either you or Brother Ilg would be acting as a chaperone."

"Well, I—"

Clearly Berta had taken my mother by surprise. She shot me a please-help-me look, but I squelched any feelings of sympathy. When I'd sent out my silent plea only a short time ago, she had ignored me. Besides, having Berta and Rudolf along would ease my discomfort. Rudolf could fish with Carl, and Berta would keep us entertained with her antics.

Before my mother could regain her composure, I said, "Of course. You're welcome to come along, Berta. And Rudolf, too."

My mother squeezed my arm. "I'm not certain that's what . . . Well, I don't think—"

"Carl will enjoy having Rudolf as a fishing companion, don't you think, Mutter?"

"I don't think either of us should speak for Carl. We can't be sure what he would enjoy."

"Oh, Carl said he didn't mind," Berta interjected. "We've already asked him."

Mother frowned and heaved a sigh. By day's end Mother would understand that dealing with Berta was not so easy—the girl could transform any event to her own liking.

When I saw the buggy waiting in front of our house, I knew Carl and Father had made the fishing arrangements in advance. Normally the buggy wouldn't have been used for such a frivolous outing. And though Father seldom took advantage, using a wagon or buggy was a privilege of his position as a farm Baas. Either Carl or my father had hitched the horses earlier in the day. Yes, this had been arranged earlier. But I couldn't understand why my parents would push me toward Carl. Our religion clearly stated that whenever possible, it was better to remain unmarried. Could my father's desire to replace Wilhelm be so strong that he would make no effort to mask his efforts?

Berta had tucked herself beside Rudolf in the rear seat. Father hadn't planned on five passengers or he would have selected a larger buggy. Berta scooted closer to Rudolf and waved to my mother. "There's room back here for you, Sister Ilg.

"Or for me," I said, approaching the buggy.

Berta shook her head with such vehemence, her cap nearly dislodged from her head. "Your mother is a better fit."

I pressed my hands down the sides of my hips. "Are you saying I'm too large to fit back there with you?"

"No, of course not, but . . ."

My mother inched around me. "I will sit between Rudolf and Berta. You climb up front with Carl." She motioned for Berta to step down. "Hurry now, Berta, or we'll waste the afternoon getting ourselves arranged."

A frown stretched across Berta's face, but she followed Mother's instruction. I didn't know why, but irritation niggled at me. Perhaps because Berta had given in so easily and I knew she would have argued with me.

As he rounded the buggy, Carl ran his palm down the side of the horse's muzzle in an affectionate gesture. "Let me help you up," he said as he approached me. His voice was gentle.

He grasped my elbow, and a surprising tingle raced up my arm. I chided myself for such foolishness and wriggled onto the buggy seat. With practiced ease, Carl hoisted himself up beside me. His arm brushed against me as he flicked the reins. Another shiver coursed through my body, and when he glanced at me, my stomach fluttered. I turned away, fearful my embarrassment would be obvious.

"Your cheeks are as red as a ripe tomato. You should have worn your sunbonnet instead of only your cap." Berta giggled and squeezed my shoulder. "Unless it's something other than the sun that's causing your rosy complexion."

I wanted to throttle her. The girl took far too much pleasure in causing others embarrassment. "I'm fine, thank you. My sunbonnet is in my sewing basket. I'll put it on once we arrive at the river."

"I'll find a place in the shade for you to sit," Carl said. "In springtime, the sunshine can cause sunburn before you know it."

Between the two of them, they'd made me sound like a frail flower that might wilt in the out-of-doors. "I am accustomed to working in the sunshine, Carl. I help with the onion and potato harvest, and I'm even able to hang clothes on the line without fainting."

He lowered his chin. "I am sorry if I offended you. It wasn't my intention. I only wanted to offer protection."

I wanted to tell him I didn't need protection, that I'd managed just fine for all of my twenty-one years, that I was quite capable of finding my own shade, but something stopped me. Perhaps it was the pained look in his eyes. Or perhaps it was the memory of his hand on my elbow. "Thank you, Carl. I appreciate your concern."

Although I couldn't discern their conversation, I could hear Berta and Rudolf chattering throughout the remainder of the drive. My mother attempted to interrupt them several times, but her efforts proved futile. Smiling, I pictured the scene in the back of the buggy—Berta bending forward and leaning across Mother so that Rudolf wouldn't miss a word she was saying while Mother struggled to gain control. I knew I'd hear a full report later from Mother.

"Here we are," Carl said, pulling back on the reins and bringing the horse to a stop.

I wasn't surprised at the choice of fishing location. It had been one of Wilhelm's favorites, as well. Though nearly everyone in all of the villages considered Indian Dam the very best place to catch fish, time wouldn't permit such a distant visit today. Both Berta and I would be expected back at the kitchen to help prepare Sunday supper before the evening church meeting.

A few other families had spread their blankets nearby. Several of the children had removed their stockings and were dipping their toes in the cold river water. Carl pointed to a distant spot where the leafy branches of two thick trees provided ample shade. "A gut spot, ja?"

Sister Zewald was staring in our direction, likely wondering why we were secluding ourselves from the other families.

"The children will frighten the fish away with their splashing and squealing." Carl had obviously noticed Sister Zewald's watching us. My mother's lack of concern surprised me, for normally she worried about appearances. When Wilhelm had moved from the community, she'd fretted for months. At times I wondered if it was because she missed him or because she feared other members of the society might think she'd failed as a parent.

I remained planted beside the buggy. "What do you think, Mutter? Do you want to visit with Sister Zewald or sit near the stand of trees?"

"Under the trees will be better. I can rest my back while I'm doing my needlework."

Berta hadn't waited for my mother's decision. She bounded out of the buggy and was close on Rudolf's heels, both of them headed toward the river. She stopped long enough to look over her shoulder and wave me forward. "Come on, Johanna. Put on your sunbonnet and let's see if we can catch more fish than either of the fellows. Rudolf said he'd bait my hook."

While Carl helped my mother settle beneath the trees, I strolled down to the edge of the water, where Rudolf was threading a scrawny worm onto a hook. "What a skinny little worm you're giving her," I commented. "Only a minnow would nibble on such a paltry worm." I lifted the lid on Rudolf's can of bait and worked my fingers through the dirt. "What about this one?" I grasped a fat earthworm between my thumb and index finger and hoisted it into the air.

Rudolf looked at me and then at the worm he'd threaded onto the hook. "I already baited her hook."

"You can switch poles with her. Give me that other pole, Berta."

She grinned at Rudolf and handed me the pole. "You're not going to do that yourself, are you?"

"Of course. The first time I asked my brother to take me fishing, he said I had to bait my own hook and take any fish I caught off the hook. I promised that if he'd show me one time, I'd do it myself." With surprising ease, I worked the wiggly worm onto the hook. "I've been doing it ever since."

Berta wrinkled her nose. "I don't think I want to hold a worm."

"Then you better not plan on winning a fishing contest, because I'm not going to stop and bait your hook each time you catch a fish or lose your bait." I nodded toward the river. "Toss your line out there in the deeper water. If you feel a tug on the line, jerk back."

Carl sauntered toward me while I was baiting another hook. "I thought you brought some mending you planned to work on while I fished."

I'd completely forgotten my earlier remark. I shrugged and glanced toward the trees. "Maybe Mutter will take pity on me and do my mending instead of her fancywork."

"You did a gut job with that worm. Let's see how gut you are at catching fish," he said with a grin as he tossed his line into the water.

I stepped around him and moved a short distance before I tossed out my line. "I think you'll discover I'm better than you or Rudolf." My remark was far too smug for a proper young woman, yet he didn't appear offended.

"And what is the prize for the winner?" he teased, and I could feel the heat rise in my cheeks.

"The losers bait hooks for the winners next Sunday afternoon."

Berta had shouted out an answer before I could even begin to think of a response. I glared across the expanse of rock-laden riverbank that separated us. "I believe he was asking me, Berta."

She ignored my remark and laughed. "What do you think, Carl? Do you think the reward suitable?"

He touched two fingers to the brim of his straw hat. "Your offer is accepted."

Before I could object, Berta cried out and pulled back on her pole. "I've got one, Johanna. Help me before it gets away!"

Rudolf reached out to grab Berta's pole, but she turned her back to keep the pole from his reach. "Don't you try to make me lose my fish, Rudolf Stilson. Hurry, Johanna."

Carl extended his hand. "I'll hold your pole while you help Berta." He smiled and promised he wouldn't cheat.

Had Berta or Rudolf made such a promise, I wouldn't have believed them, but for some reason I believed Carl. Maybe it was the set of his square jaw or the soft yet firm tone of his voice. Then again, maybe it was the sincerity that shone in his blue eyes. I wasn't sure why, but I trusted him.

Within moments I was at Berta's side. Though she proved more of a hindrance than a help, we finally managed to land the fish. Berta took a backward step while the fish flopped on the riverbank. "Is it in pain?"

I met her worried eyes. "I don't know if fish feel pain, but if they do, I would imagine that it is in pain. Do you want to throw it back in?"

Brow furrowed, she stared at the flopping whiskered catfish.

"I've got one!" Rudolf shouted, jerking on his pole.

His proclamation was enough to make Berta's decision clear. "Take the hook out and put another worm on," she commanded.

"Lean down here and watch me take the hook out. It's up to you to take care of the next one." Though she flinched several times, she watched me remove the hook and place the fish on the stringer. I did my best to rinse the fishy smell from my hands at the edge of the river before I pointed to the bait. "Get busy and get a worm on there. Looks like Rudolf's fish got away."

Holding his empty line in one hand, Rudolf cast a disgruntled look at us. "And it took my bait, too," he grumbled.

Berta's laughter followed me as I hurried back to retrieve my pole from Carl. "No bites?"

He shook his head. "Not yet. Maybe the one that got away from Rudolf will swim down here."

The words had barely escaped his lips when I felt a stiff tug on my line. I yanked back to lodge the hook in the fish's mouth. The simple movement was enough to let my foot slip into the mud. Without warning, my other foot slid forward and I let out a yelp. Carl dropped his pole and took a sideward step as I toppled in a giant heap and landed directly on top of him. My mud-streaked skirt splayed across his legs as I fought to gain a foothold. I struggled to a sitting position, horrified when I realized I was sitting between Carl's legs. Again I struggled for a foothold.

"Quit wiggling." With a firm grip, Carl grabbed me around the waist and pulled me backward until we were on the grass. The warmth of his chest rested against my back, and even after he released his hold, I could feel the strength of his arm around me. Leaning back, he pushed to a stand and reached for my hand. "That was truly fisherman's luck." He pointed at the river's edge.

Lying on the bank was my pole with a giant fish still on the hook. "I'll let you count that one," I said and hesitated only a moment before adding, "as thanks for saving me."

He flashed a grin and shook his head. "As thanks, I would like you to come fishing with me each Sunday in June. What do you think about that?"

I thought of his strong arms around me, and the idea appealed more than I cared to admit. Thoughts swirled in my head while I considered his offer. "You will need to discuss that with my Vater. I do not think he will approve. Even more, I doubt the Bruderrat will approve."

He appeared unconvinced. "Why should they object? We are only fishing."

The gleam in his eye belied the words he spoke. I knew this was more than fishing.

# CHAPTER 10

A week later the door to my bedroom burst open without warning. In one frantic motion I twisted on the bed and shoved the magazine behind my pillow. From the gleam in Berta's eyes, I knew I hadn't been quick enough. "Don't you know it's rude to walk into someone's room without knocking? What if I had been changing clothes?"

Berta plopped down on the edge of the bed. "It wouldn't have bothered me in the least. Besides, you wouldn't be changing clothes at this time of day."

Why had Mother permitted her to enter my room without notice? Her gaze remained fastened upon my bed pillows, and I knew it was only a matter of time before she made her move. "I thought you were going to spend the afternoon with your father."

My Sunday afternoon fishing trip with Carl had been canceled due to the rain, and I had anticipated being alone until time to prepare supper.

"He had to go care for one of the Stuke boys. He fell out of a tree."

I clasped a hand to my chest. "Was it Luther?" I was certain of the answer before I asked. Luther was one of those children who had a new injury with each passing week.

Berta bobbed her head, her gaze still fixed upon my pillow. "From what his brother said, it sounded like a broken leg. I decided it would be more fun to spend the afternoon visiting with you."

"Did you speak to my Mutter in the parlor?"

"She and your father are on the front porch. Whispering together." Mischief danced in her eyes. "I would be glad to tell you what they were saying if you let me look at that magazine you've hidden behind your pillow."

Rain pattered on my bedroom window and spiraled downward in streaming rivulets. Although the front porch had a roof, I couldn't imagine my parents sitting out there while it rained. "They're sitting in the rain?"

"No. They were standing—very close together. Under the roof. Whispering about a letter."

My interest heightened, but I didn't completely trust Berta. To get her way, she'd go to most any length—even tell a lie. If I expressed a modicum of disbelief, perhaps she'd tell me more. "I don't know why they would whisper about a letter."

"Maybe because they don't want you to know what it says." Like the juicy apple offered to Eve in the garden, Berta enticed me with her words.

"And why did they permit you to listen in on their conversation?"

She flopped backward and stretched across the width of the bed. "I was eavesdropping. They didn't know I was listening."

I didn't doubt that Berta would eavesdrop on a private conversation, but I didn't believe she'd heard my parents talking on the front porch. She wanted to see my magazine. If I showed her, I didn't trust she'd keep her lips sealed, but if she truly had heard something about a letter, I wanted to know. "What makes you think I have a magazine?"

"I know that's not your Bible or *Psalter-Spiel* you shoved behind the pillow. They're too cumbersome. Is it *Peterson's Magazine* or *Godey's Lady's Book*?" She rolled to her side and rested her chin on her fist. "I do hope it's *Godey's*. It's my favorite."

"Mine too," I blurted without thinking.

The inky blue quilted bedspread rumpled beneath her as she rolled to her back and clapped her hands. "I knew it! I knew it! Let me see."

She lunged at the pillows, but I blocked her move. "I didn't say it was *Godey's*. I merely agreed that *Godey's* is my favorite magazine."

"But how would you even know about *Godey's* if you didn't have a copy? Where did you get it?"

I clasped her wrist and held her at bay. "Tell me what my parents said, and perhaps I'll tell you how I know about *Godey's*." I wasn't yet ready to admit I had a copy of the magazine. "I'm not certain I trust you."

"In that case, I don't know if I can trust you, either." She pushed her lower lip out and formed a childish pout. When I didn't respond, she finally relented. "They received a letter from Wilhelm."

My excitement secretly escalated, but I did my best to appear nonchalant. "And?"

She folded her arms across her waist and shot me a defiant look. "Is it *Godey's*?"

We were at a stalemate. It made no sense that my parents would hide a letter from Wilhelm. Perhaps Berta didn't know more than she'd told me. I wrestled with the thought. Finally, I relented. "Yes, but it's an old copy. I'm sure you saw it before you came to Amana. Now tell me what you heard."

"Will you let me look at it?"

"Only if you promise you won't tell I have them."

"Them? You have more than one?" she shrieked.

I slapped my palm across her mouth. "Shh. Keep your voice down."

"I promise I won't tell anyone." Using her index finger, she crossed an X on her bodice.

I'd never before seen anyone do such a thing, but I assumed it meant she'd keep her word. "Yes, I have more than one, but I'm not telling you anything more until you tell me everything you heard."

"Oh, all right." She settled on the bed. "Wilhelm said he is coming for a visit, and he has something important to discuss with your parents."

"What?"

"I didn't hear everything. They said something about Louisa. Do you know anyone named Louisa?"

"She's Mutter's younger sister. After my Oma died, she lived with my family. She and Wilhelm and Pieter were very close."

Berta scooted closer. "What about you? Were you close to her, too?"

"She moved away before I was born. She's never come back. Mutter and Vater don't speak of her, but Wilhelm told me a little about her. He loved her very much, and said she was like an older sister to him. When he spoke of her, he would always become very sad." I forced my thoughts back to the present. "Did they say Louisa is coming to visit, too? She lives in Chicago now."

"I don't think so, but maybe. I couldn't hear very well." She hesitated for a moment. "Your mother started to cry."

"Maybe Louisa died," I whispered. "That would be a terrible thing. They haven't seen her for all these years, and if she died . . ." The words choked in my throat. How would Mutter feel in such a circumstance? Even though I'd never met *Tante* Louisa, I had always hoped that one day she would return for a visit with the family. The very idea that she might have died was like a weight on my chest. "What else did you hear, Berta? Surely you must have heard something more. When is Wilhelm scheduled to arrive?"

"I've told you everything I heard. I moved, and the floorboard creaked. Your mother turned around and saw me. I said I was looking for you. That's when I saw her wipe her eyes."

I now understood how Berta had managed to burst into my room without knocking. I longed to know when Wilhelm would arrive, but I dared not ask my mother. For once, I wished Berta had been more skillful with her snooping.

Berta pointed toward the headboard. "It's time to let me see."

I reached beneath the pillow. "Only this one." Berta could beg all she wanted, but I wasn't going to divulge my hiding place.

Instead of grabbing the magazine, she held it between her hands in a reverent manner and traced her index finger around the title. Her eyes appeared to glaze as she slowly turned the pages and devoured each one. "This is an old edition, but it's still wonderful." She glanced up at me. "How did you get it? I know they don't have these at the general store."

Wilhelm wouldn't care if I told, but if my parents discovered he'd been bringing me magazines, they would be angry with him. And even if Berta gave me her word, she was an impulsive young girl who might unintentionally blurt out my secret. "I'd rather not say. Isn't it enough that you get to look at it?"

"You don't need to tell me. I've figured it out for myself.

Wilhelm is the only one who would bring them to you." With an impish grin, she turned another page. "I think I would like Wilhelm very much. I believe he must be a lot like me."

"No, he's not. Not in the least." There was no need to defend my brother's character, yet I felt obligated. Perhaps because bringing the magazines had been my plan. I'd captured a glimpse of *Godey's* when a visitor brought a copy into the Küche. The next time Wilhelm arrived for a visit and asked what gift he could bring me, I requested the periodical. At first, he opposed the idea, but I pressed him until he finally relented. Now and then I experienced a pang of guilt for reading something other than the Bible, but mostly I enjoyed studying the fashions and reading the articles and short stories.

Berta flipped another page, apparently unaffected by my outburst. "Is Wilhelm married?"

"Yes. Her name is Larissa, but I've not met her. She's never come with him on his visits, but I've urged him to bring her." Perhaps that was what the letter had contained. Something regarding Wilhelm's wife, Larissa, rather than my aunt Louisa. Maybe Berta had misunderstood.

Berta pointed to a flowing lavender gown. "This one is very pretty, don't you think?" She waited for my approval, and after I nodded, she said, "Wilhelm's wife is probably very stylish. Maybe he fears she would consider life in Amana quite odd." She gathered the magazine close to her chest. "Or maybe he thinks she'd be afraid he'd want to move back to Iowa. That would be awful for her! Do you think Wilhelm would do such a thing?"

Ever dramatic, Berta clearly had envisioned a scene worthy of the stage. The girl could squeeze a story to life from one simple comment. "No. Wilhelm has no desire to live here again. I'm certain he assured Larissa of that before they married." I, too, had given thought to the fact that Larissa might find our way of life odd, but

I remained silent. If I agreed with Berta, she would develop yet another sensational story.

"Larissa. That's a lovely name. What does her family think of Wilhelm?"

"I have no idea. Do you think you may have heard the name Larissa rather than Louisa when my parents were discussing Wilhelm's visit?"

Berta continued thumbing through the magazine. "No. I'm certain it was Louisa."

Questions invaded my thoughts. The minute one question was answered, another would spring up to take its place. Would Larissa come with Wilhelm? Had something tragic happened to Tante Louisa? Why were my parents keeping Wilhelm's letter a secret?

"May I take this to my room?"

"What?" Berta's question jerked me from my musings. "No. Of course not."

"That's selfish. If I had some magazines, I would lend them to you for as long as you wanted."

"We shall never know about that, for you don't have any magazines. And even if you did, I would never ask. I'm sorry if you think I'm selfish, but I won't take a chance on the magazines being seen by anyone else."

With a frustrated huff, Berta slapped the magazine atop the bed. "Then you should at least let me look at one more while I'm in your room."

"This one is enough for today. If it's raining next Sunday afternoon, you can look at another."

A scowl creased Berta's face. "But there's plenty of time before we must return to the Küche."

There was no denying the girl had determination. No wonder her parents found it difficult to tell her no. She could wear down the nap on a rug in no time. "I'm not going to change my mind, Berta."

"Even if I told you another secret?"

I didn't believe she knew anything more. She was egging me on, yet I couldn't squelch my curiosity. "You have to tell me something more than that before I can decide. What kind of secret? More about what you heard from my parents on the porch or about something different?"

A wicked gleam shone in her eyes. "A little of both. I heard it from your parents, but it's not about Wilhelm or his letter."

The girl was a tease of the worst sort, and I was no match. She knew she had gained my attention. I could see it in the way she angled her head and grinned at me. Even in her plain calico, Berta appeared far worldlier than any seventeen-year-old girl I'd ever known.

After weighing my decision, I cultivated an idea of my own. "I will let you look at another magazine if you tell me."

"Today. You must let me see it today."

"I will let you see another magazine today." The girl was impossible. "Now tell me what you heard."

She scooted along the edge of the bed and tipped her head close to my ear. Her behavior made me feel as though we'd joined together in a dark conspiracy. "They talked about you and Carl."

I reared back at the unexpected declaration. Immediately suspicious, I narrowed my eyes and attempted my fiercest look. "You are fibbing to me, Berta Schumacher. If you think I'm going to give you another magazine when you make up stories, you're mistaken."

She flinched as if I'd slapped her. "It isn't a lie. I heard your mother say she thought you should marry Carl."

I shook my head. "You forget that you told me this story once before, but last time you said it was Vater who was arranging my marriage."

Berta jumped up from the bed and assumed a rigid stance. "I *am* telling you the truth. If you want to say I'm a liar, I can't stop you. But I know what I heard."

Her haughty glare was intended to defy my challenge. Such behavior might work with her parents, but it didn't convince me. Still, I worried there might be a snippet of truth in what she'd said. Mother had carefully avoided my questions about marriage and Carl the previous Sunday. On the other hand, Berta wanted those periodicals, and she would invent any story to get what she wanted. If I denied her, she might tell someone I had the magazines. I didn't think she'd go to my parents, but she'd likely confide in Rudolf. And who could know whether he'd remain silent. I was cornered and needed an escape.

"I'm not certain if you're telling me the truth, but since I can't be sure, I'm going to keep my word. If I discover you've lied to me—"

"I'm not lying. I promise." She rubbed her hands together and smiled, obviously eager for her prize.

Her grin disappeared when I pointed to the door. "You can wait in the parlor while I retrieve the magazine."

"But what if your parents are out there? What will I say? I'm waiting for Johanna to remove a magazine from its hiding place?"

Berta never disappointed. She was always quick with a rejoinder. "Tell them you're going to the outhouse and will return in a few minutes. If reading another magazine is truly important, I doubt that a few raindrops will deter you."

She stomped across the floor and slammed the door behind her as she left the room—a clue that the parlor was empty. I hurried to the large walnut wardrobe. Not a moment too soon, I unearthed another magazine.

Without so much as a knock on the door, she poked her nose back into the room. "Ready?" she chirped.

Pulling the magazine from behind my back, I held it in the air. "Ready."

She bounded across the room and plunked down on the edge of the bed. "Since you kept your word, I've decided to tell you one more thing I overheard. But I'll wait until I want to see another magazine."

Berta had dropped the luring temptation in front of me like a baited fishhook. Although I managed to maintain my dignity and didn't beg, the girl's assertion hung heavy in my mind. I was torn among dread and anticipation and disbelief. Had she truly overheard more of my parents' conversation? And if she had, did she hear something I would consider good news or bad?

# CHAPTER 11

Berta Schumacher

Over the next few days I decided my plan had failed. Johanna hadn't said one word about my other secret. I had hoped she would come to me. That way I could strike a bargain. One that would let me see more of her magazines and possibly convince her to let me borrow them. But not once had she mentioned our conversation. With each passing day I became more annoyed. How could she possess so much patience and I so little?

Yesterday I had done my best to lure her with a mention of the ruined fishing expedition with Carl last Sunday. Her only reaction had been to murmur that God controlled the weather. And each time I had attempted a visit with her after prayer services, she had demurred. Her declinations had been kind but firm. And always in her mother's presence. Her way of avoiding any argument from me—at least that was what I'd decided.

Even on our way to work each morning, she controlled the conversation with talk of kitchen chores, but last night I decided upon a new tack. On our way home from work today, I would drop a few mentions of Carl and see if she took the bait. If so, I would insist upon two or three of her magazines as a reward. I would return them, of course, but she could part with them for a few days.

I was lost in my thoughts of the latest fashion plates when Sister Muhlbach poked my shoulder.

"Where are your manners, Berta? It is rude to ignore people when they speak to you."

Startled, I wheeled around, and the crock of cottage cheese I was carrying across the room slipped from my hands and landed on the wooden floor with a heavy thud. Except for chips along the rim, the crock remained intact, and for that I was thankful. Cottage cheese was everywhere. It had ejected from the crock like a wintry explosion. Keeping my eyelids at half-mast, I peeked at Sister Muhlbach. Her lips remained fixed in a giant oval while she surveyed the area. My clothing and the floor had received the worst of it, but there were also splashes on the worktable legs, on Sister Muhlbach's shoes, and on the hem of her skirt. A few curds had even landed in the older woman's graying hair, a sight that caused me to grin.

"This is not funny. Look at the waste of gut food," Sister Muhlbach said.

"No. There's, there's . . ." I pointed to her hair.

She brushed her hand across the top of her head, but her fingers stopped when they touched the wet curds. "Ach! I'm going to my room to clean up while you scrub the kitchen floor." She pointed to the edges of the cabinets and table legs. "And don't miss any of it. If I haven't returned by the time you finish, go home and change your clothes." Sister Muhlbach sent a warning look to the other workers. "No one is to help her. You all have your own work to finish."

The minute Sister Muhlbach was out of earshot, the other women offered their support but not their help. They knew better. Even Johanna maintained a safe distance, but when I'd finally completed the task, she agreed to inspect the area. I impatiently waited while she ran her fingers beneath the cabinet's edge and around each leg of the worktable.

"You've done a fine job, Berta. I don't think Sister Muhlbach can find any fault with your work." Johanna's words of encouragement bolstered my spirits.

I sidled close to her. "I wouldn't have dropped the cottage cheese if Sister Muhlbach hadn't frightened me out of my wits. This is more her fault than mine."

Johanna gazed heavenward and sighed. "You shouldn't place blame on others, Berta. What does the Bible say about such behavior?"

"I doubt it says anything. As far as I know, they didn't have cottage cheese back then." From the disappointed look on Johanna's face, I knew my answer hadn't pleased her. On the other hand, she knew I had little knowledge of the Bible. What kind of answer had she expected?

"Go home and do as Sister Muhlbach instructed."

Johanna's voice lacked its usual warmth. Unless I could somehow draw myself into her good graces, I'd ruined any chance of looking at her magazines. Once again my tongue had gotten ahead of my brain, and I silently chided myself on the walk home.

Streaks of sunshine filtered through the trees and danced across my stained clothing, but even the thought of scrubbing out dried cottage cheese didn't detract from the beauty of the day. Though the distance to home wasn't far, there was something surprisingly intoxicating about strolling down the street at this time of day. No watchful eyes, no harsh commands, no looming schedule. Nothing but freedom to go home and change clothes.

The walk home had taken longer than necessary. I'd stopped to smell blooming flowers and admired a bird's nest along the way. Nothing I would have done while living in Chicago, yet here in Amana the actions proved strangely satisfying. I pressed down on the metal latch and entered the front hallway. The house was eerily quiet. I'd never before entered the house when no one else was at home. I closed the door and leaned against the hardwood door, listening. Not a sound.

I plodded upstairs, through the parlor, and into my bedroom. It didn't take long to change my skirt and apron, but my shoes were in need of cleaning. I'd emptied my water pitcher that morning, but perhaps I'd find water in my parents' room. I pulled open the door and crossed the room, grateful when I spied a few inches of water in the bottom of the china pitcher. I poured it into the bowl and glanced around the room for a cloth. I pulled open the top drawer of Father's chest. One of his handkerchiefs would do.

When I'd cleaned the shoes to my satisfaction, I wadded up the handkerchief. I would wash it with my apron next Monday. Reaching to close the drawer, I stopped short when something gleamed in the rear corner of the drawer. Pushing aside the handkerchiefs, my breath caught at the sight. Two gold coins lay near a leather pouch that had fallen open. One peek inside told me that my father hadn't turned over all of his assets when we'd joined the community.

In addition to several more gold pieces, the pouch contained loose gems and what appeared to be gold nuggets, though I couldn't be certain. My breath came in short spasms, and confusion invaded every corner of my mind. What did this mean? Was our time here merely a trial period? Had Father lied to the elders about our assets, or was it common practice to withhold funds? Did Mother know?

Still holding one of the gold coins, I dropped to the chair and stared across the room, focusing on nothing. Until I heard the lowing of the cows lumbering down the street on their way to the barn, I couldn't force myself to break the trance. What if Brother Ilg was with the cattle and stopped in at the house? My mouth turned dry. Jumping to my feet, I shoved the drawer closed and dropped the coin into my apron pocket.

There was no need to panic. Sister Muhlbach had sent me home to change clothes. If Brother Ilg came into the house, I had an approved reason for being there. After assuring myself I'd set things aright in my parents' room, I waited in the parlor until the street cleared and then departed.

Shoving my hand into my apron pocket, my fingers curled around the gold coin. How lovely it would be to peruse the items in the general store and purchase something special, something Johanna might want to trade for a magazine. The thought brought me to a halt, and I turned back toward the house. If I skirted along the back of the houses, I wouldn't be seen.

Moving with stealth and speed, I scuttled through the yards, keeping myself hidden along the bushes and trees. Though most folks were at work, some mothers remained at home with their children until they were old enough for Kinderschule. If one of them caught sight of me, I'd surely be reported to the elders or, even worse, to Sister Muhlbach.

The bell above the front door jingled in friendly greeting as I entered the store.

"*Guten Tag*, Sister Berta."

Brother Kohler's greeting was enough to set my thoughts awhirl.

I hadn't considered he might reveal I'd been here. "Guten Tag, Brother Kohler."

"Sister Muhlbach has given you a rest from your duties in the Küche?"

He'd made an assumption. I didn't agree or disagree. Instead, I let my gaze wander the store. "I was looking for a magazine or a book. Do you have anything like that?"

His back stiffened until it was as straight as a poker. "Periodicals and magazines? Not unless you want to read one of the farm journals. Brother Ilg has copies of those you could borrow." His frown deepened. "Why would you have need of periodicals?"

"For my cousin's birthday. I wanted to send her a gift." It was, of course, a lie, but what was I to do? He shouldn't have asked the question. Then I wouldn't have had to lie.

He scratched his bald head and scanned the room. "What about a sewing kit in a leather case?"

"No. She isn't keen on sewing."

He gasped as though I'd pierced his heart. "Then she should learn! Every young woman needs to know how to sew. It would be the perfect gift for her."

"I'm hoping to find something very unusual."

"Maybe your cousin would like some of this lace I just received from Chicago."

I shook my head. Johanna couldn't possibly be enticed with lace. Amana women didn't wear fancy trim on their clothes. "No," I mumbled and continued down the aisle. Then, on one of the top shelves, I spotted what appeared to be a book. "What is that?" I pointed to the shelf.

My shout startled Brother Kohler, and he took a backward step before he glanced upward. He shook his head. "Oh, that is a book that was forgotten by a salesman last year. I thought he would return, but—"

"I want to buy it."

"It isn't for sale, Berta. What if the man should return?"

"You can give him the money if he returns. But if he hasn't been back for a year, I doubt he'll show up, don't you?"

His frown deepened. "It may be unsuitable for your cousin, ja?"

"We won't know until we look." I wanted to grab the ladder and scale the wall myself, but I managed to maintain my decorum.

Though he huffed and puffed, Brother Kohler climbed the ladder and retrieved the book. He glanced at the cover as he stepped off the last rung of the ladder. "It is a book of poems and sonnets. At least that's what the cover says." He flipped open the book and nodded his head. "Poetry. In my estimation, she'd be better off reading the book of Psalms."

"May I look at it?" I extended my open hand.

His jowls sagged, and his fingers tightened around the volume. "I don't know if this is a good idea."

Before he could further consider, I stretched forward and grasped the book from his clutches. It was in pristine condition, probably never opened by the salesman. I wondered if he'd purchased it as a gift for his wife or sweetheart. He'd probably removed it from his sales case while talking to Brother Kohler and accidentally left it behind. By now he would have purchased another gift. In my mind the matter had been resolved completely.

I looked inside the front cover and discovered I had enough money to purchase the book. "I'll take it." I pulled the coin from my pocket and thrust it toward him.

He stared at the coin. "How do you happen to have money, Berta?"

I swallowed hard. Yet another problematic question. "It was a gift from a relative." *Another lie*. If Brother Kohler didn't quit asking me questions, I was going to burn in hell. I should have realized he would be suspicious when I produced money to pay for the purchase. Only visitors paid with cash. Nobody who lived in Amana used money—our purchases were listed as credits by our names and deducted from the yearly stipend allotted to each family.

Brother Kohler pressed his thick thumb across the coin, and I wondered if he was going to clamp it between his teeth to determine if it was genuine. He was watching me from beneath hooded eyes, assessing my every move. I steadied myself and forced myself to look confident. At least I hoped that was how I appeared.

"I cannot give you any funds in return, but I can add the difference to your family's account in the ledger. This would suit you?"

"No, that isn't necessary. To have a nice gift to give to my cousin is all I wanted."

"Then I will wrap it up and send it to her." He rested his beefy palms on the counter. "That's the least I could do, ja?"

"Oh, I'd much rather give it to her in person. I'm going to wait until we go back to Chicago or until she comes here for a visit." His brows furrowed, and I was certain I detected a hint of disbelief in his eyes. "But if my father thinks I should mail it, I'll bring it back to the store and have you take care of it for me. Thank you for the kind offer."

I made a slight curtsy, which appeared to further confuse him. Book in hand, I attempted to make my escape. I'd nearly made it to the door when his shout echoed in my ears.

"Wait! Come back, Berta."

I stopped in my tracks and made a slow pirouette. "Yes?" I clenched my fingers around the thick book cover as fear took up residence in the pit of my stomach.

He tapped the wooden cubbyholes where mail was distributed to the town's residents. "I have a letter for your Vater. You can take it to him, ja?"

I exhaled a puff of air, and relief flooded over me. I hastened back to the counter, retrieved the letter, and hurried out of the store. I was on my way to the Küche when I realized I couldn't take the book with me. I'd have to return home. I'd better have a good story ready for Sister Muhlbach, for she would surely question how long I'd been gone.

I retraced my steps along the rear of the neighbors' houses until I reached home. Once inside, I scuttled up the stairs to my room. Panting for breath, I lifted the lid to the small leather trunk at the foot of my bed and buried the book beneath the clothing stored inside. I decided to prop Father's letter on the small table in the parlor and examined the handwriting on the envelope as I carried it into the other room. I'd never before seen the delicate script. There was no name to indicate who it was from, only a street address in Chicago—one I didn't recognize. I traced my fingernail over the beautifully shaped lines that formed my father's name. Nobody but family knew we'd moved to Amana—that's what Mother had told me the week after we'd arrived. Had father told someone else of our whereabouts?

Curiosity plagued me. I didn't have time to weigh my decision right now, but the letter was too enticing to leave behind. I tucked the envelope into my skirt pocket. After I returned to work, I'd have time to think about what I should do.

# CHAPTER 12

The smell of sausage wafted through the air and greeted me as I rounded the corner of the Küche. One whiff and my mouth watered. But at the sight of a glowering Sister Muhlbach standing on the back porch, my mouth turned as dry as parched dirt. There would be no slipping into the kitchen unobserved.

She examined everything from my shoes to the top of my head. "Did you have to sew a new skirt?"

The question unnerved me. "N-n-n-no." I pressed my hand down the front of the calico. Of all the things she could have asked, I hadn't expected such a silly inquiry. "You've seen this skirt before."

She narrowed her eyes. "Ja, but you were gone so long I thought you decided to make a new frock."

I'd missed her earlier sarcasm, but now it came through loud and clear. Why hadn't she simply asked what had taken so long? When I opened my mouth to respond, she wagged her finger in front of my nose and pointed at the kitchen door.

"You can explain later. Right now, there is work piling up because of your selfish behavior."

Selfish? I wasn't selfish. A remembrance of my visit to the general store niggled at my conscience. Maybe I was a little selfish, but there were enough women in the kitchen to complete the work without me. Since my first day Sister Muhlbach had acted as though my presence was more hindrance than help. Strange that my brief absence should create such havoc.

In five elongated steps Johanna crossed the kitchen, her lips tightened into a pinched frown. "Where have you been, Berta?" Johanna's question harbored no sarcasm. Instead, it bore accusation and anger. "Your selfish actions have set us behind in our preparations."

Selfish? There was that word again. Had she and Sister Muhlbach been discussing me? "I'm sorry, but it took longer than—"

She waved me to silence. "I don't want to hear your excuses. I wouldn't believe you anyway. Get busy with the potatoes. They need to be peeled and shredded."

In a valiant effort to locate the shredder from among the variety of gadgets and tools that hung on the racks, I scanned the hanging metal equipment. There might be a shortage of workers in the kitchen, but there was no lack of tools. Since my arrival, Johanna had attempted to teach me the name and proper usage of each item, but the lessons held little interest. The only part I'd enjoyed had been a trip to the tinsmith's shop to deliver several items that had required repair. I'd been amazed at the items the man created, but I still didn't know the difference between a cheese mold and a pudding mold or a cheese grater and a potato shredder.

I'd almost gathered my courage to ask which one of the graters I should use when Johanna reached overhead and yanked the utensil off the hook. She held it in front of my nose. "Potato grater." She thrust it toward my hand. "Don't cut your finger. Sister Muhlbach might take pleasure in seeing you bleed a little." She swiveled on the heel of her well-worn shoe.

"And you?" I asked.

Her features softened. "I don't want you to hurt yourself, Berta, but I do want you to act like a responsible young woman. We'll talk later. After the work is completed."

Like it or not, I was in trouble. Even Johanna was unhappy with me. Maybe I should present her with the book of poetry when we get home from work. I wouldn't even try to bribe her for the magazines—unless I change my mind by the time we get home. After tying the apron around my waist, I set to work peeling the potatoes. One look at the tub of vegetables and my shoulders sagged. Why hadn't someone else started this job an hour ago? I couldn't possibly finish in time, but I dared not complain. It seemed the others were hard at work, though a quick head count revealed several of the ladies were missing.

A short time later Johanna dragged a chair beside the table and picked up a potato. "You're going to have to work faster."

"I'm working as quickly as I can. Where are the sisters? Can't they help?"

"Sister Dickel is ill, and Sister Bader was called to the school. Her son fell from one of the trees, and the teacher feared the boy broke his arm. They took him to your father for treatment."

Both of the women had been in the kitchen earlier. No wonder Sister Muhlbach was in a sour mood. "Maybe Sister Muhlbach should have been peeling potatoes instead of standing on the porch watching for me," I whispered.

Johanna clucked her tongue. "And maybe you should have

been back here in fifteen minutes instead of an hour." She lowered her head and leaned close. "I know how long it takes to get to our house, and so does Sister Muhlbach. Fifteen minutes would have been ample time to go home and change your skirt."

I pointed the tip of the paring knife at my shoes. "I had to clean my shoes, too."

"Then twenty minutes. That doesn't account for the rest of the time. Did you take a nap?" Johanna leaned back in the chair and pierced me with a fierce glare. "You went to visit Rudolf, didn't you?"

Finally an accusation I could deny—and I wouldn't be telling a lie. "No! How could you think such a thing?"

She arched her brows. "Then where were you?"

Should I tell her the truth? If she promised not to tell anyone, it would be the best possible solution. "Promise you won't tell?"

After a moment of hesitation, she agreed. While we continued to peel and grate the potatoes, I explained what I'd done. "If only you'd agreed to let me see your other magazines, I wouldn't have gone running off to the general store to purchase you a gift."

"Once again you are placing blame where it doesn't belong. This is not my fault, Berta. You are an impetuous girl who is determined to always have her way. One day you are going to have to admit that your actions are solely your responsibility, not the fault of others." Johanna reached for the grater and forced the potato along the uneven metal. "There are things I'd prefer to do, places I'd like to see, people I want to meet, but I can't simply give in to my own selfish desires."

"Why not? What's wrong with living your life in a manner that pleases you? Isn't that why this community was formed? So the members could live in a way that pleased them? Why can't you do the same? If you want to see what's beyond Amana, why not do it?" I stopped peeling the potatoes and scooted to the edge of my chair. Maybe I could convince Johanna she should follow her heart instead of the rules. The idea excited me.

She sighed and shook her head. "Even though I've tried to explain, you still don't understand why we came together in this communal living situation. Though I long to visit my brother in Chicago and maybe see more of the world, I find comfort in my life here. Where else is there more opportunity to seek and find Christ through prayerful fellowship with like-minded believers? Remember, time is a gift. Wise people do not—"

"Squander their gifts." I'd heard that from Sister Muhlbach at least once a day since I'd arrived in her kitchen. "If time is a gift, and you want to see other places, aren't you squandering your gift?"

"The allotment of time on this earth is given for us to draw closer to Christ—not to fulfill our own desires." Johanna motioned toward the knife. "Keep peeling, Berta." She continued grating another potato. "I'm curious about this book you mentioned. I'm surprised Brother Kohler would permit such a purchase."

"I think he liked the idea of keeping the change from my gold coin." The moment the words had slipped off my tongue, I wanted to take them back. But it was too late. Johanna's eyes shone with interest.

"I'm somewhat fearful to hear your answer, but how did you happen to have a gold coin in your possession?"

Deciding upon my answers had become a balancing act: truth or lie. This time, truth would win. I needed to tell someone about the letter. While we continued to pare and grate, I divulged the information. Johanna appeared aghast that I would enter my parents' room without permission, and I thought she might faint when I admitted to taking the coin from my father's drawer. She stared at me, her mouth wide open. Had a fly been in the room, it could have taken up residence.

"Close your mouth, Johanna," I hissed.

Her lips snapped shut, but her focus remained fixed upon me.

"It isn't like I stole the money. It belonged to our family."

"It belonged to your father, and you didn't have his permission. If it isn't stealing, what do you call it?"

At this rate I was never going to get around to telling her about the letter. "I borrowed it to purchase a gift for you. I'll tell him I used the money to purchase a book. He won't care in the least." I carefully avoided any reference to when I might tell him and pressed on before she could stop me with another question or condemnation. "But here's the important part." I sucked in a gulp of air and explained the letter Brother Kohler had given me. "What do you think I should do?"

Her brow crinkled and a V formed between her eyebrows. "Don't try to shift blame by saying you stole the money to purchase a gift for me. I would never accept a gift that was purchased with stolen money, so you can keep the poetry book or return it to Brother Kohler at the store. As for the letter, it isn't a difficult decision. You need to hand it over to your father."

That wasn't what I wanted to hear. "But what if—"

"If the contents were meant for your eyes, the letter would be addressed to you. It wasn't." She shoved the grater and knives into the crock of mounded potatoes. "Let's get these drained."

I grasped one of the large sieves made by the village tinsmith, my wrists aching by the time we'd completely squeezed all of the liquid from the potatoes. While I beat the eggs, Johanna mixed flour, salt, baking powder, and pepper. "Eggs are ready," I said.

She dumped the flour mixture into the potatoes and motioned for me to add the eggs. "Go ahead and stir them. I'll heat the skillets." When the lard was sizzling in the skillets, she motioned for the bowl of potatoes. "Be certain to set out bowls of applesauce. Potato pancakes are not their very best without applesauce."

I thought applesauce on top of the potato pancakes ruined the flavor, but I kept that thought to myself. Right now I didn't need another disagreement with Johanna. For the next hour I scuttled about the kitchen and performed my duties as best I could and received a favorable nod from Sister Muhlbach when the meal had been delivered to the tables. Good job or not, I was the one who remained late to clean the kitchen.

"It's the right thing," Sister Muhlbach said. "While the others worked, you were sitting at home. Now they will rest while you work."

There was no need to argue. I wouldn't win. Besides, I'd come to a decision. Once the others were out of the kitchen, I would steam open the envelope and read the letter. I'd never before tried such a thing, but when we lived in Chicago, John Underwood had told me of steaming open letters his sister had received from a beau. From what he'd told me, it didn't sound all that difficult.

The letter proved an incentive to perform my tasks with haste. Sister Muhlbach would have been stunned to see how quickly I could scrub pots and pans and set the kitchen aright. I placed a kettle of water atop the stove while I scrubbed the wooden floor—an effort in futility as far as I was concerned. It would only get dirty again. But I knew Sister Muhlbach would return and examine my work before morning, so I scrubbed—except for the far corners of the dining room. Nobody walked there anyway.

By the time the floor was cleaned, steam was rising from the kettle in a swirling pattern that twisted toward the ceiling. I removed the letter from my pocket and reexamined the lovely script. My palms turned damp, and I swiped them down the front of my apron. I dared not wait too long or Sister Muhlbach would return and interrupt me. Any attempt to explain would surely fall upon deaf ears.

Keeping my fingers free of the steam, I held the envelope above the boiling water, but my first attempt to open the missive failed. Undeterred, I returned the envelope to the warm mist and slowly moved it back and forth. This time, using the tip of a knife to aid in my effort, the glue released and the envelope popped open. My fingers trembled as I removed the pages and dropped to a chair near the kitchen door. From this vantage point I would gain the most daylight and could also hear if someone approached.

My stomach clenched into a knot as I scanned the rows of neat script.

> My darling Herman,
>
> How I have missed you, my love. My heart aches for you, and I don't know how I shall survive until you return to me. For more than a week I have been expecting to hear your familiar knock on my door but have been sorely disappointed. When you departed, you promised you would return once Helen and Berta were settled in Iowa.
>
> If you truly love me—as you so often have said—then why do you linger? Know that I love you, but I will not wait forever.

My stomach roiled, and I swallowed hard. I couldn't bear to read any more of this painful entreaty. I turned to the last page and looked at the signature. *Lovingly yours, Caroline*. I rubbed my forehead, hoping to relieve the pressure that pounded behind my eyes. So many questions, but who would answer them? Not my father. And I couldn't ask my mother. Anger mixed with fear as I considered the letter's contents. I wanted to believe the woman didn't exist, but memories of arguments between my parents and the many nights my father had been absent from our home in Chicago paraded through my mind. And then I remembered the leather pouch.

Was that why he had the money hidden away? So he could return to her? Did he care so little for Mother and me? I folded the letter, returned it to the envelope, and dipped my finger in a pitcher of water. With a light touch, I daubed the water onto the seal and pressed it back in place. Once I was certain it held fast, I tucked the letter into my pocket and walked out the kitchen door, down the street to our house, and up the stairs to our rooms.

My father was sitting on the upholstered chair thumbing through one of his medical books. He glanced up when I entered the room. "I wondered if you would return in time for prayer service."

"Where is Mother?"

"She went back to the Kinderschule and said she would join us at prayer service."

I couldn't imagine why she'd go back there, but I was pleased. Without further conversation, I removed the letter from my pocket and stretched it forward. "This letter came for you in the mail."

His complexion turned ashen. "How do you happen to have this?"

There was a noticeable tremor in his voice that confirmed my worst fears—and probably his, as well. "I was at the general store, and Brother Kohler gave it to me."

"I see." He shoved the envelope into his pocket.

"Who is it from, Father? I don't recognize the address."

"Nobody you know, Berta. Just one of my patients from Chicago."

My heart turned cold when I heard my father's calculated lie.

# CHAPTER 13

Johanna Ilg

There was little doubt I had offended Berta with my recriminations, but I hadn't expected the silence and isolation she'd exhibited for the remainder of the week. Never before had she held a grudge. In fact, she'd always been rather indifferent when chastised—except for her attempts to blame others.

For the past several days I'd done my best to cheer her, but her responses had been no more than one or two words. The girl's silence had become as frustrating as her earlier penchant for chatter. I'd never been inclined to delve into the business of others, but I'd been assigned to train Berta, and it somehow seemed right to pursue the matter.

When she'd continued her unresponsive nature on our walk to work this morning, I decided that after work I would ask her to go fishing with Carl and me on Sunday. I hoped the invitation would break down the invisible barrier she'd placed between herself and the rest of the world. Even Sister Muhlbach had expressed confusion over the girl's quiet demeanor.

The morning passed without incident, but I expected to observe a hint of excitement when Sister Muhlbach sent Berta outdoors to meet the milk wagon. But when Rudolf arrived, she remained subdued. The fact that the handsome young man couldn't bring a glint to her eyes created even more worry.

At day's end Berta hurried out the door and started home without me. I waved a hasty good-bye to Sister Muhlbach and trotted around the side of the house, calling to her. "Wait for me, Berta! I need to speak to you." With a brief glance over her shoulder, she slowed her pace, but she didn't stop.

Panting when I finally reached her side, I looped my hand into the crook of her arm. Part of me feared she might bolt, yet I knew it was a silly thought. Where would she run to? "Berta, I want to invite you to go fishing with Carl and me on Sunday. We can go as soon as we complete the noonday meal."

Silence.

I squeezed her arm. "Berta? Would you like to go fishing with us? We can invite Rudolf to come along if you'd like." I hoped she would hear the genuine enthusiasm in my voice, for I truly wanted her to join us.

Her gaze remained fixed on the road ahead. "No."

I waited, certain she'd explain her refusal. But she didn't. That was the sum total of her response. *No.* I didn't know whether to laugh or cry or shout. I tugged her to a halt and took a firm hold on her upper arms. "Look at me, Berta." When she raised her chin, I said, "I want you to come with us." I bobbed my head. "I really do want you to, Berta."

A single tear escaped one eye and rolled down her cheek. She dabbed at it with the corner of her apron. "If you're worried I'm angry, you can set aside your concern. This has nothing to do with you, Johanna."

"Then will you come with us? If you say you'll come along, I promise I won't ply you with questions."

"Why would you want me to? I'm nothing but a nuisance to everyone I've ever known. Except maybe John Underwood."

I grinned. "And Rudolf. And your parents. And—"

Her eyes turned dark. "No. Only John. Rudolf finds me a nuisance at times. My mother prefers the children at the Kinderschule, and my father has no use for either my mother or me."

The dramatic commentary slipped from her lips with far too much ease. "You don't believe that, Berta. Your parents love you very much. I'm not a doctor, but it seems you're suffering from a bout of melancholy. I'd guess you've been remembering springtime in Chicago and you're missing your friends and the many festivities you enjoyed at this time of year. Come fishing with us, and we'll make some memories of our own. What do you say?"

She shrugged one shoulder.

I couldn't tell if it was an agreement or if she simply wanted me to remove my hold on her. I bent down until we were eye to eye. "So you'll come?"

"Maybe."

I released her arms and matched her stride. We were nearing home when I was struck by a fresh idea. Why hadn't I thought of it earlier? I clasped her hand. "If you want to stop by my room before prayer service, you can look at another magazine."

She shook her head. "I'm going to rest for a while."

I couldn't believe my ears. She wanted to rest rather than look at the *Godey's* magazine. I reached to touch her forehead. "Are you ill?"

"In a way," she murmured.

"Then we should stop by your father's office."

"No." She turned to face me, her eyes as cold as a winter day. "He's the last person I want to see."

I didn't understand, but it was obvious she wouldn't welcome any questions. At least not now. Eventually I would uncover the cause of this mysterious change. I opened the front door, and Berta climbed the stairs, each movement slow and plodding. She had turned into an old woman before my eyes. Had Berta's mother noticed this difference in her daughter, or was she as detached as Berta alleged?

Pushing down on the latch, I entered the parlor and greeted my mother with a kiss on the cheek. "I'm surprised to see you at home before me."

She pressed her palm against her lower back. "And glad I am to be here. Each year I forget about the aching muscles I suffer when we transfer plants from the hotbeds. Sister Rosina sent me home to rest."

"I'm astounded she was so compassionate." Neither Sister Muhlbach nor Sister Nusser was known to possess a sympathetic disposition.

"I told her if I remained at work and strained my back over-much, I might miss several days work instead of an hour or two. She sent me home and said she'd see me in the morning."

I bent forward and removed the mending from her hands. "Then you should go in and rest before prayer meeting. It would be better for your back."

"If you will come and visit with me," she said. "Otherwise, I will fall asleep, and then I will be wide awake all night long."

Sewing basket in hand, I followed her into the room and settled into a chair beside my parents' bed. Holding the fabric taut, I drew the needle through the material and formed tiny stitches as

I worked to repair the frayed seam. "Have you visited with Berta's mother recently?"

"Only a little. Why do you ask?"

"I think Berta misses having her mother's attention. She says Sister Schumacher is at the Kinderschule a great deal."

My mother pursed her lips. "She told me she likes to be around the little children. After Berta was born, they hoped for a son, but it didn't happen. I think that's why she enjoys the little children so much."

"But Berta needs her, too. She's been sad these last few days, and she won't tell me what's bothering her. I thought maybe Sister Schumacher might have said something."

"No. She hasn't mentioned Berta at all." My mother shifted her head on the pillow. "I am pleased you and Carl are going fishing on Sunday. He is a fine young man."

A glint shone in her eyes. Perhaps Berta had been telling the truth. "Aren't all of the men in our village fine men?"

"Ja, that is true. But Carl is special. Your Vater says he is a good worker and eager to please." Her eyelids fluttered. "And nice to look at, as well, ja?"

"Mutter!" My cheeks felt as though they'd been touched by a hot poker. "I cannot believe you said such a thing."

"Come now, Johanna. I am not blind, and neither are you." She lifted her head from the pillow. "He would make a fine husband for you."

My mother had now erased all doubt. Berta had spoken the truth. She and Father had been discussing marriage. My marriage. To Carl Froehlich. To tell her that Carl's glance made my heart race and his touch caused my hands to tremble would only reinforce her determination. Why this sudden plan that I should wed? I could understand my father wanting Carl's help in the barns. I could even understand his desire to embrace Carl as a son. He missed

Wilhelm. Of that there was no doubt. But why would my mother support this idea of marriage? There had to be something more involved. Although the elders usually approved marriages, Amana parents didn't encourage or arrange them. At least that's what I'd been taught since I was a little girl.

While I had a modicum of courage, I asked the questions searing my mind. "Why are you suddenly pushing me toward marriage? Is it because Vater hopes to replace Wilhelm and make Carl his son, or is it because you know I want to go to Chicago and visit Wilhelm?"

Once again I saw the glimmer of fear that shone in her eyes whenever I mentioned Chicago. She clutched her handkerchief tight in her fist. "No person ever replaces another. Nobody will ever replace Pieter or Wilhelm. And Vater and I have told you over and over there is nothing gut for you in Chicago." She placed her palm across her forehead.

No doubt my questions had caused her a headache to go along with her backache. I patted her hand, but I didn't want her to think I'd given up on a visit with Wilhelm. "I thought we would hear from Wilhelm now that spring has arrived. Each day I hope there will be a letter from him saying he will arrive for a visit."

The fear returned and shadowed my mother's dark eyes. Her brows dipped low as she studied me for a brief moment. "Did your Vater mention a visit from Wilhelm?"

A prickling sensation coursed across my shoulders. Either she'd heard from Wilhelm or she hadn't, but from her guarded response, I now was certain my brother had written. I wanted to shout a resounding yes, but the response stuck in my throat. I couldn't lie to my mother. "No," I mumbled.

She covered her eyes with her forearm. "We received a letter from Wilhelm saying he would visit tomorrow."

I dropped my mending and clapped my hands together. "Why

didn't you tell me? I must let Carl know I won't be going fishing with him after all."

Strands of hair fanned across the pillow as she shook her head. Slowly, she lowered her arm. "You can still go fishing. Wilhelm will not be arriving tomorrow. I wrote to him and told him he should wait awhile longer before he comes."

"But why would you ask him to wait?" My voice bore the shrill tone that frequently emerged when I was overcome by fear or distress.

"There are some things that are private, Johanna. This is one of them."

"Private? We are a family. When I was a little girl, you told me that families shared and always helped one another. I want to know why you would discourage a visit from Wilhelm."

Astonishment and anger combined to pinch my mother's features into a surprised frown. My parents were unaccustomed to confrontation, especially from me. When Wilhelm left home, he hadn't confronted my parents. He'd simply stated his intentions, packed his bags, and departed. There had been no argument, no discussion, no pleading. Just a slamming door and then silence. That heavy silence had returned. Like a bolted door, it separated my mother and me. But I remained steadfast. I wanted an answer.

"Emilie? Johanna? Where are you?"

At the sound of my father's voice, relief flooded my mother's eyes. She pushed the hair from her forehead and peered toward the doorway. "We're in the bedroom, Frank."

My father's hurried footsteps were muffled by the carpet, but he now stood framed in the doorway staring at my mother. "You are ill, Emilie?"

"My back is aching, as it does every spring."

"Ach! Sister Rosina should have the younger women bending and stooping. Every year she does this, and every year you suffer."

"Not every year, Frank. You may remember there was a time when I was young."

My mother shifted to her hip and pointed in my direction. She attempted to hide the gesture, but I recognized the signal—an indicator to my father that trouble was brewing.

Well, if she wanted to alert my father, then I'd just as well speak up. "Mutter tells me Wilhelm wrote that he was coming for a visit. She also tells me she asked him not to come."

My mother lifted on one elbow. "That is *not* what I said, Johanna! I said I wrote and told him to wait and come later."

"The same thing." I sounded more like Berta than myself.

My father shook his head. "You know it isn't the same, Johanna. You are angry because you want to see your brother. If you want to cast blame, you should direct it at me rather than your Mutter. I am the one who thought we could better enjoy Wilhelm's visit a little later in the season. After spring planting is completed and we aren't so busy."

"And weary," my mother added.

They were telling me half-truths. Granted, we would have more time with Wilhelm after spring planting was completed, but there had been much more to their decision. Berta had seen my mother crying, and Louisa's name had been mentioned. Strange, but at the moment I believed more of what Berta had told me than what I'd just heard from my parents.

The descending sun cast shadows across the room, and my father nodded toward the door. "We should leave for prayer meeting in a few minutes." He leaned down to touch my mother's arm. "Do you feel well enough to attend?"

Both his concern for my mother and the mention of prayer service combined to annoy me. His behavior didn't fool me in the least. My father wanted to close the door to further discussion of Wilhelm's visit.

Shifting her legs, my mother eased to a sitting position. She arched and rubbed her palm along the small of her back. "I will be fine."

Eyebrows knit in concern, my father shook his head. "You remain here. Rest is the best thing for an aching back. Johanna and I will attend without you."

After gathering his Bible, he motioned me to the parlor. "You can wait for Berta and her mother. I'll go on ahead. I need to speak to one of the elders."

I didn't argue. My parents could avoid my questions for this evening, but eventually they would need to answer. Then again, perhaps it would be easier if I wrote a letter of my own—a letter to Wilhelm asking for the truth and asking if I could come to Chicago for a visit. Yes. That's exactly what I would do.

The next morning Berta and I walked to the garden with a basket containing thick slices of buttered bread, a small crock of grape jam, and jugs of coffee and water. Although the fare varied, each Küche delivered a midmorning and midafternoon repast to their garden workers every day—a task assigned to Berta and me. Though I normally disliked the chore, today it would fit into my plan.

As we rounded the bend, Sister Nusser waved us toward the shed. We marched past the rows that had been carefully planted with onions, radishes, spinach, salsify, and peas, then on past the cauliflower, beets, cabbage, and carrots. Even some of the pole beans and celeriac were now in the ground, although Sister Nusser wouldn't be happy until all the plots had received their spring planting. The women who worked for the Gartebaas joked that she would have them planting by moonlight if the elders would grant permission.

My mother swiped her hands on her apron as she and the other women made their way toward the garden shed, where they would gather to enjoy their refreshments. I waved but didn't linger. She might say something that would deter me from my decision.

Once we'd deposited the basket and jugs in the shed, I hurried Berta toward the road and motioned for her to follow me in a different direction. I was surprised when she didn't ask questions. Until recently Berta had always been full of questions. But this morning the only sounds were the scuffle of our shoes on the dirt road and the twitter of birds as they constructed nests in the cedar trees.

"Would you tell me your other secret?" Berta's startled reaction reminded me of a marionette that had been jerked to life with the pull of a few strings. Had she forgotten she'd promised to tell me more if she could look at my other magazines? "You recall, don't you? You said you heard more about Wilhelm's letter and my parents' conversation on the front porch."

"Oh. I'd forgotten. There was something about Louisa's baby, but I really didn't hear anything other than that."

I yanked her to a halt. "What baby? Louisa doesn't have any children."

Berta's eyes remained as dull as the overcast day. "All I can tell you is what I heard. Maybe Louisa has a child and they didn't tell you. They weren't going to tell you about Wilhelm's letter, so there could be other things you don't know. I've decided that parents keep lots of secrets from their children."

"What is wrong with you, Berta? You're not the same girl who arrived here in March."

"There's nothing I can tell you right now. Maybe someday, but not now." She immediately retreated into her own thoughts.

I wouldn't pry. When she was ready, Berta would come to

me. At the moment my mind was still reeling from the news that Louisa had a baby of her own—after all these years. It seemed impossible. But Sister Bader had given birth to a healthy little boy last year, and she must be at least forty years of age—a little older than Louisa, for certain.

I tugged on Berta's sleeve when we neared the turn that would take us toward town. "I need to stop at the general store and post a letter. You won't tell, will you?"

Finally something I said ignited a spark of interest. "Who are you writing to?"

I inhaled a deep breath of fresh spring air. "Wilhelm. I do wish I'd known about Louisa's baby before I penned the letter. I would have asked him about the child, but maybe he'll tell me when he answers."

Her eyes widened with surprise. "Why are you writing to Wilhelm?"

"To discover the truth. My parents won't tell me why they've delayed his visit." I didn't tell her I'd also asked Wilhelm if I could come for a visit. Telling Berta too much would make it even more difficult for her to keep my secret.

She gasped. "You didn't tell them—"

I shook my head. "They don't know a thing about your over-hearing their conversation."

"Then how—?"

"I asked if there had been any news from Wilhelm. They don't suspect that you are involved in any way." I inched closer. "But I know they aren't telling me everything. Instead of trying to pry it out of them, I decided I would write and ask Wilhelm."

"You think he will tell you the truth?"

I gave a confident nod, but Berta didn't appear particularly convinced. "Why? Do you think he will hide the truth from me, too?"

"Who can say what another person will do. We never really know anyone else. Not deep down." Her shoulders sagged, as though she were carrying the weight of the world. "I won't tell that you've sent him the letter, but you never know about Brother Kohler. You should tell him you're planning a surprise so he doesn't say something to your father or mother."

"Oh, that's a good suggestion. Thank you, Berta."

"And tell him that if a letter arrives addressed to you, he shouldn't give it to anyone else. You wouldn't want your reply to fall into the wrong hands."

Helping plan my ruse lightened Berta's mood, and she listened intently while I instructed Brother Kohler.

The storekeeper sucked in a breath. "I always put the mail in the proper slots."

I'd offended him. Of that there was no doubt. Before I could apologize, Berta took a step forward and placed her palms on the counter. "Not always, Brother Kohler."

Realization struck, and he slowly bobbed his head. "Ja. You are right, Berta. Sometimes I give the mail to a family member." He turned and looked me in the eye. "But I will be sure any letter addressed to you is delivered only to you."

"*Danke.* You can deduct the postage from my father's account. I am most thankful for your help."

"No," Berta said. "You can deduct it from the extra money I paid you when I purchased the book, Brother Kohler."

"Ja. I can do that." He glanced back and forth between Berta and me. When I didn't object, he slapped his hand on the counter. "Then it is settled. I will mail your letter today." He lifted a finger to his lips. "And the three of us will keep this our secret."

His eyes twinkled with anticipation, but I offered no further explanation. I would never consider taking Brother Kohler into my confidence. I'd only included Berta because she'd heard my parents' conversation, and because I couldn't have stopped at the store without her. If Berta had returned to the Küche alone, Sister Muhlbach would have questioned my whereabouts.

Like it or not, Berta and I had become partners in deception.

Later that evening during prayer service, it felt as though God's hand reached down from heaven and opened the Scriptures. Brother Mauer had taken his place before us and announced he would read from chapter four of Second Corinthians. His choice hadn't bothered me in the least. Mostly because I had no idea what was written there. After clearing his voice and glancing about the room, he read:

> "Therefore seeing we have this ministry, as we have received mercy, we faint not; But have renounced the hidden things of dishonesty, not walking in craftiness, nor handling the word of God deceitfully; but by manifestation of the truth commending ourselves to every man's conscience in the sight of God."

I didn't hear the remainder of the chapter. My palms turned damp with perspiration, and pinpricks marched down my spine. In the past I could have stood before the elders and said that I had renounced hidden things of dishonesty—all except for my *Godey's* magazines, which of course could be considered hidden and dishonest. However, I thought the magazines suitable reading material and hadn't asked for the forgiveness of the elders. Or of God, for that matter. And I certainly hadn't considered myself to be walking in craftiness or handling the Word of God deceitfully. At least not until today. But the letter to Wilhelm had been all of those things. It had been hidden, dishonest, crafty, and deceitful— indeed it had been very deceitful. On the other hand, if my parents had simply told me the truth, I wouldn't have been forced to take deceptive measures.

My breath caught, and I clasped a hand to my chest. I sounded just like Berta!

# CHAPTER 14

Berta Schumacher

Though I'd done my best to stay at home, Johanna, Carl, and Rudolf had banded together and insisted I join them for their afternoon of fishing. I would have feigned a headache, but Father had made it clear that he planned to spend the afternoon in the parlor with his medical books. Unless he was called out for some sort of emergency, an unlikely event on a Sunday afternoon, there would be no opportunity for private conversation with my mother.

I didn't plan to mention the letter from my father's lady friend—that would give rise to questions I didn't want to answer—but I did want to explore my parents' true reason for the move to Amana. I was now convinced that my behavior had been a pretense they had used to hide the truth. I didn't know if I possessed the skill to lead my mother into an honest conversation, but I wanted to make an attempt. The idea offered the first glimmer of hope since I'd read Caroline's letter. Perhaps if we could have a truthful discussion, there might be hope for our family. Otherwise, I wasn't so sure.

While I changed out of the black calico I'd worn to church, I considered Caroline's letter to my father. I wasn't an authority on romance, but there was little doubt she believed he was going to return to Chicago—and to her. My scalp tingled at the idea. Would my father do such a thing? He'd been distant and aloof toward Mother—even I had noticed their lack of affection, and they seldom spoke to each other. What would Mother do if he made such a choice? And what would the elders and other residents of Amana think? More important, what would God think? Would He deal harshly with my father if he chose Caroline over Mother? The thoughts marched through my mind like an army of ants.

"You'd better hurry or the others will leave without you," my mother called from the parlor.

A few weeks ago that warning would have caused me to race down the stairs. But not today. If I didn't go fishing, it would be no great loss. Nothing seemed to matter as much as it had a few weeks ago—nothing except my father's secret and what it would mean for our family if he left us. What it would mean for me! The thought took my breath away, and I dropped to the side of my bed. If Father left us, would I ever see him again?

Caroline knew Mother and I existed. Still, she'd encouraged him to leave his family. What kind of woman did such a thing? And what kind of man wanted such a woman? There was a time when I thought I knew my father quite well, but now I realized I'd never known him at all. If what Caroline had written in her letter was true, my father had agreed to this ugly plan. And where would

I belong? I doubted Caroline would want me to be a part of their new life—and remaining in Amana with Mother would be no life at all. I'd be a reminder of our former life, and she'd turn all of her attention to the children in the Kinderschule, a process she'd already begun. Was Mother already preparing herself for Father's departure? Did she know?

"Berta! What are you doing in there?"

I forced myself up from the bed and shuffled to the bedroom door.

My mother glanced up when I entered the parlor. "What took you so long?" Her features knotted into a deep-set frown. "That shirtwaist is stained, and the hem has come loose on the right side of your skirt." Her lips puckered, and she made a *tsk*ing sound. "Hurry and change into something more presentable. I'll ask Johanna to wait on you."

"We're going fishing, Mother. People don't wear good clothes to go out in the woods or to sit on the riverbank." Apparently I'd spoken with enough authority that she didn't argue when I continued toward the door.

Rudolf was waiting in the downstairs foyer. A wide grin split his face when I appeared at the top of the steps. "I was beginning to wonder if you'd forgotten," he said. "Carl and Johanna are waiting outside."

Having the use of a buggy or wagon for Sunday afternoons was one of the privileges afforded us because Johanna's father managed the livestock and barns. I climbed into the buggy while Carl located a suitable spot for the fishing poles and his tin of worms. Johanna held a food basket on her lap, and there were two jugs of water resting by her feet. I was acutely aware that I'd brought nothing but myself. Then again, I hadn't planned this expedition. In fact, I hadn't even wanted to join them. Those thoughts helped assuage my feelings of guilt.

During the ride Johanna and Carl were unusually talkative, while I was unusually quiet. Rudolf attempted to engage me in conversation, but I cared little about the new calves and lambs being born or the laying hens that were disappearing from the coop behind one of the other kitchen houses. What I wanted was peace and quiet, an opportunity to be alone with my thoughts of Caroline's unwanted intrusion in my life and what the future held for me. I couldn't help but wonder if my father would sneak off in the night, just as I'd crept out to meet John Underwood when we lived in Chicago. I wanted to believe Father would tell me—that he wouldn't simply walk out of my life. That I'd have an opportunity to beg him to stay, to promise I'd behave in a proper manner, to convince him he needed us more than he wanted Caroline. If only he would give our family another chance, maybe he would be happy. Maybe.

"Berta and I get the spot by the big rock!" Rudolf nudged me when I didn't immediately reach for his hand. "Come on, Berta." He poked Carl's shoulder and pointed to a grassy slope a short distance away. "That would be a good place for you and Johanna."

Carl laughed and shook his head. "I can choose my own spot, thank you."

"Grab the tin of worms, Berta," Rudolf said as he helped me out of the buggy.

I followed his instruction and trailed behind him. Once he'd settled on the rock, I handed him the tin. "I don't feel much like fishing. I'm going to go hunt for mushrooms. I'll be back in a while."

He made several fervent requests for me to remain and fish with him, but I declined. After my final refusal he dropped his fishing pole to the ground and jumped to his feet. "Then I'll go hunt mushrooms with you."

"No. Absolutely not." I pointed to the rock. "Sit down and fish." Confusion shone in his eyes. "This has nothing to do with you, Rudolf. I need some time alone to think." I forced a smile and leaned forward to squeeze his shoulder. "Maybe when I return I'll feel more like fishing."

Though he didn't appear totally convinced, he sat down. "Here. You'd better take this for your mushrooms." He pulled a burlap bag from beneath him. "I don't need it. Brought it along in case we wanted to sit in the grass."

I thanked him and hurried off before he could change his mind. Sister Muhlbach had collected some morel mushrooms last Sunday and cooked them for the kitchen workers as a special treat. Fried in her buttered iron skillet, they had melted in my mouth. While I searched for the golden sponge-topped morels, my thoughts returned to Caroline's letter and how I could save our family.

I pushed aside an early growth of plants that had begun to take hold in the wooded area and smiled with satisfaction when I spied several of the yellowish mushrooms poking through the weeds. Like vigilant sentinels they appeared to be standing guard over the woodland floor. I dropped them into the burlap bag and continued my search. Sister Muhlbach had told me the mushrooms were difficult to find, but after tasting the delicacies, I knew they were worth the effort.

I'd located several of the mushrooms' hiding spots when I heard the rustle of approaching footsteps. I expected to see Rudolf. Instead, I caught a glimpse of Johanna as she pushed aside an overhanging branch.

"Any luck with the mushrooms?"

Strange. When I wanted company no one came around, but when I needed time to think, there wasn't a quiet place to be found.

Holding the bag shoulder high, I gave a nod. "Not nearly as many as Sister Muhlbach picked last week."

Johanna peeked inside the bag. "But there's enough that we could have a tasty treat when we do the laundry tomorrow. We can borrow a skillet from the Küche and fry them over the stove in the washhouse. What do you think? That would be a nice reward for doing the laundry."

I wasn't certain Johanna's mother would agree. She seemed far too stern to enjoy frying mushrooms in the washhouse. "Do you think your mother would agree?"

"Of course. She enjoys mushrooms as much as I do."

"Any luck catching fish?"

Johanna shook her head. "Not for me, but Carl and Rudolf have each caught two. I think they're in competition." She stooped down and looked beneath the undergrowth and pulled out a large mushroom. Smiling, she stood and dropped it into the bag. "I keep meaning to ask you what your father said about that letter he received. Did he tell you who had written to him?"

My throat constricted. I gasped for a breath of air and choked out my answer. "He said it was from one of his patients in Chicago."

"There, you see? No need for concern."

I hadn't planned to tell Johanna my secret, but I could no longer hold the ugly story inside. "He lied!"

Her eyes opened wide at my shouted accusation. "That's a serious statement, Berta. What makes you think he lied?"

"Because I read the letter. The woman wasn't one of his patients. She loves my father. Even worse, I fear that he loves her." Without warning my tears spilled over and plopped onto my stained shirt-waist. I sniffled and wiped my eyes with the heel of my hand.

Unless tears were being used for the purpose of manipulation in a difficult situation, I detested them. Long ago I'd learned that women who cried were considered frail and defenseless. I never wanted to be considered either of those things.

"Oh, Berta." Johanna pulled me close and wrapped me in a warm embrace. "I'm very sorry. This is why you've been so quiet and withdrawn, isn't it."

Her soft cotton dress rubbed against my cheek. "Yes. I wish I had followed your advice. It would be better if I didn't know."

"Have you spoken to your mother?"

I took a backward step. "Not yet, but I think she may know."

"You should be very careful, Berta. You don't want to hurt your mother. You should seek God's direction. A mistake could create problems that might never be resolved."

Johanna was right. This was more serious than peeking at presents before Christmas morning arrived. Saying or doing the wrong thing could ruin the rest of our lives. "If I tell my mother and there is an argument, I fear Father will leave Amana for good. And I'm certain he won't take Mother or me with him. What would you do?"

"I don't know, Berta. That's why you must pray for God to give you the direction you need."

Later that afternoon, I listened to my father's footsteps as he descended the stairs. Once I heard the front door close, I glanced toward my mother. We were seldom alone nowadays. If we weren't at work, we were at church. And when we were at home, Father generally sat in the parlor reading his medical journals while Mother stitched on her needlepoint. Even now she held her handwork, though she did appear distracted. She hadn't taken a stitch since I'd looked in her direction. With Father off to check on a patient, I decided this would be the perfect time to ask some questions.

I crossed the room and settled into the chair beside her. "That's a lovely piece you're working on."

"What?" Her focus darted to the needlepoint. "Oh, this?" She dangled the fabric in the air. "It's a canvas I started before our move to Amana."

Her response gave me the perfect opening. "How well are you enjoying our new life in Iowa, Mother?"

She measured and snipped a length of yarn. "I believe we're adjusting quite well. Don't you?"

I lifted my weight and pulled the chair closer. "When we first arrived, I thought Father was the one who wanted to move here, especially since he has a distant cousin living in Middle Amana." I was going to ask her if we would ever meet the unknown relative, but immediately pushed the idea aside. I didn't want to veer from the important questions. I couldn't be sure when Father would return. "Now I'm wondering if you're the one who made the choice to move here."

She stared at me for a moment. "It was a joint decision. We both knew it would be best for all of us to move away from Chicago."

"So you admit we didn't move here because you feared I'd run off with John Underwood."

"Not entirely. We were very worried about your behavior prior to our departure. You are easily influenced by others—especially young men. And that's not a good thing. Amana is a safe haven for all of us."

"But why is this place good for you and Father? You were happy in Chicago, and Father had a good medical practice with lots of patients. This move makes little sense, and Father doesn't appear particularly happy here. What if he should decide to leave?

Would you go with him? Would you permit me to go if he wanted to move back to Chicago?"

My mother shifted in her chair. I could see my questions made her uncomfortable.

"None of us is going to leave Amana. We are a happy and content family. Besides, we have sold all of our possessions, and the money was turned over to the society when we moved here. Even if your father wanted to return, he has no way to rebuild his life in Chicago. It would be far too difficult."

I swallowed hard as I remembered the contents of the leather pouch in my father's dresser. Had Mother never seen it when she placed clean laundry in his dresser? Then I remembered that she'd assigned each of us the task of putting away our own laundry when she started working at the Kinderschule. Still, I wondered if she knew about the leather pouch and had chosen to ignore my father's dishonesty.

"Were you unhappy in Chicago, Mother?"

Her fingers trembled as she attempted to thread her needle. "Why all this talk of Chicago? I thought we'd settled this discussion long ago." She narrowed her eyes and pinned me with a hard look. "Is there something you need to tell me, Berta?"

I wagged my head back and forth, but my mother's gaze remained steadfast. If I turned away, she'd know I was lying. "No, nothing I can think of at the moment."

She placed the needlework in her lap. "I realize you still find life here in Amana difficult. But if you will open your heart to God and listen to His Word at Sunday meetings and during our prayer services, you will feel His presence and the blessing He can bring to your life."

Who was this woman? She didn't sound like my mother. In all the years we'd lived in Chicago, I'd never heard her speak of God's presence. Her conversations had consisted of fashion, artwork, and her friends' latest acquisitions. There had been no talk of blessings—other than a bargain she'd discovered when purchasing fabric for a new gown.

Disbelief assailed me. Did she truly think this had been a good choice? "You enjoy attending all the church services and sitting with me and the other women rather than beside your husband? You like going to the Kinderschule every day and teaching children how to knit mittens and scarves? You like wiping their runny noses and buttoning their jackets? You enjoy taking your meals in a room full of strangers rather than eating in the privacy of your own dining room? You enjoy washing our dirty clothes every Monday, and you enjoy the routine we must follow each day? You like living in these rooms, and you're pleased we moved here?" With dramatic flair, I created a sweeping motion that embraced the cramped living quarters.

She looked at me as though I were the slow child in her Kinderschule class. "Yes. I think it was a wise decision—for all of us. However, I could do without eating the doughnuts, waffles, and cream puffs every Tuesday. It isn't good for my waistline." Leaning toward me, she clasped my hand. "If you remain unhappy and want to move away when you are older, I won't object. Of course, such a move would prove difficult, since your father and I couldn't provide any financial assistance." She released my hand and offered a bright smile. "But I have a feeling you'll steal some young man's heart, get married, and remain in Amana. You'll have a good life here, Berta. No worries about other women coveting what is yours."

"What's coveting?"

"That's when you want something that belongs to someone else. Like a nice home or pretty jewelry, or—"

"Your husband?"

"Ouch!" Mother lifted her finger to her mouth and held it there for a moment. "I pricked my finger."

Had she intentionally poked herself in order to avoid my question? I remained silent and waited to see if she would answer me.

She yanked her handkerchief from her pocket and wrapped it around the finger. Moments later she arched her brows and glanced up at me. "Now, what were we talking about?"

"A woman coveting your husband," I said.

She sputtered and coughed. "I didn't mean that in the literal sense, my dear."

We locked gazes, and I knew that she was lying.

On Tuesday, while I tipped the bowl of doughy Spätzle mixture over boiling beef stock and cut the batter into noodle-sized portions with a sharp knife, I came to a decision. I was going to follow Johanna's lead and write a letter of my own. I didn't know Caroline's last name, but the return address on the envelope remained emblazoned in my mind. Though I hadn't prayed for direction, I was certain Johanna had done so before she penned her letter. If God's answer to her had been to write a letter, He would surely tell me the same thing. At least that's what I told myself, because that's what I wanted to believe.

For the remainder of the day I considered the contents of the letter. My first idea was to send a threatening missive; the second, a heartfelt plea. The third concept was more businesslike—a statement of the facts. I settled on the third idea. If the woman knew my father was without money to provide for a wonderful life, she'd surely leave him alone. If all went well, I would write the letter that evening and post it in the morning.

On the way home I stopped along the way and picked up a few small rocks and pebbles. I bundled them in a handkerchief and tucked it into my pocket. I would need the pebbles when the time was right.

When my parents decided to visit with the Ilgs after prayer service that evening, I was certain God was on my side. With a quick wave I hurried upstairs and slipped into my parents' bedroom. My heart pounded beneath my dark calico. If I looked in a mirror, I'd likely see my bodice ripple with each resounding thud. I opened the dresser drawer and slipped my hand to the back of the drawer. Suddenly afraid the pouch wouldn't be there, I held my breath until the familiar leather bag was in my hand. I shoved it into my skirt pocket, pushed the socks back in place, closed the drawer, and escaped the room. I rushed to my bedroom as if the devil were on my heels.

I leaned against the closed door and forced myself to breathe normally. Then I extracted the leather bag from my pocket. The lumps inside indicated my father hadn't removed the contents, but I wanted firsthand knowledge. How I wished my bedroom door had a lock; I'd feel so much safer. I tiptoed across the room, listening for any sound in the outside hallway. I had learned long ago that you could never be too careful. Especially when any form of subterfuge was involved. All remained quiet. God truly wanted me to succeed!

After emptying the contents of the bag onto my bed, I sighed with relief. It didn't appear that my father had removed anything. I retrieved the bundle of pebbles and stones from my dresser and unknotted the handkerchief. While uttering a fleeting prayer that my parents wouldn't return within the next few minutes, I dumped the stones into the bag and returned the pouch to my father's dresser drawer. The entire exchange was conducted without a snag.

My temples pounded as blood raced through my veins, but I couldn't relax just yet. With a swoop of my hand, I gathered up the jewels and money from my bed, the remains of my father's inheritance from my grandmother, tied them into the hand-kerchief, and tucked them into the bottom of my trunk for safekeeping. The deed completed, I dropped to the side of the bed. My father wasn't going to leave this place—at least not without me.

Now I would write to Caroline.

I retrieved my small writing desk, propped it on my lap, and leaned against my pillows while I considered exactly how I should address such a woman. I didn't know her last name, and I certainly wouldn't greet her by her first name. I tapped my fingers on the sheet of stationery and considered a greeting of *Dear Coveting Woman*, but that wouldn't do. After several more minutes I decided against any salutation at all—a woman such as Caroline didn't deserve a formal greeting!

In a careful script I wrote the date at the top of the page, but formulating my thoughts took longer than I'd expected. Finally I put pen to paper.

> My name is Berta Schumacher. I am the daughter of Herman and Helen Schumacher. We have never been introduced, but I know who you are. You are the woman who hopes to steal my father away from my mother and me. My reason for writing to you is simple. You should leave my father alone. He belongs with his family, not with you. Though you may think otherwise, my father no longer has any money. Nor does he have any gold or jewels. All that he inherited from his mother is now gone. I have determined you are a woman of social position. I'm sure you want to continue your life of comfort. Unless you plan to use your personal funds, my father would come to you without status or position and in need of financial support. I suggest you find a wealthy man, one without a wife!

Tipping my head, I looked up at the ceiling. What else could I say to convince this woman? In a flash it came to me.

One thing more: If my father would leave my mother and come to you, could you ever trust that he would not do the same to you? In addition, please know that your secret is not safe with me.

Berta Schumacher

I hadn't given Caroline the courtesy of a salutation, and I wouldn't give her the courtesy of a formal closing to the letter, either. I folded the piece of paper and tucked it into an envelope. Now I had to trust that my words would be enough to terminate her plans for a future with my father.

# CHAPTER 15

Johanna Ilg

Alone in the backyard, I counted how many days had passed since I'd written to Wilhelm. Two and a half weeks. During that time, my mother had turned increasingly detached. Recent attempts at conversation had proved stilted and forced, and I worried she knew I'd written to Wilhelm. Yet how could she? I'd been clear in the letter to my brother that he wasn't to tell our parents that I'd written. And when I'd checked to see if any mail had arrived at the general store, Brother Kohler assured me he hadn't told anyone I'd mailed a letter. My conscience nagged like a pecking hen. Perhaps I shouldn't have written to Wilhelm.

"Here you are," my father called. "We wondered where you could be."

Both of my parents rounded the side of the house and approached with determined steps. Their serious demeanor was enough to tell me something was amiss. I braced myself for accusations that I had betrayed them by writing to Wilhelm without their knowledge.

Forcing a smile, I said, "I decided to remain outdoors after I returned from the Küche. I hope I didn't worry you."

My father surveyed the yard. "No, but we wanted to speak with you privately. Are you alone?"

Such a silly question. He'd just scanned the entire yard. Did he think someone was hiding in the washhouse? "I'm alone." Curiosity on the alert, I scooted out of the sun's glare. I wanted a good view of my parents' expressions when they spoke to me.

Hunching his shoulders, my father bent down to walk beneath the drooping clotheslines. My mother followed close on his heels, slipping beneath the sagging ropes with only a tip of her head.

I patted the grassy spot beside me, but my parents declined. Both of them stared down at me with somber faces. "We have some good news," my father said.

Good news? He looked like he had come to tell me there'd been a death in the family. "And what is that?"

He rubbed his large callused hands together. "Carl has asked permission to court you. We told him we would be very pleased to welcome him into our family." He cleared his throat and forced a smile. "I believe he hopes to marry you, but I don't think he will rush you to a decision."

"M-m-marry? M-m-me?" The sputtered words caught between my lips. "But we barely know each other. And you both know about my desire to travel, to see other places. The whole country is outside the borders of our villages. I want to see part of it before I settle here in Amana for the rest of my life. More than anything, I want to visit Wilhelm and Larissa in Chicago."

My mother gasped, and my father's smile disappeared. His weathered features settled into a frown. "We have all heard enough about Chicago from Wilhelm. A visit isn't necessary to know it isn't the place for us."

"But that's not the same as—"

My father lifted his hand to silence me. "Since you were a little girl, you have asked questions about other places, but that doesn't mean we would ever give our approval. And who would you travel with, daughter? Even if we gave our permission, you couldn't travel by yourself. It's improper."

"And dangerous," my mother added. The fear in her eyes matched the warning in her tone.

"Wilhelm could accompany me to Chicago, and I would stay at his home. There would be no danger in that. It is my wish that you would give me permission to go and visit with him. Then we can speak of my future." I clasped my hands together and squeezed until my fingers ached. "You know I will return, Mutter. I don't want to live in the big city. I just want to go and see it for myself."

Grief replaced the fear that had shone in my mother's eyes only a short time ago. "Ja. That is what Wilhelm said, too. First Pieter, then Wilhelm, now you. Am I to lose all of my children?"

"You haven't lost Wilhelm. He is—"

My mother flapped her handkerchief. "Pieter didn't choose to leave us, but Wilhelm—" She bobbed her head. "Ja. He wanted to go. And now you."

Tears rimmed Mother's eyes, and my father pinned me with an accusatory stare. My insides wrapped into a tight knot, but I didn't change my mind. I wanted to see Chicago. "So this is why you have given Carl permission to court me. You fear I'll leave here. But if I marry Carl, you will no longer have to worry. That's it, isn't it?"

My father leaned his back against the tree with his shoulders hunched forward like an old man. "Carl has become like a member of the family—visiting with us in the evenings after prayer meetings and on Sunday afternoons. You have gone fishing with him, and he tells us the two of you have become gut friends." The frown deepened. "He hasn't spoken lies to me, has he?"

Everything my father had said was true. Carl and I had gone fishing on Sundays, we'd visited in my parents' parlor each evening after prayer meetings, we'd enjoyed Sunday afternoon walks with Rudolf and Berta, and we had formed a friendship. I enjoyed Carl's company and found his easy laughter and gentle nature agreeable. I didn't doubt he could be a good husband. But I wasn't looking for a husband. And Carl had never mentioned marriage. He hadn't even mentioned love. "We are friends, and I enjoy his company. Carl knows I want to see Chicago and maybe even New York City—I've told him so. And what of our church doctrine that says to remain single is best?"

My mother drew closer. "But marriage is acceptable when approved by the Bruderrat."

My heart pounded an erratic rhythm. "Have you already spoken to the other members of the Bruderrat?"

My father shook his head. "No. Unless you are willing to accept Carl's marriage proposal, there is no reason to speak to them yet." His brows lifted in an expectant arch.

"We would be required to wait at least a year, and Carl would likely be sent to another village during our engagement. You would be without him to help you with the work."

"That's not for sure," my father said.

Had he forgotten the procedures ordered by the Grossebruderrat once an engagement was approved? The couple was separated for a year in order to make certain they truly loved each other. He and my mother had endured such a separation. Secretly, I thought it was because the elders hoped the couple would change their minds when faced with a year of separation.

"I believe the Bruderrat would agree there are circumstances that prohibit Carl from moving to another village. The elders know that

I am in dire need of his help. Rules in our community are fitted to circumstances and can be broken when there is gut reason."

From my father's quick response, I surmised the three of them had been planning for longer than I cared to think about. I found the fact that Carl and my parents had taken it upon themselves to plan my future quite annoying, yet I wouldn't be disrespectful. "I wish you would have talked to me before you gave Carl your permission, but . . ." I let my comment hang in the air for a long moment. Now might be a good time for some delicate persuasion. "If I agree to the courtship, would you give permission for me to visit Wilhelm in Chicago for a week or two?"

"Children do not bargain with their parents!" My mother's sharp words further reflected her fear.

Could I ever convince her that a visit to Chicago didn't mean she'd lose me? "I am your daughter, but I am no longer a child. I hope you and Vater will consider my request. I don't want to go against your wishes." Using the trunk of the tree for support, I pushed to my feet and shook the leaves from my skirt. An argument with my mother would only make matters worse. If I remained in the yard, I might say something I would regret. "We all need time to think on this. I am going to my room."

My parents didn't argue. I knew they were disappointed with my reaction, but what had they expected?

When Wilhelm had written to tell them he was getting married, my mother had cried for a week. Not continuously, of course, but she'd shed enough tears to sink a small rowboat. She'd thought marriage a terrible idea. Granted, Wilhelm had married a girl from the outside—a fact that they still had not completely accepted. I had hoped my agreement to court Carl would relieve their fears and they'd agree to let me visit Chicago. After seeing Mother's reaction, I now doubted anything would change their minds.

When I stepped around the corner of the house, Carl was

waiting on the front porch. He beamed at me. "Your parents talked to you?"

"Ja."

"The arrangement suits you?" Another broad smile split his face.

Warmth flooded my cheeks. I wasn't certain how I should answer. "We are still talking about some other matters, but I am willing to continue our friendship."

"Friendship?" Carl rocked back on his heels. "I spoke to your father about more than friendship, Johanna. Did your father make that clear?"

"Yes, but there are other things . . ." My words trailed off in a whisper. I didn't know what to say.

The spark in his eyes flickered and died. He squared his shoulders, but he dropped his gaze to the ground. "Did I misunderstand your feelings, Johanna? I thought you had grown to care for me."

I bobbed my head. "I care for you, Carl. But I'm not yet ready for such a . . ." Once again, words failed me.

"Commitment?"

"Yes. A lifetime commitment. We've known each other such a short time."

He relaxed his shoulders and clasped my hand. "That's why I suggested we court for a time before we ask the Bruderrat for permission to marry. After that, we will have to wait another year. I don't intend to rush you, but I worried some other man might speak to your Vater and I would miss my opportunity."

I didn't miss the expectancy in his voice, but I needed to be honest. "Do you remember I told you I wanted to travel and see some large cities? Places like Chicago?"

Wrinkles creased his forehead. "Ja, I remember."

"I still want to travel—at least to Chicago. I've asked my parents to give me permission to visit Wilhelm."

Carl's head jerked as though I'd slapped him. "For how long?"

"That's yet to be determined, but we could speak of courtship when I return."

"So your parents have agreed?"

"Not yet, but I believe they will. I told them I will return to live in Amana, but I'm not sure Mutter is convinced. She thinks I'll be like Wilhelm."

He shoved his hands into his trouser pockets. "And will you?"

"No. I'll return. Why doesn't anyone believe me when I say I'll return?"

He hitched his right shoulder. "Maybe because we know there is temptation in other places, things that are difficult to resist. You can't be certain it won't happen to you, Johanna."

I couldn't deny that possibility existed, but it didn't change my mind. "Ja, you may be correct, but my heart tells me I will return to Amana."

Carl's smile made a slow return. "Then you should probably go to Chicago and see for yourself. It would be best to know this before we begin a courtship." He gently squeezed my hand.

My heart fluttered at his touch—the same feeling I'd experienced when he'd held my hand at the river. He was the first to understand and agree with me. Perhaps I did love him. Nobody had ever explained how you'd know if you were in love with someone. It had been a natural occurrence to love my parents and brothers. But how did one know if they were truly in love with a stranger?

Two days later I settled my gaze on Brother Kohler while I served breakfast. We'd developed a routine. Each day when I looked at him, he would shake his head—his signal that no letter had arrived. But today he gave an emphatic nod—one that couldn't be denied. Had a letter truly arrived? I bobbed my head in return, just to be certain. His broad smile told me what I'd hoped for.

The early morning chores seemed endless. For once I was eager to deliver the midmorning refreshments to the garden workers. I motioned for Berta to join me and then grabbed one of the baskets. "Come on," I urged when she dawdled longer than necessary.

"What's your hurry? The quicker we leave, the quicker we'll be back here preparing for the next meal."

"We need to stop at the general store." I kept my voice low and waited until we were away from the Küche before I said more. "Brother Kohler signaled me during breakfast."

"Did he say if there was any mail for me?"

"No." I slowed my gait. "I didn't know you were expecting a letter. Something important?"

"I wrote to that woman and told her my father no longer had any money. I said she should find a wealthy man—one without a wife. I thought she might respond, but she'll probably write to my father instead."

"Oh, Berta. If she writes to your father, you'll be in a great deal of trouble."

She kicked and sent a stone flying down the street. "What difference does it make? My parents ignore each other, and both of them ignore me. At least when my father is angry, he remembers I'm alive."

Compassion stirred in my breast. Even though my parents wanted to control my future, there had never been a time when I felt unloved or ignored by either of them. I could always count on their help and comfort whenever needed. They were dependable, caring, and above all else, truthful. I couldn't imagine parents who lived with lies and deceit—parents who would hide painful secrets.

"I doubt she will write to you, either. We should pray for her."

"Pray for her?" Berta stopped in the middle of the road. "If I pray for her, it will be that she dies and goes to hell."

"Berta! You should never pray for such a thing. We are supposed to pray for our enemies. If God would touch Caroline's heart and make her realize what a terrible thing she has done, it would change everything. She would become a different person and wouldn't want to be with your father. She'd be sorry for her sin." I touched Berta's sleeve. "And we should pray for your father, too." I doubted she wanted to hear me speak against him, yet he bore responsibility, as well.

"I know he is wrong, too, but it's easier to blame her. I'll pray for my father, but I'm not yet ready to pray for Caroline."

"Then until you're able, I shall do it for you," I said.

I saw my mother wave from the far side of the garden as we approached. I gestured in return but continued into the shed, where we placed the baskets and jugs on the table and then hurried off. If we remained for even a short visit, there wouldn't be time to stop at the general store. Returning down the path at a near run, we didn't slow our pace until we were outside the store. Only then did fear descend and hold me in an unyielding grip. My feet wouldn't move.

Berta grabbed hold of my arm and tried to tug me forward. "Come on!"

There was no denying the urgency in Berta's voice, but my feet wouldn't follow my brain's command. Once more she yanked my arm. My torso bent forward, but my shoes remained stuck to the ground. If I didn't move them, I'd fall flat on my face. That thought seemed to do the trick. I did a quick shuffle that brought my body into alignment with my feet just as I neared the step leading inside. With a slight hop I entered without mishap.

Brother Kohler stood behind the counter and waved the letter overhead. I wended my way between shelves filled with calicos and woolen fabric while Berta forged ahead of me. Had it not been for Brother Kohler's quick reflexes, she would have snatched the letter from his hand.

"This isn't addressed to you, Berta." He stretched forward, and I accepted the missive.

The minute I set eyes on the writing I knew it was from Wilhelm. Finally! "Danke, Brother Kohler."

"You're welcome." He tucked his thumbs beneath his suspenders and grinned. "There is one for your parents, as well, but I will give it to your father." He glanced at Berta. "I don't want to be accused of giving mail to the wrong person."

She ignored his comment and gestured toward the boxes behind him. "Is there anything for me or my family?"

"Nothing has come for your father except one of those medical journals he is so fond of receiving."

"May I see the letter to my parents, Brother Kohler?" I asked. When he hesitated, I said, "I only want to see if their letter is from the same person."

He pulled the envelope from the box and placed it alongside mine. "Ja. You see, the writing is the same." And so was the return address. Both of the letters were from Wilhelm.

"You won't mention my letter when my father comes in, will you?"

He shook his head. "I gave my word. Your secret is safe with me."

Fingers trembling, I opened the envelope and scanned the contents as we exited the store.

Berta danced in front of me, her excitement contagious. "Tell me what it says, please."

I continued to scan, but I couldn't resist her request. It was the most animated I'd seen her for days. There didn't seem to be any mention of my coming for a visit, but then I stopped in my tracks. "He's coming! Wilhelm is coming for a visit. He'll arrive next Wednesday." I clapped my hand to my mouth. Beneath his signature, he'd added that we would discuss a visit to Chicago once he arrived in Amana. "Oh, Berta! He's going to bring his wife with him. Finally I'll meet Larissa." I grabbed her hands, and the two of us swung around in a circle. "Isn't it wonderful?"

"It is wonderful. I hope you'll introduce me to them."

The breeze tugged on the strings of my lightweight bonnet as I tucked the letter into my skirt pocket. Until I knew for certain I would make the journey to Chicago, there was no need to tell Berta. "The letter says he also wrote to my parents and told them he was coming for a visit, but he didn't tell them I had written to him."

"Do you think your mother will write to him again and tell him he must wait even longer?"

"I don't think so. It would be very rude, since he plans to bring his wife along. What would his wife think of us? My mother isn't pleased Wilhelm married an outsider, but she wouldn't want his wife to think we are rude."

"Do you think they will bring you presents?" Berta asked.

"Maybe," I said, but I didn't care if they brought me a gift. More than a present, I wanted to meet my brother's wife and have time to visit and make plans with Wilhelm and Larissa—alone.

# CHAPTER 16

Carl appeared at our door the following evening after I had returned from the Küche. Hair damp and freshly combed, he sat down in the parlor.

Soon after, my mother made an excuse to go outside. "I think I will sit on the porch. The fresh air will be nice."

Once she'd made her exit, Carl nudged me. "She wants to give us time alone, I think."

I laughed. "Since she's been outdoors working in the garden all day, I think you're right. I doubt she needs more fresh air." I kept my voice low.

"She hopes I will convince you the best thing is to get married and never again think of the outside world."

"She told you that?"

He shook his head, his damp hair flying in all directions. "No, but your Vater asked me if we had talked."

"What did you tell him?" My heart picked up speed.

He hesitated. "I hope you won't think me a coward, but I told him it would be better if he spoke to you."

"And what did he say?"

"He said he respected my wish to keep our conversation private. I'm sure he wants to know what you told me, so you should be prepared with your answers." Carl brushed a thread from his pant leg. "It would be good if you let me know what you tell him. I want to avoid any confusion."

"So you didn't tell him anything? Not about my going to Chicago or waiting until I return to discuss our courtship—nothing?"

"Nothing. If you tell your Vater of our talk, you can assure him I have agreed to wait until you come back from Chicago. Perhaps that will help him make his decision."

"Thank you, Carl. You're very kind." His thoughtfulness touched me. I wanted to squeeze his hand, but I could never be so bold. "My brother Wilhelm and his wife are coming for a visit very soon. I hope to return to Chicago with them. I don't know if Wilhelm or my parents will agree, but I am hopeful."

A light breeze drifted in the window, carrying the scent of spring flowers. He leaned back as if to capture the smell. "To have them as travel companions would be a gut thing. And the sooner you go, the sooner you will come back home. At least that is my prayer."

"Ja. And then we can learn more about each other." I offered a tentative smile. "I don't know much about your life before you came here."

He glanced at the clock. "We don't have to wait until then. There is time for us to begin to know each other right now." His smile deepened and revealed a dimple in his right cheek that I'd never before noticed. "I think it is most important that a husband and wife always tell each other the truth. That is why I'm pleased you told me about Chicago. Even though I don't want you to go, it pleases me that you were honest. What do you think is most important in a marriage?" Head held high, blue eyes seeking, he waited for my answer.

"Love. They must love each other very much."

He leaned a little closer. "Ja. Love for sure, but what else?"

I'd never given much thought to such a question, but the sound of footsteps in the rooms overhead were a reminder of Dr. Schumacher and his woman in Chicago. "Trust. I think trust is very important in a marriage."

"That is gut, too. People in love should always be able to tell the truth and trust each other. Such love builds strong families, ja?"

A flash of heat warmed my cheeks. The mention of family meant children, and I didn't want to discuss children when nothing had yet been settled about a courtship. I searched my mind for something, anything, that had to do with families but nothing to do with children. Finally I said, "I was surprised your Mutter didn't come with you when you moved here."

He rubbed his palm across the light growth of stubble that shadowed his jaw. "I would have liked that, but she didn't want to leave High. It has been her home ever since the move from Buffalo. She is comfortable with her friends and knows everyone in High. It would be hard for her, but she encouraged me to move. She knew it was best."

"Because of working with my Vater?"

"Ja, that and something else, too."

His jaw twitched. What else was there that would make him want to move away from the village where he'd lived all his life? I arched my brows, anticipating whether he would tell me.

He clasped his sizeable work-worn hands together. "I have

said truth is important. I also think it is gut if there are no secrets between a man and woman." His voice faltered, and he cleared his throat. "Since you told me about your secret wish to see other places, maybe I should tell you something more about me. About my past few years in High."

I didn't realize I'd been holding my breath until I inhaled a deep gulp of air. His somber eyes made me even more curious. "Only if you want to." Yet, for some unknown reason, I secretly wanted him to confide in me.

"Through all of my years growing up in High Amana, my parents were close friends with another family. Their rooms were in the same house as ours. They had a daughter, Karin, who was a few years younger than me."

I bobbed my head. "Ja. Like Rudolf living in our same house."

"Not exactly." He cleared his throat. "Because our parents spent much time together, Karin and I became close friends. Her parents and my parents always expected we would marry. And from the time we were small children, I thought the same thing."

"What happened? Did she die?"

"*Nein!* She is very much alive and well. She still lives with her parents in the same house where my Mutter lives." He unclasped his hands and rested them on his knees. "As Karin neared the age when we could ask permission to marry, I knew that I didn't love her in the way a man loves a wife. I cared deeply for her but more like a sister or a cousin."

"You told her this?"

"Ja, but she insisted we could still have a good marriage. I told her it would be better to stay single than marry without love." He massaged his forehead with the palm of his hand. "Each day we would argue. And my Mutter wasn't happy with my decision, either. She loved Karin, and I think she felt guilty about it." He glanced toward the window. "I tried to explain it was my decision, and it wouldn't change things between her and Karin's family, but it did."

"So when there was a job with my Vater, you—"

"I begged for the chance to come here and work with him. Even though this had continued for over two years, Karin still thought I would change my mind. I think she can better accept that we won't marry if I am gone from there." He looked deep into my eyes. "I didn't want to hurt her, but a marriage without love is not gut. That's why you must find out what you want." He pointed to my heart. "I want you to marry me only if you know you have love in your heart for me and are sure you want to live in Amana."

"Thank you, Carl." I glanced out the window, where several children were running down the street, their shoes kicking up trails of dust. His words surprised me. This was truly a good man. A man who wouldn't force himself upon me. A man who wanted to marry for the proper reasons. A considerate man who wanted only the best for those he cared about.

Maybe he was a man I could love.

# CHAPTER 17

Berta Schumacher

"He's leaving!"

My stomach roiled as I spoke the words.

I clutched Johanna's arm with a ferocity that brought her to an immediate halt and caused her to yelp in pain. "Did you hear me, Johanna?" Ignoring her cry, I held fast to her arm, determined to make her listen.

"Who is leaving? Rudolf?" One by one Johanna pried my fingers loose and rubbed her arm. "You hurt me. I'm going to have bruises by this afternoon."

We were approaching the Küche when I stepped in front of her. If I blocked her path, she'd have to listen. "Don't you understand? This is more important than a bruised arm. This is going to change my life, forever—even more than when we moved here."

My admission felt like a blow to the stomach. Instinctively I crossed my arms tight against my waist.

Johanna grasped my hand. "Come on. Let's get into the kitchen. We'll talk there." Once inside I dropped to one of the long wooden benches. Johanna sat down beside me, gathered my hands between her own, and focused her attention upon me. "Now tell me what has happened."

"My father is leaving us and going to Chicago."

"For good? He is leaving your mother and you?"

She squeezed my hands, and I could see the sorrow that shone in her eyes. For once I was glad no one else had yet arrived for work. "He's leaving the day after tomorrow. He says he'll be gone for six weeks, maybe two months. He asked the elders to send him to Chicago for some additional medical training regarding a new procedure or something. I don't believe a word of it."

"But, Berta, he wouldn't lie about such a thing. Before the Grossebruderrat would send him, your father would have shown them proof of his reason for going and explained how it would benefit the colonies. Their approval isn't such an unusual thing."

"Isn't it more important that the doctor be in the village to care for the sick?"

"There is a doctor in Middle Amana who can come when needed. We were without a physician for almost a year before your family arrived. This must be something of value or the Grossebruderrat wouldn't grant permission."

"He's probably been scanning those medical periodicals looking for any reason he can use to get away from us." I jumped up from the bench and began to pace the length of the kitchen. "How could he do this? Bring us here and then return to that woman?"

"You don't know that he's doing anything of the sort, and you'll accomplish nothing by working yourself into a frenzy. If you truly believe he's never going to come back, I think you should talk to him this evening—ask him your questions."

That wouldn't work. I didn't want to have a discussion in front of my mother. If she believed he was merely going off to study some new technique, I didn't want to be the one who dashed her hopes. Then again, maybe she did know and was trying to soften the blow for me. Maybe she'd developed a plan to tell me after he was gone, when I couldn't create a scene and beg to go with him.

I explained my concern to Johanna, at least the portion about not wanting to talk in front of my mother. "I need to talk to him this morning. Do you think you could go to the garden yourself and then stop at my father's office after you've delivered the food to the workers?" She frowned, and I knew my suggestion had given rise to concern. Johanna wouldn't want to lie, and Sister Nusser would be sure to ask about my whereabouts. "If anyone asks where I am, you can say that I needed to see the doctor. That would be true."

"But they will think you are ill."

"Exactly!" I squared my shoulders. "At least I'm not asking you to lie. All you need to do is take the baskets to the shed, wave, and then leave before the women come in from the garden plot. It shouldn't be a problem."

"I'll do my best, but I won't lie." Johanna pushed to her feet and held out her hand. "Come on. We need to begin breakfast preparations."

When the village bell clanged to announce breakfast, I kept watch for my father's arrival. I stood at the kitchen doorway looking for any sign of him while Johanna took over my duties frying the potatoes. I held on to the doorjamb and lifted on tiptoe, hoping to catch a glimpse of him. My mother entered, circled around to her usual table, and sat down beside Sister Ilg, but there was no sign of my father.

I bowed my head while we recited the morning prayer, but

the moment the prayer ended, I scurried to my mother's side. The strings of her black cap hung down on either side of her neck. How strange to see the small black cap take the place of a fashionable feather-bedecked chapeau—the kind of hat Mother used to perch upon her beautifully coiffed hair before leaving our house in Chicago. Other than daily brushing, her hair received little attention nowadays. Like most of the women, she parted it down the middle, fastened it into a knot at the nape of her neck, and covered it with her cap.

"Where is Father?" I glanced toward his table to emphasize the empty space.

"I don't know. He went to his office early." She shrugged. "He may have been detained." The serving girls arrived at the tables with the pitchers of milk and coffee, and my mother nodded toward the kitchen. "Aren't you supposed to be working?"

"I have been working, but when I didn't see Father come in, I was concerned he had already left for Chicago."

With a sigh she shook her head. "I told you he is scheduled to leave tomorrow, Berta. You better go back to work before you get into trouble. I'm sure your father will be here soon," she said, her eyes flitting around the table as she spoke to me in hushed tones. "If not, you'll see him at the midday meal."

There was no use questioning her further. If my mother knew anything, she wasn't going to tell me. Her curt response didn't ease my suspicions, but I returned to the kitchen. "Thank you for your help with the potatoes, Johanna."

"Is your father here?"

"No. And my mother was no help. She says she doesn't know where he is." I tilted my head closer to Johanna. "To tell you the truth, I don't think she cares. She doesn't appear concerned in the least that he is going back to that woman."

"You don't know he's doing any such thing. Besides, what can she do? Go to the elders and state her objection? I think she would be too embarrassed to tell them why she wanted them to change their plans."

I ladled two heaping scoops of fried potatoes into a bowl and handed it to one of the servers. "I suppose you're right, but she is far too calm."

"Perhaps the Lord has given her a peaceful spirit about the situation. I would imagine she has asked God for guidance and protection."

I wrinkled my nose. "My mother isn't one to ask God to guide her. She's always relied upon my father or her own intuition when she was uncertain what to do."

"But she has changed since coming here. More than you or your father, she has embraced our way of life and appears content. A heavy burden is lifted when we trust the Lord to meet our needs. I think she has learned there is power in prayer and trusting God." Johanna removed the skillet from the stove. "You should try it, Berta."

I hitched my shoulder and turned away. The last thing I wanted was another person preaching to me. I already had enough of that every evening as well as on Wednesdays, Saturdays, and Sundays. Johanna said no more. Perhaps I'd offended her, or maybe she was simply trying to complete her chores as quickly as possible to permit me additional time with my father.

While the rest of us finished cleaning the kitchen and began preparations for the noonday meal, Sister Muhlbach cut thick slices of bread and tucked a jar of apple butter into the basket we would deliver to the workers. Though the bread was a favorite of some, others preferred leftover coffee cake or some other sweet with their coffee. Should Johanna not get away from the garden shed before the workers arrived, she would receive more than a few questions about my whereabouts, and she would receive complaints about the bread and apple butter, as well.

We diverted from our usual route, but Johanna insisted upon waiting until I was certain my father was in his office. "If he's not there, you should come with me, and we'll check again on the way back to the Küche."

Johanna's idea didn't hold any appeal, so I offered a speedy prayer—the only kind I'd ever uttered—asking God to ensure that my father was in his office when we arrived. In my opinion a rapid request might help, and it certainly couldn't hurt.

My pulse quickened as we neared the office, and I hurried ahead of Johanna. Reaching the door, I glanced over my shoulder. "Wait out here," I said.

The small bell over the door jangled when I entered the building. No one was waiting in the outer office, and though I waited for a moment, I didn't hear any sound from the adjoining room. After a moment longer I tapped lightly. I didn't want to walk in if he was examining a patient. "Father! Are you in there?" When there was no immediate response, I knocked a little louder.

"Who is it?"

*Who is it?* How many people called him *Father?* "It's me, Berta, your daughter."

"I'm with someone. You'll need to return later."

His voice sounded strained, and I wondered if his patient was going to die. The thought was enough to send me scurrying to the door. I peered down the street, but Johanna was nowhere in sight. Should I follow and meet her somewhere along the road? What if she took a different route and I missed her?

I closed the door and plopped instead onto one of the hard, straight-backed chairs. Leaning forward, I rested my chin in the palm of my hand and counted the rows in the rug that was striped in blue, brown, and gray. Next I counted how many blue stripes there were and then the gray. I was in the midst of counting the brown stripes when the heavy metal latch clacked and the door leading to my father's office opened.

A woman, looking as though she'd stepped from the pages of *Godey's* magazine, stood framed in the doorway. Sunlight filtered through the windows and encircled her in a radiant glow. Her gown, the shade of ripe plums, was an immediate reminder of the pink silk skirt I'd worn when we first arrived in Amana. She carried a parasol in her lace-gloved hands, and thin plum-colored ribbons swirled atop her chapeau.

Instantly I knew.

*Caroline.*

I jumped to my feet, my heart pumping as though I'd been running for hours. "What are you doing here?" I hadn't expected to shout, but the sight of her caused a surge of dread and panic like nothing I'd ever before experienced. "You're Caroline, aren't you?" I choked out the question and prayed she'd refute my question and tell me she was a visitor who'd become ill while taking a tour of the village. *Please, God.*

Before she'd said a word, my father appeared behind her and grasped the woman's shoulders. Instinctively she stepped forward, and he moved to her side. Had it not been for the horror that shone in his eyes, they would have looked like the perfect married couple: he in his suit and white shirt, she in her elegant walking dress.

"What are you doing here, Berta?"

His tone was harsh and unfamiliar, and I struggled to understand why he'd spoken to me in such a manner. Arriving at his office unexpectedly couldn't be considered improper. I was, after all, his daughter. He should have been pleased to see me.

"I had hoped to have a brief chat, but I see you're busy." I met the woman's steady gaze. "With Caroline."

I waited for him to respond, but it was the woman who extended her hand. "I'm Mrs. Harwell, and I am very pleased to meet you, Berta. Your father has spoken highly of you. I hope to see you again in the future."

*See me again?* I gasped at the outrageous remark. "Well, I don't want to ever—"

My father grabbed my wrist and gave me a warning look. "I'll see you to the door, Mrs. Harwell. The buggy will arrive at the general store to return you to the train depot in Homestead shortly."

She bobbed her head. "I hope to have time to pick up a few gifts before I leave." With a glance over her shoulder, she lifted her gloved hand and waved. "Good-bye, Berta."

I glowered in return. How dare she wave at me and sashay out the door as though we were best friends. I considered shouting after her that she wouldn't see me or my father again if I had anything to do about it.

The moment my father closed the door, he wheeled around on his heel. "How dare you speak to a guest in such a rude manner." He narrowed his eyes until they were no more than slits. "I have never been so embarrassed in my life. And why did you address Mrs. Harwell as Caroline? Who is Caroline?"

Anger churned in my belly. He was going to play a game of denial with me. "Caroline is the woman who wrote you the letter I delivered. I believe you said she was one of your patients who lives in Chicago."

"Oh yes. Now I remember." He removed his handkerchief and wiped the perspiration from his forehead. "It's warm in here, don't you think?"

"I hadn't noticed." My response wasn't completely true. I thought he should open a window. The waiting room could use a breath of fresh air, but I wasn't going to tell him. Besides, it was his own guilt that was making him warm. Of that much I was certain, for when trapped in one of my own lies, I'd experienced the very same feeling.

He seemed to regain his composure as he tucked the handkerchief into his pocket. "Exactly what did you want to discuss with me? Aren't you supposed to be at work?"

"Each day at midmorning and midafternoon, I deliver food to the garden workers. I asked Johanna to make the delivery so that I could stop here. Mother tells me you are going to Chicago to some sort of school."

"Yes, that's correct, but couldn't we discuss this when I get home this evening?"

"There's nobody waiting to see you, and I told Johanna I would meet her here on her return from the garden. I didn't want to talk in front of Mother."

He crossed the room and leaned against the doorjamb leading into his office. "Whyever not? We have no secrets."

"Really?" I laughed.

He straightened at the sound of my derisive laughter. "Are you mocking me?"

Instead of answering, I asked a question of my own. "Exactly who is Mrs. Harwell? Another patient from Chicago?"

"No, of course not." He pointed to one of the chairs. "Why don't we sit down." His complexion had turned a sickly gray that reminded me of the ashes I removed from the stove each day, and I wondered if he might faint. He didn't wait for me to be seated before he dropped into one of the chairs.

"Would you open one of the windows, Berta?"

I did as he requested, but he wasn't going to deter me. "You haven't yet told me who she is, Father."

"Her name is Mrs. Phillip Harwell, and she is the proprietor of a finishing school. I know you have been unhappy here in Amana. After investigating the school, I planned to talk to your mother about the possibility of sending you there to complete your education."

"And what is the name of Mrs. Phillip Harwell's finishing school? Caroline's School for Educating Young Girls on the Fine Art of Stealing Someone Else's Husband?"

My father's complexion remained pasty, but he pointed his finger at me. "You watch your tongue, young lady. I will not be spoken to in such a manner. And why do you keep referring to Caroline?"

"Because I know all about her, Father. I read the letter. Let me see if I can remember the exact words." I tapped my finger to my lips. "Ah yes. I believe this is a portion of it: 'If you truly love me—as you so often have said—then why do you linger? Know that I love you, but I will not wait forever. Lovingly, Caroline.' Does that sound vaguely familiar?"

Once again perspiration dotted his forehead. "Caroline and Mrs. Harwell are two different people. Mrs. Harwell is the proprietor of Harwell's Finishing School for Young Ladies."

"In Chicago?"

"No. The school is located in her home in Iowa City. Her husband teaches at the university, and she has decided the area is in need of a finishing school. She is seeking pupils."

I didn't believe a word he was saying. "And how did you happen to discover Mrs. Harwell and her finishing school? A strange coincidence?"

"No coincidence at all. I'd been looking to locate a place even before we arrived in Amana. One that wasn't too far away. I saw an advertisement in the Iowa City newspaper."

"And where did you see a copy of the newspaper?" I folded my arms across my waist, pleased I'd been able to catch him in another lie.

"You'll find a stack of old copies in my office. And before you rush to conclusions, I have the Bruderrats' permission to have them. Go on." He nodded toward his office door. "I can see you don't believe me."

I considered saying I believed him, but I simply had to look for myself. Diverting my gaze, I walked past him and entered the other room. In the far corner I spotted a pile of newspapers, and I shuffled through them. Although I saw one or two from Chicago, the rest were copies of the *Iowa State Press*, the Iowa City newspaper. I returned to the outer office.

We both turned when the bell jangled and the front door opened. Johanna stood framed in the doorway. After a quick greeting to my father, she waved me forward. "We need to return."

My father managed to get to his feet, his complexion still pale. "Give us just a minute longer, Johanna."

She nodded and closed the door.

"We don't have much time. We'll take a walk after prayer service, when we can talk, but say that you believe me, Berta. I'm telling you the truth. This is the first time I've ever seen Mrs. Harwell, and I don't know her first name."

"Even if I believe you about the finishing school, that doesn't explain Caroline or your plans for Chicago." I took a step toward the door and then stopped. "Does Mother know about the finishing school, or is that another one of your secrets?"

"She knows, but she doesn't agree that you should attend. Her preference would be that you remain here in Amana."

"And what do you think Caroline would prefer? That you have no wife or daughter at all?" I turned and ran from the room, tears forming in the corners of my eyes before my feet hit the sidewalk.

# CHAPTER 18

Dark splotches dotted the front of my dress where my tears had fallen. Swiping fingers beneath one eye and then the other, I sobbed as Johanna drew me into an embrace.

"Tell me what happened."

I glanced toward my father's office and could see him looking out the window. He was watching—probably worried I'd tell Johanna about that woman.

While keeping one arm around my shoulder, Johanna urged me forward. "Let's go down the street a distance. We'll sit down under the trees, where you can have a good cry."

"I'm not going to cry anymore!" I sniffled and wiped my nose on the handkerchief I'd removed from her pocket. "But he better not try to send me off to any finishing school. I'll run away and they'll never see me again."

Johanna lifted my chin with the tips of her fingers. Concern shone in her eyes. "Tell me what you're talking about."

Between sniffles, I sputtered the story of Mrs. Harwell, her finishing school, and the questions that still remained unanswered—ones about Caroline and whether my father planned to remain in Chicago. "I still believe Mrs. Harwell is Caroline."

"But you saw the newspapers from Iowa City, didn't you?"

"What does that prove?" I snatched loose from Johanna's hold. Couldn't she see that my father's mention of the newspapers had been a feeble attempt to wriggle out of his lies? "Just because he read about a finishing school in Iowa City doesn't mean that the woman in his office was the owner, or that she even knows the finishing school exists. Why are you defending him?"

"I'm not, but I think you need to give him the benefit of the doubt. You still have as many questions as you had before you walked into his office. Maybe more."

I jammed the handkerchief into my pocket. "You're right about that." We circled toward the rear of the house. "Are my eyes puffy?"

Johanna laughed and shook her head. "No. You're perfectly beautiful—as usual."

What would I ever do if I didn't have Johanna? She never failed to say a kind word or compliment me when I most needed encouragement. "I'm so thankful I have you, Johanna. You're the only person who even tries to understand me."

"God understands you, Berta. He created you, and He loves you. You must always remember that."

I clasped her hand. "I'll try. And I'm sorry I snapped at you before. Please forgive me."

Her face brightened, and she sniffed the air. "I think I smell Sister Muhlbach's honey cookies."

Since my first taste of honey cookies, I'd developed a special fondness for them. I sent a fleeting glance in Johanna's direction.

She laughed and nodded, already knowing I was hoping she'd give me her cookie. "Yes, you can have mine," she said.

I grabbed her around the neck and hugged her. "Oh, thank you, Johanna. You are so good to me. I know I can always count on you."

"God is the one you can always count on," Johanna called to me as I made a pell-mell dash for the kitchen door.

Deep inside I knew God was out there somewhere, but Johanna was far more real to me. It was her shoulder I cried upon, not God's.

For the remainder of the day I pushed thoughts of the woman and the exchange with my father to the back of my mind. I had no choice. Sister Muhlbach decided this would be the day I would learn to make the filled noodles I'd tasted only once since we'd arrived in Amana. On that occasion there had been visiting elders in the village who'd chosen to eat in our Küche. A special honor, I'd been told at the time, but I hadn't understood why having extra plates to fill could be an honor. And though I still didn't understand every event that signified importance within the community, I had learned that visiting elders always called for a special meal.

After Sister Muhlbach sent Johanna and Sister Dickel to the other side of the kitchen, where they would chop and mix the filling, she carried two large mixing crocks to the table and smiled. "One for you and one for me." Her smile disarmed me. "Do not worry. I will lead you through the process, and when we are done, no one will be able to tell my noodles from yours." She laughed. "Except maybe for me."

Her pleasant demeanor and kind assurance were enough to

make me think she'd taken leave of her senses. "How is that possible? You've been making these noodles for years. I've eaten them only once. I don't think mine will compare—except in a bad way. I should watch you make them."

She shook her head. "We learn by doing. First you must break your eggs in the crock and whisk them with the water. Like this." She completed the task and then pointed to the eggs. "Now you."

One by one I cracked the eggs on the edge of the crock and emptied the slippery contents into my bowl. I was on the last egg when part of the shell dropped into the crock. I gulped and glanced at Sister Muhlbach. "Now what?"

She shrugged. "Take it out."

I'd expected her to shout at me, but she handed me a spoon and patiently watched while I chased the piece of shell. Each time I thought I had it captured, it slipped away. "I can't get it," I said and thrust the spoon toward her.

With a gentle push she guided my hand back toward the bowl. "Work it toward the edge of the bowl and then slide it up the side." After two more attempts, I caught the eggshell, and she gave me a satisfied nod. "Gut. Now beat the eggs with the water, and then we will measure the flour."

Once we'd finished mixing, she covered my bowl with a cloth. "You watch while I roll out my dough. Then you will roll yours. This is the hard part. The dough must be thin enough to make it tender but thick enough that it won't tear when we put the filling inside and seal the edges."

The very thought made me quake. I watched intently, certain I would fail. When she finished rolling, she had me touch the dough to feel its thickness. "Now we cut the dough into squares." Her knife slid through the dough in straight lines that created perfect four-inch squares. She covered the squares with a damp cloth and motioned me toward the other table. "You will roll your dough here. We will wait to fill the noodles until you have your dough ready. Johanna can help you, and Sister Dickel will assist me."

I swiped my moist palms down the front of my apron before picking up a portion of the dough. After patting it onto the board, I took up the rolling pin and pushed first one way and then the other, flattening the dough into a giant square.

"Put the kettles of water on the stove to boil," Sister Muhlbach called to one of the kitchen workers while she continued to watch my technique. "You are doing fine." She leaned forward and lifted one corner between her thumb and forefinger. "Needs to be a little thinner, and then you can cut your squares."

My lines weren't nearly as straight as Sister Muhlbach's, but she laughed and showed me how to push the dough together and cut again. I thought I might burst with satisfaction when the older woman gave a nod of approval. "Do you think they'll hold together?"

"Ja! If they are made in my Küche, they will be perfect." She motioned Johanna to bring her bowl of filling to my table. "You help Berta. Sister Dickel will work with me."

The procedure proved time-consuming, and my first attempts at sealing the filled squares of dough were less than perfect. Johanna came behind me and made certain all the edges had been properly sealed. By the time the first batch was completed and ready to boil in the large kettle of salted water, I'd improved my technique.

"You did gut work today," Sister Muhlbach said as she placed browned bread crumbs atop the boiled puffed squares and motioned for the servers to pick up the platters and take them to the tables. "Our people will leave our Küche with happy stomachs tonight."

As the women placed the platters on the dining tables, fear replaced my earlier excitement. I nudged Johanna. "What if my noodles are tough and Sister Muhlbach receives complaints?"

"You have no reason to worry. Sister Muhlbach tasted a noodle from each of your batches before they were served." Johanna chuckled. "She tastes all food before it goes to the tables. If she has declared them worthy to be served in the Muhlbach Küche, there will be no complaints."

Indeed there were only compliments, and for our work, Johanna and I were relieved of any cleaning duties. "Go on and enjoy some time before prayer service," the Küchebaas instructed. "And return ready to work in the morning," she added as we hurried out the door.

I picked a handful of blooming wild flowers as we proceeded toward home. "Sister Muhlbach seemed like a different person today, don't you think?"

"She's always more strident when someone new begins work in her kitchen. I think she wants to be certain each worker understands that she is in charge."

Johanna's explanation caused me to giggle. "Well, she does a good job. I think we all know she commands the Küche."

We continued on in silence, and the thoughts of the finishing school and Caroline that had fled my mind while I worked in the kitchen once again haunted me. A bank of darkening clouds hovered on the horizon. "I hope it doesn't rain. My father promised we would go for a walk after prayer service. Alone."

"Gut. I'm glad you're going to have time to talk some more before he leaves for Chicago." Johanna tapped my shoulder. "Be careful that you don't say anything you'll regret. Try to think before you speak. Even though you are angry with him, your father deserves your respect."

I murmured my assent, but in my heart I didn't agree. How could I respect my father after what I'd learned about him?

Most of the clouds had disappeared by the time we left home

to attend prayer service. I uttered a silent, fleeting prayer of thanks for the clearing skies. Although not completely successful, I'd been trying to remember to pray more often. Usually my prayers were about the things I wanted to do, and I did my best to thank Him when things went my way. But mostly I remembered Him when He didn't answer the way I wanted. On those occasions He was always scheduled to receive one of my "If you loved me, you wouldn't have denied me what I wanted" prayers. Early on I'd discovered that tack didn't work as well with God as it always had with my parents, but it hadn't stopped me from trying.

Even though I attempted to remain quiet and prayerful, I fidgeted throughout most of the meeting. In truth, I thought it would never end. The moment we were dismissed, I hurried outdoors. When my mother approached, I glanced at the cluster of men. "Father said he would go for a walk with me so we could talk." I hesitated a moment. "Alone."

My mother patted me on the hand. "So he told me. I hope his answers will ease your mind," she said before turning toward home.

His features somber, my father joined me a few minutes later. "I believe I'm ready for our walk."

From his glum appearance, he wasn't looking forward to our time together. Neither of us spoke again until we'd distanced ourselves from our neighbors. I didn't want our conversation to be overheard. Doubtless my father concurred, for he escorted me toward the cemetery.

"I know you have many questions, Berta, and I'm willing to answer them. However, there is no way I can make you believe me. I cannot prove the truth of my answers."

He didn't carry himself with his usual crisp vigor, and I discerned sorrow in his voice, but I wasn't going to let him off so easily. "I want to know about Caroline."

His shoulders slumped forward, but he didn't avoid the question. He admitted what the letter had already told me—Caroline was more than a friend or acquaintance. She was the reason my parents had moved to Amana. My mother hadn't believed his promise that he would stop seeing her. "Not that I can blame your mother. I'm ashamed to admit that I've broken that same promise on several occasions."

"Then why doesn't she object to your trip to Chicago?"

He shrugged. "It would give rise to questions from the elders if I refused to go. She doesn't want them to know about our past—*my* past."

"She probably didn't want them to know that I'm a headstrong, willful daughter, either, but I took care of that."

"I don't think you've caused her undue concern since we've come to Amana." He turned toward me and smiled, but his smile lacked its usual charm. "I want to assure you that the woman you met in my office this morning was not Caroline. I've told your mother about the incident, and she knows the schoolmistress was in my office. She can confirm that Mrs. Harwell looks nothing like Caroline."

I tried to remain calm, but I was incredulous. "Mother has met Caroline?"

"No, but she has seen her. She can attest to the fact that the two women don't resemble each other in the least."

He grasped my elbow, and we continued to stroll along the outer edge of the cemetery. A perfectly aligned white headstone perched over each of the graves like a ghostly sentinel.

"You may ask her if you don't believe me."

I wondered where the two women had encountered each other, but there were other questions of greater importance. I wanted my father's assurance he would return to Amana, and I wanted a promise he wouldn't send me to Iowa City. Without mincing words, I told him so.

His hurried response of "I'll do my best" was followed by a question of his own. "When I was packing my bag for the trip, I noticed something missing from one of my drawers. Would you know anything about the contents of a leather pouch that I'd placed in my dresser?"

I swallowed hard. "What did it look like?"

He frowned. "It's brown leather, and it has a tie at the top. It looks like a leather pouch. Were you in my dresser for any reason?"

I shook my head back and forth. "No, I don't think so."

"You don't *think* so? What kind of answer is that? Either you were or you weren't. It isn't a difficult question, Berta." He clenched his jaw and stared at me.

I met his anger head on. "No! I wasn't in your dresser, and I don't know anything about your leather pouch." The only reason he would want the contents of that leather pouch was if he wasn't returning to Amana, and I wasn't going to assist him with his plan. He'd have to discover some other means of financing his escapade. Surely God would overlook a lie in this circumstance.

"I'm not sure I believe you," he said.

"And I'm not sure I believe you, either." I wrenched my arm from his grasp and ran home.

# CHAPTER 19

Johanna Ilg

Even Berta's dour countenance wasn't enough to allay my excitement. Wilhelm and Larissa were due to arrive at any moment if all went according to plan. Sister Muhlbach had agreed I could take the evening meal to our house and join the family. Though the practice of eating at home was common when relatives came to the village for a visit, I needed the older woman's permission to be away from the kitchen. Berta had agreed to assume extra work both this evening and tomorrow while I visited with my family.

Berta stood nearby while I lined the basket with a linen towel. "I hope they've arrived. I don't want the food to be cold for them."

"I'm sure it will be fine. They won't care if the food isn't hot.

They've come to see you, not to judge our food." She wrapped thick slices of bread in a cloth napkin and handed it to me. "I'm going to miss having you here in the kitchen."

"It's only for this evening and tomorrow." I knew my answer didn't help. Since her father's departure two days ago, Berta had been despondent. Nothing I said or did persuaded her he would return. She remained convinced she'd never see him again. Though their time together in Amana had been limited by work schedules, from what she'd told me, they had seen even less of each other when they'd lived in Chicago. And her mother hadn't proved much help, either. Sister Schumacher seemed even more withdrawn since Dr. Schumacher had left town. "You can rely on Sister Muhlbach to answer any questions or help you. She's been very pleased with you of late."

Berta grimaced. "Sister Muhlbach isn't like having you in the kitchen." She tucked a jar of strawberry preserves into the basket. "Still, I'm glad you're going to see Wilhelm. It's too bad they weren't here when we made the filled noodles."

"I'm sure Wilhelm will enjoy Sister Muhlbach's creamed chicken and potato dumplings. He was always fond of those." I chuckled. "And most anything else served in the Küche—except the liver dumplings. He didn't like those at all."

My anticipation mounted as memories of Wilhelm's years in Amana flooded my mind. He'd taught me how to climb trees and how to catch fish. He'd taught me how to paddle a canoe and row a boat. He'd even taught me how to swim—just in case the boat should tip. He'd been a wonderful big brother to me. I finished packing the basket and covered the contents with a clean towel.

"I'd like to meet them sometime while they are here," Berta said, following me to the door.

"Of course! I want them to meet you, as well. Father received permission for us to miss prayer service this evening, but you will meet them tomorrow for sure." After a quick hug, I hurried out the door without looking back. Seeing the despair in Berta's eyes would make me feel guilty, and I wanted to feel joy instead of guilt.

I had rounded the side of the Küche when I spied a buggy stopped in front of our house. My heart jumped into quickstep. I tried to relax, but the marching beat continued to hammer my chest. In the distance I could see Wilhelm assisting his wife from the carriage. If I hadn't been burdened with the food baskets, I would have run to meet them.

When I arrived at the front door, they were greeting Mother in the hallway. She looked up when I entered the door, and I detected what appeared to be disappointment, and it was directed at me. Why should she be unhappy that I had appeared? Perhaps she and Father had wanted to visit with Wilhelm and Larissa before I arrived home. I clenched the basket handles until my hands ached and forced me to relax my hold.

Wilhelm turned and flashed a bright smile. "Johanna!" I immediately placed the baskets on the floor and held out my arms to receive his embrace. His hug was warm and fierce, all at the same time.

When he released me, he turned to his wife. "I want you to meet my wife, Larissa. She's eager to become acquainted with you." He glanced at my parents. "With all of you."

"The feeling is mutual. I am very pleased to finally meet you, Larissa." She was a pretty woman with hair the shade of brewed coffee and pale blue eyes that contradicted the dark hair and olive complexion. I guessed she was probably five or six years older than I and at least two inches shorter. If she removed her hat and Wilhelm held out his arm, she could probably pass beneath. Her appearance was much different from what I'd expected. I had always pictured

Wilhelm's wife with blond hair, blue eyes, and a pale complexion. At least I'd gotten the eye color correct.

Mother had pushed together two side tables and covered them with a cloth to create a makeshift dining table. She hurried us to sit down before the food became cold, and I could sense her discomfort as we prayed. It continued for the remainder of the meal. We weren't accustomed to entertaining, especially outsiders.

While we cleared the table after the meal, Larissa and I did our best to make conversation. "There was a flavor I couldn't distinguish in the creamed chicken," she commented.

My mother stepped closer. "You didn't like it?"

Larissa continued scraping remnants from the dinner plates, but the color in her cheeks deepened. "I liked it very much. I simply couldn't determine the flavor."

"Nutmeg. I think that may be it. Nutmeg gives a different flavor to the dish," I said, hoping to relieve Larissa's obvious embarrassment.

"Oh yes. Now that you've told me, I realize that is the seasoning I tasted. The entire meal was quite delicious. I can't remember the last time I had creamed chicken."

My mother gathered the corners of the tablecloth together. "We don't eat fancy here, but we serve gut hearty meals. We work hard and need food that fills the stomach and sticks to the bones."

My mother seemed compelled to defend our ways to Wilhelm's wife. Tablecloth in hand, she marched out the back door to shake off the crumbs. I rounded the table and leaned close to Larissa. "I think Mutter is concerned you will find our food and surroundings quite plain."

I decided it must be the strain of having Wilhelm's wife visit with us for the first time. At least I hoped that was all that was bothering Mother, for I thought Wilhelm's wife very nice—and quite fashionable. Berta would approve of Larissa's pale plum walking dress with black satin piping. Gold and plum earrings dangled from her earlobes, and a bar-shaped pin was fastened atop an ecru jabot.

"I'm sure it's difficult for her. Wilhelm warned me she wasn't happy he'd married me," Larissa whispered.

"It's not you, Larissa. Mutter hoped Wilhelm would come back to Amana. Once he married, she knew he would never return—at least not to live here. Give her time. Once she gets to know you, she'll be fine." I didn't want Larissa to feel unwelcome. It had taken Wilhelm far too long to bring her to meet us. If the visit didn't go well, she'd likely never return. "I've been given permission to take the day off work tomorrow. If you'd like, I can take you around the village. I'll give you a grand tour if Wilhelm doesn't have other plans."

Wilhelm and my father were sitting in the far corner with their heads together. At the mention of his name, he looked up and grinned. "Are you talking about me, Johanna?"

"Only to ask if you have plans for tomorrow. I have a day away from the Küche and would like to take Larissa for a tour of the village."

Wilhelm withdrew a pipe from his pocket and filled the bowl with tobacco. "Of course. I'm going to ride over to Homestead with Vater. I'm sure Larissa would prefer to see the village and visit with you. Thank you, Johanna."

While Larissa couldn't comprehend the significance of being granted a day off work, or how seldom such a request was made, my brother understood. And I heard the appreciation in his voice. "We'll have great fun," I told Larissa. "I'll take you to see how our baskets and brooms are made, and we'll go visit the mill—you might even want to purchase some fabric for a new dress."

My mother returned while I was outlining our possible activities. Larissa smiled in her direction. "Will you be joining us, Mrs. Ilg?"

"It's our busy time in the garden. I must be at work, but I'm sure Johanna will make certain you see everything," she replied, folding the tablecloth into a perfect square. "If you all are in agreement, we will eat our meals in the Küche tomorrow."

Wilhelm pushed to his feet. "That will be fine, Mutter. I look forward to visiting with some of the men." He motioned to Larissa. "We've had a long day of travel, and we need to get settled at the hotel. There will be time to visit tomorrow. I don't want you to miss prayer service."

Although I didn't want them to leave so early in the evening, I understood they'd had a long day. How I wished we had an extra bedroom so they could stay with us, but we'd been assigned smaller quarters when Wilhelm moved to Chicago. Still, the hotel was nearby, and visitors to our village said the rooms were neat and clean.

After they'd departed, my mother removed her apron and smoothed the front of her dress. "If we hurry, we can arrive at prayer service before they begin."

I wanted to shout that we had permission to miss the service this evening, but I refrained. Instead, I met her determined gaze. "Why were you so unfriendly to Larissa?"

She gasped. "I was not unfriendly."

"You were. Wasn't she, Vater?"

He cleared his throat, obviously uncomfortable I'd put him in the middle of the disagreement. "Maybe *unfriendly* is too strong a word, but you weren't very warm toward her, Emilie. She seems like a nice woman, and Wilhelm is happy with her. Isn't that most important?"

"And if Wilhelm hadn't married her, he might have returned

here to us." She wrapped her shawl around her shoulders and tucked the ends into the waistband of her skirt. "Come along, Johanna. Get your shawl. We're going to be late."

My father grasped her elbow. "This isn't like you, Emilie. You're placing blame where it doesn't belong. If you want to be angry, be angry with your son. Even if he hadn't married Larissa, he wouldn't have returned. He chose to live in Chicago long before he met her."

"But he might have changed his mind."

My father shook his head. "That's not true, Emilie. He was already set in the ways of the outside world. Wife or no, he would not have returned."

I ventured a sidelong glance at my mother as we hurried down the sidewalk, our shoes clacking on the wooden boards. She didn't appear convinced.

When I sat down at prayer service, Berta whispered to me, but I shook my head. "I'll explain later." She fidgeted throughout the meeting, and the moment we walked out the door, she bombarded me with questions.

"Where are they? Did they go home already? What happened? I thought you had permission to miss prayer services this evening." She inhaled a deep breath. "Well, tell me!"

"If you stop asking questions, I will tell you." I waved her back a few steps so that my mother wouldn't hear. She wouldn't approve of my telling Berta our business. In a hushed voice I quickly explained what had happened. "I hope things will go better tomorrow."

Berta nodded. "Sometimes it's difficult to understand parents, don't you agree?"

I chuckled at her question. "Indeed it is, even when you're as old as I am. I said a special prayer that Mutter would soften her heart toward Larissa."

"If she's going to be unhappy with either of them, I think it should be Wilhelm. He's the one who chose to leave the community. Poor Larissa," Berta lamented. "I feel sorry for her. For your sake I hope they don't decide to leave bright and early tomorrow." She hesitated. "Do you think they might have left this evening instead of going to the hotel?"

"No, of course not. They were tired from a day of travel. Besides, Wilhelm would never leave without saying good-bye."

I'd uttered the rebuttal with great confidence, but when I crawled into bed later that night, Berta's words plagued me. I fell asleep with her thoughts nipping at the fringes of my consciousness like a troublesome puppy. I awakened the next morning, fraught with memories of unpleasant dreams about Larissa begging Wilhelm to take her home.

When the bell tolled to announce breakfast, I walked with my parents to the Küche feeling completely out of place. I'd asked for permission to go to the hotel and accompany Wilhelm and Larissa, but my mother had refused. "You have the entire day to be with them. Besides, I doubt Larissa will rise early enough to eat breakfast. She may be one of those society ladies who sleep late."

I didn't know how my mother would know about society ladies or if they even slept late, but her comment annoyed me. "Look! There they are." I waved gaily as Wilhelm and Larissa approached in the distance. "You see? She doesn't sleep late. Let's wait for them," I said, coming to a halt. "Larissa won't know where to sit."

"You and your father can wait. I'll go inside and save two extra places at the table."

My father pushed his hat back on his head and winked at me. "You could take Larissa to the barns and introduce her to Carl."

"We'll see," I said.

I wasn't certain why my father was going to Homestead, but I assumed there was a piece of new farm equipment due to arrive on the train. Our people prided themselves on using the most modern methods and equipment in all of our work. If it saved time, we would use it. More free time meant more time to commune with the Lord, a virtue we strived to attain. I was pleased my father and Wilhelm would have time to visit alone. I hoped I would have the same opportunity.

"I think it would be a gut thing to have them meet, don't you?"

"I don't know how much time we'll have. There are lots of places I'd like to take her. If we decide to go see the lambs over in East, could I use a buggy?"

"Ja, of course. I'll tell Carl he should get one ready for you."

"No. I'd rather you just tell him that I have permission to take a buggy, and I'll let him know if I need one. I wouldn't want him to go to the trouble if we don't need it."

"Don't need what?" Wilhelm asked as he and Larissa approached.

While we walked up the steps to the kitchen, my father explained to Wilhelm. Larissa glanced over her shoulder toward our house. "Where's your mother?"

"She went inside to save a place for us at one of the women's tables."

Larissa smiled. "That's very kind of her."

Once we entered the dining room, I reached for Larissa's hand. "Over this way." I strained to see if my mother was in her usual place. When I spotted her, I hurried Larissa across the room. "Here we are," I said. "Isn't Larissa's gown pretty?" The bodice of the pale blue gown boasted narrow pleats that perfectly matched the pleating around each of the dress sleeves.

"Ja. It is very nice."

Why couldn't my mother offer a little more conversation, a little more warmth? Berta offered a tentative wave from the kitchen door, and I smiled in return. I continued to hold Larissa's hand while we recited our prayer. "I hope you will like the breakfast."

"Nothing fancy," my mother said.

"I know. Just good, hearty food," Larissa replied. "You told me last night."

I almost giggled out loud. Berta approached our table carrying a platter of fried potatoes in one hand and sausages in the other. Apparently she'd been on good behavior or she wouldn't have been permitted to serve a table where guests were seated. "This is my friend Berta Schumacher, who works with me in the kitchen each day. Berta, this is Wilhelm's wife, Larissa Ilg."

Berta gave a tiny curtsy. "I'm pleased to meet you, Mrs. Ilg. I hope you enjoy your visit."

"Thank you, Miss Schumacher. It's nice to make your acquaintance."

"Your dress is lovely. It's a near perfect match for your eyes," Berta said before scurrying back to the kitchen.

"She seems like a sweet young lady with fine manners," Larissa said.

My mother frowned. "Ja. She understands the ways of the world, but she hasn't learned to conform to our ways."

Larissa spooned a serving of potatoes onto her plate. "She's so polite. That's hard to believe." Without waiting for a response from my mother, she passed the china platter. "Potatoes, Johanna?"

My mother curled her lips into a thin seam and remained silent for the rest of the meal. As soon as the after-breakfast prayer had been recited, she bid us a brief and hurried farewell. I exhaled a sigh of relief. My mother hadn't been particularly agreeable, but at least she hadn't said anything unkind to Larissa.

"Wilhelm says your mother thinks I'm the reason he hasn't returned to Amana. That's why he's never wanted me to come here. He didn't think she'd welcome me." Sadness shadowed her eyes. "I suppose he was correct."

"Deep in her heart she knows he wouldn't have returned. One day she will accept his new life and be happy for him." Though I spoke the words with authority, I wasn't truly convinced.

One thing was certain: With Mother at work, the remainder of the day would be more pleasant.

# CHAPTER 20

Before we departed the dining room, I took Larissa to the kitchen and introduced her to Sister Muhlbach and the other workers. Larissa's eyes grew wide at the sight of the huge brick stove and wood-fired oven.

"Such a large sink," she said when I pointed out the six-foot-long trough and washstand.

Berta chuckled. "We need lots of room to stack all the dishes before we wash them, don't we, Johanna?"

I quickly agreed. Then Larissa questioned me about the cheese molds and noodle boards. "All of the tools we use in the kitchen are made here in the village. The cooper makes our wooden buckets and barrels, and the large casks we use for wine making. The tinsmith makes our pails and pudding molds, even our cookie cutters, the big ladles, and spoons."

"He does a fine job, too," Sister Muhlbach said. "And you'll not find a better broom maker or basket weaver than those who live in Amana. You might want to see some of the fine calico we have at the general store. Our woolens and calicos are the finest you can buy anywhere."

One of the paring-knife sisters passed through the kitchen as Sister Muhlbach was extolling the products and shook her head. "Those are mighty prideful words, Sister Muhlbach."

"But true," the Küchebaas replied with a hearty laugh. "Make sure you return in time for the noonday meal. We'll have a special dessert."

"They all seem very nice," Larissa said after we headed off toward one of the shops.

"Amana is a fine place to live. Not like what you're used to, of course, but I think you'll find our shops and people all interesting," I said as we entered the broom maker's shop. We watched while he completed one of the small brushes used to wipe crumbs from the table. Though he spoke when we entered, his focus remained fixed upon his work. To my surprise Larissa appeared quite interested and asked several questions before we departed for the basket-making shop. Her eyes shone with delight when she surveyed the varying sizes and shapes perched on a shelf and hanging from wooden hooks awaiting delivery to households in the village. There were bread baskets, laundry baskets, apple baskets, and every other size and shape in between.

"The ones on the shelf are display baskets. When visitors come to the village they can see the sizes and shapes that are made," I explained.

"Let's make the general store our last stop. I know I'll want to purchase some fabric to take to friends in Chicago, and I promised

Louisa I would bring her one of those cookie cutters you mentioned. I hope to take her a rabbit-shaped one. Each Easter since Wilhelm and I have been married, she's told me about how all of the Amana children love those rabbit cookies. Even Wilhelm agreed, and he seldom mentions his childhood."

"Really?" The comment surprised me. "Only our woolens and calicos are for sale, but if the tinsmith has extras, perhaps he will be kind enough to give you one."

"Oh, I do hope so. Louisa will be terribly disappointed if she doesn't receive her cookie cutter."

At Larissa's mention of my mother's sister, my thoughts wandered back to the conversation Berta had overheard on our front porch. I would wait until after we visited the tinsmith, and then I'd ask Larissa about the baby. Perhaps the birth of a child had fueled Tante Louisa's desire for the cookie cutter.

Larissa watched the tinsmith at work, but mostly she looked at all the wares he had on display. Her eyes shone with delight when we stopped in front of a wooden box filled with cookie cutters—lambs, chickens, cows, horses, and rabbits were only a few of the many shapes. She lifted one of the rabbits from the box and held it in her palm. "I was hoping to take one of these to a relative," she said to the tinsmith. "Is there any possibility . . . ?" The question hung in the air.

Eyebrows raised, the tinsmith glanced in my direction. "This is for a member of your family, Johanna?"

"Yes. My aunt who lives in Chicago."

He grinned. "Then I think we could spare one cookie cutter, ja?"

"Thank you. My family is most grateful for your kindness."

A short time later as we exited the tinsmith's shop, Larissa clasped my hand. "I had hoped to purchase several, but at least I have this one to take to Louisa. Let's go to the general store so I can pick out some fabric. We can take my parcels to the hotel, eat our noonday meal, and then go see the lambs. I think that would be great fun."

I agreed. Besides, it would take a few minutes to walk to the store, and the time alone would provide an opportunity to ask my questions. But before I could formulate exactly how I wanted to broach the subject of Louisa and her baby, Larissa launched into talk of Chicago and her life with Wilhelm. "I would guess that Wilhelm has never told you how we met, has he?"

"No. I know he visited a lot of places when he used to work as a salesman for our woolen and calico goods. Did he meet you in one of the stores where he sold our fabrics?"

"That's a good guess, but it's not right. We met on a very cold day when I was ice-skating on the Chicago River with a large group of friends. I had left the ice and was headed toward a fire to warm myself when I tripped and literally fell into Wilhelm's arms." She giggled. "I'm not sure who was more embarrassed, Wilhelm or me, but I'm very glad that accident occurred. Otherwise, I doubt I would have ever met him."

Her story surprised me. Of course, that was many years ago. "Were you injured?"

"Oh no, though if I'd fallen, I'm sure I would have suffered bruises and perhaps a broken bone. After the rest of my group finished skating, we invited Wilhelm to join us for hot chocolate at one of my friend's homes. He agreed, and I can't tell you how pleased I am that he did. Wilhelm is a fine husband."

"And a fine brother, as well."

Her smile faded. "I don't think he considers himself a good brother. He laments the fact that he seldom sees you, and Pieter's death continues to plague him."

Her comment surprised me, but I'd been so young when Pieter died that my memories of him were only stories I'd heard from my parents and Pieter's friends. "Wilhelm can do nothing to change Pieter's death, but he could visit Amana more often. I think it would help him."

"That's exactly what I've told him, but he says his visits make him sad. He knows he disappointed your parents by leaving. Still, he says he'll never return. I hope they don't think I've convinced him to stay away, for I'd never do such a thing." She swept her arms wide as though she could embrace the entire community. "I don't believe I could live here, but I think Amana is charming, and I would love to visit more often."

We stepped inside the general store, and Larissa sauntered down one aisle and then another, stopping to examine items as she moved along. "I want to see all of the fabrics before I make my final choices." She picked up several of the trims and laces and piled them into the crook of her arm.

"Those aren't made here," I whispered. "They are sold to us by salesmen from Chicago."

She shrugged. "I like them, and who can say when I'd find exactly the same items back home."

"Then let me take them to the counter for you. Brother Kohler will keep them together until you've completed your shopping." I gathered the items from her arm, and while she continued to examine the array of goods, I piled the lace and trims in front of Brother Kohler. "She hasn't completed her shopping. There will be more items."

"I was pleased to see Wilhelm has come for a visit. We don't see him often enough. And is this young lady a friend of the family?"

"She's Wilhelm's wife."

I took a backward step, but before I could move any further, he leaned forward and rested his arms on the counter. "I don't believe I was ever told that Wilhelm had taken a wife. When did he marry?"

"I don't recall the exact date, but this is their first visit to Amana." I took another backward step and glanced toward Larissa. "If you'll excuse me, I should see if she has any questions." I hurried off before he could ply me with further questions. Brother Kohler did a fine job keeping the store shelves stocked, but he also managed to extricate information from every customer who shopped there. He prided himself on knowing everyone in the community, as well as every event that affected each of us. He was obviously flustered that Wilhelm's marriage had gotten by him.

I picked up one of the large hand-woven baskets the store provided for use by the customers and carried it with me. "This should help," I said, approaching Larissa, who now held several jars in her arm. One by one I placed the containers in the basket.

"I've chosen some fabrics, too." She waved me forward. Holding the corner of two different fabrics, she said, "What do you think? Which would be better for a new dress?"

I stared at the bold plaid cloth that we manufactured for outsiders. Never before had I considered such shades for a dress. "I'm accustomed to the dark calicos and woolens. You would know how to make a better choice. Maybe you should pick whichever color you don't already have." While she contemplated her choices, I rested the basket atop a pile of neatly folded blankets and daydreamed about what kind of life Larissa must have in Chicago.

"I think that should be everything I want."

Her remark startled me back to the present. The basket brimmed with a variety of goods, and I knew Brother Kohler would be pleased. On the other hand I wondered if Wilhelm would be unhappy with his wife's many purchases. I hoped his job paid him well.

Brother Kohler's eyes shone with delight as we approached with the overflowing basket. He picked up his pencil and pad, ready to begin his calculations. It would take him some time to enter and tally the items, and he'd likely ask questions if we remained at the counter.

I hoisted the basket onto the counter and pointed to the lace. "Don't forget to add in the lace and trims. We're going over to the barns for a short time, and we'll return to pay for the purchases in a little while."

"Won't take me that long," he said. I could read the disappointment in his eyes and was certain he'd been assembling a list of questions for Larissa.

I flashed a smile in his direction. "We don't want to be late for the noonday meal, and we need to stop by the hotel beforehand." Giving him no opportunity to protest, I strode quickly toward the door, Larissa following close on my heels.

"Do you think Wilhelm will worry that you purchased too many items?" I hoped my brother wouldn't hold me responsible.

Larissa laughed. "No. He doesn't worry over such things as a little shopping. Besides, I have money of my own."

Her announcement surprised me, since Berta had told me few married women worked. "Where do you work?"

"Oh, I'm not employed. My grandfather was quite wealthy, and prior to his death he arranged a trust fund for me. I receive money from it several times a year. In truth, Wilhelm wouldn't need to work, but he's too proud to use any of my inheritance. He insists upon paying our monthly living expenses from his earnings. I think he'd be happy if I'd give the money to the poor."

"Do your parents live in Chicago?" Secretly I wondered why her grandfather hadn't bequeathed the money to them instead of Larissa.

"Part of the time. They travel a great deal. Currently they're in Europe. Thanks to Wilhelm, they can travel at their leisure."

"Thanks to Wilhelm?" Wilhelm had always been vague when

my parents inquired about his work in Chicago, and I assumed he continued to work as a salesman of some sort, probably in the textile industry. "He works for your father?"

"My grandfather was a financier who invested in many profitable companies. My father inherited those holdings, and now Wilhelm has taken charge. Father says he is the most astute businessman he's ever met—even more brilliant than my grandfather."

The news surprised me. I thought it strange that Wilhelm, who had been reared in a community where money was seldom needed for anything, would now be deeply involved in the business of finances and banking. Though I wanted to hear more about Wilhelm's work, my attention wavered when I caught sight of Carl entering the barn with a woman at his side. My stomach tightened, and I shaded my eyes. It was impossible to see her face at this distance. Why would a woman be going into the barn with Carl? I silently chastised myself for questioning something that clearly wasn't my business. After all, permission was granted to use a buggy or wagon when needed for important business or a family emergency. Still, it was odd to see a woman enter the barn for such a purpose.

When we reached the door leading into the barn, I hesitated. "If you want to wait out here, I can go in and request the buggy." I glanced at the hem of Larissa's gown. "I wouldn't want you to ruin your dress."

"Don't be silly. I want to see inside so I have an idea where Wilhelm used to spend some of his childhood days."

I heard a woman's soft laughter as we entered. I squinted, forcing my eyes to adjust to the dim light. Carl said something indistinguishable, and once again the woman laughed. Following the sound of their voices, I continued around the horse stalls but stopped in my tracks at the sight that greeted me.

I gasped, took a backward step, and landed atop Larissa's shoe.

"Ouch! That's my foot you're standing on, Johanna."

Carl and the woman jumped apart and swirled in our direction. "Johanna!"

The woman stared at me for a moment and then turned her head. I'd never before seen her. She wasn't from our village, of that I was certain. Anger and disappointment collided as I attempted to maintain a calm demeanor.

"I will need a buggy ready for use after we have eaten our noonday meal." The strangled words were as much as I could manage before turning on my heel and motioning Larissa outside.

"That was rather embarrassing," Larissa said. "Still, it's refreshing to know that love finds a way, even in Amana."

"Refreshing, indeed." And I had thought the rest of the day was going to be pleasant.

# CHAPTER 21

During our return to the general store, I remained in a haze, unable to comprehend the entirety of what I'd observed in the barn. While Larissa chattered aimlessly about young people in love, I attempted to push aside feelings of anger and betrayal. If Carl and that girl in the barn were an example of young love, I wasn't certain what that said about his talk of a future with me and truthfulness between a man and woman who planned to marry. Of course, I hadn't committed to Carl, but he'd been clear that he cared for me—at least I thought he had. I was thankful I'd not mentioned Carl to Larissa earlier. My humiliation would have been complete.

Since we'd spent little time in the barn, Larissa and I arrived at the Küche a short time before the noonday meal was due to be served. We circled around so we could sit and wait on the back porch without disturbing the meal preparations. We hadn't been there long when Berta scurried out the door and motioned me toward the shed.

"Please excuse us for a moment, Mrs. Ilg. I have a matter I need to discuss privately with Johanna."

"Yes, of course," Larissa said.

I nearly laughed aloud at Berta's perfect manners. She obviously knew how to act the perfect lady when she wanted to impress. I pushed to my feet and excused myself before following Berta. She wheeled toward me. "Did you see her?"

"See *who*?" I'd been working through a haze for the past thirty minutes, and now Berta wanted to play games.

The sparkle disappeared from her eyes. "You don't need to snap at me."

"I'm sorry, Berta. It's been a difficult morning. Who was I supposed to see?"

"Karin—the woman from High—Carl's friend. She's here. Rudolf told me. He met her when he stopped to get the wagon and take it to the dairy barn before his deliveries."

My stomach tightened into a knot, and my hands quivered. He'd told me his feelings for Karin were brotherly, but his actions belied his words. "Why is she here? Did Rudolf tell you?" I clasped my hands together to keep them from shaking. I tried to understand these feelings that were boiling like a bubbling pot of water. Shouldn't I be pleased to know Carl wasn't what he'd pretended before I'd pledged my love? My head said yes, but the pain in my heart told me I already cared.

"Rudolf said she arrived with her father and that he went to the calico mill to help repair something."

Berta's explanation made sense. Occasionally men from another village would come to assist when there was difficulty repairing a machine. I guessed that her father's help had been requested and that Karin had convinced him to bring her along. Yet why would she come here if Carl had been clear with her? And why were they locked in an embrace? In spite of the warm day, I shivered at the remembrance. I hoped that Karin and her father would eat lunch in another Küche.

"Berta!" Both of us turned toward the back porch. Obviously annoyed, Sister Muhlbach swiped her hands on her apron and motioned Berta to come. "I need you in the kitchen."

I pushed Berta forward. "Go on. You'll get in trouble on my account, and I don't want that to happen." I called an apology to Sister Muhlbach and relaxed when the older woman's features softened with a smile. Returning to the back porch, I attempted to digest Berta's news, but my mind jumped from one thought to another.

"I like your friend Berta," Larissa said as I took a seat.

Her comment yanked me from my jumbled thoughts. "Yes. She's a nice girl." I was thankful to hear the bell toll in the distance. Conversation had become difficult since our visit to the barn, and the thought of returning for the buggy made matters all the worse. How could I possibly look at Carl? And what would he say?

I stood. "We should go around and enter the dining room from the front with the others." Silently I prayed Karin wouldn't be anywhere in sight. As we rounded the corner of the house, I scanned the crowd and released a relieved breath. No strangers were visible, nor was Carl. Perhaps he'd gained permission to join them at another Küche. I hoped so, for I didn't want to see him, either.

As we entered the dining room, I saw my mother waiting at her table. She smiled and waved us forward. "You had a pleasant time this morning?"

"Yes. I've enjoyed myself very much," Larissa said.

Mother nudged my arm. "Where did you go?"

I hastily listed the shops we had visited.

"I found some lovely gifts to take home. Louisa asked that I bring her one of the rabbit cookie cutters. The tinsmith was especially kind and gave me one to take to her. She's going to be very pleased."

At the mention of Tante Louisa, my Mutter's smile disappeared. "I'm surprised she talks about Amana. What else has she told you?"

"Not much. She said she has fond memories of her life in Amana, especially the holidays." Larissa glanced at me. "Don't forget to tell your mother that we stopped at the livery barn. We're going to go see the lambs this afternoon."

My mother brightened. "So you met Carl? A nice young man, don't you think? He's asked to court Johanna."

There wasn't time for Larissa to respond before we bowed our heads to pray, but she clutched my hand and squeezed until the final amen. "You didn't tell me," she hissed in my ear.

"He's a fine young man and nice looking, too, don't you think?" My mother spooned a helping of cottage cheese onto her plate.

Once again Larissa clamped on to my hand. "He was quite busy, so I didn't meet him," Larissa replied.

"We can have this conversation another time," I whispered to my mother. "We don't want to break the rules just because we have a guest."

My mother didn't appear pleased by my suggestion, but at least I'd silenced any further mention of Carl.

"We'll talk later," my mother said when we parted outside the dining room. "Give my regards to Carl. And introduce Larissa."

I didn't intend to do either of those things, but I didn't say so. Instead, I smiled and bid her farewell. "Come on, Larissa. We'll see if the buggy is ready." I hoped Carl had left it outside, and I wouldn't have to see him.

"Now that your mother is gone, are you going to tell me about Carl?" Her wispy fringe of bangs fluttered in the light afternoon breeze.

Though I didn't want to talk about Carl, I could hardly ignore Larissa's pointed question. I made my explanation brief and hoped she wouldn't ask too many questions.

She arched her brows. "So this is an arranged courtship."

"Not exactly, but my parents have been involved. I haven't committed to Carl. I wanted to wait awhile."

"And from what we saw this morning, it would appear Carl isn't completely committed to the idea, either."

I was thankful she didn't ask why I hadn't committed before now. I didn't think it proper to bring up my letter to Wilhelm and my desire to visit Chicago before I decided upon marriage. What if Wilhelm hadn't mentioned my request? Or what if she didn't think it a good idea? We would both be embarrassed.

Even though my love for Carl remained uncertain, I had thought him kind and truthful, a man I could easily love. Perhaps that's why Larissa's comment stung more than I'd expected. I couldn't quell the anger and rejection that now stirred deep inside. How would I ever forget the sight of him in the barn with Karin in his arms? What if Rudolf or one of the other young men had seen them? My cheeks turned warm at the thought. Carl wasn't what he'd pretended to be—he had made a fool of me.

To my disappointment the buggy wasn't waiting outside the barn when we arrived. Larissa hesitated at the door. "Would you prefer to speak to Carl alone? I can wait out here if you'd like."

"No. I don't want to talk to him right now. If you're with me, it will be easier."

Carl was waiting near the doors, and the moment we entered he rushed to my side. "We need to talk," he whispered.

"Is the buggy ready for us? We need to be on our way." I stared straight ahead, unable to look at him.

"Johanna, please. I can explain."

"The buggy," I said from between clenched teeth. My stomach roiled, and I wished I hadn't eaten lunch.

"The horse is already hitched. I'll get it for you."

I turned on my heel. "We'll wait outside."

"He seems genuinely sorry," Larissa said while we stood waiting outside the barn.

"Sorry? Had that been Wilhelm with another woman, would you be so easily charmed?"

Her smile faded. "No. I don't suppose I would. Still, you said you hadn't committed to Carl."

"And for that I am most thankful."

Moments later Carl drove the buggy through the double door opening and gently pulled back on the reins. "Whoa, boy," he crooned. He jumped down from the buggy and grasped my elbow to assist me.

Twisting free of his hold, I moved toward the buggy. "Assist Larissa. I can get in and out of a buggy without your help."

He took a step closer. "Please say you'll talk to me later this evening," he whispered.

I hoisted myself up into the buggy, no longer caring if Larissa heard our conversation. "You have nothing to say that interests me." I turned toward Larissa, who was concentrating on straightening her skirt. "Ready?"

"Yes. Whenever you are."

I slapped the lines against the horse's back. "Walk, Jack."

"He understands you." Larissa grinned, obviously impressed the horse had followed my command.

"Too bad Carl isn't as well behaved as this horse," I muttered.

For so long I had looked forward to meeting Larissa, and now it seemed nothing would go right. Between Mother and Carl, the excitement of this visit had lost much of the anticipated luster. At least there should be no unexpected surprises on the visit to East, and seeing the lambs would provide a good diversion—and an opportunity to ask about Louisa's baby.

We were well on the way when I gathered my courage. "I wondered if Tante Louise wanted the cookie cutter because she will one day want to make the rabbit cookies for her baby."

Larissa stared at me. "A baby? Louisa?"

I nodded. "I understand she has a baby."

"Wherever did you hear such a thing? You're the only baby Louisa has ever had."

I gasped. "What did you say?"

She clapped a hand to her mouth and shook her head. "I'm sorry." She continued to repeat the muffled apology until I yanked her hand away from her mouth.

"What do you mean? Tell me!" I pulled back on the reins. "Whoa, Jack." The horse clopped to a halt, and I turned to face Larissa. "Are you telling me that you think Louisa is my mother?"

Larissa stared at me, her eyes brimming with tears. "I'm so sorry. I promised I'd never tell. And I didn't mean to. It slipped out. Oh, what am I going to do? Wilhelm will never forgive me. Your parents will never forgive me. Your mother will never speak to me again."

"Stop!"

She gulped a breath of air. "Please forgive me."

"Larissa, I want you to quit asking me to forgive you and tell me what you're talking about. Louisa is my mother? Are you certain?"

She bobbed her head. "Yes. The family agreed you would grow up as Frank and Emilie's daughter. No one was ever to know. Louisa left Amana and went to Iowa City until you were born. About a year after your birth, she left Iowa City and moved to Chicago."

I felt as though I might faint. None of this could be true. Surely it was impossible. How could I have grown up in Amana and been blind to the truth? Never had I heard an inkling of gossip, nothing that had ever caused me to wonder about my parents. I cupped my forehead in my hand. "Who knows this?"

Perspiration dotted Larissa's face, and she reached into her reticule for a handkerchief. "I don't think anyone but your family."

That made no sense. Others had to have known. My parents couldn't have suddenly appeared with a baby. Questions would have been asked. My mind reeled, and once again I felt lightheaded. My entire life was a lie.

Larissa wrung the handkerchief around her fingers. "Maybe I misunderstood. Let's don't say anything and pretend I never mentioned a word of this."

I looked directly into her pale blue eyes, incredulous she could even put voice to such a farfetched comment. "I'm sorry, Larissa, but I can't simply push this from my thoughts. I know you didn't intend to break your confidence or to hurt me in any way, but this is something I must discuss with my parents." I picked up the reins and flicked the horse's rump. "Walk, Jack."

"They'll never forgive me," she whispered. "I know they won't. I can only hope that Wilhelm won't hold this against me."

I ignored her plaintive remarks. She was trying to sway my decision, but I couldn't disregard what she'd told me. Yet if there was any possibility she'd misunderstood, great damage could be done if I wrongfully accused my parents. "Perhaps I should speak to Wilhelm before I say anything to my parents. Just to be sure."

She bobbed her head. "Yes, that might be better. Maybe if he answers your questions, it won't be necessary to say anything to your mother and father."

I didn't agree, but I didn't say so. If my parents weren't really my mother and father, there was nothing Wilhelm could say or do to suppress the need for a confrontation with them. If Larissa was correct and my entire life was based upon deceit and lies, whom could I trust? Throughout the remainder of the afternoon, I considered what questions I would ask Wilhelm and what I would do if Larissa's claim was true. At first I told myself it changed everything. Later, I thought it might change nothing.

Wilhelm and my father were scheduled to return by late afternoon. I hoped Father would be at the barn by the time we returned the buggy. Carl wouldn't dare say anything in front of him. And though the pleasure of seeing the new lambs had diminished, we remained in East for several hours—until I thought Wilhelm and Father would be back in Middle.

"You need to arrange for me to speak alone with Wilhelm. Could you suggest he go to the hotel so we could talk there?"

Larissa agreed the hotel would be best. "Let's hope your father doesn't decide to come along."

"He won't. After being gone from work all day, he'll want to make certain everything is in order upon his return."

I sighed with relief when I saw Wilhelm standing next to my father outside the barn. At least one thing had gone as planned. Larissa smiled and waved to Wilhelm, though I could see her smile was forced. She kissed his cheek as he helped her down from the buggy.

Wilhelm's brows furrowed. "You feel warm. I hope you didn't get too much sun. Are you feeling ill?"

"Just a bit tired. I was hoping you would escort Johanna and me to the hotel. She's had little time to visit with you, and we thought it would be nice if the three of us could spend some time together." She turned to my father. "I'm sure you have work that needs your attention before supper."

"Ja. The three of you go to the hotel and have your visit. I need to speak with Carl and make certain there were no problems while I was gone."

I grinned at Larissa. If nothing else, at least I'd been correct about my father's reaction. While we walked to the hotel, Larissa regaled Wilhelm with tales of our shopping and the places we had visited. I thought she sounded artificial and insincere, but Wilhelm didn't seem to notice. He hung on her every word and appeared amused to hear about the lambs.

"I'm pleased you enjoyed yourself. And how about you, Johanna? Did you have a pleasant day?"

"It has been one of the most memorable days of my life."

"I'm very glad to hear my two favorite ladies have become friends," he said, unlocking the door to their hotel rooms. He stepped back and waited while Larissa and I entered.

"Johanna met with some unexpected news on many fronts," Larissa said. She glanced in my direction as Wilhelm directed her toward the divan.

His eyes shone with delight when he looked at her. "Then you must tell me what happened, Johanna. Life in Amana doesn't usually present surprises."

Though I'd been told all of the hotel rooms were nice, this one boasted a finely appointed sitting room that was larger than the one in our home. I was certain they had rented the most expensive rooms in the hotel. Larissa and Wilhelm sat side by side on the upholstered horsehair sofa. I chose a chair to Wilhelm's right. I looked to Larissa for direction, but she kept her gaze fastened to the floor.

"You met Carl when you were at the barns?" I asked.

Wilhelm nodded. "I did. Father seems to like him very much, says he's a good worker and a good man."

"Ja. I thought he was a good man, too." I blurted what I'd seen in the barn, the picture still vivid in my mind. "I was overcome and thankful to have Larissa with me."

"I'm sorry, Johanna." I heard the concern in his voice. "Have you thought that maybe there's more to what happened? You should consider speaking to Carl. There may be some explanation. Larissa can tell you that men sometimes make foolish mistakes."

Larissa patted her husband's hand. "Johanna needs time to come to her own decision, Wilhelm. This has been a difficult day. Give her time."

Wilhelm nodded and squeezed Larissa's hand. "I'm pleased that the two of you have gotten on so well. I told Larissa the two of you would become fast friends, but I don't think she believed me."

"Indeed, Larissa and I have become friends, Wilhelm. We've had much to talk about. She's told me many things about Chicago."

"Today it was me who made a foolish mistake, Wilhelm." Larissa reached for his hand. "I told her about Louisa. It was a mistake—I swear I didn't mean to. We were talking, and it just slipped out."

A deafening silence fell over the room. Not a muscle in my brother's body moved as he stared at her. Finally he turned, and I saw the horror in his eyes. It was true. All these years they'd hidden my identity. All these years I'd thought my parents were honest, and truthful, and dependable. This moment that image shattered.

Wilhelm's complexion paled, and he scooted to the edge of the sofa. "Listen to me, Johanna. They thought it was best—for everyone. For you, for Louisa, for Mutter and Vater. I understand that to find out like this is a terrible blow, but you know that they love you the same as they love me. They think of you as their own. What Larissa has told you changes nothing."

I stared at him in disbelief. "Changes nothing? It changes everything, Wilhelm! I don't even know my own Mutter. And who is my Vater?"

He shook his head. "I don't know. Louisa never told me."

"She's never even bothered to come and see me." The profundity shook me to the core. How could she ignore her own flesh and blood? Never care to speak to me or know my thoughts.

"Don't blame her too much. She was unmarried when you were born, and she wanted to be certain you would have good parents. She asked Mutter and Vater to raise you as their own. They agreed on the condition that she would remain out of your life and no one know you were her child."

I cupped my hands over my face, unable to fathom the totality of what I was hearing. "Why didn't anyone in Amana ever tell me? Others had to know. If this is true, one of them would have mentioned this to me years ago." How could something so impossible be true?

"Louisa moved to Iowa City as soon as she realized she was pregnant. After the agreement was made, Mutter told several women she was expecting a child. As time passed, she added some padding here and there. No one suspected anything. Vater and I went to Iowa City and brought you home. Any questions were easily explained away."

"And Louisa went off to live a good life in Chicago."

"No. She had a very difficult time for the first few years of your life. She wanted to return, but she'd given her word. And if she had asked to return and live in one of the other villages, people would have asked questions." He rested his arms atop his legs. "Louisa has a comfortable life, but she has paid dearly for her past. She and her husband have never been able to have another child. None of us meant to hurt you." Shoulders bent low and head bowed, Wilhelm clasped his hands together.

After years of lies, his words rang hollow. Forgiveness for any of them didn't rise to the surface. But in that moment one thing became clear: I must meet Louisa, talk to her, and learn for myself the entire truth of this unbelievable tale. I couldn't grasp the depth of what I'd heard. My stomach churned, and I pressed my palm to my midsection.

"When you answered my letter, you didn't say anything about having me come to Chicago for a visit. Why is that, Wilhelm?"

"It would be difficult—for everyone." Slowly he lifted his head. "Larissa and I would enjoy your company. She has spoken of nothing else since she learned of your request, but—"

"But what, Wilhelm? Mutter and Vater wouldn't approve? Are you afraid they'll be angry with you? What about me? All of you have kept this secret from me. Don't I have a right to meet Louisa? To at least spend a little time with her?"

Beads of perspiration dotted Wilhelm's forehead, and he reached for his handkerchief. "Now that you know, it might be better if Louisa came here. I can speak to her and to Mother and Father— see if they all agree."

"If *they* all agree? This should be *my* choice." Tears threatened and I swallowed hard. I didn't want to cry. "I am not a child. This would be the perfect time for me to visit Chicago. It will help me forget about Carl and Karin, I can meet Louisa, and I can travel with you and Larissa. How can you deny this isn't the best time?"

He waivered for a moment, and I thought he was going to agree. "If you appeared without any notice, it would come as a terrible shock to Louisa."

My resolve failed, and a tear trickled down my cheek. "And you think this has not been a shock to me, Wilhelm? I think they did what was easy for them, not what was gut for me."

# CHAPTER 22

I listened and tried to understand Wilhelm's pleas and explanations. He did his best to convince me that Louisa wanted to meet me; that her sorrow ran deep; that she'd done the best she could under the circumstances; that had she remained in Amana, her disgrace would have been unbearable.

"You need to remember that people make mistakes. Our parents thought they were doing what was best for you. You became their daughter. I don't know what Mother would have done if she hadn't had you when Pieter died."

One after another the excuses rolled off his tongue. One after another I dismissed them and wondered what other family secrets I might discover before I died.

Anger and pain joined forces and settled on my chest with

an unbearable weight. I tried to inhale a full breath but instead managed only a ragged, shallow gasp. Except for a few hours of shopping, the entire day had been a disaster. I gave in to my emotions and permitted the tears to roll down my cheeks unchecked. Wilhelm folded my hands between his and gently squeezed, a gesture I considered his silent plea to forgive all of them.

"To remain locked in anger won't change the past, Johanna. Nothing any of us say or do can roll back time and start again."

"I understand nothing can change the past, but I thought our family lived a life based on truth. We grew up being told we should never lie or deceive others. My entire life is a lie, Wilhelm. Can't you see that? And you chose Louisa over me. For all these years you thought it more important to protect her lie rather than speak the truth."

He shook his head. "I have protected you, as well, Johanna. Learning the truth has created nothing but havoc. It would have done the same if you'd heard it when you were a young girl—the time never would have been right to disclose the truth. No matter your age, you would have suffered from pain and confusion. I thought it better that you go to the grave never knowing. But we can't change what has happened."

"I'm so sorry, Wilhelm," Larissa murmured. "Your parents will never forgive me. They'll never want me to come back here again."

Wilhelm sat back and stared across the room. "I'll take responsibility. It's because of me that this happened. I'm the one who told you, so the blame should fall upon my shoulders."

I swiped the tears from my cheeks. "Half-truths, lies, and secrets. Is that what our family has become? Are we so unsure of our love for one another that we must tell lies to protect our bond? That doesn't say much for the faith we proclaim as the center of our lives."

Wilhelm clenched his jaw. "Don't preach to me about faith, Johanna. I don't see you following the Bible's teachings in regard to forgiveness."

His words were like a sharp blow. How could he speak about my lack of forgiveness only minutes after I'd heard this shattering news? "You're right. I don't feel any forgiveness. Perhaps one day I will. Perhaps," I whispered.

Larissa clutched Wilhelm's arm. "I think Johanna should come with us to Chicago. After she speaks to Louisa, she might more fully understand." There was a tremor in her voice.

I believe Larissa wanted to help right the wrong.

Wilhelm nodded. "You may be right. Let me think on this awhile longer."

The supper bell tolled, and the three of us paraded out of the room, each of us burdened by the conversation that must take place later. After this evening I knew nothing would ever be the same between my parents and me. Would our bond grow stronger or be permanently broken? Only time could tell.

I was thankful conversation was frowned upon during meal-time. With only clanking utensils breaking the stillness in the din-ing room, I wanted nothing more than silence and time to think. Though my thoughts remained a jumble of confusion, I tried my best to assemble my questions.

We were on the way home after supper when my father motioned me to walk beside him. "Carl tells me he needs to talk to you about what happened today."

"Did he explain what occurred?"

Vater pushed his straw hat further back on his head. "He said you came into the barn while he was talking to one of his friends from High and that you became angry."

"Ach! Talking to one of his friends? Is that what he said?"

"Ja. There is more?"

"Of course there is more. Why would I be angry if he was talking to a friend? He was embracing a woman—and not just any woman. It was Karin. The woman who had hoped to marry him before he moved to our village." I kicked a pebble and watched it drop between the wood slats of the walkway.

He pulled me to a halt. "This is true?"

I heard the disbelief in his voice.

His gaze turned cold. "Carl never spoke of unsuitable behavior with another woman."

"Would I say such a thing if it wasn't true? I wouldn't invent such a story. Why would I want to?" My anger boiled beneath the surface. Why hadn't my father questioned Carl's story instead of mine, his own daughter's? "You can believe Carl or you can believe me. The choice is yours."

I yanked away from him and hurried to catch up with Larissa and Wilhelm. "I told Vater about Carl," I whispered to Larissa. "I don't know if he believes me." There wasn't time to elaborate any further.

Mother glanced over her shoulder. "Why all the whispering?"

"We were speaking about Carl," I said.

My mother smiled. The mention of Carl was enough to allay any further questions from her. I doubted she'd be so pleased when I told her about his behavior earlier in the day. We filed into the parlor and sat down.

"You still plan to leave Saturday, Wilhelm?" My father leaned forward in his chair and rested his arms across his thighs.

My brother nodded. "I thought we'd leave for Homestead Saturday after the noonday meal. I want to visit some of the folks over there. Larissa and I will stay overnight at the hotel and leave for Chicago the following morning." Wilhelm glanced in my direction. "We have invited Johanna to return with us—for a visit."

I couldn't believe my ears. Wilhelm had decided in my favor. I flashed him a smile.

My mother paled. "You see, Frank? I told you this would happen."

Wilhelm scooted forward on his chair. "What would happen, Mutter?"

"I told your Vater that Johanna would leave us one day. Just like you, she'll go off to the city, marry someone who will keep her away from her family, and never look back." Her voice cracked with emotion. "I'll grow old without any of my children."

"Larissa isn't the reason I haven't returned to visit. She's encouraged me to visit and has asked to come and meet you. Place the blame on my shoulders, not hers. This is not her fault. Even before we married, I didn't come home but once or twice. You know that is true."

My mother's lips tightened into a knot. She didn't want to acknowledge the truth of what he'd said. She wanted to blame Larissa. It was easier than thinking her son didn't want to visit his family. Ignoring his explanation, she turned in my direction. "You have agreed to go with them?"

"Ja. I want to see the city, and I want to meet Louisa."

Mother's hands trembled as she looked at Wilhelm.

"She knows about Louisa, Mutter," Wilhelm said.

"Of course she does. She has always known that her Tante Louisa lives in Chicago. Haven't you, Johanna?"

Wilhelm stretched forward and touched her hand. "Johanna knows Louisa is her Mutter."

She jerked away. "*I* am Johanna's Mutter. I have cared for her since her birth." Her eyes implored me to take stock of what she'd said. "Do you hear me, Johanna? I am your Mutter. Even if I didn't give birth to you, I am your Mutter, not Louisa." Tears rimmed her eyes. "I told you, Frank, this would happen." Suddenly she turned on Wilhelm. "Why have you done this to me, Wilhelm? It was Louisa, wasn't it? She wanted you to tell Johanna?"

Larissa grasped Wilhelm's sleeve. "It wasn't Wilhelm's fault. I told Johanna—by mistake. I didn't mean to. I'm so very sorry. It just slipped out." She rattled on like a frightened child.

My mother rocked back in her chair and pinned Wilhelm with a glare. "You told Larissa about Johanna?"

"She's my wife. We don't keep secrets. Besides, we see Louisa and her husband frequently, and—"

She held up her hand and interrupted him. "So Louisa's husband knows, as well?"

"He does."

My mother massaged her forehead with the tips of her fingers. "This is awful. Both you and Louisa promised to never tell anyone. Both of you broke your promise. Now we must suffer the consequences."

"If you had told the truth from the beginning, none of this would have happened," I said. "There is enough blame to go around, Mutter."

"But since you are going to Chicago, it is your Vater and me who will be punished."

"I'm not trying to punish anyone. I want to meet Louisa. I want to get away from Carl. I need time to think and decide about my future."

"Why do you need to get away from Carl?"

Once again I explained what had happened in the barn. Once again there was an air of disbelief that Carl could do such a thing. In truth, I'd been as overwhelmed by his behavior as my parents were now. If I hadn't seen for myself, I wouldn't have believed it. His actions had been in direct opposition to everything he'd said and done since arriving in the village.

"I think it will be best for me to be away for a time. When I return, maybe Carl will have moved back to High. That would be better for his Mutter—and for me." I wanted to add that it would probably please Karin, as well, but I held my tongue.

"It would not be so gut for your Vater. He has grown to depend upon Carl. And the elders would ask for some explanation." She knew I'd understand that she didn't want to face the embarrassment Carl's departure would create. There would be questions if Carl moved back to High. Questions she'd find difficult to answer.

"Maybe he should tell them the truth. If Carl has had a change of heart and loves Karin, he should tell the elders he wants to marry her and return to High."

"What if he wants to marry Karin and remain here? Will you still come home?" My mother's knuckles faded to pure white as she locked her fingers in a tight grip.

"I don't know what will happen in Chicago, but I will return home before I make a final decision." My response wasn't exactly what my mother wanted, but it appeased her for the moment.

"We can't stop you from going with your brother, Johanna, but I hope you will speak to Carl before you leave for Chicago," Father said.

"There is nothing I want to say to him."

I saw the disappointment in my father's eyes. Normally that look would be enough to change my mind. Normally I would apologize. Normally I would acquiesce to his wishes. But not today, not this time.

The following evening brought a flutter of activity. While my parents and Wilhelm attended prayer service, Larissa and I stayed at home. I was certain Carl would be at prayer service, and that alone proved enough to keep me home. With Larissa's help, I packed for the journey. By the time we'd completed the task, enough cloth-ing remained in my drawers and wardrobe to assure my parents I would return.

Suddenly a knock sounded at the door. I glanced at the clock. It was time for prayer service to have ended. Surely Carl wouldn't come to the door and expect me to speak with him. I considered asking Larissa to answer, but the pounding became more insistent, so I flung open the door.

Berta doubled forward and panted for breath. "Please tell me it's a lie," she gasped.

I encircled her waist and led her into the parlor. "Sit down and catch your breath." I pulled her down beside me.

She inhaled, long and deep. "Tell me you're not going to Chi-cago." She paused long enough to gasp another breath of air. "Please tell me I misunderstood." She clung to my hand while she uttered the panic-filled plea.

"I won't be gone very long. Maybe three weeks."

She dropped against the back of the sofa. "You're planning to visit Chicago for that long?" When I nodded my head, she groaned. "If you stay three weeks, you'll never come back." She glared at Larissa. "You know I'm right."

Larissa shrunk at the accusation. "She's coming back. I don't know if she'll remain here for the rest of her life, but Johanna has promised her parents that she will return. I know she'll keep her word."

"First my father and now you. There is no one I can rely upon. And don't tell me I can depend on my mother. Now that my father is in Chicago for his training, she's home even less. And when she's home, she's withdrawn." Berta's angry words sliced through the air like a sharp knife.

I leaned toward Berta and pulled her into an embrace. "You have made great strides, Berta. It's not me you should rely upon—it's

God who will provide you the comfort you need. Unlike me, He will always be there."

She yanked free of my hold. "That's not the same, and you know it. God doesn't answer my questions or calm Sister Muhlbach. God doesn't walk to work with me each morning or teach me how to wash clothes."

"You're correct about the clothes washing—I don't believe God has an instruction manual for that. But He does answer prayers if you'll take time to talk to Him. And you must admit that Sister Muhlbach has been much kinder and more helpful to you of late. I believe God has softened her heart toward you." I squeezed her hand. "Of course, it has helped that your behavior has improved, and I hope that won't change while I'm gone. Promise me you'll do your very best."

Berta pinched her lips into a tight seam and glared at me.

"Please?"

She slowly wilted and gave a faint nod. "I promise to try, but you know it will be hard with you gone."

I leaned to the side and pulled her into an embrace. "Thank you, Berta. I know you'll make me proud."

The muffled sound of my parents' voices drifted through the open windows, and Berta jumped up from the sofa, her cheeks streaked with tears. "If you have time, I'd like to talk to you before you leave. I have a gift for you, and I want an address where I can write to you."

"I'll write it down and give it to you at breakfast tomorrow," Larissa said, her voice bubbling with enthusiasm. Obviously, she hoped the gesture would appease Berta and help to make amends.

"Thank you." Head hung low, Berta shuffled to the door. She turned to face me, her unfastened bonnet strings draped against her bodice. "I'll miss you, Johanna. More than you can ever imagine."

The pain and sadness in her face pierced my heart. "I'll be back, Berta. I promise you, I'll be back."

# CHAPTER 23

## Chicago, Illinois

The journey to Chicago was exciting, although my thoughts had traveled back to Amana with the frequency of the changing scenery. During the early portion of the trip I read some of the poems in the leather-bound book Berta had given me at breakfast. She'd wrapped it in brown paper and tied a twine bow in the center. When I'd tried to refuse it, she'd insisted and told me she had planned to use the gift as an enticement to get some of my *Godey's* periodicals. But since I was leaving, she wanted me to have it for the train ride. "You can't open it until you're on the train," she'd told me. I unwrapped the package only a short distance from Amana and was touched by her thoughtfulness, though I still wondered where she'd gotten it.

The poems proved a quiet diversion for a time, but soon the

rhythmic clack of the train's wheels began to sound like my mother's anguished pleas at the Homestead train station. *Promise you'll return. Promise you'll return. Please don't go. Please don't go.* Over and over the words thrummed with the rhythm of the chugging train. Larissa maintained a stream of conversation, but it wasn't enough to keep my thoughts from the painful good-bye with my parents or the meeting that lay ahead with Louisa. Finally the swaying motion lulled me into a restless sleep.

Larissa nudged my arm. "Look out the window. We're almost there. You're going to find Chicago magnificent. We're going to attend the theatre, go to concerts, visit friends, enjoy parties, and have a gay time. I've been planning our entertainment the whole way home. There are always lots of festivities going on, even though many of our friends are starting to leave the city for their summer homes."

With my nose pressed to the window glass, I was only half listening to her. Soon the prairie faded from sight and the train moved onto a causeway bordering the lake. Further along there were grand houses, followed by tall buildings, and grain elevators loomed larger than anything I could have imagined. The train chugged and jerked as we slowed and rumbled into the huge limestone depot. I continued to stare out the window until we lurched to a complete stop.

"Come along, Johanna." Wilhelm grinned down at me. "You'll have a much better view once you get off the train."

We stepped onto the platform as trains continued to enter the station on myriad tracks. I'd never heard so much noise in my life. The sound of hissing engines mixed with the shouts of conductors as passengers in their fancy dresses and silk hats hurried to board the trains. I wanted to wrap my arms around myself. I'd never witnessed so much turmoil. Larissa tugged on my arm.

"Come along. We'll go inside the station. Wilhelm will see to our baggage, and then we'll be on our way."

I permitted Larissa to pull me along while I cast my gaze toward the ceiling of the cavernous train depot. "I've never seen anything so huge."

She giggled. "This is nothing. Wait until you see the rest of the city."

Wilhelm took charge of our baggage, and soon we were in a carriage and on our way. The sounds of the city seemed as loud and hectic as the noise in the train station. Everywhere I looked there were drays, carriages, snorting horses, and people—so many people. The smells and sounds assaulted me on every side.

Larissa spoke of the fire that had leveled much of the city six years earlier and how the rebuilding continued. "Soon we'll be even bigger than New York City."

Wilhelm grinned. "I think it may be a few more years before that occurs."

If New York City was larger than the city that loomed around me on all sides, I would be rethinking any plans to visit. How did anyone learn to navigate through all these streets? You could walk all day and never see a familiar face. Chicago was a far cry from the boardwalks, dirt streets, and friendly greetings that abounded in Amana. How had Wilhelm ever become comfortable in this vast city?

I continued to peer out the window, but my thoughts drifted back to Louisa. Would she be pleased to see me? Wilhelm said she would be very pleased. Yet if that were true, why did he feel the need to speak with Louisa privately before we met? I told myself it was only common courtesy. Walking in unannounced would be rude. She might even faint. Over and over I told myself that, but thoughts that she might not want to meet me, that Wilhelm was giving her time to make an escape, or that she'd be aloof and unfriendly all niggled at the fringes of my mind. I thought it would be better to meet her this very day, before my fear and anger continued to build, but I wasn't in charge, so I would wait and try to remain patient.

When the carriage stopped in front of Wilhelm and Larissa's house on Calumet Avenue, I couldn't believe my eyes. I looked at my brother. "This is where you live?" I'd never before seen a home of such grandeur. The rooms I'd thought so beautiful in the Homestead Hotel must have seemed paltry to them.

Wilhelm dipped his head and gave a slight nod. "It's far more room than we need, but—"

"But I insisted. I love this house," Larissa said. "And you've grown to love it, too, haven't you, Wilhelm?"

My brother nodded, but I didn't miss the embarrassment that flashed in his eyes when he assisted me out of the carriage.

The interior of the house was as grand as the brick and stone exterior. Everyone in our neighborhood would fit inside this house—with room to spare. The sitting room alone was larger than all of the space we occupied in our Amana apartment, and the furnishings were beyond imagination. And when I was introduced to their hired workers, I knew I had entered another world. There was a man who met us at the door to take our wraps, a woman to help us get dressed and undressed as well as clean the upstairs rooms, another woman in charge of preparing the meals and cleaning the downstairs rooms—she had a girl to help—and a gardener to care for their flowers and yard. With all this help, I was curious about what Larissa did to occupy her time.

"Just wait until tomorrow. You'll see how busy I am," she said.

The following morning I shooed the maid and told her I wasn't accustomed to help with my clothing. I didn't want to seem ungrateful, but the mere thought of someone assisting me in and out of my simple attire caused discomfort. After donning my dark calico and cap, I hurried down the hallway. It had taken hours for me to finally fall asleep, and even then my sleep had been fraught with unpleasant images of a frightening confrontation with Louisa. I felt as though I'd had no rest at all. Possibly I could convince Wilhelm to change his mind. I would much prefer meeting with Louisa today or tomorrow. But it was Larissa who greeted me when I descended the steps.

"We'll have our breakfast and then we can plan our morning. I think several stops along State Street, then we'll have lunch and—"

"Is Wilhelm having breakfast with us?"

Her curls bobbed when she shook her head. "No. He left more than an hour ago. Work, work, work. He's not happy unless he can be at his desk by eight o'clock."

"And does he come home for his noonday meal? Maybe I could speak with him then."

"No, not often. It takes him away from his work for too long— at least that's what he says. I think it's because I'm usually busy with my activities or lunching with friends. I work with several charitable groups." She beamed at me as though I'd understand.

But her routine was foreign to me, and I couldn't understand why Wilhelm wouldn't eat his meals with his wife in this luxurious home where they paid someone to prepare their food. Larissa waved me toward the dining room, and I pushed aside any hope of speaking to Wilhelm. It wasn't until she once again mentioned going to State Street that I had another thought.

"Perhaps we could stop by and say hello to Wilhelm before we go shopping."

Larissa looked up from her plate of scrambled eggs and buttered bread. "There won't be time. I've planned a busy day. We're going to have great fun. Would you like to guess what we'll be doing this afternoon?"

"I can't even imagine. Tell me," I said, attempting to hide my disappointment over Wilhelm.

"There is an operetta at McVicker's Theatre this afternoon. It's a benefit for the Hahnemann Homeopathic Hospital—a special adaptation of *Little Red Riding Hood*. A perfect afternoon of entertainment and all for a wonderful cause. Isn't that grand?"

"Yes, it sounds exciting." I didn't add that I would have preferred a few minutes with Wilhelm. It was obvious Larissa was doing her best to provide me with an exciting visit, and I didn't want to appear ungrateful. "Does Louisa attend these events, as well?"

"She's involved in charity work, but you need not worry. We won't see her. I made certain Wilhelm knew the events we would attend, and he's going to advise Louisa of our plans."

"So he's already met with her?" My heart skipped a beat, and the smell of the breakfast sausages suddenly made my stomach lurch.

"He was going to stop on his way to work this morning. Louisa and her husband are early risers, and he wanted to give them as much time as possible to prepare for meeting with you."

Why did he think it was so important to give Louisa time? Hadn't she had twenty-one years to prepare to see me? If she hadn't managed to gain the fortitude to meet me before now, would two more days really matter? My anger mounted. Why wasn't Wilhelm concerned about the effects this waiting was having upon me? The longer I waited, the deeper my anxiety.

Larissa didn't give me much time to consider Wilhelm's decision. We were soon off for our morning of shopping at Field and Leiter. I gaped at the gas chandeliers, the frescoed ceilings, and the glass dome that permitted additional light to shine down on the variety of goods. We made an odd pair, she in her beautiful walking dress and me in my dark calico. We received more than a few stares as we wended our way among the counters of perfectly arranged gloves, jewelry, ties, ribbons, undergarments, hose, collars, and fabric of every imaginable color and weave. On one of the upper floors we saw rugs of all shapes and sizes, and there was little doubt this store employed more workers than all the residents of my Amana village. With all these choices, how could anyone ever decide what to purchase? Yet ladies in all their finery seemed to have little difficulty. One after another, they pointed to the items they desired and quickly moved on to the next counter.

"When we finish here, we can go to Stewart's Emporium. It isn't as fancy as this, but they have some fine choices, too."

But Larissa dallied at the counters far too long, and by the time we departed, she declared we'd save the trip to Stewart's until the next day. The decision pleased me. I didn't know if my senses could withstand another such emporium in one day.

Once outside the towering store, Larissa signaled for the carriage. "We'll have a leisurely lunch and then go directly to the theatre." She clutched my arm. "I'm so pleased you're here, Johanna. Isn't this fun?"

I agreed, but I didn't think it was something I would enjoy every day. Even now I couldn't fully enjoy myself. Although Wilhelm had notified Louisa of our whereabouts, I found myself looking at each woman we passed in the aisles of the store, wondering if we might see her.

Our lunch in the hotel restaurant was no less magnificent than the store where we'd shopped. But my discomfort increased as soon as we entered the restaurant. I was sorely out of place in my plain clothes and black cap. The man who'd taken Larissa's name assumed I was her maid and said I could wait in a room off to the side of the dining area. I don't know who was more embarrassed—the waiter, Larissa, or I.

"Tomorrow we'll purchase you a new dress," Larissa said as we departed the restaurant after our meal.

I didn't reply. There was no need for another dress. Mine was perfectly fine. Larissa gave the carriage driver instructions to deliver us to McVicker's Theatre on Madison Street. We arrived none too early. The sidewalk was already lined with ladies in their fine attire, small groups visiting as they waited their turn to enter the stone-arched brick building.

I stared at the decorative ironwork that adorned the second-floor windows, and while Larissa waved to several acquaintances, I examined the playbills enclosed in wood and glass cases outside the doors. Once we entered the foyer of the theatre, two of Larissa's friends approached. I didn't fail to see their censure as they eyed my clothing. Even after our introduction, these women were cold and aloof toward me. I considered the many visitors who passed through our villages dressed in fine clothing. We treated them with kindness and respect, even though they looked different from us. Society might consider these women well-mannered, but their actions spoke louder than words. I thought them far less gracious than the people in our villages.

When we finally took our seats, I studied the program while Larissa visited with a woman seated behind us. When the hand-painted stage curtains finally opened, I heaved a sigh of relief. Soon the orchestra sounded, and the stage was filled with young children dressed in bright fairy and bird costumes of every variety. They danced in circles, flapping their sparkle-bedecked wings until the queen of the fairies and the queen of the birds arrived on stage. While the queens danced, the smaller fairies and birds looked on in admiration. When the dance ended, the fairies departed the stage while the birds migrated toward the painted woodland scene.

As the orchestra began the next song, Red Riding Hood made her appearance to great applause. She sang several songs before a smaller curtain was pulled back to reveal the wolf in her grand-mother's bed. I laughed at the sight of the wolf wearing the huge sleeping cap. Those around me hissed when the wolf sang a gruff song about eating a good lunch and pointed his furry claw at Red Riding Hood. Some time later the queen of the fairies emerged to save Red Riding Hood, and the audience jumped to their feet, cheering. All thoughts of Louisa escaped my mind as I sat mes-merized. Not in all my life had I seen anything that compared to the show. It wasn't until the performance ended that my anxiety returned with a vengeance.

Larissa was apologetic when she explained we'd be dining at home two nights in a row. "Wilhelm thought you might not want to overdo your first few days. I told him he was being silly, but I finally agreed. I hope you aren't disappointed. I do wish I hadn't planned a dinner party for tomorrow evening, but the invitations went out long before our trip to Amana. Still, Wilhelm will make certain you have sufficient time to visit with Louisa before the other guests arrive."

"Wilhelm is right. I'm not accustomed to so much activity. I'd much prefer to remain at home this evening. I'll need to rest myself for tomorrow." I wasn't physically tired; I was accustomed to hard work. But the nagging fear and anxiety accompanied me like a heavy weight and exhausted me. And I, too, wished my first meeting with Louisa wouldn't be followed by a dinner party. Secretly I wondered if Wilhelm had planned it that way. Perhaps he thought the pending arrival of dinner guests would curtail any emotional outbursts when Louisa and I finally met.

After another day of shopping, visiting a museum, and walking through an enormous library filled with so many books I couldn't begin to count them, we returned home to prepare for dinner.

I'd seen so many things in the past two days, I didn't know how I would remember it all. Last night I had written notes to help me recall. Berta would want a full report. And I hoped Mother would be curious for details, as well.

Though I would have foregone all of the day's events for an earlier meeting with Louisa, Wilhelm had been clear. He wanted to be present when Louisa and I met for the first time. I climbed the steps to my room, my heartbeat picking up speed as the time of our meeting approached. Waves of nausea attacked as I slipped into my clean frock. The same style as the one I'd worn earlier in the day, but this one was dark blue with a smattering of white dots.

After combing my hair and fashioning it into a loose knot that rested at my neckline, I tucked my dark blue shawl into the band of my skirt and settled my cap on the back of my head. For a brief moment I considered yanking back the bedcovers and hiding beneath them. I chided myself for the silly thought and padded across the carpet.

My apprehension remained unchecked as I continued down-stairs. How would I act? What would I say? Did Louisa harbor ill feelings toward Mother and Father? How would her husband act toward me? And would I be able to withhold my anger? Both Larissa and Wilhelm had done their best to set my mind at ease, but I was stepping into uncharted waters, and even they couldn't be certain what would occur.

"You're positively pale," Larissa said when I met her in the parlor.

"I'm worried this won't go well."

"It will be fine," Larissa said as she pinched my cheeks. "You need some color." She appraised my dark calico. "I do wish you would have permitted me to purchase a new dress for you—or that you'd consider wearing one of mine. We're the same size, and

I'm certain I can find a dress in my wardrobe that's a color you wouldn't find objectionable."

"I don't find any of your dresses objectionable, Larissa, but I've already told you that I would be uncomfortable wearing anything other than my own clothing." Our gazes met in the beveled mirror that hung above the mantel, and I grinned. "And I promise I won't ask you to wear any of my dresses the next time you visit Amana."

Larissa touched a finger to her head. "Must you wear the cap?"

She sounded apologetic rather than aloof, and I silently guessed her concern was to protect me. Probably she feared the possible stares and whispers of the additional guests she'd invited to join us later in the evening would create an air of discomfort for me. "I don't suppose that I have to, but I would feel strange not wearing it. Do you mind too much?"

Larissa stepped forward and hugged me. "No, of course not. You look perfect."

I knew that wasn't true, but I didn't argue. I could hear guests arriving in the front foyer. "Do you think that's Tante Louisa?"

She nodded. "Yes. And her husband, Bertrand. Everyone calls him Bernie. The other guests aren't due to arrive until seven thirty."

"I believe I'll call him Mr. Williams until we're better acquainted." I thought it odd that Wilhelm and Larissa didn't refer to the man as *Onkel* Bernie, but I didn't inquire. At the moment my concerns ran much deeper. "Do you think he will join Tante Louisa and me while we become acquainted?"

"I'm certain he'll give the two of you privacy. I imagine he and Wilhelm will retire to the library and enjoy a cigar while they chat about the wonders of Chicago."

Her answer dispelled a portion of my concern, but not all. I stepped near the entrance to the parlor and peeked into the foyer. The woman didn't appear near old enough to be my mother. "She's beautiful," I whispered.

"You're quite pretty, as well, Johanna. It's the clothing. If you'd wear styles that fit your figure in shades that lend color to your complexion and permit my maid to fashion your hair, you'd put the rest of us to shame."

I shook my head. Larissa and her guests would have to settle for my simple clothes and plain hairstyle, for I wasn't eager for her suggested transformation. Larissa tugged me forward, and the couple turned in our direction as Wilhelm bounded down the stairs. A smile transformed Louisa's stately countenance, and she gestured for us to hurry.

Before Wilhelm could introduce us, Louisa pulled me into a warm embrace. "It is wonderful to finally meet you, Johanna. I am your Tante Louisa." Holding my upper arms, she leaned back a few inches and stared into my eyes. "I would know you anywhere. You have my hair and eyes."

While it was true we both possessed blue eyes, hers were as dark as indigo, while mine were as pale as a summer sky. And her hair was far lighter than my own. Mine had been as white as corn silk during my childhood, but the flaxen color had given way to streaks of light brown and little of the blond remained.

Once again she wrapped her arms around me. "I'm so glad you finally know the truth."

I took a backward step. "I suppose time will tell if it was a good decision. It has proved quite difficult for Mutter and Vater, not to mention my own feelings."

She winced at my words but forced a smile as I looked up at her husband. He was quite tall, with strands of gray interspersed in his thick dark hair. He was quite dignified appearing, and I guessed him to be considerably older than Louisa. Then again, I wasn't particularly good at estimating age. Perhaps it was the gray hair that created the illusion of age.

Louisa touched her husband's arm. "I'd like you to meet my husband, Bertrand."

He flashed a bright smile. "I'm pleased to meet you, Johanna."

"My pleasure, Mr. Williams."

"No, no," he said, shaking his head. "Please don't address me as Mr. Williams. I feel far too ancient as it is. Everyone calls me Bernie. You must do the same."

"I couldn't, Mr. Williams."

"Then how about Uncle Bernie. Is that better?" He chuckled and handed his hat to the maid.

Neither Bernie nor Uncle Bernie would be easy for me, but everyone remained silent as if awaiting my response. "Yes. That will do." I could only hope I wouldn't have to address him by name, for I'd surely stumble.

"I'll leave you ladies to your visiting and join Wilhelm in the library. Louisa tells me Larissa has planned some time for the two of you to visit by yourselves." He patted Louisa's hand. "I look forward to rejoining you ladies at supper."

As he strode down the hall, Larissa waved us toward the sitting room. "You two go in and become acquainted. I'm going to see about the meal preparations. The other guests won't arrive until seven thirty, so you have more than two hours."

Once we'd entered the sitting room, Larissa closed the pocket doors. I could hear the click of her shoes on the tile floor as Louisa and I sat down opposite each other. "I know this is difficult, Johanna. Wilhelm tells me he has explained the agreement I made with Emilie and Frank. I hope you understand it was a very difficult decision for me. I wanted to be certain you'd have a good home with parents who would love you." She leaned forward, and I could see the beseeching look in her eyes, begging me to believe.

"I don't doubt it was hard, but what I don't understand is why the three of you decided I shouldn't be told. How unfair it was that I should hear such news from Wilhelm's wife. Larissa knew about my birth, but I didn't." My voice escalated, and I caught my lower lip between my teeth to hold my anger in check.

She held up her hand. "I understand what you're saying, and you're correct. It was grossly unfair. Nobody ever intended for you to find out this way."

I gripped the arms of the chair. "Nobody ever intended I find out at all. That's the truth, isn't it? You all planned to keep your secret hidden. After all, why should I, of all people, know anything about this?" She reached to touch my hand, but I yanked away. None of them grasped the depth of my pain.

"I'm sure you feel as though your entire world has crumbled and your life has been sustained by nothing more than a pack of lies." She folded her hands in her lap. "I thought having this extra time before we met would give you an opportunity to consider our decisions and accept that they were made out of love and concern rather than with any intent to hurt you. Our hope was to give you the best life possible. You have been dearly loved by Emilie and Frank. And I've held you in my heart for all these years, too."

Words, nothing but words. It was easy for her to sit there and say she'd held me in her heart while she went on about her life as though I didn't exist. "That may be true, but even if my parents objected, you should have come to visit. You're family. No one would have suspected anything if you'd come to see us, least of all me."

She leaned back in the chair. "Your father and mother refused my request to visit, and I had given them my word, Johanna. If I broke my word to your parents, could I expect them to keep theirs? They feared I would return when I was financially able to care for you and that I'd take you away from them. To be honest, the thought crossed my mind on several occasions, but they had come to my aid when I was in need—when both of us were in need. It would have been the wrong thing to do."

I could agree that she shouldn't break her word, but it didn't change the pain in my heart. I should have been told. "You may be correct, but they could have at least told me."

"I did tell them I wouldn't object if they one day decided to tell you the truth, but I knew they wouldn't. As time passes, telling family secrets becomes more and more difficult." Tears rimmed her eyes. "There would have been no right time to tell you, Johanna. At a young age you wouldn't have comprehended the situation, and as you became older, your resentment and anger would be exactly what it is at this moment. I know what you feel. It's called betrayal—I've experienced it myself."

I tightened my jaw. She had no idea how I felt. "How were you betrayed? Your mother didn't abandon you."

She flinched. "No, I wasn't abandoned as an infant, but I was abandoned by your birth father. He said he loved me and wanted to marry me, but the moment he discovered I was going to have a baby, he fled in the dark of the night. I've never seen or heard from him since." She bowed her head. A single teardrop escaped her eye and left a dark circle on the skirt of her yellow silk dress. She continued to stare at her clasped hands. "I've never felt as alone in my life as that day when I left Amana and went to live in Iowa City. I thought I would die." She lifted her head. "As you can see, I didn't die. But the scars remain."

"It seems you moved on and have recovered quite well." Pain shone in her eyes, and my conscience screamed to forgive, but I ignored the silent advice. I wanted to hurt her as deeply as I'd been hurt.

"You're right. In time I did move on. Bernie and I married a number of years later, after I had moved to Chicago. We met while I was working in a dress shop his mother frequented. For some reason she took a liking to me and introduced us. You've probably guessed that he is somewhat older than I, but we have been very happy." Her brows pulled into a sad frown. "Except that we had desperately hoped to have children, and that never happened."

"What did he think when you told him about me?" I waited for her to say that she hadn't told him until after they were married.

With a wistful smile she touched the rings on her left hand. "Bernie invited me to attend an afternoon concert. Afterward, as we walked through the park, I told him about you. I never hid your existence from him. It didn't change his feelings for me. Later, when he asked me to marry him, he wanted to bring you to Chicago to live with us. I explained his suggestion was impossible."

I couldn't imagine having grown up living in such surroundings, and having Louisa and Mr. Williams as my parents. The thought gave me pause. To leave Amana as a young child and move to Chicago would have terrified me. Perhaps the decision they'd made hadn't been so terrible.

"I can't change the past, Johanna." She edged forward on her chair and met my gaze. "I can tell you of my grief, but that's the most I can do. My scars are not visible for you to see. I had choices to make for your future and for my own, and I made them. Now you are a woman, and you have choices to make. You can remain angry and bitter, or you can accept that the decisions we made were the best we could do at the time. Ultimately, the choice is yours."

Louisa was right. Only I could decide how I would live the rest of my life. Over the past days, I had developed a deep yearning that couldn't be satiated. Nothing had filled the aching hollow beneath my heart. And I realized nothing would until I put aside my bitterness and anger. In time, and with God's help, forgiveness and love could fill the void, yet I didn't know how we would all begin.

As if she'd read my thoughts, Louisa patted my hand. "Maybe now Bernie and I can come and visit. I would like for him to meet Emilie and Frank. It has been far too long since I've seen my sister."

I didn't know if my mother would welcome Bernie or Louisa, though I hoped she would relent. "Maybe we could pray about it each day and see where God leads."

Louisa opened her fan and nodded. "I would be pleased to join you in praying about such a plan. I know Emilie is frightened she will lose you, and I understand her fear, but I want her to know that it isn't my intent to steal you away from her. All I want is to be a small part of your life—as your Tante Louisa, not your Mutter."

Relief swelled in my heart. Maybe if Mother realized that Louisa didn't want me to come and live in Chicago, that she only wanted to visit from time to time and exchange occasional letters, perhaps she would set aside her fears. "Maybe if you wrote her a letter, I could take it back with me. That might help."

Dust motes danced across the carpet as the late afternoon sun cast shards of light through the parlor window. "That's an excellent idea, Johanna." She waved the glossy hand-painted fan in front of her face. "This room is far too warm. Let's open some windows." Without waiting for my response, she strode across the room, pushed aside the lace curtains, and lifted one of the windows. "You open one on the other side, and we'll get a cross breeze." She grinned. "At least I hope we will." After she'd once again settled in her chair, she said, "Now tell me about your life. I want to hear everything—especially what made you decide to accept Wilhelm and Larissa's invitation to come for a visit."

I gulped. How did one go about relating her entire life? I would bore her to death. At least she understood life in Amana so I wouldn't need to explain all of those details. I decided a brief overview would be best. When I finished, she appeared relieved and satisfied.

"It sounds much like the life I had as a young girl—except I had to deal with the death of my parents. But Frank and Emilie were good to me, and I enjoyed my years with Wilhelm and little Pieter. He was so young when I left, but such a sweet boy. I doubt you remember him at all."

I shook my head. "I was only two when he died, but I know he and Wilhelm were very close. Vater still talks about what good friends they were—not like lots of boys who fight with their brothers. He told me Wilhelm always protected Pieter, from the time he was a baby."

Once again her eyes clouded. "I'm sure that's why Wilhelm left Amana. He couldn't live with the guilt." She placed her fan on the side table. "Guilt is such a terrible thing—it destroys us from the inside out. Bernie's mother was the one who helped me realize I needed to ask for God's forgiveness and relieve myself of the guilt I'd lived with since the day you were born. Once I was able to do that, my past was easier to bear."

I was trying to follow the conversation but wasn't having much success. What guilt had caused Wilhelm to leave Amana? Was it due to the secret about me? I was doubtful he'd be moved to such extreme measures when he'd played no part in the decision.

"I've tried to convince Wilhelm that prayer is the answer, but he isn't convinced. Instead, he tried to ease his guilt about Pieter by leaving Amana. Unfortunately, he replaced one guilt with another. Now he struggles because he feels he deserted the rest of the family."

I tried to digest what Louisa had said, but her explanation made no sense. "Pieter? Why would Wilhelm feel any guilt about Pieter?"

Louisa's brow pinched together. "You don't know how Pieter died?"

"Yes, of course. He drowned when he fell through the ice while skating, but Wilhelm wasn't responsible."

Louisa sighed. "The day Pieter died, your father and some of the other men had gone to the river early in the morning to cut ice. The river wasn't completely frozen in the areas farther from the bank. After school, Pieter told Wilhelm he was going to go ice-skating and asked Wilhelm to tell your mother and father. Wilhelm did as Pieter requested, but your father sent him after Pieter to warn him not to go on the river. On the way, several of Wilhelm's friends called to him, and he stopped to talk with them for a few minutes. By the time Wilhelm arrived at the river, Pieter had fallen through the ice and drowned." Louisa's voice faltered. "He raced for help, but it was too late."

"But he can't blame himself—"

"When your father asked if he'd gone and warned Pieter, Wilhelm said that he'd gone directly to the river, but Pieter had ignored him. So you see, it's not only the fact that Wilhelm believes he could have saved Wilhelm but also the lie he has lived with all these years that drove him away from Amana and your parents. Each time he goes home, he relives that incident, and a deeper wedge is driven between him and your parents and the life he'd enjoyed for all those years.

I sat back, stunned at the revelation. Yet another secret from the past had reared its ugly head—a secret that should have been exposed many years ago. How could forgiveness and healing ever come to pass in the midst of lies and deceit? My heart ached for Wilhelm, and it ached for my parents, as well. All these years they had somehow blamed themselves for Wilhelm's departure, always wondering what they had done and why they'd lost both of their sons.

"How very sad." Though I did my best, I couldn't summon anything more to say. I longed to embrace Wilhelm and tell him our parents would forgive him if he'd simply ask—that *God* would forgive him if he'd simply ask. Why had he chosen all these years of pain rather than telling the truth?

"Yet he told you," I said.

She nodded. "I was safe. I had secrets of my own. Besides, he knew I'd never return to Amana and tell your parents. And you must not tell them, either, Johanna. This is Wilhelm's heartache. He is the one who must decide how it will be resolved."

I knew she was correct, but I wondered if I would be as good at keeping secrets as the rest of my family. I would do my best to keep Wilhelm's confidence, yet I didn't believe we should continue this legacy of deceit.

# CHAPTER 24

Amana Colonies, Iowa
Berta Schumacher

Johanna had been gone only three days, yet it seemed much longer because I'd already suffered loneliness while her brother and his wife were here visiting. Sister Muhlbach permitted me time for a brief visit with Johanna before she left town, but it wasn't long enough to say all the things that were on my heart. And I'd never been able to question her about Karin's visit, which annoyed me in the extreme—especially since Rudolf came bearing tales of Carl's broken heart the day after Johanna departed.

I'd tried to question Sister Ilg, but she sealed her lips at the mere mention of Johanna's name. There was little doubt she was keeping a secret, but I couldn't convince her to talk to me. Rudolf promised to question Carl about Karin's visit, but with less help in the Küche, my time with Rudolf was limited. When he delivered the milk earlier in the morning, he whispered to meet him near the dairy barn on my way to the garden this afternoon. I hoped he could shed some light on what had happened.

No doubt I'd need to be mindful of my time away from the Küche. If Sister Muhlbach had her way, there wouldn't be time for any visiting or a stop at the store. Three new families, a total of fourteen additional mouths to feed, had been assigned to our kitchen over the past few days, and the demand was taking its toll on all of us.

Sister Muhlbach banged a metal serving spoon against one of the soup pots. "You're daydreaming again, Berta. Put those potatoes on to cook, or we won't have food to serve when the bell rings!"

There was no denying both Sister Muhlbach and I had resorted to our old ways. She shouted and nagged, and I was sullen and lazy. Guilt nagged from time to time. I had promised Johanna I'd do my best, but I no longer wanted to please Sister Muhlbach or hear her kind words. Instead, I wanted to be released from the daily drudgery inside the kitchen. I longed for some sort of normalcy, though I no longer could define what that might be. More than anything, I wanted my father and Johanna to return.

Each day as I delivered the midafternoon repast to the garden workers, I stopped at the general store to see if a letter had arrived from my father. Each day I was disappointed. To make matters worse, my mother provided little solace. Father's absence didn't appear to bother her in the least.

"Did you hear me, Berta?" Once again Sister Muhlbach's voice interrupted my thoughts. I glared into the pan of potatoes. Instead of hollering across the kitchen, she could have looked at the stove and seen that I'd followed her order.

Heat from the stove spiraled upward, and perspiration beaded across my forehead. "I don't have the power to make the water boil any faster."

Using a long-handled spoon, Sister Muhlbach pointed in my direction. "You need to tame that tongue of yours, Berta."

I grabbed the basket of lettuce, carried it to the dry sink, and dumped the contents into a bucket of water. Before I could begin to wash the leaves, Sister Muhlbach stomped to my side.

"Now look what you've done. You poured all the dirt from the basket into the clean water." Cupping her hands together, she scooped the dripping lettuce out of the bucket. "Empty this dirty water and refill the bucket. And be quick about it."

Bucket in hand, I walked into the backyard and heaved the dirty water toward the shed.

"Hey! Watch where you're throwing that water."

I took a backward step as a man I'd never before seen stepped forward. The legs of his britches were wet from the knees downward.

"I'm s-s-sorry," I stammered. "What are you doing back there?" I guessed he must be one of the hobos who passed through town looking for occasional work and a free meal. Either that or he'd recently been hired as summer help and no one had bothered to tell me.

"Got hired this morning. Sister Muhlbach set me to work cleaning the chicken coop."

"From the outside in?"

He laughed. "I was sitting out here resting for a while." Using his thumb, he gestured over his shoulder toward the chicken coop. "How long's it been since that coop was cleaned?"

"Not so long that you'd need to rest before you got the job done. You better not let Sister Muhlbach catch you sitting around or you won't be working here for long." The warning didn't seem to bother him much, because he didn't move an inch. "What's your name?"

"Henry. Henry Barton." He pushed his floppy-brimmed hat

back on his head. "I been working around here for three or four summers now—then I head south for the winter. Don't much like the cold weather. Last summer I worked at the dairy barn over in South. Nice folks over there. They didn't throw water at me."

"If they were so nice, how come you didn't go back there this summer?"

"Figured there might be something different to see here. Don't like to stay in the same place twice unless I have to." He grinned. "And if I would have stayed in South, I never would have met you."

I squared my shoulders. "You still haven't met me, Mr. Barton."

"Berta! Where's that water?" Sister Muhlbach's question echoed from the kitchen door.

"Coming," I shouted in return.

In five long strides Mr. Barton was at the pump. "You hold the bucket, and I'll have it full for ya in no time."

Once the bucket was full, I lifted it by the handle. "Thank you for your help."

"You're welcome. Nice to meet you, Sister Berta." He tipped his hat and chuckled.

His laughter was a welcome sound to my ears. I hadn't heard the pleasing sound for far too long. I suppressed the grin that twitched in my cheek and hurried back inside. I lifted the sloshing bucket of water into the sink. While I cleaned the lettuce, I decided Mr. Barton might provide a welcome change to my tiresome daily schedule. His presence had already improved my spirits.

During the kitchen cleaning that followed the noonday meal, I remained focused on my work. I didn't want my delivery job assigned to someone else. I scoured the pots and pans, and when all the utensils had been dried, I hung them from their assigned hooks along the wall. I didn't even complain when Sister Muhlbach told me I'd be scrubbing the cheese rounds.

"If you don't daydream, you'll have time to complete the task before you go to the garden. I'll send two of the young girls to help." She ordered me to the cellar to begin lugging the crocks upstairs. "If you don't get done, Sister Dickel can make the garden delivery."

Everyone disliked scrubbing the rounds of hand cheese, and it seemed I'd been assigned the smelly job more often than not. This batch of cheese had been made before I arrived in Amana, but Johanna had explained the procedure to me. I was glad I had missed the process, but I'd soon decided scrubbing the rounds was as bad as pressing milk curds through a sieve, adding salt, and kneading the mixture until it reached the proper consistency.

The cheese rounds were flattened and set to dry before being packed in crocks that were stored in the cellar, where they remained until mold formed. After that first mold had been scraped from the cheese, the crocks were returned to the cellar. Only when the second batch of mold appeared did I learn of the washing process.

Johanna had taught me how to scrub the rounds with a stiff brush, a time-consuming and smelly process that had to be repeated once or twice a week until Sister Muhlbach declared the cheese rind had attained the proper golden color. Only she could decide when the cheese had properly aged. And obviously it hadn't turned the proper shade just yet. I hoped the cheese would soon attain the proper glow, for I quickly tired of this job.

"Have the new man fill the tub. His name is Mr. Barton," Sister Muhlbach called after me as I walked outside.

Mr. Barton apparently heard her, as well, for he loped across the yard and doffed his hat in greeting. "Need some help filling that tub, I hear."

"Yes, thank you. How's your work in the chicken coop coming along? Done yet?"

He should have completed the job long before we'd served the noonday meal, but most of the hired men didn't exert themselves too much. Still, at times such as this, their strong arms and backs were appreciated.

With a crooked grin he grasped the pump handle. "I'll have it done by this evening, for sure. Don't wanna disturb the chickens too much, or they'll quit laying."

I laughed as water splattered into the tub. "I don't know if Sister Muhlbach will accept that excuse, but it's a good one. Once you finish you can set that tub over on the table." It wasn't a table in the true sense of the word, but a heavy wood board had been bolted onto sawhorses, and it served the purpose. The heavy cheese crocks were placed at one end to balance the washtub at the other.

Mr. Barton disappeared once he'd lifted the tub into place. I didn't blame him. The smell of the chicken coop would be preferable to the odor of this reeking cheese.

"I wish I could plug my nose while we do this," one of the girls said.

"We could try one of the clothes pegs, but I think it would hurt," the other one replied.

"Breathe through your mouth instead of your nose. That's the only thing that helps me. The faster we work, the sooner we can get away from the smell."

I kept the two girls working at a steady pace until they had to return and help with summer sessions at the school. We'd finished all but two crocks when they left me on my own. If I fell behind, Sister Dickel would be on her way to the garden instead of me, and I wasn't going to let that happen. My hands were rough and red by the time I'd finished all but the final crock. One look at the position of the sun and I knew I had to make a decision. There wasn't time to scrub the cheese rounds in the final crock.

"Mr. Barton! Could you come and help me?"

The hired man poked his head from inside the chicken coop. "You call me?"

"Yes. Could you empty the water and carry these crocks to the cellar for me?"

He sauntered to the worktable and surveyed the area. "What about that one down there?" He pointed to the final crock at the end of the table. "You gonna wash those?"

"They're already done," I said.

He furrowed his brows, and I knew he didn't believe me. "If you say so. Any special place you want me to put 'em in the cellar?"

I quickly explained where they should go and asked him to dump the wash water and to store the table in the shed. I thanked him and turned on my heel.

"You sure you washed the rounds in that last crock? Don't look like it's moved an inch since you brought it up here."

His insistent questions annoyed me. I stomped over to the crock and moved it several inches. "There! Does that make you feel better?"

He doffed his hat and dropped it atop the table. "Ain't me you need to make feel better. You're the one who said Sister Muhlbach didn't accept excuses. Just trying to look out for ya."

"Just carry the crocks to the cellar, Mr. Barton. I'll worry about Sister Muhlbach."

He scratched his head and slapped the felt hat back on his head. "Whatever you say."

There wasn't time for an argument. I hurried inside. "I'm done. Should I pack the basket?"

Sister Muhlbach shook her head, and for a moment I thought she was going to tell me Sister Dickel had already gone to the garden. Instead, she motioned toward the far table. "I've already packed it. You can go now." I retrieved the basket and was at the door when she said, "Don't waste any time. There's much work that needs to be finished before supper."

I didn't reply. If I'd said what I was thinking, I'd be in trouble for weeks. However, I didn't plan on hurrying. I'd worked hard all day. Besides, it had been far too long since I'd visited with Rudolf. Now that I was getting out of the kitchen, I had no plans to rush my visit.

I hummed a tune as I strode toward the garden, glad for freedom from my boring chores. To my great pleasure, Sister Nusser was out in the garden with the other workers when I arrived. I placed the basket inside the shed on a worktable and turned to leave. I heard Sister Nusser call to me, but the wide brim of my sunbonnet blocked her from view. Keeping my head bowed low, I continued to walk away from the garden. I didn't have time for Sister Nusser and her nosy questions—not today.

Once I was out of earshot, I slowed my pace and cut around to the far side of the dairy barn, where I caught sight of Rudolf. He was slouched against the siding with his arms folded across his chest. When he saw me approach, he pushed away and straightened his shoulders.

I peeked around the doorway. "Is anyone in there?"

"We're alone, but it's probably better if we stay out here so we can hear anyone coming this way." He pointed toward an old wagon that was sitting in the shade of the barn. "Want to sit over there?"

I nodded and followed him, surprised when he turned and lifted me onto the back of the wagon. He hoisted himself up beside me and grinned. "You haven't been yourself lately. I've been worried about you." He touched my cheek with his finger. "I miss seeing you smile."

"There hasn't been much to smile about." It didn't take much prodding for me to sing my tale of woe. I ended the sad story with the cheese-scrubbing incident from only a short while ago. "I can't get along with Sister Muhlbach. One day she's nice, and the next day she's mad as a wet hen."

"I can just see her flying around that kitchen." He made a clucking noise and flapped his arms up and down until I laughed at his silly gyrations. "That's better. I finally hear some laughter."

"If only Johanna would come back," I lamented.

"You sound just like Carl. That's all I hear from him, too. It's not even a week since she left. Let her enjoy her time in Chicago. She'll be back." The odors from the barn carried on the breeze, and he grinned when I wrinkled my nose. "Don't like the smell, do you?"

"It doesn't smell as bad as the *Handkäse* I had to scrub earlier today." I scooted a little closer. "I want to know what happened between Johanna and Carl before she left. What has he told you?"

"It wasn't gut." He wasted no time in telling me that Johanna had walked in and caught Karin and Carl in an embrace.

I slapped my hand across my lips, unable to believe Carl would do such a thing. "I thought he truly cared for Johanna."

"It wasn't what it looked like. Carl and Karin have been dear friends since they were small children. Karin confided that her mother has developed problems with her mind." Rudolf touched his index finger to his head. "She's become confused, and part of the time she doesn't even know Karin. As she was explaining her mother's condition, Karin began to cry. Carl was just trying to comfort her."

I curled my lip. "He should have comforted her from a distance. Then he wouldn't be in such a pickle."

"Johanna should have permitted him an opportunity to explain; then there wouldn't be all this misunderstanding." He cupped my chin and gently turned my head. "You would have given me a chance to explain, wouldn't you?"

"I would have kicked you in the shins. Then, maybe, I would have given you a chance to state your case. We're different from

Johanna and Carl—we're good friends. But Carl had stated his intent to court Johanna. And Carl and Karin had been much more than childhood friends; they had talked of marriage. To discover them locked in an embrace would be dreadful. I can only imagine Johanna's humiliation."

Rudolf sighed. "Only Karin talked of marriage—not Carl. Besides, I told you it wasn't like that."

"You don't have to convince me. It's Johanna that needs to be swayed. And he better not wait too long, or she'll decide to remain in Chicago."

What a shambles Carl had created. Why hadn't he beaten on the Ilgs' apartment door until Johanna let him come in and explain? If he'd been persistent, maybe Johanna wouldn't have gone to Chicago.

"Carl wrote a letter and explained. Now he must wait to see if she'll believe him. Sister Ilg gave him Wilhelm's address," Rudolf said.

I was no expert on matters of the heart, but I thought it would take more than a written explanation to convince Johanna. "Promise you'll tell me if Carl receives a letter, and I'll tell you if she writes to me and mentions him."

"Agreed."

"I'd like to stay and talk, but I want to stop by the store to see if there's any mail from my father. I've already been gone longer than usual, and Sister Muhlbach won't be happy."

Rudolf jumped from the wagon bed and assisted me down. "I'll let you know the next time I'll be here in the afternoon so we can meet and talk some more." He grinned. "Unless you want to meet me out in the backyard again."

I shook my head. "My mother isn't sleeping well, and she paces the parlor half the night. She'd catch me, for sure. Besides, it's too hard for me to get up and go to work if I'm up during the night."

"That's because you've become an old woman."

I gave him a lighthearted slap on the arm. "If so, it's because I'm required to work hard and put in longer hours than the hired help."

He chuckled and gestured toward the dairy barn. "After you've tried working in there, I'll be happy to listen to your complaints about kitchen duties."

"I'll pass on that offer," I said and skipped off toward the general store with guarded hope that I'd find a letter from my father.

# CHAPTER 25

My life hadn't been going well of late. At least not according to Sister Muhlbach. I'd taken far too long returning from the garden the past two days. She had threatened to speak with the elders if my unruly behavior continued. It wasn't her threat that gave me pause but a remembrance of my promise to Johanna. Last evening at prayer service I asked God to forgive me. Not for anything I'd done, but for breaking my promise to my friend. Truth be told, I'd been confused about how to pray.

I hadn't promised God I'd try to do better; I'd promised Johanna. Yet God was the one who offered ultimate forgiveness. This whole prayer and forgiveness thing could be quite confusing. Finally I'd silently told God I was sorry I hadn't kept my word to Johanna. And I was sorry. I just wasn't certain I could do better.

With each passing day, I resolved to do better. I truly wanted to keep my word, but determination took flight when boredom or loneliness set in. Johanna would be disappointed when she discovered my lack of success. God already knew my misdeeds, and He was probably disappointed, too.

From my vantage point at the window above the kitchen sink, I could see Sister Dickel and Sister Muhlbach in the backyard. They were deep in conversation and looked in my direction. I held my breath and waited. I knew I would soon be required to join them.

"Berta!" The older sister shouted so loud the chickens squawked and raced around the yard as if they feared they might be chosen for the stewpot. With halting steps I exited the Küche. Sister Muhlbach glowered and waved me forward. "Come down here. Now!"

My heart thumped into a quickstep as I joined the two women in the yard. There was no doubt my offense had been discovered. They exchanged a look, but it was Sister Muhlbach who bent forward, reached into one of the crocks, and lifted a cheese round. She thrust the moldy round forward and held it beneath my nose. One whiff of the cheese and I turned my head, opened my mouth, and gulped a breath of fresh air. I stared at Sister Muhlbach and waited. I'd had enough confrontations in my early years to learn the worst thing one could do was to blurt out an apology or confess to a transgression.

Sister Muhlbach shoved the round a little closer. "Do you have anything to say for yourself, Berta?"

I shook my head.

She heaved a disgusted sigh and removed another round from one of the crocks. "Do you notice a difference between these two rounds of cheese?"

"Maybe a little," I said, determined to remain noncommittal.

She turned and plunked the cheese on the table with a thud. At that exact moment Mr. Barton appeared from inside the shed. Sister Muhlbach jolted to attention. "Come over here, Mr. Barton."

Shoulders slouched, the handyman shuffled across the yard. I did my best to capture his attention, but he wouldn't look my way. I could only hope he'd protect me.

Sister Muhlbach pointed to the two rounds of cheese she'd placed on the table. "Do you see any difference in these two pieces of cheese?"

" 'Course I do," he muttered.

"And what would that be, Mr. Barton?"

He tapped one of the rounds. "That one's got more mold on it."

"Thank you, Mr. Barton. You may go and finish your chores." Sister Muhlbach straightened her shoulders and rested her fists on her ample hips. "Well, Berta? Do you admit that you didn't scrub the rounds in that crock?"

"It would appear that I didn't." All thought of trying to do better fled from my mind as I attempted to contrive an answer. And then it came to me. "I see that there are six crocks of cheese. I must have missed one when I carried them upstairs. I thought there were only five."

"Don't compound your bad behavior with a lie, Berta. You are only making matters worse." She waved Sister Dickel toward the back porch. "Go inside. I want to speak to Berta alone."

"I don't care if she stays out here. I'm not changing my story," I said.

Sister Muhlbach ignored my remark, but Sister Dickel slowed her departure, obviously eager to hear the rest of our conversation. "Go on, Sister Ursula. You can finish washing the dishes," the older woman said.

Once we were alone, Sister Muhlbach urged me to tell the truth, but I held fast to my lie. She gazed heavenward and shook her head. "I'm going to go speak with Mr. Barton and ask him how many of these crocks he carried to the cellar for you the other day." She turned on her heel and huffed across the yard. I hoped Mr. Barton wouldn't remember, or that he would be willing to tell a small untruth to protect me. When I saw the self-satisfied look on Sister Muhlbach's face as she marched toward me, my hopes faltered.

Though my insides churned, I did my best to appear confident. "Shall I go back to my dishwashing?" I longed to escape the angry diatribe that was sure to come my way.

"No, you shall not! You stay right where you are." She planted her feet firmly in the soft grass and looked me directly in the eye. "Mr. Barton tells me he carried *six* crocks to the cellar."

"Does he? Then he must be mistaken, for there were only five. I don't think his memory is very good." I leaned a bit closer. "He drinks while he's supposed to be working."

"I can see that you're unwilling to confess the truth, so you leave me no choice. I'll be forced to speak to the elders about your recent behavior."

"Do what you must." I truly didn't care if she talked to my mother, the Bruderrat, or even the Grossebruderrat. No punishment they would mete out could compare to my loneliness and concern for Johanna and my father. Johanna said God would bring me comfort, but that hadn't occurred.

Apparently Sister Muhlbach considered my remark a sign of defiance rather than one of resignation, for she stomped up the back stairs with me following slowly. She untied her apron, shouting that she would return in short order, before continuing through the dining room and departing. When the front door closed the women turned to look at me, alarm evident in their eyes. It was obvious they would be mortified to be in my situation. But then, none of them ever broke the rules.

After the women returned to their work, I marched outside to locate Mr. Barton, who had disappeared from sight after his betrayal. Hoping to catch him by surprise, I circled to the side of the chicken coop and peeked inside. He wasn't there. I glanced at the tool shed, then dashed across the expanse and yanked open the door.

"Taking a nap, are you, traitor?" I spat the words into the shed as my eyes adjusted to the darkness. Shuffling sounds were enough to confirm the handyman was hiding here.

"Why you callin' me a traitor? Didn't I warn you about that cheese?"

Plunking one fist on my hip, I leaned forward and pointed my other finger under his nose. "You have no loyalty, Mr. Barton. I would have come to your defense, but you can be certain I won't help you in the future."

"I'm as loyal as they come, Berta, but you shouldn't expect me to defend you when the lie you're telling is as plain as the nose on your face. I never promised to keep your secret. Sister Muhlbach woulda sent me packing without a second thought. And I need this job."

"I didn't realize hobos held their jobs in such high esteem."

He chuckled. "You shouldn't lump us all together. I work all summer and make enough money to enjoy winters down south. When my money runs low, I know it's time to head north. I might not be your typical hobo, but you're not a typical Amana sister, either."

That much was true. I couldn't be easily lumped together with the other women in the village. And I hadn't asked him to lie for me. Still, any fool would know that's what I'd expected. Only the future would tell if Mr. Barton could be trusted.

Upon her return, Sister Muhlbach took me aside and explained she would meet with the Bruderrat on Saturday morning. "You are welcome to come along and state your case. In fact, I would suggest that you do so. It's always best for the elders to hear both sides of any controversy."

"No thank you. You can tell them whatever you want, and they can make their decision based upon your report. I have nothing to say."

I'd arrived at my decision without hesitation. If I attended the meeting, I'd need to confess that I'd been lying. Or I'd have to tell additional lies to support my earlier fabrications. I knew the elders would believe Sister Muhlbach, for she'd be the one speaking the truth. I did wonder if Mr. Barton would be called upon to repeat his story. Probably not. They wouldn't need a hobo to confirm my misdeeds. Besides, it mattered little what the elders said. Their punishment wouldn't change my behavior.

I was surprised when Sister Muhlbach ordered me to deliver the afternoon repast to the garden. She knew I enjoyed the task, and I'd expected her to permanently assign the deliveries to Sister Dickel. "I'd tell you to hurry back, but I'm certain you'll do as you please." She shrugged and shook her head, obviously resigned to the fact that nothing would change until I'd been properly punished.

Basket in hand, I hurried out the door before she could change her mind. On the way I decided she'd sent me because I'd been of little use in the kitchen. Either way, I was glad to be outdoors. Maybe Sister Muhlbach would ask the elders to assign me to the garden or the calico mill. Or maybe they would send me to work with my mother at the Kinderschule. I wouldn't mind that so much. Playing games with the children would be fun, and I could go visit Rudolf whenever I wanted. Mother wouldn't care.

I stopped by the dairy barn after I'd handed over the basket to Sister Nusser, but Rudolf hadn't returned from his afternoon deliveries. My stop at the general store was as brief as the one to the dairy barn. No mail for me or for my mother. A weight settled in my stomach. Why didn't Father write? Couldn't he take a few minutes to pen a note to us and tell us all was well and he missed us? I wandered aimlessly down the sidewalk, unwilling to return to the Küche just yet. When nothing of particular interest came to mind, I decided to go home and rest for a while before returning to work.

It wasn't until I entered the front door and glanced toward the Ilgs' apartment that I knew what I would do with my time. After tapping on the door to make certain no one was home, I entered the parlor. "Sister Ilg?" I hadn't seen Johanna's mother at the garden, and I wanted to be sure she hadn't taken to her bed with an illness of some sort. I tried to remember if I'd seen her at breakfast, but I couldn't recall. Better to be safe.

"It's me, Berta Schumacher." I tiptoed through the parlor and peeked into the bedroom. Empty. I heaved a sigh and opened the door to Johanna's bedroom. A nagging guilt tiptoed into the room behind me, but I pushed it aside. Johanna wouldn't mind if I borrowed her magazines. After all, I'd given her the poetry book before she left for Chicago. She'd think it a fair exchange. I carefully examined her wardrobe and dresser, but a search of both revealed nothing. Perhaps she'd taken them with her.

My excitement plummeted. I was about to leave the room when I spied the small trunk at the foot of her bed. The chest was filled with mementoes from Johanna's childhood. A few hand-carved toys, a doll, an old blanket, and a flour sack. My breath caught in my throat the minute I saw it. Even before I shoved my hand inside, a piece of the pink silk escaped the bag's opening. Johanna had never destroyed my skirt. She'd either forgotten about it or she'd intentionally decided to keep it. Either way, I was pleased. I dug a little deeper, but still no magazines.

I stood in the doorway and studied the room. Where would I hide magazines in this room? I'd checked in each piece of furniture, looked behind the wardrobe, and under the bed. Where else could they be? My gaze settled on the carpet. I dropped to my knees alongside the bed and then lay down on the carpet. Reaching beneath the bed, I traced my palm over the rug until I felt an unexpected rise in the carpet. She'd shoved the magazines beneath the rug so that if anyone looked under her bed, the magazines wouldn't be detected. My delight mounted when I lifted the edge of the rug and was able to retrieve them. I tossed the magazines atop the bed, patted the edge of the rug into place, and got to my feet, pleased with my success.

I rolled the magazines and tucked them inside the flour bag with my pink silk skirt. After one quick glance to ensure all was in order, I exited the bedroom, crossed the parlor, and peeked out the door before making my final escape into the foyer and up the stairs. My palms were damp with perspiration, and my breathing came in rapid spurts as I pushed open our parlor door.

"Is that you, Berta?"

I clapped my hand over my mouth to force back the shriek in my throat.

"Berta?" My mother's voice drifted from the bedroom.

"Yes, Mother. Are you ill?" Panic held me captive as I heard her approaching footsteps. I needed to hide the bag, but before I could force my feet to move, she was in the room.

She pointed to the cloth bag held tight in my arm. "What do you have there?"

"Oh, nothing. It's an old flour sack that I use when I take food to the garden workers."

She nodded as though what I'd said was entirely believable. There was no reason for her to think I would lie about a flour bag. She continued toward the door and then stopped. Her brows pulled into a frown. "Why are you at home?"

My thoughts swirled. "I need to change my shoes. This pair

pinches my toes." I took a step toward my bedroom. "Have you heard anything from Father?"

She shook her head. "No, of course not. I've told you, Berta, that your father has never been a man to write letters. If I received any word from him, I'm certain it would be bad news. When he is away from home, I know that no news is good news." She pointed toward the bedroom. "Don't take long. I don't want you to get into trouble."

I didn't know if I believed her, but she waved and was out the door. I could only wonder what she would think when she discovered I was already in trouble. I expected Sister Muhlbach or one of the elders to mention the meeting to my mother. Then again, I didn't really know how such matters were handled. Maybe Mother wouldn't be advised until the elders rendered their final decision.

I tugged and wiggled one of my dresser drawers until it had opened wide enough to shove the flour sack inside, but then I stopped. There was no reason to hurry back to the kitchen. I was already in trouble, so why not relax at home awhile longer. I dumped the contents of the bag onto my bed, reveling in the color and feel of the pink silk. Lifting the fabric, I draped it over my head and let it fall over my face, enjoying the feel of the soft, cool silk against my skin. Could I possibly repair it?

Jumping to my feet, I spread the skirt across the bed. My hopes deflated as I traced my fingers along the jagged rip. I had hoped for a split seam that could easily be repaired, but the rip was four inches above the hem and right in the center. I doubted even a practiced seamstress could repair the frayed fabric to its previous glory. I stood back and took stock of what could be salvaged.

Making a decision, I retrieved Mother's sewing box, removed the scissors, and set to work. The first cut proved the most difficult, but after that initial snip I sliced through the fabric with ease. Had I been more talented with a needle and thread, I would have developed a more intricate plan, but this would have to do. Besides, no one would see my slipshod handiwork. After separating the upper portion of the skirt, I set it aside and cut the ripped portion from the lower half. Feeling satisfied with my plan, I retrieved a muslin petticoat from my dresser and arranged the pieces of pink silk over the muslin. I stood back and studied the effect. The wide strip of white muslin between the two pieces of silk would do nicely.

After I'd stitched the silk to the upper portion of the petticoat, my concentration waned. Even this mischievous project couldn't increase my interest in sewing. I didn't understand why so many women claimed handwork a pleasurable activity. Sewing would never rank high on my list of favorite pastimes.

My conscience began to prick a bit, and I thought I'd better return to the kitchen. I could finish the sewing that evening. After tucking my project into the dresser drawer, I scurried downstairs. A fleeting remembrance of my promise to Johanna flashed to mind, but I pushed aside the twinge of guilt and thought about the pink silk instead. How could something so lovely be considered improper?

# CHAPTER 26

My sewing had gone quite well last evening. In fact, I had finished it by bedtime. Granted, my stitches were far from perfect. Where most women would have used five or six stitches, I used only one. But the appearance didn't matter all that much. The pink silk was a memory of my past life, a time when my mother and father enjoyed my company and doted upon me. After tying it around my waist this morning, I stood before the mirror and stared at my lopsided handiwork. I traced my fingers along the soft fabric and longed to feel my father's or my mother's arms around me. Johanna said God loved me, but I couldn't feel His embrace, either.

It seemed an eternity since we'd come to Amana—an eternity since I'd worn my lovely pink silk. I fastened my dark calico skirt atop the petticoat and turned to make certain none of the pink fabric could be seen. Assured the silk was well hidden, I departed for the Küche. Since arranging for the meeting with the elders, Sister Muhlbach said nothing when I was late or if I didn't complete my assigned tasks. However, I was certain she was keeping a mental record of all my wrongdoings. A list she would gladly present to the elders. A list of which I was secretly ashamed, though I'd never admit such a thing to her—she wouldn't believe me anyway. Besides, my behavior didn't reflect the remorse and guilt that had become more frequent since I'd made my promise to Johanna.

Today she and Sister Dickel would go to the general store to choose the provisions for next week's meals. The fact that she would be gone for a good long time pleased me. No doubt she'd leave a list of tasks for me to complete in her absence. And no doubt I'd ignore them. The weather was far too nice to remain indoors.

We had completed washing the breakfast dishes and the young girls were sweeping the dining room floor when Sister Muhlbach signaled us to gather in the kitchen. The young helpers hastened to do her bidding, while I followed at a much slower pace. "I will be gone most of the morning, and I expect the noonday preparations to be completed when I return. I am depending upon you." She hesitated and glanced at Sister Dickel. "Perhaps I should leave you here and take Berta with me."

Disappointment clouded Sister Dickel's eyes, and her lips drooped into a frown. I was just as unhappy with the suggested change of plan. Shopping with Sister Muhlbach didn't rank high on my list of fun ways to spend a morning.

"But it's my turn to go," Sister Dickel said.

"You're right. I shouldn't change the schedule. I worry too much." Sister Muhlbach looked at me as she spoke.

She obviously hoped I would give her some sign that I'd be on my best behavior during her absence, but I didn't bite. After gathering their shopping baskets, the two of them departed. I briefly considered leading the junior girls in a rebellion but doubted I could convince them. Besides, they'd be afraid to truly enjoy the experience. Instead, I wandered outside. It wasn't long before I spotted the handyman near the toolshed.

"What are you doing, Mr. Barton?" I strolled across the cushion of soft grass and stopped beside him.

He lifted a saw in the air. "Cleaning the tools. Looks like the fella who worked here before me didn't think it was important."

"When did it become important to you? From what I've seen, you wouldn't win any prizes for hard work."

He glanced up at me as he rubbed an oiled cloth along the metal blade. "You're sure a feisty gal. None of the other women say a word to me, but you're always ready to say whatever comes to mind."

"I haven't lived here as long as they have. And just so you know, I still haven't completely forgiven you for not siding with me against Sister Muhlbach."

Even though the brim of his floppy hat shaded his face, he squinted against the shard of sun that reflected off the saw blade. "I already explained why I couldn't come to your defense. Doesn't mean I don't think you're a fine young lady." He grinned. "How come you're not inside helping fix the noon meal?"

"Sister Muhlbach and Sister Dickel went to the general store, and I intend to enjoy this fine morning."

He examined the saw and gave a nod. "Well, I've about finished up in here. How you planning to enjoy your morning?"

I hadn't given the matter much thought, but when I spied a long-handled mallet in the shed, I smiled. "How about some croquet?"

He shook his head. "Don't know what that is."

"I've only seen it played a few times, but we can make up our own rules." After I explained the game and what was needed, Mr.

Barton twisted some pieces of wire to make wickets. "We'll have to share the mallet. It may be a bit short for you, but it will be a little long for me, so that should make us equal."

"You have wooden balls for us to use in this game?"

I paced back and forth as I attempted to come up with a solution. "I know! I'll bring some of the onions from the cellar. We can use those."

Before Mr. Barton could express an opinion, I raced back across the yard and down the cellar steps. I stopped on the bottom step to give my eyes time to adjust to the darkness before working my way through the dank room. My previous trips to the cellar proved helpful, and I soon located a basket of onions. Mr. Barton was poking the pieces of wire into the grass when I returned.

"Those look like they're in the right place?"

I hitched my shoulders. "I don't really recall. It doesn't matter. We can make up the rules as we go along. That's more fun anyway."

He tipped his hat back on his head. "Kind of the way you're going through life, right? Just making up your own rules as you go along?"

I plopped the basket of onions beside one of the wire wickets. "Exactly. I think fun is what's most important. 'A merry heart doeth good like a medicine: but a broken spirit drieth the bones.' In case you didn't know, that's from the Bible."

Mr. Barton leaned down and retrieved one of the onions. "Is it now? I'd never guess you'd be one to quote the Word of God, Berta."

"I only have a few passages committed to memory." No need to have him thinking I was a Bible scholar.

"And from the sound of it, the verses you've memorized are ones that best fit your idea of how you want to behave."

His comment annoyed me. Probably because I'd been plagued

by moments of remorse and guilt of late. "You want to give this a try or not?"

"Just makin' an observation. No need to get surly." He nodded toward the mallet. "You go first so I can see how it's done."

Only the top of the onion peeked out from the grass, but I aligned myself and gave it a whack. The onion didn't move far, but my effort destroyed a small clump of grass. "Maybe a potato would work better."

He took the mallet. "I don't think a potato is gonna work any better than an onion. Here, let me give it a try." His swing produced no better effort than my own.

"The onion is too small and the mallet is too big. What about a head of cabbage?"

Mr. Barton shook his head. "They won't fit through those wires."

"We don't need to use the wickets. We can lean a board against the shed and aim the head of cabbage at it. Whoever comes closest will win. What do you say?"

"I'll get these wires out of the yard and see if I can find something we can use for a target." He pointed to the basket of onions. "Might as well take that basket of onions with you to the cellar."

I grabbed the basket handles and returned to the cellar. Each year most of the cabbage was made into sauerkraut, but I knew Sister Muhlbach kept some in reserve. I just couldn't remember where I'd seen it. After several minutes of searching and feeling inside the baskets, I discovered cabbage. With a grunt, I lifted the heavy basket, waddled toward the steps, and called to Mr. Barton.

When he poked his head above the door opening, I motioned him forward. "You need to carry this—it's too heavy."

In no time he'd retrieved the basket and carried it to a grassy spot a distance from the shed. "What do you think? Is that going to work for our target?"

"Looks good to me," I said, positioning a head of cabbage on the ground. "Hope this doesn't break the mallet."

"I don't think you're quite that strong."

I took the remark as a challenge and thumped the head of cabbage with a mighty wallop that landed it just short of the target. Mr. Barton reached for the mallet, but I pulled away, grabbed another cabbage from the basket, and placed it in position. "I get two hits and then you get two."

"Right. I forgot you make up the rules as we go along." He held up his hand. "If you miss this time, does it go up to three times before I take a swing?"

The man could certainly be aggravating with his offhand remarks. "No, it won't be increased. We each get two swings before we hand over the mallet." I settled into position, swung, and kept my focus on the flying cabbage. "Good one!" I jumped up and down, delighted that I'd met with success.

"It only grazed the side of the board. I don't think it should count as a direct hit."

"You're jealous because you didn't think I'd succeed." I pointed to the mallet. "Go ahead. Let me see you do any better."

Snatching a cabbage from the basket, he dropped it to the ground.

"Wait! You have to move farther back. My arms are shorter than yours." I extended my arm to prove I was right.

Using the toe of his boot, he moved the cabbage to the spot I picked. "You sure this is where you want me?"

I nodded.

"You're not gonna change your mind once I have the mallet in the air, are ya?"

I narrowed my eyes and glared at him. "I said I wasn't going to change my mind. Quit holding up the game and hit the cabbage."

"I'm not the one changing the rules," he muttered as he took aim and swung the mallet. The cabbage careened through the air and landed against the shed with a splattering force.

"Excellent! I want to do that with mine."

"You're gonna have to hit it harder next time." He positioned his second head of cabbage and once again met with the same success. Pieces of cabbage flew in all directions.

"Since I think I'm gonna win this game, I'll let you move closer so you can have more fun."

"Why, thank you, Mr. Barton. That's very kind." I was elated when I met with success after another try.

I wasn't certain how long we'd been playing our game when Sister Muhlbach and Sister Dickel returned. And I don't know who was most surprised. I hadn't watched the time, but I didn't think they'd be back for at least another thirty minutes.

I could see the anger in Sister Muhlbach's eyes as she stomped toward us. "Are those my cabbages you've destroyed?"

"They're cabbages from the cellar." I didn't think Sister Muhlbach should consider them hers. To my way of thinking, they belonged to everyone who ate in the Küche. "You can consider the ones I've ruined as my portion. I won't eat any sauerkraut, either." I didn't mention my offer wasn't a great sacrifice on my part—I didn't like either one.

She glared.

"I'm sure Mr. Barton will sacrifice his portions, as well," I said. Maybe if we both relinquished our share it would lessen her anger.

"Mr. Barton doesn't have a share to give." She pointed at the street. "Gather your belongings, Mr. Barton. You won't be needed any longer. You can go and speak to Brother Kohler at the general store. He'll give you information so that you can collect any wages due to you."

"Wait! You can't do that. It isn't his fault. It was my idea." I grappled for something to say that would halt her decision.

Sister Muhlbach shook her head. "Mr. Barton is a grown man. He could have refused. In fact, he should have encouraged you to go back inside and perform your duties. Instead, he joined you."

With his head bowed and chin resting on his chest, Mr. Barton headed back toward the shed. "I'd be more than willing to clean up this mess before I go if you'd like, Sister Muhlbach."

"That won't be necessary, Mr. Barton. Berta will be in charge of cleaning the mess." She looked directly into my eyes. "After she's finished her other chores."

I wanted to run after Mr. Barton and apologize, but Sister Muhlbach was holding my arm in a viselike grip. Seeing the handyman lose his job was much more painful than the tongue-lashing that followed. She escorted me into the kitchen and pointed to the baskets. "You can begin by putting the supplies away. I tell you, Berta, I am glad I will meet with the elders tomorrow. I have done my best to teach you, but I cannot. You are as changeable as the weather. One week you are willing, the next you are defiant. Let the elders decide what will come of your unruly behavior."

For the remainder of the day I followed most of Sister Muhlbach's orders. I was outside picking up the pieces of mangled cabbage when Rudolf arrived with his afternoon milk delivery. When he jumped off the wagon and waved, I ran to his side, eager to explain Sister Muhlbach's unjust discharge of the handyman.

I'd completed only a few words when he stopped me. "I already know. Brother Kohler told me when I stopped at the general store."

"Brother Kohler tells everything he knows. He's a bigger gossip than most women," I said.

"You're in big trouble, Berta. I hear Sister Muhlbach is going to talk to the elders tomorrow morning."

"I know. She decided to go to them earlier in the week, before any of this happened." I shrugged. "Now she has more to tell them. Maybe they'll tell Mother that we must leave."

Rudolf hoisted one of the milk cans from the wagon. "That's what you want, isn't it? To leave without really giving this new life a chance to work."

"I would miss you, Rudolf, but there's little else to hold me here. I can't be certain my father will return. I miss Johanna, but even if she does return, she'll have no time for me—not after she and Carl are married."

He set the can on the porch and returned for another. "By then you'll have made other friends, and you'll be more accustomed to our way of life. Your parents seem content, especially your mother."

Before I could comment, Sister Muhlbach stepped out of the kitchen door and motioned to Rudolf. "Berta doesn't have time for visiting. Leave the milk and get along with your deliveries."

Rudolf didn't argue, and neither did I.

The following afternoon Sister Muhlbach waved for me to follow her into the dining room. "Sit down." I settled on one of the benches and waited to hear the outcome of her meeting. "The elders have ordered that you will not attend any further meetings until your behavior improves. No evening prayer services, no Sunday morning or evening services."

"I understand." I failed to withhold my smile.

Sister Muhlbach grimaced. "I told the elders their punishment would please you, but they remained steadfast. Do not think that you will have nothing to do during those times when others are in meetings. You will work in the Küche, and if you fail to perform the tasks as expected, you'll remain until they are completed—even if I am required to oversee you until after bedtime each night." She folded her hands in her lap. "If you can't pare the vegetables while we're at meeting on Sunday morning, then you will do it on Saturday night. Do I speak plain enough that you understand?"

"Yes, Sister Muhlbach. I've understood every word."

"Gut. Then you will begin tomorrow morning during Sunday meeting. I will have only one junior girl in the Küche to help you. We will see if you understood what I expect."

I pushed up from the bench, pleased with the outcome of her meeting.

"One other thing, Berta. Brother Ilg has gone to the Kinderschule to speak with your mother. The elders believe she must be made aware of your behavior as well as the punishment they've ordered."

The fact that Brother Ilg would tell my mother didn't bother me in the least. Granted, Mother would be annoyed with me—mostly because others would soon know of my misdeeds. Otherwise it wouldn't change anything in her life. Except for a few rare occasions, she'd forgotten I existed.

The remainder of the day passed without incident, but it soon became obvious the others knew what had happened. They spoke in whispers and clucked their tongues when I passed by. However, it was my mother who surprised me that evening. She did more than cluck her tongue or whisper. In fact, I'm certain Brother and Sister Ilg could hear her downstairs.

After listening to her explain how I had embarrassed her beyond belief, she dealt a final blow. "If you get into trouble one more time before your father returns, I will take it upon myself to immediately send you to the boarding school in Iowa City. You leave me no choice, Berta. I won't permit you to continue this unruly behavior."

I stared at her in disbelief. "You would never do such a thing."

"Please don't test me, Berta. This is no idle warning."

I turned on my heel and stalked into my bedroom. How could my mother threaten such a punishment!

For the rest of the evening I remained in my room. I heard my mother leave for evening prayer service, and I heard her return, but we didn't speak. After I had gone to bed, I wondered where Mr. Barton would be sleeping and if he'd soon find another job. I lapsed in and out of a fitful sleep fraught with dreams of Mr. Barton without food to eat and begging Sister Muhlbach for a crust of bread.

The following morning I arose early, unwilling to subject myself to any further disturbing dreams. I pulled my calico over the pink-trimmed petticoat and departed for work while Mother prepared for church. Sister Muhlbach appeared surprised when I arrived at the kitchen a full ten minutes ahead of time. She was even more surprised when I immediately set to work. Sunday mornings we served coffee cake for breakfast, so while she measured the ingredients, I went and gathered eggs.

She thanked me but eyed me with suspicion. "Your mother spoke to you last evening?"

"She did."

"Gut. I can see that she has influence upon you. I should have spoken to her long ago."

I didn't reply. My good behavior had nothing to do with my mother or her threat. I simply wanted to get as much work accomplished as possible before the others left for church. That way I could enjoy the time alone—well, almost alone. One of the junior girls would be with me, but that was almost the same as being alone. I hoped it would be Lydia. I'd visited with her on a few occasions, and I was certain she would enjoy having a bit of fun while the others were gone.

"You have questions about the preparations?"

"I should be able to do it if you write down the measurements for the *Kuchen*." I'd read the menu: crumb soup, cooked carrots, boiled potatoes, roast beef, rhubarb kuchen, and coffee. The rhubarb cake was the only thing that worried me.

"I'll assign Lydia. She's a good baker."

I tucked my lower lip between my teeth to keep from smiling. At least something had gone my way. While the others bid us good-bye, Lydia lifted a crock from the shelf and began to mix the cake ingredients. I cleaned and pared the rhubarb, then set to work on the potatoes and carrots. We visited while we worked, and although Lydia was only twelve years old, she seemed more my age. Probably because she'd been taught to work hard and assume responsibility from an early age. However, she was a curious girl and was delighted she'd been chosen to work alongside me.

Lydia pointed toward one of the large kettles. "Don't forget we must put the broth on to heat for the soup."

I thanked her for the reminder and, once I'd completed the task, returned to paring carrots. "Have you ever traveled outside of the villages, Lydia?"

"No, but my Mutter said that one day we will go to Iowa City." She stared out the kitchen window for a moment. "Would you tell me about the city where you lived before moving here? What was it like?" Her voice rang with excitement. When I hesitated, she hurried to the dry sink and grasped my arm. "Please. I would like to know what it looked like, and what you did, and how it was different from Amana."

Lydia didn't realize how difficult it would be to explain the differences. I started by telling her about our home, the maids, the shopping and, of course, the many parties.

"But what about school?"

"I attended school, but that was never my favorite thing. School is school—they're all alike." I stopped short at what I'd said and added, "Unless it's boarding school. That's when your parents send you away and you live at the school. Some of my friends went away, but I convinced my father it wouldn't be a good fit for me." At the thought of boarding school, I shuddered. "Boarding schools are horrid places. You never get to see your friends or family, and they are run by people who insist upon rules."

She appeared confused. "Rules help us learn right from wrong. They aren't a bad thing."

I didn't respond to that comment—better to change the subject than use our time arguing about the good and evil of rules. "You would enjoy seeing all of the shops and the variety of items to choose from. Some of the stores are so large they need five or six floors to display everything that's available."

"I think it would be difficult if you had so many choices. I doubt I'd ever make up my mind what I wanted." Lydia poured the cake batter into the large metal pans and shoved them into the oven. "Now what?"

She didn't seem to grasp what wonders could be had outside the village. Instead of my explanations enticing her, they had the opposite effect. Then I had an idea. I lifted my calico skirt several inches and watched Lydia's eyes fill with awe.

Stepping closer, she leaned forward. "May I touch it?"

"Of course. You can even wear it for a while, but you mustn't tell." Reaching beneath the calico skirt, I untied my petticoat and let it slide to the floor. "Come here. You can wear it overtop your calico, and I'll teach you some dance steps."

A smile as bright as summer sunshine lit her face. She rubbed the silk between her fingers. "It feels as soft as a baby's skin, doesn't it?"

I agreed, although I had no idea how soft a baby's skin might be—I'd never been around any babies. At least not long enough to touch or hold one. Lydia stepped into the petticoat, and I tied it around her waist while she lifted the silk to more closely examine it—at least I thought that was what she was doing until I stepped around and faced her.

"Did you sew this?" She traced her fingers along the uneven stitches.

"I was in a hurry. Besides, I don't like to sew."

She appeared dismayed by my confession. "You don't? I thought all girls liked to sew. Maybe I could teach you how to make better stitches, and you can teach me how to dance."

"Agreed," I said. "But remember, you can't tell anyone about our dancing or the petticoat."

"Can I wear it each time we dance?"

"As long as no one will see." I covered the potatoes and carrots with water and placed them on the stove, pleased that everything was in order and Lydia and I had time to enjoy ourselves. "First I'll teach you how to hold your partner, and then we'll attempt a waltz."

It took longer than expected for her to learn the steps. With each movement she looked at her feet until I threatened to blindfold her. "Now I'm going to teach you how to do a sweeping turn." We practiced several times, and when I thought she'd perfected the steps, we moved to the far end of the dining room. "We'll dance down the center of the dining room, enter the kitchen, turn around near the stove, and dance back into the dining room. I'll try to hum a tune to help with the rhythm."

The sweet aroma of the rhubarb cake filled the kitchen, and Lydia scurried to the oven. "I'd better take the cakes out of the oven first."

I was thankful she'd remembered. A burned dessert wouldn't

be appreciated. We took our places near the dining room door. At my signal we waltzed our way into the kitchen, where I took a wide sideways step. Lydia tripped and her shoe caught in the petticoat. I watched in horror as she tumbled toward the stove.

"Watch out for that pot of boiling broth," I shouted. Her eyes opened wide and glistened with fear as she crashed into the pot. Her scream echoed in my ears as I rushed forward and yanked her toward me. The pot clattered to the brick floor, the scalding broth flying in all directions.

"My arm! I hit it on the side of the kettle. It's burned and I think it broke when I hit the floor."

I raced outside to the pump, wet a towel with cold water, returned inside, and placed it on her arm. "Stay here. I'll go to the church and get help."

I sprinted down the street, my heart racing. Perspiration beaded across my upper lip, and my breath came in short gasps. Giving no thought to what might be happening inside, I flung open the doors. "We need help in the Küche! Lydia's injured." Benches scraped against the wooden floors, but I didn't wait to see who would come and lend aid. I raced back to the kitchen to comfort Lydia.

A fresh surge of shame and guilt washed over me. Once again my selfish need to misbehave had caused trouble. Tears stung my eyes, but the tears weren't for me. Lydia would suffer pain and scars—all because I had given in to my own selfish desires. Would Lydia forgive me? Would Johanna forgive me? As I neared the kitchen door, I wondered if God could forgive me.

# CHAPTER 27

Shame and guilt nipped at my heels like a dog after a bone. My foolish dancing and need to rebel had placed Lydia in grave danger. Not only had she been burned yesterday, but her arm was broken, as well. Memories of the accident, of the angry red burns and Lydia's arm splayed in an ungainly position, flashed through my mind. No one in this village would ever forgive me, of that I was certain. My mother had ranted at me until she'd nearly lost her voice. And Sister Ilg couldn't even look me in the eye. Not that I blamed anyone but myself. If I'd kept my promise to Johanna, this wouldn't have happened. It would be best for everyone concerned if I left this place.

I'd been hiding in my room ever since the incident. Sister Muhlbach had sent word to my mother that I should remain at home until the elders decided upon a new work assignment for me. Before she'd left for the Kinderschule this morning, my mother had given me strict instructions that I should remain in the house. I'd heeded her word, pacing the floor for most of the morning. I watched as the milk wagon passed below my window to make deliveries to the Küche. I considered yelling to Rudolf but stopped myself. Hadn't I created enough havoc?

I sat down and forced myself to develop a plan. I was deep in thought when a tap sounded at the door. Probably the elders wanting to question me.

Inhaling a deep breath, I opened the door. "Rudolf! What are you doing here?"

"I came to see how you are doing. Do you need anything?"

I nodded and yanked him inside. "I've decided to leave. Are you willing to help me?"

He gulped and stepped inside. "That's not the answer, Berta. You should stay and see this thing through. You'll be forgiven."

I shook my head. "No, not for this. It's too much. Maybe if it had been my first offense, but I've gone too far. It was an accident, but if I hadn't insisted on showing Lydia how to dance, it wouldn't have happened. It's best this way, Rudolf. For everyone."

"Not for me. Where will you go?"

"If you'll help me get to Homestead, I'll board a train for Chicago." I clutched his arm. "Please say you'll help."

He leaned against the doorjamb and stared at the floor. "To do this would be hard, Berta. We'll need to secure a wagon, and with the night watchman on duty, getting out of town without being seen will be hard."

I brightened. He'd said "will be" not "would be." He was going to help me. "We can do it. I promise I'll follow your instructions without question, but we need to leave tonight, before my mother or the elders make any decisions about my future."

His brows furrowed. "Like what?"

Maybe I'd misunderstood. Maybe he wasn't willing to help. "Like my mother sending me off to boarding school or the elders sending our family to another village. It could be anything."

"I don't know about your Mutter, but the elders won't send you away. Of this I am sure."

He might be sure, but I couldn't withstand the embarrassment of remaining here. Seeing Lydia and her parents, eating at Sister Muhlbach's Küche and seeing the other workers every day—I couldn't withstand such pain. And to be moved to another village would be just as bad. Word traveled among the villages. They would know what belligerent Berta Schumacher had done. "Please say you'll help me, Rudolf."

He rubbed his jaw, and I could see he was thinking, considering the possibilities. He was beginning to waver. I held my tongue, fearful anything I said might cause him to change his mind. Finally he looked up and met my steady gaze. "As soon as it is dark enough that you won't be seen, you must sneak out of the house and meet me at the edge of town beyond the mill. Cut behind the houses, and be careful you don't make a sound. Better to go slow than to fall or make noise and get caught."

My heart thumped so hard I thought it would jump from my chest. "You'll get a wagon?"

He shook his head. "Only a horse. I could never manage a wagon. We would be caught, for sure. You'll have to ride behind me on the horse. Besides, a horse will get us there faster than a wagon."

I swallowed hard. I'd never ridden a horse, and the thought frightened me, but I didn't say so. I didn't want to give Rudolf any excuse to change his mind. This would be my only chance of getting to the train depot.

I nodded my agreement. "You promise you'll be there?"

"Ja. I will do it. After prayer service I'll tell my Mutter I must go to the barn to check the milk wagon. I'll remain at the barn. Mutter always goes to bed directly after we come home from prayer service. She won't wait up for me."

"As soon as it's dark, I'll sneak out."

He pushed away from the doorjamb and straightened his shoulders. "Remember, you must leave your belongings. We won't be able to carry them with us."

"Nothing?"

"Only what you can hold on to while we're riding."

I agreed. After all, there wasn't much I wanted. Besides, my mother would make certain the mother-of-pearl dresser set that had belonged to my grandmother would be well cared for, and I didn't want my work clothes.

At the top of the steps he turned. "How will you purchase a train ticket?"

"I have money."

"I should have known." Disappointment clouded his eyes.

For some reason his comment stung, but I didn't reply. Even Rudolf considered me a devious troublemaker. Well, he wouldn't have to put up with me for much longer. If he'd get me to the train station, I'd be out of all of their lives. My conscience nagged, and I remembered something Brother Mauer spoke about in a service many weeks ago. He'd said problems weren't solved by turning our backs or running from them. Instead, we needed to take them to God and seek guidance. I hadn't gone to God for guidance, but I had asked to be forgiven. I wasn't brave enough to go to Lydia and her parents and ask for their forgiveness, but I had asked God. Strange how it was easier to ask God to forgive me than to ask Lydia. I knew I couldn't bear to see the pain in Lydia's eyes. With God it was different. I couldn't see His sorrow.

❖

Once my mother had eaten her supper in the dining hall, she delivered my meal to our house. She and Sister Muhlbach agreed it would be best. I wasn't certain whose idea it had been, but I knew it decreased my mother's embarrassment to have me hidden away in these rooms. I'd become a prisoner. Not that I didn't deserve much worse punishment, but I was glad I'd be gone come nightfall.

"I'll be home after prayer service. Once you've finished your supper, you can read the Bible or go to bed."

I ate my supper and gathered items that I could shove into a small bag. The only things of importance were the contents of my father's leather pouch. I tucked the bag beneath my covers, slipped my nightgown over my clothes, and crawled into bed.

When my mother returned, she poked her head into my room and bid me good-night. I hoped she would go to bed quickly and fall into a deep sleep—and that I would remain wide awake.

It seemed an eternity before the last vestige of daylight gave way to darkness. Hands shaking, I stood beside my bedroom door and listened for any sound before I turned the knob. I held my breath, hoping the door hinge wouldn't squawk in protest. With the bag hanging from my wrist, I carried my shoes and tiptoed to the parlor door. I stepped into the hallway and carefully closed the door. The door latch clunked. I stood frozen in place until I was certain all remained quiet. Shortly after our arrival, I'd learned where to place my foot on each step in order to avoid making any creaking sounds. Tonight I was thankful for that skill.

My breathing remained shallow until I made it to the backyard. I dropped beneath the tree and shoved my feet into my shoes. Now if I could make it to the edge of town without being seen. I picked my way through the backyards, careful to watch for anyone who might be making a nighttime trip to the outhouse. The air was still and heavy from the rains earlier in the week, and I gasped for a deep breath of air as I continued onward.

A sense of relief washed over me when I finally caught a glimpse of the mill. I didn't permit myself to think that Rudolf might fail me. There was no alternate plan. I couldn't get to Homestead without him, but I wouldn't go back. At every sound my heart raced, and my head throbbed with pain. Slowly I edged toward the road and strained to catch a glimpse of Rudolf. My palms turned moist as I hunkered down along the road. *Where is he?*

The shrubs crackled, and I poked my head a little higher to get a better view. In the shadows along the side of the mill, I saw Rudolf emerge leading a horse. I glanced at the watchtower. Keeping low, I scuttled across the road and soon was at Rudolf's side. "I was afraid you weren't going to come."

He pressed his finger to my lips. "Better to keep quiet until we are farther away. We'll walk the horse down this way and then take to the road, where the watchman can't see us," he whispered.

For once I followed instructions without question. When Rudolf finally pointed his thumb toward the road, I followed. He hoisted himself into the saddle and then held his hand down to help me. It took three tries before I was finally astride the horse.

"It's gut I chose a gentle horse," Rudolf said when I was settled behind him.

We didn't talk much on the way. I rested my head against his back and asked God to protect Rudolf. I didn't want him to get in trouble for helping me.

# CHAPTER 28

Chicago, Illinois
Johanna Ilg

The days were passing in a flurry of activity. Both Larissa and Louisa treated me to experiences I'd never imagined. More shopping in the lovely stores along State Street, tea and luncheons with a variety of their friends and acquaintances, concerts—all of it had been exciting. And though I took great pleasure in the myriad activities, I felt like an outsider, trespassing in a world where I didn't fit.

With each passing day, I asked God to show me where I belonged. The answer didn't come to me in a jolting revelation. Rather, it seeped into my consciousness through gentle reminders of the life I would be forced to leave behind. While I'd experienced great pleasure during this visit, I'd come to know that I didn't belong. I doubted I could ever integrate into this way of life—certainly not the way Wilhelm had. I needed a quiet, well-planned existence. A way of life where I could best serve God.

Of course, there had been several letters from Amana that prodded my memories of home: The ones from my mother expressed her love and concern. The ones from Berta chastised me for leaving her and told of her many problems with Sister Muhlbach. And the ones from Carl I still needed to answer.

My prayers regarding Carl had been flying heavenward ever since his first letter arrived. After reading the pages of bold script, I knew he'd spoken from his heart, and I needed to respond. Carl was a good man—a man who loved God, and he'd shown me nothing but kindness and respect. In the letter I received yesterday, he'd once again said he hoped I would return, but he wanted only what was best for me. The same words he'd whispered when he came to the train depot to bid me farewell. I still marveled that he'd come to say good-bye, and I still recalled the pain I'd seen in his eyes while he stood on the station platform beside my father. I didn't doubt he truly cared for me.

I unfolded the letter and traced a finger over the page, recalling the touch of Carl's hand and his quick smile as I once again read his words.

Dear Johanna,

Please know that I care for you in a very special way, and I hope you will return to Amana so that we can spend more time together. It is my hope that as we learn more about each other, a deep love will grow between us—a love that might lead to our marriage. Although it would break my heart, I would never want you to marry me unless you loved me. I have been praying that this time away has provided you with all you need to make your decision.

Brother Kohler grows weary of my daily visits asking if I've received a letter from you. I believe he has taken pity on me. Yesterday he gave me a piece of candy before relaying the sad news. He also said I should tell you to hurry home before he depletes his supply of candy. I would be most thankful if you would write and tell me of your plans. Your father says you have written to them but haven't said for sure when you will return.

I look forward with great anticipation to seeing you again.

With great fondness,

Carl

*With great fondness.* Warmth flooded my cheeks as I whispered the words into the empty room and pictured Carl in my mind—his sandy hair and the twinkle of his blue eyes, his broad shoulders and work-worn hands. I missed his kind voice and gentle spirit.

"Here you are! I thought you'd gone outside to enjoy the lovely weather, but instead you remain in this stuffy sitting room." Larissa glanced at the writing paper spread atop the hand-carved parlor desk. "Writing letters?"

"I've been making a feeble attempt to answer Carl."

"I don't understand why you're having so much difficulty putting pen to paper. You've decided you're not interested in living anywhere other than Amana. Isn't that correct?"

"Yes, but—"

"And you believe Carl's explanation, correct?"

"Well, yes, but there's more to it than—"

Larissa held up her hand. "Do let me finish, Johanna."

Lips sealed into a tight seam, I leaned back in my chair and waited.

"I know you were plagued by feelings of jealousy when you observed Karin and Carl in the barn that day. I believe if you didn't care for Carl, you would have merely been surprised or startled when you saw them. After all, it isn't an everyday occurrence to see a young couple locked in an embrace in Amana, correct?"

I wasn't certain if I should answer. Only a minute ago she'd told me to remain silent, but when she continued to stare at me, I nodded. "Correct."

"There you have it. You're in love with Carl."

"I am?"

Larissa sighed. "Yes. You've been longing to set matters right between the two of you, or you wouldn't be sitting in this airless parlor staring at a blank sheet of paper." She pointed to the piece of stationery. "I could dictate the letter if it would make it easier for you."

"No thank you. I'll manage."

"You're making it far too difficult. All you must do is tell him you're sorry there was a misunderstanding between the two of you, that you accept his apology and look forward to seeing him, when you can discuss the future in person." She gulped for air. "You see? Simple. Now write that down or leave the desk and let's go to the park. We'll visit the gardens and enjoy the day. Which will it be?"

I glanced out the window. The day was indeed far too lovely to remain indoors. "Both. I'll write the letter, and then we can go post it and stop at the park afterward."

Larissa clapped her hands together. "Perfect. I'll arrange for the carriage and fetch my hat while you write your letter. Hurry, now."

Using my best penmanship, I followed Larissa's instructions. She'd been correct. I added a bit more than Larissa had suggested— enough to let Carl know that I was eager to see him and willing to see where the future would lead.

I had completed the letter and was sealing the envelope when Larissa returned. "I may arrive in Amana before the letter," I said. My departure date had been moved up a week due to Wilhelm's schedule. He'd promised Mother he would accompany me home. After all, an unmarried woman traveling alone would be highly frowned upon, and having Wilhelm along would provide great comfort.

"Then you should stay until Wilhelm returns from his business meetings in New York," Larissa said as we left the house. "Louisa and I would both be delighted to have several more weeks to enjoy your company. And I don't think Wilhelm would object. Why don't I speak to him this evening?"

The driver assisted me into the carriage, and once I'd taken my seat, I shook my head. "No. Please don't do that. Mutter would be troubled if I delayed my return. I've already written and told her I'll be coming home earlier than expected. Her last letter expressed their delight. I think any change would cause my parents undue worry. I've had a lovely visit, and if I never return, I'll have the memories to sustain me." I grasped her hand. "And you must promise you'll return to Amana."

Her smile was as bright as the summer day. "If not before, I promise to be there when you marry Carl. By that time I hope your mother will be happier to see me." Her smile faded a bit. "I do hope she'll come to believe that it was Wilhelm's choice to remain in Chicago long before he ever met me. Even though he explained, I believe she still holds me accountable."

"She never completely accepted his decision to live elsewhere. After he left, she continued to hope and pray for his return. Once he married she knew that wouldn't happen. She doesn't dislike you, Larissa. She's simply sad she's lost both her sons."

Larissa stared out the carriage window while I retreated into my own thoughts. We'd posted the letter and were on our way to the park when Larissa remembered her parasol. "I left it in the foyer, and I can't possibly go out in this sun without protection. Do you mind overmuch if we return home first?"

"Of course not. We have the remainder of the afternoon."

She assured me we'd be on our way to the park in no time. I truly hadn't cared—she was the one who wanted to visit the gardens. During the carriage ride, we chatted about Carl.

"I'm eager to visit with him the next time I'm in Amana," she said as the driver brought the horses to a halt in front of the house and jumped down.

"Shall I go inside and fetch your parasol, Mrs. Ilg?" he asked.

"Yes, thank you. You'll find it on the chair in the foyer."

He walked to the house and up the front steps but soon returned at a hasty clip. I glanced out the window. "The driver doesn't have your parasol, but it appears you have a guest."

Larissa stretched forward and peeked out the window. "He's directly in front of her. All I can see is the woman's skirt."

The driver stepped to the right, and that's when I saw her. "Berta!" Her name exploded from my lips in a frantic whoosh. "What is she doing here?"

"I'm sure I don't know, but I believe we're going to find out. Would you prefer to stay here, or do you want to go to the park?"

"I don't know which would be better. Let me speak with her and see what has happened."

Arms flung wide, Berta lunged at me and nearly sent me toppling to the ground. "I'm so happy to see you, Johanna. I know I shouldn't have simply appeared on your brother's doorstep, but there was nothing else for me to do."

She rattled off the list of offenses she had committed since she'd last written. My anger flared when I learned she'd been searching through my personal belongings, but I held my tongue. Tears threatened as she told me about Lydia. "Both the handyman and Lydia have suffered because I was determined to have fun rather than work. Sister Muhlbach immediately discharged him, and I don't know if Lydia's burns will heal without scars or her arm will properly mend. When Sister Muhlbach discovered what had happened, she banished me from the kitchen." She bowed her head. "And here I am."

"You should have gone to Lydia's home to apologize and inquire about her condition, Berta."

"I know, but I was afraid her parents would say horrid things." She met my gaze. "They had every right to confront me, but I couldn't make myself go. Over and over I've condemned myself for my ghastly conduct. I asked God to forgive me, but I couldn't ask Lydia." She wilted like a flower in need of water. "It's better I'm gone from Amana. They are good people and don't deserve the likes of me running amok and causing problems at every turn."

I thought I'd heard the worst of it, but when she admitted she'd pilfered money from her father's bureau drawer and used a portion of it to pay for her train ticket, I became more dismayed. Even worse, she'd convinced Rudolf to sneak into the barn and take her to the train station in Homestead during the night.

"I'm surprised the night watchman didn't see the two of you."

Berta shifted to her other foot. "Rudolf figured out that part. I asked God to protect him. If I could have figured out any other plan, I wouldn't have involved Rudolf—or God." She sent a beseeching look in Larissa's direction. "I hoped you would consider helping me."

Larissa had remained at a distance. I wasn't certain how much she'd heard, but I waved her forward and stifled a smile when Berta made a tiny curtsy. "It's good to see you again, Mrs. Ilg."

"It's good to see you, as well, Berta. I wish it were under other circumstances, as it's quite clear you're distraught. Tell me how I can assist you."

Berta dug in her reticule and withdrew a piece of paper. "Can you help me locate this address?" She thrust the paper toward Larissa.

Stretching forward, I peered at the address and wheeled around. "I thought you wanted to locate your father. Isn't that Caroline's address?"

"You're right!" Larissa said. "I was certain I knew who lived at that address, but until you said Caroline, I couldn't recall. Yes, that's the address of Caroline Rohrer's home. A lovely place—and a beautiful widow."

"Widow? You're acquainted with her?" Berta asked.

"Not well. Caroline's father was somewhat older than my own father, but they formed a business relationship years ago. My father owes some of his success to Mr. Rohrer. Both of Caroline's parents are deceased. At her mother's death, she became very wealthy in her own right."

"Would you be willing to take me there?" Berta was already inching toward the carriage.

"I would, but the house is closed for the summer. Caroline sailed for Europe and won't return to Chicago until September. I understand she made a last-minute decision to sail to Europe before returning to the family's summer home at the shore."

Berta leaned against me, and I thought she might faint. "Why don't we go inside to finish this conversation."

"But I must find my father. I was certain he would be with Caroline." Fear shone in her eyes as sudden realization hit. "Do you think he sailed to Europe with her? Or maybe he's gone to meet her at the shore?" Berta blurted the questions as though she expected us to know.

Larissa grasped Berta's sleeve and nodded toward the porch. "Come along. You need to sit down. And let's don't assume the worst."

I nodded in agreement. "I'm sure we can find your father. He said he would be attending medical training here in Chicago. It shouldn't be difficult to locate him."

While leading Berta to a chair in the parlor, Larissa assented. "Yes, we'll find your father. Wilhelm will know what to do."

My final days in Chicago weren't at all what I'd expected. Instead of another visit to the museum or library, instead of enjoying a concert or play, instead of attending a tea or party, my time was consumed with Berta and Dr. Schumacher. Wilhelm had been more than willing to lend his assistance in locating the doctor but thought it best if I accompany him rather than Berta. "It's better you explain her circumstances so that Dr. Schumacher has time to consider how he should handle his daughter." His idea was well founded, and I didn't argue. Berta, however, hadn't agreed.

But she'd been forced to acquiesce when Wilhelm announced the matter would be handled his way or not at all. The afternoon after Berta had arrived, our carriage driver delivered us to an address some distance away. A sign on the porch rail proclaimed the place was a boardinghouse serving fine food. "I'm surprised Dr. Schumacher is staying here. I thought he'd stay at a hotel. Or maybe with a doctor he'd known when he lived here."

"It's close to the medical school. And I'd guess Dr. Schumacher's old acquaintances aren't as interested in his friendship now that he's living in Amana. Folks don't understand our ways, Johanna."

"Our ways? Are they still your ways, Wilhelm?"

His shoulders sagged, and I detected the pain in his eyes. I hadn't meant to hurt him.

"I still believe everything I was taught, but I can't live in Amana." He folded his hands together. "Living in such opulence may not confirm what I say, but Larissa is accustomed to luxury. I can't deny her." He glanced at the boardinghouse. "Shall we see if Dr. Schumacher is in?"

The boardinghouse keeper answered the door on Wilhelm's first knock. Her hair was pulled into a tight bun at the back of her head, and she assessed us with pursed lips. "I'm full up, but I can give you the address of another boardinghouse."

Wilhelm shook his head. "We're not in need of a room. Is Dr. Schumacher here at the present time?"

She waved us inside. "He returned from the school a short time ago and went up to his room to study his books until suppertime. I'll fetch him."

"She's certainly a fount of information," Wilhelm said with a grin.

From the startled look on Dr. Schumacher's face when he first set eyes on me, I knew Wilhelm had made the proper decision. Seeing Berta would have likely sent him into a panic. "Johanna! I never imagined I'd see you here. Has something happened to my wife?" He hesitated a moment. "Or Berta?" The landlady stood behind him on the steps as he clutched the newel post and waited.

"They are both fine," I assured him. "Is there someplace where we could speak privately?"

The boardinghouse keeper pushed her way around Dr. Schumacher. "You can use the parlor. Feel free to close the doors. I'll see to my supper preparations."

Though it hadn't been my intent, I'd clearly offended the woman. Dr. Schumacher didn't seem to notice, for he hurried us toward the room and immediately closed the doors. "Please, sit down." He wheeled around and dropped into one of the overstuffed chairs, his brows furrowed. "Tell me what brings you here."

"It's Berta."

He lurched forward at the mention of her name, and I waved him back.

"She is perfectly fine, but she's here in Chicago."

His jaw dropped, and he stared at me, then looked at Wilhelm, obviously wanting confirmation I hadn't lost my mind.

"She arrived yesterday and wanted to come here with us.

However, I thought it would lessen the shock for you and also give you a little time to think about how to . . . well, decide what you want to do." Wilhelm turned toward me. "You go ahead and explain, Johanna."

I briefly told him about the dancing and Lydia's burns and broken arm, but I didn't detail all that Berta had told me. "There is more, but she didn't believe she could remain in Amana any longer. She came here to find you, but she had my brother's address and knew I was visiting him."

He nodded, but confusion still clouded his eyes. "Until I talk to her and discover the full extent of what has occurred, I won't be able to make a decision about the future. Needless to say, I'll need to talk to her mother, as well. This all comes as quite a shock."

After speaking privately with Berta, Dr. Schumacher determined it would be best to leave Chicago before his training was completed. Both Wilhelm and I had agreed with his decision. Berta had been less enthusiastic. She thought they should remain in Chicago and send for her mother, but she didn't win the argument. Instead, after a talk with her father, they decided she should visit the boarding school in Iowa and then return to Amana with her father so the family could discuss her future.

Berta and her father departed early in the morning the same day Wilhelm and I left for Amana. Larissa accompanied all of us to the train station. Berta bid us a tearful farewell and promised she'd see me soon. I couldn't be sure if she had already come to some decision about her future or if she simply didn't want to say good-bye.

As the train heaved and chugged out of the station, Berta waved from the open window.

"Her parents do have their hands full with that young lady, but you can't help but like her," Larissa said.

"I don't know if everyone in Amana would agree with that. However, she is a sweet girl who longs for attention. Unfortunately, she goes to great lengths in order to get what she wants."

Larissa nodded. "She reminds me of myself when I was younger. My parents had time for everything except me—at least that was how it seemed at the time. I didn't go to Berta's extremes, but they were quite unhappy with me on several occasions. After my father finally refused me several things I wanted, I outgrew my penchant for such mischief."

"Berta has difficulty abiding by rules. She'd never before been forced to follow them, so living in Amana has been a challenge. Though I would miss her, perhaps the boarding school would be best for her." I looped arms with Wilhelm once the train was out of sight. "We'd better hurry or we'll miss our own train." When I said good-bye to Larissa it would be with the hope that my mother and father would eventually welcome Louisa back home and would accept Larissa with genuine love.

# CHAPTER 29

Wilhelm hurried ahead to see if our train was on schedule while Larissa and I waited with the baggage. She withdrew an envelope from her reticule. "Please don't give this to your mother until after Wilhelm has departed for New York."

"I don't think he would object to you writing our parents," I said.

"He knows I planned to write, but I don't want the time consumed with talk about me. I'd like for him to use the time with them to heal the wounds from his past."

"Have you encouraged him to do that?"

Her melancholy smile told me she hadn't. "I was hoping you might find some way to talk with him on the train. Tell him how much your parents have missed him and that you know I want to visit more often. See if he will confide in you."

The noise in the station escalated as a wave of people disembarked an arriving train and flooded inside. "I'm not very good at such things, but I'll do my best."

She leaned forward and kissed my cheek. "You'll find a way."

I wasn't so certain. "Only if God gives me the right words. I have no idea how to broach the subject without raising suspicion that we've discussed his past."

"Then we must pray that God will give you the words—and the proper timing."

The train had entered Iowa when I turned to Wilhelm. "Tell me about Pieter. I have no memories of him. I always think Mutter or Vater will become sad if I ask about him."

He jerked away, as if my words had wounded him. "And you think talking about Pieter's death doesn't make me sad?"

His harsh tone surprised me. "I didn't ask about his death. I asked about Pieter. Unlike the rest of the family, I don't remember him at all. I wondered if he was bright in school or liked to be outdoors. Did he go fishing with you like I did before you left Amana, or did he prefer to play with his friends?"

Wilhelm leaned his head against the seat and closed his eyes. "Pieter was a fine boy. He loved doing all the things young boys in Amana enjoy: fishing, picking apples, sitting on the levee watching the dredge boat shovel muck from the millrace, climbing trees." Wilhelm opened his eyes. "He was energetic and full of life from the day he entered the world. If not for me, he would have become a wonderful man."

"What do you mean, 'if not for me'?" I hoped my gentle prodding would convince my brother to finally tell me the story my sister-in-law had already related.

Pain contorted Wilhelm's strong features. "Mutter and Vater didn't tell you I was the cause of Pieter's death?"

"No. They would never say such a thing. They said Pieter drowned while he was ice-skating. It's why they never permitted me to go skating with my friends when I was young." I touched his arm. "They said it was an accident, Wilhelm."

He shook his head, and shame contorted his features. In a halting voice he related the ice-skating incident and how he'd failed to warn Pieter of the thin ice and then lied to our parents. "You can't imagine the guilt I feel each time I look into their eyes. I stayed in Amana until I could no longer bear to live with the constant feelings of shame." His feelings gushed forth like a torrent of rain thundering across a parched desert.

Elbows on his knees, he covered his face with his palms. I leaned against his arm and rested my head on his shoulder. "You've buried this inside for too long, Wilhelm. Promise me you will talk to Mutter and Vater. They love you. It is time to heal these memories that haunt you." Softly I nudged his arm. "Promise me you will talk to them. Please, Wilhelm. Family secrets aren't a good thing."

He nodded. "You're right. It has been long enough. They deserve to know the truth. Long ago I received God's forgiveness, but I need their forgiveness, too. Otherwise I'll never be free from the past." He leaned sideways and kissed my forehead. "Thank you, Johanna."

I clutched his arm for the remainder of the journey. I'd never felt such a close kinship with my brother, and I wanted to cherish each moment.

As the train rumbled into Homestead, I spied Father standing on the platform and waved from the train window. He signaled in return, and a broad smile transformed his usually sober face.

The moment I stepped down from the train, he hurried to my side and pulled me into a rib-clenching embrace that forced the breath out of me.

"It is gut to have you home, Johanna."

He released me, and I inhaled a deep breath of air and rubbed my side. "And I am pleased to be here." I glanced around. "Mutter didn't come with you?"

"She had to choose if she would be away from her work in the garden this morning or this afternoon. She chose to come home early this afternoon so she will have more time to visit with Wilhelm."

Wilhelm stretched forward, and the two men shook hands. From my angle I thought both of them feared rejection if the other should reach out to embrace. Wilhelm gestured toward the luggage. "I'll get the bags, and we can be on our way."

Vater wanted to hear about what all I'd done during my stay in Chicago. I shook my head and laughed. "You must wait until Mutter is with us. Otherwise you'll listen to the same story two times."

He agreed as he flicked the reins, and we headed toward Amana. "I do have some news that will make you very sad." My Vater glanced over his shoulder and looked at me. "Your friend Berta has disappeared. Run away. Poor Sister Helen has been very worried."

I wasn't certain why, but I assumed Berta had left a note telling her mother she'd gone to Chicago. I never imagined that she would leave her mother to worry over her whereabouts. Dr. Schumacher had given me a note for his wife, but I thought the contents revealed his plans to take Berta to Iowa City before returning home.

"Berta is safe. She's with her father, but I must speak to Sister Schumacher as soon as we arrive in Amana. Could you take me to the Kinderschule? I have a letter for her, and I believe I can set her mind at ease about Berta."

"How do you know all of this? Did Berta send you a letter?"

I explained Berta's arrival in Chicago. "Dr. Schumacher said he will need to meet with the Bruderrat when he returns from Iowa City later tonight—to explain his inability to complete the medical training."

"That Berta is always busy stirring up trouble. You would not believe the problems she has caused for Sister Muhlbach." He *tsk*ed and wagged his head. "She makes me thank God for my wonderful children."

Wilhelm shot me a look of apprehension.

"We are not perfect children, Vater. Both Wilhelm and I have made our share of bad choices. Your memory is short because we are older now."

"Ja. I suppose that is true. And even old folks like me still make mistakes. I need to have a more forgiving spirit with Berta, but it hasn't been easy watching Sister Schumacher suffer with worry and concern for her daughter. Or listening to Sister Muhlbach rant and rave about the girl's bad behavior." He chuckled. "I don't know how one girl could think of so many ways to annoy the Küchebaas. Your Mutter says Berta has a special gift for trouble."

I didn't think her assessment was correct, but I didn't argue. While Vater and Wilhelm talked about the woolen mill and work at the barn, I relaxed and enjoyed the colors that had transformed the bleak timbered hills and valleys after a long, hard winter into breathtaking beauty. As our villages came into view, I marveled at their unfolding loveliness. Breathing a gentle sigh, I knew I'd come home to the place where I belonged.

Mutter was already at home when we arrived. She scurried to the front door to welcome us. After carrying the baggage into the house, Wilhelm and Father decided they would return the buggy to the barn.

"I need to see if there have been any problems while I was gone," my father said.

The moment they'd departed, my mother enfolded me in another embrace. "I missed you so much, Johanna."

Her eyes brimmed with tears, and I patted her shoulder. "There's no need for tears, Mutter. I'm home to stay, but I'm glad that I went to spend time in Chicago and to meet Tante Louisa."

The mention of Louisa brought a flood of fearful questions. I answered them one by one.

Finally she gulped a deep breath and asked, "Do you still harbor anger at me for not telling you?"

"The anger is gone, Mutter, but family secrets are not good. I know your fears ran deep, but you should have trusted me enough to know that my love for you would have outweighed any secret about my birth. My anger was because you hid the truth from me."

"I know now that you're right, but I didn't ever want to lose you; and once you discovered the truth, it confirmed all of my fears." A tear trickled down her weathered cheek. "But after a while I realized it wasn't the truth that caused you to leave but rather the lie we'd been living for all these years."

With a gentle touch I wiped the tear from her cheek. "There's no need for crying. You will always be my Mutter." I pulled her into an embrace.

"What about Louisa? Is she angry with me?"

"Louisa sends nothing but love to you. She said she will be writing, and if you and Vater won't come to Chicago for a short visit, she would like to bring her husband to Amana for a few days." I leaned back to look in her eyes. "Do you think that would be a gut idea?"

She shook her head. "Not to go to Chicago, but I would like her to come to Amana. We need to put the past behind us and become sisters once again." She inhaled a deep breath. "Now tell me all the things you did in Chicago. Did you have a gut time?"

"Vater asked me that same question on the ride home, and I told him he must wait until you were present. So now we must wait for him."

Mother laughed and the wrinkles deepened around her eyes. "Then I will try to be patient. Sister Thekla will be glad that you are home. She has missed you, but not as much as Carl did. I know he is hoping to see you very soon."

"And I'm eager to see him. But I think it would be best if I wait until we have enough time to talk at length. Will we be eating at home or at the Küche?"

"I asked Sister Thekla to prepare a basket for us, but if you want to go over to the Küche and visit with the other women until suppertime, I won't object." She gestured toward the hand-carved cabinet where she kept the dishes that had belonged to my Oma. "I'll arrange the table, and when the basket is ready, you can bring our supper."

We had finished eating when my brother leaned forward in his chair and folded his hands together on the table. "There is something I need to tell both of you."

His tone was serious, and my Mutter's smile waned. "You are sick?" I could hear the concern in her voice.

"No, Mutter. This is about Pieter's death." Rather than looking at Wilhelm, my parents glanced at each other.

Worry twitched around my father's lips. "Pieter's death? Why do we need to talk of sadness from long ago?"

Wilhelm clenched his hands even tighter. "Because I've been living with a lie since the day he died, and I can't go on any longer.

ohanna has convinced me that living with secrets has separated our family. I don't want that anymore."

My father was obviously bewildered, but he nodded his agreement. "Ja, then have your say, Wilhelm. Tell us what secret you have been keeping."

With his gazed fixed upon the table, the story slowly unfolded. Then he looked up at our father. "I lied to you. I stopped to visit with my friends before I went to the river. When I got there, Pieter had already fallen through the ice. If I had gone when you told me, Pieter would still be alive. I lived in Amana as long as I could, but the guilt was too much, so I had to leave. I need your forgiveness."

My father gasped for air. "Ach! This can't be true." There was disbelief in his voice. "That is why you left us?" He shook his head and stared at my mother. "You should have told us, Wilhelm. All these years you never knew the truth."

"It is you who didn't know the truth," Wilhelm said. "Didn't you hear what I told you?"

"Ja, but if you had gone and told Pieter, it would have changed nothing. At the funeral Brother Samuel told me he had seen Pieter skating and warned him to get off of the ice."

Mother dropped to her knees in front of Wilhelm and clasped his hands. "Pieter knew the danger, but he ignored Brother Samuel's warning. It wasn't your fault, Wilhelm." A stream of tears flowed down her cheeks. She kissed his clenched fists. "All these years you could have been here with us—if only you'd told us." She rocked back on her heels and looked up at him. "There is nothing to forgive, Wilhelm. You are our son, and we love you."

My thoughts swirled as I digested what my parents had told Wilhelm. Misunderstandings, secrets, words left unsaid—I'd been guilty, as well. I'd run off to Chicago instead of talking to Carl. I'd made incorrect assumptions and seized them as truth. What if

Carl hadn't written to me? Just like Wilhelm's, my life could have been altered forever.

"And I owe my own apology," my mother said, "to you and to Larissa. I wish she were here to receive it in person, but I will write a letter that you can take to her. I treated her with unkindness. She is a good woman, and I can see that she loves you. I placed blame on her because I didn't want to believe you would choose to stay away from your family."

"I know, Mutter. She understands."

My mother shook her head. "Still, she needs my apology."

My father leaned forward on his chair. "And you worried that Wilhelm and Larissa would convince Johanna to live in Chicago, too," he added.

"Ja, but so did you."

"So you will make your apology letter for both of us, and I will sign my name, as well." He slapped his palm on the table. "It is settled."

# CHAPTER 30

Berta Schumacher

Once the train had pulled away from the Chicago station, my father leaned back in his seat. I thought he was going to take a nap. Instead, he quietly said, "We've discussed everything that occurred while I was gone, but there's one thing you haven't mentioned, Berta. I asked about this before I left for Chicago, but I feel I must ask again."

I snapped to attention. "And what is that, Father?"

"It's about the contents of the small leather bag that was in my dresser drawer. It contained some jewels, gold coins, and nuggets. The contents were removed and replaced with pebbles and stones. Can you tell me anything about this?" He reached forward and lifted my chin and looked into my eyes.

"Yes. I'm sorry, Father. I took them. When you asked me before,

I lied because I was afraid you were going to leave us. I thought if I had your valuables, you'd have to stay in Amana." I opened my reticule and removed the knotted handkerchief that contained most of the valuables. "I used one of the coins for my train ticket and to buy Johanna a book of poetry and to pay for some postage at the general store. Otherwise, it's all here." I didn't immediately hand it to him. "Were you planning to use this to go and make a new life with Caroline?"

"To be perfectly honest, Berta, I'm not certain. When we moved to Amana, I had promised Caroline I would settle you and your mother in Amana and then return to Chicago. I had also promised your mother I would remain in Amana for two years, and if we weren't happy then, we would leave and return to Chicago. Either way, I would need finances in order to begin life anew. The valuables in that pouch were my inheritance from your grandmother. I turned over all the rest of our assets to the elders when we were given permission to move to Amana."

"So you had considered leaving us?"

He bowed his head. "I had. But after we were settled and I was away from Chicago, I knew that I couldn't leave you or your mother. I corresponded with Caroline for a short time. She continued to write and encouraged me to leave Amana. I won't deny that I was tempted."

"Did you see her when you arrived in Chicago?"

"No, Berta. I didn't see her."

"Did you go to her house?" He hesitated for a moment too long, and I knew. "You did, didn't you!"

"Yes. But not to reunite with her. I needed to return something to her, a gift she'd given to me—a watch that had belonged to her father." He glanced out the train window and then looked back at me. "I left the watch with the housekeeper. She told me Caroline had sailed for Europe two days before my arrival."

"Were you surprised she was gone?"

"As a matter of fact, I was. In her earlier letters, she'd indicated she was going to her summer home later in the season. There'd been no mention of Europe." He unclasped his hands and rested his palms on his pant legs.

Something had caused Caroline's early departure. I wondered if my letter had been the reason, but I didn't suppose I'd ever know. And probably it was just as well.

"Now what will happen? Between you and Mother?"

My father brushed a lock of hair from my forehead. "You must remember that it takes time to heal, Berta. Your mother will not soon forget the pain I have caused her. Trust isn't easily restored when you've wronged someone. Although you're still young, you need to remember what I'm telling you so that you will more care-fully weigh the choices you make in the future."

My father's words weren't as necessary as he probably thought. Ever since the incident in the kitchen when Lydia was injured, I'd been dwelling on my past behavior and the consequences others had suffered because of me. More than once the shame had been almost too much to bear. I'd been trying to remember that no sin was too great for God's forgiveness—at least that's what Johanna had told me. She'd even shown me the verses in the Bible. But I knew I must do more in order to find complete peace in my heart.

"Iowa City! Iowa City!" The conductor's shout awakened me, and I rubbed the sleep from my eyes.

Once we got off the train, Father gathered our baggage. While I stood watch over his trunk and my meager belongings, he walked to the livery and rented a horse and carriage. He helped me inside and then took the reins.

We'd gone only a short distance when I decided to ask his

opinion regarding my future. "Do you think I should attend the boarding school?"

"I think you should view the school with an open mind before you make your choice. Afterward, if you're still having difficulty deciding what to do, we'll talk."

"Then you think I should go to the school."

My father chuckled. "That's not what I said, Berta. If you choose based upon what I want, you won't be committed to the decision. I want you to pick the place where you believe you will be happy and flourish."

Now that I'd been granted a say in the matter, making choices didn't seem such a grand idea. There would be no one else to blame for my unhappy lot in life. And I was certain I'd *flourish* in either place—whatever that was supposed to mean. "I do think Chicago is the best choice for all of us, but I don't suppose that's an option."

"Not at the moment. I gave your mother my word that I would remain in Amana for at least two full years. Like you, I wasn't completely committed to the decision when we arrived, but during my time in Chicago I met a man who helped me understand that I need to go beyond honoring my word; I need to do it with an open heart and an open mind. That's what you must do, as well, Berta."

We continued down the streets of Iowa City. Though it couldn't compare to Chicago, it seemed a nice enough town, with sturdy brick-and-frame storefronts and a stone capitol building that likely was considered the crowning glory of the town. My father mentioned that the capital was moved to Des Moines some twenty years ago. The carriage slowed as we approached a sprawling two-story brick-and-stone edifice outside the confines of the town.

I stared at the mansion. "This seems somewhat out of place."

My father agreed. "Mrs. Harwell tells me that it was constructed by a wealthy Easterner when he moved to the area, but after his wife died, he couldn't bear to live in the house any longer. He returned to his former home, and the place sat vacant for a number of years. Finally he decided it should be sold."

After tying the reins, Father assisted me down from the carriage. "Let's go in and see if Mrs. Harwell is here. If not, we may have to take a room at the hotel."

I wasn't certain which I would prefer—an immediate tour of the school or a delay of the process. However, I didn't have to worry for long. A bell jangled when we entered the front door. Soon Mrs. Harwell appeared in the foyer, and after a brief meeting our tour began. While we proceeded through classrooms and living quarters, Mrs. Harwell explained the variety of opportunities afforded her students.

"You share your room with one other young lady, and we do our best to see that your personalities are compatible. Sharing a room may prove difficult for a short time, but acquiring the ability to live in harmony is a useful skill—and our rooms are large." She opened the door to one of the unoccupied rooms as if to prove her point. The sun-filled room was cheery and more than adequate for two girls. "We have a large library and study room downstairs, and our grounds provide a lovely respite for those times when the girls want some solitude."

The place itself appealed, but I wasn't convinced it would hold my interest for long. "I've already taken many of the classes you offer, Mrs. Harwell. I'm not certain the school teaches much that would be new for me. My father will confirm that I bore easily."

Her laughter echoed down the long hallway. "Then this is indeed the perfect place for you, Berta. Because my husband is an instructor at the university, we have enlisted the aid of several teachers from the college. They come to our school and instruct young ladies like you who are prepared for more advanced classwork. I believe you would find the classes a challenge."

"Your students live here—even in the summer?"

She nodded. "Some of them do, especially if their parents are traveling or live in Europe. Others go on holiday with their parents for the summer months. We have a schedule that permits whatever is needed by the girl and her family. It is a choice you and your parents will make if you decide to come here."

We walked to the rear veranda, and Mrs. Harwell waved to several girls sitting beneath a leafy elm tree. "Let me introduce you to some of the girls. You can visit with them for a while, and I'll go over paper work with your father."

"But I haven't—"

She patted my shoulder. "I know you haven't made up your mind, but if you decide to attend, I'll have already answered your father's questions." She glanced at my father. "I'll be right back. You can wait here on the veranda."

After the introductions were made, Mrs. Harwell left me on my own. I was wary of the welcoming friendliness of the girls. At first I was convinced they'd been threatened with punishment if they didn't make potential students feel wanted, but as we continued to visit, I changed my opinion.

"Whether you stay all year or for only a portion of the year, I think you will be happy here, Berta," one of the girls said. "I go home to be with my family during the Christmas holidays and for a few weeks during the summer, but I much prefer being here. And some of the girls who stay here through the Christmas holiday can tell you that Mrs. Harwell makes it quite special."

The girls had few complaints—mostly they weren't particularly fond of the meals. "We had a wonderful cook, but she left us to move west with her husband. The new cook has been less than stellar, but Mrs. Harwell is seeking a replacement. She does listen to our complaints and makes every attempt to create an enjoyable life for us."

"Her husband is quite nice, as well. Somewhat older, but unlike my parents, they seem devoted to each other," another said.

When they had answered all the questions I could think of, I excused myself. "I think I should join my father."

"It was nice to meet you, Berta. I hope you'll return and become one of us," still another said.

As I made my way across the grassy expanse, I turned to wave at the girls. Could I be happy here? Would it be better than living in Amana? I wasn't certain.

Mrs. Harwell greeted me as I returned to the house. "What do you think, Berta?"

"The girls are very nice, and I don't think any other school in the area offers as many classes or such lovely rooms, but I'm still unsure that I want to live away from my parents. Must I decide today?"

"No, of course not. I'm sure your father agrees that this isn't a decision you should enter into until you feel comfortable with your choice, isn't that correct, Dr. Schumacher?"

"Indeed." My father lightly squeezed my shoulder. "We can talk on the way home. After we return to Amana and visit with your mother, there will be plenty of time to decide."

"And if you don't want to enroll until September, that's fine, as well," Mrs. Harwell said. "I've told your father that we currently have two openings. I'm continuing to advertise to fill those vacancies, but we'll trust that if you decide to return, an opening will be available." A train whistle sounded in the distance and Mrs. Harwell looked at the grandfather clock that stood guard in the foyer. "If you hurry, you can get to the station before the train departs for Amana."

We said hasty good-byes, and although Father did his best to prod the horse to a trot, the animal seemed determined to keep his pace at a walk. When we arrived at the train station, Father removed our baggage. "You go inside and purchase our tickets while I return the buggy to the livery."

The train hissed and belched as I anxiously paced back and forth on the platform. I heaved a sigh of relief when I spotted Father rushing toward me. I waved him forward. "Our bags have already been loaded. I was afraid you wouldn't get here on time."

"I'm sorry, but it took longer at the livery than I anticipated," he said as we hurried aboard the train and dropped into our seats. He withdrew a handkerchief and wiped the perspiration from his forehead. "I haven't run a footrace in quite some time. That one about did me in." He grinned and tucked the handkerchief back into his pocket.

The train ride to Homestead wouldn't take long, but we'd have a carriage ride to Amana afterward. There would be more than sufficient time to consider my options.

We arrived in Main Amana well after prayer services, and Mother was surprised to see us home. The three of us talked at length, and though I saw a glimmer of warmth in my mother's eyes, I knew it would take time before trust would return.

When there was a lull in our conversation, I finally mustered my courage. "How is Lydia? Has the broken bone mended? What about the burns?"

"She is doing quite well. It will take time before she has completely healed, and she may bear some scars, but most of the broth splashed onto the floor. For that we are thankful. We can't be sure about the broken arm. It seems the bones splintered and didn't set in a proper fashion. The doctor says she may never regain full use of the arm."

My heart plummeted. "I will go visit her tomorrow. Is she able to work in the Küche?"

My mother nodded. "She has been there the past two days."

"I want to ask the elders for permission to speak at a meeting so that I can apologize and ask forgiveness for my behavior."

My mother clasped her hand across her heart. "That would be the right thing to do, Berta. No matter what you decide about your future, I think your apology would be well received."

Father scooted forward on his chair. "I'll go with you. We can ask Brother Frank if the elders will meet with you tomorrow after evening prayer service. Then you can speak before the church on Sunday."

Tomorrow was Saturday. I wouldn't have much time to change my mind. I shivered at the thought of everyone seeing me—knowing what they must think. I lowered my head and stared at the floor.

My mother had sounded confident I would be well received, but when I slipped into bed I wasn't so sure. Maybe the elders wouldn't let me speak. Even worse, what if they gave me permission and I made a fool of myself? Maybe this wasn't such a good idea. I rolled to my side and whispered a prayer that God would show me what to do. I didn't have much faith in the prayer. Why should God take time with the likes of me when there were lots of good people who needed His help?

I awakened well before dawn, dressed in the plain calico, made my way down the front steps, and hurried off toward the Küche. I don't know who was more surprised to see me, Sister Muhlbach or Lydia, for my presence rendered them speechless.

"I've come to apologize to both of you for my irresponsible behavior." Though the sleeve of her dress covered the burn, my gaze settled on Lydia's broken arm. "I hope you haven't suffered terribly, Lydia, and I'm sorry I didn't come to see you before I ran off. I just didn't have the courage. I don't deserve your forgiveness, but I want you to know that I am very sorry."

I gulped when she stepped forward and embraced me. "It isn't all your fault, Berta. I know the rules even better than you. I shouldn't have encouraged you. We both disobeyed. You could have been injured, too." She turned back the sleeve of her dress. "The burns are healing, and I don't care what the doctor says. I'm going to work with this arm until I can use it just as well as before I fell down."

My apology to Sister Muhlbach wasn't as well received.

"I am pleased to see you are in good health, Berta, but before I will agree to have you work in my Küche, I need more than words. You have apologized in the past. This time I will need to know you are willing to change." She measured out flour for the Sunday morning coffee cakes while she continued to talk. "I'm sure Sister Rosina could use more help in the garden."

"I don't expect you to want me back in the kitchen, Sister Muhlbach. I didn't come for that. I came to apologize to you and Lydia before I go before the elders and ask for permission to speak at meeting tomorrow. I want to ask forgiveness. I have caused you and Lydia the most harm, so I wanted to speak to you alone." I hesitated a moment. "And Mr. Barton. I do wish you hadn't discharged him."

She poured the bowl of cracked eggs into the flour mixture and added milk. "Mr. Barton is a grown man. He knew the rules, and I gave him more than one chance." She stirred the mixture with vigor. "Besides, we both know he was lazy. Now go and help Lydia set the table for breakfast."

I hid in the kitchen while breakfast was served. I couldn't force myself to sit at one of the women's tables.

When the meal was over, my father found me. "I told Brother Frank that you wish to speak to the elders this evening. He said he would arrange the meeting."

I didn't know whether to feel relieved or frightened. While I knew this was the right thing to do, standing before the elders would be fearsome.

That evening when my father tapped on my door, I nearly jumped out of my skin. "It's time, Berta." The elders had decided we would meet prior to prayer service. I would have fifteen minutes to say my piece.

Arriving at the meetinghouse, my father squeezed my hand and told me I should speak from my heart. "Tell the truth and remain calm."

I stared at him in disbelief. "You're going in with me, aren't you?"

He shook his head. "No. They want to speak to you alone." I wanted to turn tail and run, but my father nudged me forward. "Go on. You'll do fine."

The ten elders sat at a long wooden table facing the door. They turned in unison when I entered. Ten men with well-trimmed beards, clad in dark vests and white shirts, watched my every step as I approached. I waited, trembling. Brother Ilg broke the silence and said I could speak.

My first attempt proved futile. My mouth was so dry I could only manage a croak. I uttered a silent prayer for help. Feet shuffled beneath the table while they waited for me to gain my voice. "I've come to ask to speak before the congregation tomorrow." My voice cracked and I swallowed. "I want to apologize for my behavior and ask forgiveness. I have fought against the rules and been a bad influence upon others. I am truly sorry for my misconduct."

Silence.

The men seated at the ends of the table leaned forward and stared at those seated near the center of the group. There were murmurs, but I couldn't make out what they were saying. Finally Brother Ilg nodded toward the door. "It is better that you wait outside while we finish our talk."

My father was leaning against the brick building when I exited. He pushed himself upright and smiled. "How did it go?"

I shrugged. "I don't think they're going to agree. I'm supposed to wait until they decide."

Five minutes later I was summoned inside. "We have agreed you may take your place before the church members and speak tomorrow morning. This is permitted so that you can ask the congregation for forgiveness. Do not disappoint us by doing anything to make us regret our decision."

One or two of the men frowned at me, obviously unhappy with the decision. I offered my thanks and fled from the room. Though I should have been relieved to hear I'd be permitted to speak, fear washed over me like a spring freshet. Tomorrow would be even more difficult.

My mother sat beside me and held my hand. If I returned to live here, I'd remain in children's church. My parents had moved up, but I'd never made it out of the lowest level. Yet today I would ask the forgiveness of all—from those in children's church to the members of the Bruderrat.

It was impossible to concentrate on the beautiful harmony of song or the reading of Scripture, but when Brother Ilg called me forward, a surprising sense of calm swept over me. I took my place in front of the church, and words flowed from my lips. When I finished, I returned to my seat, unable to recall a single word I'd uttered.

"That was absolutely perfect," my mother whispered.

My heart pounded within my chest. I knew that God had

answered my prayer. He'd given me the words that would calm the turmoil I'd created in this community of loving people. Silently I thanked Him and then whispered one more prayer: *Please show me where I belong.*

# CHAPTER 31

## Johanna Ilg

When Berta requested forgiveness of the church members during Sunday morning meeting, my stomach flip-flopped, and I had to wipe my damp palms with a handkerchief several times. Her words were sweet and kind, a gentle plea for mercy. I was proud of her strength and courage, and I told her so when we left the meetinghouse.

"Thank you, Johanna." She bowed her head and grasped my arm. We strolled along the board sidewalk, remaining a short distance behind the other women. "Tell me more about what you thought of the school." We'd only had a few moments alone together the previous evening. "Do you think it's a place you would like to attend, or would you prefer to live here?"

"I'm not sure. I asked God to show me. I hope I get an answer."

Her face glowed as she leaned her head close. "I asked God to help me when I went before the church today, and He answered my prayer. I thought I would faint when I got up there, but it was as if God held me up and said the words for me. Isn't that amazing? Who would think that God would take time for Berta Schumacher!"

"We're all important to God, Berta. I'm pleased you now realize that He loves you."

Berta released her hold on my arm and shifted her *Psalter-Spiel* and Bible. "Since you mentioned love, has anything happened between you and Carl?" She giggled, a mischievous glint sparkling in her eyes.

A smile twitched in my cheek. "Some things never change with you, Berta. You think you must always know what's going on, don't you?"

"If I don't give you a little shove, you and Carl may never resolve your differences."

The sun shone clear and bright, and a slight breeze rippled the hem of my skirt as we continued toward home. We planned to leave our hymnbooks and Bibles before going to the Küche for the noon meal. It would seem strange for Berta and me—eating at the women's table instead of helping to cook and serve the meal.

"You will be pleased to know that Carl and I are going to the river this afternoon so that we can talk. Wilhelm has agreed to go with us. He wants to try his hand at fishing and will act as our chaperone."

Berta pulled me aside as we neared the house. "You're going to marry him, aren't you?"

"I haven't made up my mind, but like you, I've asked God to guide me in my decision. Making a choice to marry isn't like deciding to go on a picnic. I want to make sure marriage is the right thing for me and that Carl is the right man."

Berta glanced toward her mother and father, who were standing at the front of the house. "I wonder if you can ever be certain. Sometimes I think you have to just jump into the water."

Laughing, I shook my head. "Well, I think we'll fish this afternoon and save the jumping for another time."

Though I tried to relax, my shoulders were as tight as the metal hoops on a cooper's barrel when I greeted Carl on the front porch. My gaze traveled from his boots up to his clear blue eyes. One look into his eyes and heat climbed up my neck and warmed my cheeks with an intensity that surprised me. I was certain my complexion had turned bright pink. The thought embarrassed me, and I turned to avert Carl's intense scrutiny.

"I am very pleased you agreed to spend time with me this afternoon, Johanna. I am eager to talk about our future." He looked over my head toward the door. "Your brother is going to join us?"

"Yes. I'll tell him we're ready." I rushed inside and inhaled two deep breaths before entering our apartment, hoping to calm my nerves. "Carl is here, Wilhelm," I said. "Are you ready to go?"

My brother jumped to his feet. "I'm ready to catch some fish." He kissed my mother on the cheek and gave my father a mock salute. "I haven't been fishing for a long time, but you can believe I'll put the two of them to shame and finish the day with the biggest fish."

" 'Pride goeth before destruction, and a haughty spirit before a fall.' Proverbs 16:18," our father said with a laugh. He waved us toward the door. "Go and have fun."

Mother stepped to my side and handed me an old quilt. "You'll need something to sit on while you and Carl talk." She leaned a little closer. "Carl is a good man. Give him a chance, Johanna."

"I am seeking God's will, Mutter. We'll see what answer I receive."

"Then your Vater and I will be praying."

There was no doubt in my mind that the minute I walked out the door, the two of them would begin to pray. And they'd probably remain in prayer until our return. The thought made me smile. Mother knew what she wanted, so I knew how she'd be praying. And the same could be said for my father. Everyone seemed to know what I should do. Everyone but me.

I was pleased to have Wilhelm with us. He and Carl talked about the work at the barns, and Carl asked questions about Wilhelm's life in Chicago. I didn't have to contribute to the conversation, and for that I was grateful. However, soon after we arrived at the river, everything changed.

Wilhelm removed the fishing poles and bait from the buggy. "While the two of you talk, I'm going to go downriver a ways." He lifted the poles to shoulder height. "No sense leaving any of these for you two. I'll put all three of them in the water."

"I think that's cheating. You're certain to catch the most fish that way."

He turned on his heel, and I could hear him laughing as he walked along the river's edge.

I turned to Carl. "You better stop him or you won't have a chance with the fish."

"I'm not worried about the fish, Johanna. It's a chance to win your heart that concerns me." He reached forward and clasped my hand.

A spiraling tremor raced up my arm, and I withdrew my hand. "We shouldn't be holding hands, Carl."

"I'm sorry. You're right. But you act like a bird ready to take flight. I'm afraid you're going to fly away before I have a chance to tell you what's in my heart."

The letter he'd sent had said that he wanted to more fully apologize in person and to speak of his feelings for me. My heart fluttered at the remembrance of his words. "I promise I will listen to everything you wish to say, Carl. Why don't we sit over there?" Near a towering cottonwood, I spread the quilt and bid him sit down beside me. "I'm ready," I said, giving him my full attention.

While he repeated the details of what had occurred on the day I'd seen him with Karin, I carefully listened for any departure from what he'd written to me. I detected nothing amiss in his explanation.

"I am willing to answer any questions you have, Johanna. I give you my word that my answers will be honest and from my heart."

His offer took me by surprise, but I seized the opportunity. "If Karin lived in this village, would it cause you pain to see her with another man?"

"No, it would not. The feelings that I have for Karin come from years of friendship. But I do not love her, Johanna—not in the way that I love you."

How easily he said that he loved me. "How do you know you love me, Carl?"

"Because I can't bear the thought of living without you, because seeing your smile makes me happy, because the touch of your hand warms my heart, because you are everything I have always prayed for in a wife." He grinned. "I can go on and on if you'd like. There are so many reasons I love you, Johanna. You are a good daughter, you are obedient to the Lord, you serve others with a willing heart—"

"That's enough." His praise was embarrassing me.

He chuckled. "And because you are humble." When I didn't immediately respond, he frowned. "Please tell me that you do not plan to leave Amana."

"No. Amana is where I belong, Carl."

Relief shone in his eyes. "And do you belong with me, as well?"

He cupped my chin with his palm and looked deep into my eyes. "I love you, Johanna. I give you my word that I would never intentionally do anything to hurt or embarrass you. If you agree to marry me, I promise that I will happily honor my marriage vows and proudly call you my wife." I tried to turn away from his steady gaze, but he held my chin. "Look into my eyes and see the truth of what I'm telling you, my love."

*My love.* The words resonated deep in my soul, and I knew this was the man God intended for me. "Yes," I whispered.

"Yes, you will marry me?"

I nodded. "Yes, I will marry you."

He let out a whoop and jumped to his feet. "We need to go speak to your parents and then see if I can meet with the elders this evening. I don't want to wait any longer than necessary." His smile warmed me like the bright summer sunshine, and I took delight in his childlike enthusiasm.

Upon reflection, I couldn't decide who had been more enthusiastic: Wilhelm flaunting his string of fish or Carl announcing I'd agreed to marry him. My parents' delight had been expected, and my father gave his immediate blessing. Soon after Carl and my father left the house to meet with the elders, I went upstairs to speak with Berta.

She'd never forgive me if she wasn't one of the first to know I'd accepted Carl's proposal. Dr. Schumacher answered my knock at the door. "Come in, come in! Berta is in her room. Let me—"

Before he could complete the sentence, Berta flung open the door to her bedroom. Her eyes were bright with anticipation. "You're back." She grasped my hand and tugged me toward her room. "Come in and we'll talk. I have much to tell you, too."

Only a few hours had passed, and I wondered what could have

happened during my absence, but I was anxious to tell her my news first. "I have accepted Carl's proposal. You're the first person I've told, other than my family."

Berta's eyes shone with delight. "So you jumped into the water after all. I knew you would. Now what happens?"

"Vater and Carl have gone to meet with the elders to ask permission."

"They won't object, will they?"

"No. There's no reason they would oppose the marriage. The only question will be if we must wait the full year before we take our vows. I think Carl plans to argue against waiting so long, but I doubt he'll meet with success. I told him he shouldn't argue too much, or they'll send him to another village during the waiting period."

Berta clasped her hand to her chest. "They wouldn't! Your father needs him."

I shrugged. "Who can say? The elders could argue that Father got along without Carl's help before he arrived."

"Oh no! That would be terrible." Berta fell across the bed. The girl's flair for the dramatic didn't disappoint. "So you don't know when you will wed? We can't even begin to plan. Before Wilhelm leaves, you must tell him to have Larissa send you pictures of the latest wedding gowns that appear in *Godey's*." My laughter disarmed her. "Why are you laughing? It takes a great deal of time to plan a wedding."

I ceased laughing and clasped her hand. "I won't be wearing a wedding gown like the ones they show in *Godey's*. We don't wear white dresses when we get married. White is for burials, not weddings."

Berta's enthusiasm faded. "I'd forgotten. How very disappointing."

"The wedding won't be disappointing at all—just different

from what you're accustomed to. And if you're here, you can help Sister Muhlbach prepare the cakes and cookies to serve after the wedding."

"Even if I wasn't living here, I would return for your wedding—that's what I wanted to tell you."

I plopped down beside her on the bed. "What?"

"I've decided I'm not going to rush God to give me an answer."

Her answer made me smile. "That's good, Berta, because I don't think God is easily pushed—even by you."

She ignored my teasing remark. "I figure I have to live either here or in Iowa City while I'm waiting for God's answer. So I'm going to remain in Amana until I know for sure what I'm supposed to do. Besides, I think maybe I got a little bit of an answer already."

"Really? And what was that?"

"When I talked to Sister Muhlbach and Lydia before breakfast yesterday, Sister Muhlbach forgave me, though she said I couldn't return to work in her kitchen. But later she called me outside and said that after she'd heard me speak in the meeting, she'd had a change of heart. She said she wanted to give me another chance."

How could I possibly disagree with Berta's assumption? It did, indeed, sound as though she'd received direction on where she should live. "And are you prepared to give Sister Muhlbach your best work, Berta?" If the girl wasn't committed, Sister Muhlbach would soon regret her decision.

"Yes. I even told her she should remind me that I'd made a promise to her and to God that I would do my very best to obey the rules."

I wasn't certain a reminder would set Berta back on the right path should she veer to the right or the left, but I determined to pray that she would keep her word and that God would direct her future.

My father and Carl entered the parlor only minutes after I returned downstairs. The wide smile on both of their faces told me the elders had agreed. And though I'd had little concern that they'd permit the marriage, I was relieved the ordeal was over.

Carl stepped to my side. "Your Vater says we may go out back and talk privately for a few minutes."

I knotted my fingers together and glanced at my father for affirmation.

"Ja. Go on. You two have much to discuss. Alone is better."

Walking through the soft grassy yard, we circled the house. Carl led me to a far tree with leafy overhanging braches.

"The elders all confirmed that we may marry, and they agreed it would be best if I remained in Amana because of my work with your Vater."

I looked up at him, my heart soaring at the love radiating in his eyes.

"We must wait until the first week in March for our wedding. Not what I'd hoped for, but at least it's not a full year."

"We can wait that long, Carl. It will give us time to learn more about each other."

He raked his fingers through his sandy hair. "Just as long as you won't change your mind when you discover all of my faults."

"I doubt that will happen. I know you are a good man with a kind heart."

Without another word he captured me in a warm embrace. "Do you think your parents would be angry if I kissed you?"

"I don't think so." I wasn't sure if my voice or my hands quivered the most when I delivered my answer.

"And what about you, Johanna? Would you think me too forward if I kissed you?"

Heat flooded over me from the tips of my toes to the top of my head. I held tight to his shoulders. "I think it would be acceptable if you kissed me—to seal our engagement."

He leaned down and gently covered my lips with a tender kiss, and I knew without a doubt that I had found where I belonged.

# SPECIAL THANKS TO . . .

. . . My editor, Sharon Asmus, for her generous spirit, excellent eye for detail, and amazing ability to keep her eyes upon Jesus through all of life's adversities.

. . . My acquisitions editor, Charlene Patterson, for her enthusiastic support for this series.

. . . The entire staff of Bethany House Publishers, for their devotion to making each book they publish the best product possible. It is a privilege to work with all of you.

. . . Brandi Jones, Amana Heritage Society, for tirelessly answering my many questions, for private tours, and for reading my manuscript for technical accuracy.

. . . Lanny Haldy, Amana Heritage Society, for meeting with me and taking precious hours away from other tasks to provide information, answer questions, and make recommendations.

. . . Mary Greb-Hall for her ongoing encouragement, expertise, and sharp eye.

. . . Lori Seilstad, for her honest critiques.

. . . Mary Kay Woodford, my sister, my prayer warrior, my friend.

. . . Tracie Peterson, friend extraordinaire.

. . . Laurie Toth, for providing excellent Chicago materials.

. . . My husband, Jim, my constant encourager, supporter, and advocate, and the love of my life.

. . . Above all, thanks and praise to our Lord Jesus Christ for this miraculous opportunity to live my dream and share the wonder of His love through story.